Praise for William Gay

Little Sister Death

"Chilling, beautiful, quietly shocking...a study of the writer: his temperament, his torment, and his devil's pact for the price of a good story."
—*The Independent*

"*Little Sister Death* is not a glib meta-commentary on horror...but a personal glimpse at Gay's own life, at the way a dedicated artist does not exorcise his demons—but seeks them out, and invites them in."
—*Electric Lit*

"Gay's signature muscular prose, authentic dialogue, and vivid setting combine to make this posthumous novel a worthwhile read."
—*Publishers Weekly*

"Cannily crafted, exceptional in its storytelling and doubly seductive in its sultry Southern setting...*Little Sister Death* is literary horror of the highest order."
—*Tor.com*

"Gay takes the familiar trope of the haunted house and imbues it with a slow-burning melancholy and a sense of the inescapability of fate."
—*Big Issue*

"If you mix Stephen King with William Faulkner, the result would be the posthumous novel *Little Sister Death* by William Gay...a great read for a quiet night at home, in an empty house, with the lights off except for a lone reading lamp."
—*The Knoxville News Sentinel*

The Long Home

"Gay has created a novel of great emotional power."
—*Denver Post*

"It'll leave you breathless..."
—*Rocky Mountain News*

Provinces of Night

"Earthily idiosyncratic, spookily Gothic...an author with a powerful vision." —*The New York Times*

"An extremely seductive read." —*Washington Post Book World*

"Southern writing at its very finest, soaked through with the words and images of rural Tennessee, packed full of that which really matters, the problems of the human heart." —*Booklist*

"A writer of striking talent." —*Chicago Tribune*

"Almost a personal revival of handwork in fiction—superb—must be listened to and felt." —Barry Hannah, award-winning author of *Geronimo Rex* and *Airships*

"This is a novel from the old school. The characters are truly characters. The prose is Gothic. And the charm is big." —*The San Diego Union-Tribune*

"Writers like Flannery O'Connor or William Faulkner would welcome Gay as their peer for getting characters so entangled in the roots of a family tree." —*Star Tribune* (Minneapolis)

"[A novel] about the preciousness of hope, the fragility of dreams, interwoven with a good-sized dollop of Biblical justice and the belief that a Southern family can be cursed." —*The Miami Herald*

"Plumbs the larger things in life.... The epic and the personal unite seamlessly." —*Milwaukee Journal Sentinel*

"An old-fashioned barrel-aged shot of Tennessee storytelling. Gay's tale of ancient wrongs and men with guns is high-proof stuff." —Elwood Reid, author of *Midnight Sun* and *What Salmon Know*

"A finely wrought, moving story with a plot as old as Homer. Sometimes the old ones are the best ones."
—*The Atlanta Journal Constitution*

"William Gay is the big new name to include in the storied annals of Southern lit."
—*Esquire*

"A plot so gripping that the reader wants to fly through the pages to reach the conclusion...but the beauty and richness of Gay's language exerts a contrary pull, making the reader want to linger over every word."
—*Rocky Mountain News*

"Gay is a terrific writer."
—*The Plain Dealer*

Twilight

"Think *No Country for Old Men* by Cormac McCarthy and *Deliverance* by James Dickey...then double the impact."
—Stephen King

"There is much to admire here: breathtaking, evocative writing and a dark, sardonic humor."
—*USA Today*

"William Gay brings the daring of Flannery O'Connor and William Gaddis to his lush and violent surrealist yarns."
—*The Irish Times*

"This is Southern Gothic of the very darkest hue, dripping with atmosphere, sparkling with loquacity, and with occasional gleams of horrible humor. To be read in the broadest daylight."
—*The Times*

I Hate to See that Evening Sun Go Down

"William Gay is richly gifted: a seemingly effortless storyteller...a writer of prose that's fiercely wrought, pungent in detail yet poetic in the most welcome sense."
—*The New York Times Book Review*

The Lost Country

William Gay

DZANC BOOKS

5220 Dexter Ann Arbor Rd.
Ann Arbor, MI 48103
www.dzancbooks.org

Library of Congress Cataloging-in-Publication Data

Names: Gay, William, author.
Title: The lost country / by William Gay.
Description: First edition. | [Ann Arbor, MI] : Dzanc Books, [2017]
Identifiers: LCCN 2017059574 | ISBN 9781945814525
Classification: LCC PS3557.A985 L67 2017 | DDC 813/.6--dc23
LC record available at https://lccn.loc.gov/2017059574

First US Edition: July 2018
Jacket design by Steven Seighman
Interior design by Michelle Dotter

This is a work of fiction. Characters and names appearing in this work are a product of the author's imagination, and any similarity to real persons, living or dead, is coincidental and not intended by the author.

Printed in the United States of America

10   9   8   7   6   5   4   3   2   1

Contents

Foreword

A Good Man

by Sonny Brewer

William Gay was a good man. And they aren't that easy to find.

My great uncle got specific and said a really good man was one in ten thousand. He was a Harvard-trained minister who spent forty years in the pulpit. He was, however, pulling a thread in his clerical cloth hoping to impress me with an opportunity to be somebody just by being good.

Confucius talked about the idea of a good man. He said a good man is kind, has integrity, doesn't need much, and is willing to put himself at the disposal of other people. But more, while being an archetype, he is not rich or a politician, not a ballplayer or a celebrity—just somebody who understands others, and counts relationships with family and friends above all else. The philosopher said you could spot a good man in a crowd. Something about him, even at a casual glance, welcomes your trust. You don't have to wear a robe and chant mantras to detect something different in a good man.

The night I met William, we were in a bar in Columbia, South Carolina, in town for the Southeastern Independent Booksellers Association annual conference. It was the fall of 1999. My pal Tom Franklin had mentioned his name to me, said I'd want to get in line on Sunday morning for a signed copy of his chapbook.

"I've never heard of this guy," I said. "Is this something he self-published?"

"No. But it's independently published by a woman who lives in his hometown," Tom said. "It's one short story, in a limited run of 250 copies. All of them numbered." I had a bookstore back in Fairhope, Alabama: Over the Transom Used and Rare Books. Tom had heard my story about selling one book for more than $6,000 to a collector. "Trust me," he said, "you haven't heard of William Gay but that's about to change when his first novel comes out in November. And you *do* want to have one of these chapbooks."

The bar was crowded, people standing up, brushing past, and Tom turned to greet a man. "Hey William," he said. "I was just telling Sonny about you," and clapped me on the shoulder.

I don't know what I was expecting. First-time author, maybe a young college type. No, this writer had some miles on him. Older than me, I guessed. And with long hair, kind of curly. I couldn't see his eyes. But something about him drew me in.

"Hey, Sonny." His slow Tennessee voice was musical and had a kind of smile in it. He was wearing jeans and a rumpled black velvet-looking sport coat with broad lapels. Out of fashion.

Pretty quick I found myself sitting in a booth with the man. Just the two of us. And we fell into an easy conversation about editors. William's heavy drawl was the real version of the fake thing that actors foist on moviegoers in hillbilly movies. It belied his mercurial intelligence and an English professor's vocabulary. I asked him what he did besides writing. "I've hung some sheetrock," he said. His wit shone a light you could read by in a dark corner. I decided I liked this guy a lot.

And like two men shooting pool, we took turns across the table. Him then me. Me then him. Ratchet-jawing like drunken sailors on leave in Barcelona, Spain. A pattern we'd follow in the years to come that would distract us in the car and make us miss our turns. Like overshooting a ten-acre clean, well-lighted interstate exchange, I-95 south off I-10 eastbound, that we didn't catch until we saw the Atlantic Ocean in Jacksonville. I asked how in the hell did we do that? William did not like to drive, didn't like to merge or go over bridges, and I had the wheel on all our road trips. William said, in matter-of-fact monotone, "I reckon we were talking."

But our talking was not trifling gossip. It was on our New England trip that William explained to me why Robert Penn Warren's "Blackberry Winter" was a perfect short story. Said if you removed or added just one word from it, you'd damage it.

Same ride I quoted by heart to him a paragraph from his *The Long Home*:

Morning. A hot August sun was smoking up over a wavering treeline. Such drunks as were still about struggled up beneath the malign heat slowly as if they moved in altered time or through an atmosphere thickening to amber. The glade was absolutely breezeless and the threat of the sun imminent and horrific. The sweep of the sun lengthened. Windowpanes were lacquered with refracted fire. Sumac fronds hung wilted and benumbed as the whores and smellsmocks rose bedewed from the foxglove and nightshade. Strange creatures, averse or unused to so maledictive a sun, they were heir to a curious fragility, as if left to the depredations of the sun, their very flesh would sear and blacken, their limbs cringe and draw like those of scorched spiders.

Then I asked him how long it took him to compose those lines that scattered my mind and squeezed my chest. "Oh, however long it took me to set it down," William answered. I called bullshit. And he said, "No. I hung drywall by day when I wrote that book, and I composed whole pages in my head while hanging boards." Then he confessed that he had a photographic memory for words on pages. Even from other writers' books. I drove in silence for a mile or two. Considering this man in the passenger seat.

When, short weeks after he died, I read the handwritten manuscript of *The Lost Country*, what pages had been found by then, and I came across the paragraph that included the book's title, that time, too, my heart stumbled and I cried for the loss of my friend.

On one of our trips the bed and breakfast the college had lined up for us was, well, dainty, and heavy on the pastels. William went into his room and came right back out again. Didn't even put down his bag. "Can we go to a motel? I'm afraid I'll be swarmed and smothered in my sleep by butterflies." We left. Found a handy motel where I thought up some story for our hosts.

We couldn't blame our wrong turns on whisky. I never once saw William Gay drunk, co-piloting or not.

But he and I did belly up to a bar now and again. Like the night in Nashville we were parked on stools when three young women came to stand right beside us. They ordered drinks and scanned the room, blessing the barroom's ambience with their centerfold looks. When they left in a swirl and sway, fifteen minutes later after one round of cocktails, I said, "Did you see that? I mean, those girls were clearly looking for somebody to play with and they did not even *glance obliquely* in our direction!"

William didn't look up from his beer when he said, "I guess you ain't checked your expiration date lately, have you?"

Another night, this time on Beale Street in Memphis, it was obvious how poorly we two fit into the scene when William said to me, "I'm ready to go anytime you are. This looks like a damned dress rehearsal for the bottom level of hell."

William would always hang with me when we were out in some town. Never would he run off with a better offer to some livelier place when I was content to be that older guy and keep it low-key. He and I and Suzanne Kingsbury sat at a table together in the afternoon's late sun in Jekyll Island, Georgia, during a weekend's literary conference, and his editor came up to our table. She told William, "The car is here. It's time to go."

William said to me, "Come on, Sonny, let's go."

"Your friend can't come with us," the editor said. She did not look at me.

"We came together," William said.

"I'm sorry," she said. She told William it was, of course, okay for him to bring the lady. There were people expecting him, she said, and they really should get going. William settled back in his chair and told his editor he was not going, and took up the conversation where we'd left off. He didn't speak further to her. Neither did he look at her. Neither did he go.

I think most men would have apologized and taken the ride with the cool people to the cool place. After all, William was *expected*. But William Gay was not most men, nor like them in most ways. I once asked him did he ever feel like he was an alien when he found himself a stranger amongst people and their peculiar ways, their manner of living and speaking and behaving. "No," he told me. "I feel more like I have been set among aliens."

He was right at home in his skin, and didn't need to fix up different when company came calling, nor duck when he was caught out. When I came calling to his cabin in Hohenwald, he'd always ask me what I wanted to eat, and he'd have it homemade on the stove when I got there. He'd have clean sheets on *his* bed, all made up for me to sleep in, and wouldn't have it any other way. He'd take the couch. His dog would keep him company.

I once pushed my publisher to let me include, late in the production cycle, one more author's work in *Stories from the Blue Moon Café*. The guy, a good writer, had been on a dry spell of late and needed a break. And then that writer withdrew his story. Just days from going to press. He'd got a more prestigious offer from an iconic literary magazine, and told me he was sorry, but, quite frankly, he needed *Southern Review* more than he needed our anthology. I was pissed off, and called Tom Franklin to bitch and vent. Tom stopped me. "Well, Sonny—you and me—we both know only one writer who wouldn't have pulled their story, and, sorry, but I'm including us both in that count."

"William Gay," I said.

"William Gay," he said.

He was a superior man. Willing to sell his literary papers to help with someone else's doctor bills. Or to offer me a loan when I lost my home to a foreclosure sale on the courthouse steps in 2008.

On one of our highway runs, we made a little detour and stopped at my mother's house in rural Alabama. My brother Frankie lived with her and took care of her and wanted to meet William Gay. When we went inside, my mother was upset because Frankie had failed for four days, he admitted, to figure out what she wanted from him. Mama couldn't speak since a stroke fifteen years earlier, and could only gesture and say, "Okay, yes," or "Okay, no." I gave it a try, sat on the sofa with her while *The Price Is Right* blinked on the TV.

Mama gestured in a direction that could have indicated the hallway to her bedroom, or the bathroom, or something outside in the unknown distance. William walked into the living room to stand near my mother. He was interested in her trouble. When I shifted my *Is it bigger than a breadbox?* approach to nearby towns in the general direction of her pointing, she lit up when I said Vernon. "Okay, yes!" she said, and even gave a little laugh, relieved for some progress finally. Frankie looked on. William watched and listened. Mother even motioned to William, as if, *Please, help my dimwit sons!*

"Let's see," I said. Then, to add a bit of levity, and keep the mood going, I asked, "You want to go to the jailhouse in Vernon?" But my comedy was weak and my mother's face conveyed to me a deep frustration that quickly devolved into sadness. I thought she was going to cry. I got serious. "Do you want to go and visit Uncle Carl there?"

"Okay, no." And then her lip started to tremble and she looked down the couch and out the window. She was afraid. There was no humor at all in connecting her very sharp mind to a broken voice.

"Is Vernon the county seat?" William asked.

"Yes," Frankie answered, "same pissant courthouse on the same pissant town square as all the other county seats in this pissant state." My brother did not like government.

"Have y'all paid her land taxes? I just paid mine a while back."

Then my mother did cry out, "Okay, yes, yes, yes!" And wept and held out her hand to William, who took it. William sat down on the other side of her and settled in to looking at *The Price Is Right* on the television screen. Like there was nothing else that mattered in this world. My mother patted him on the knee and cut a smile now and then at me and her other son.

When William and I headed out later, my brother Frankie leaned over to me and said, "I like this man. Sort of figured I might. Just a feeling I had, you know?"

I do know. It's what happens sometimes when you meet a good man.

That chapbook? The one by the writer I'd never heard of? I sat in the back seat of my Ford Explorer and read it aloud to two other men, Kyle Jennings and Frank Turner Hollon. We were southbound back home, toward Alabama. A story called "The Paperhanger, The Doctor's Wife, and the Child Who Went into the Abstract." When I finished, the vehicle had slowed from seventy-five to fifty. Somebody finally said, *Damn!* And I said, "I gotta get this guy down to read in my bookstore. But I heard he doesn't drive."

"Sounds like a road trip," Kyle said.

Yes, and what a road trip it was. Here and there, over and over, again and again. Until one day almost six years ago I got the news, behind the wheel, on my way to pick up William and go to a reading at Lincoln Memorial University, that my traveling buddy had died. But, because he wrote books, and because this manuscript was finally found, the road trip continues.

Sonny Brewer

The Lost Country

Memphis
April 1955

The court had awarded her custody of the motorcycle, they were going this day to get it. Edgewater was sitting on the curb drinking orange juice from a cardboard carton when the white Ford convertible came around the corner. A Crown Victoria with the top down though the day was cool and Edgewater had been sitting in the sun for such heat as there was. The car was towing what he judged to be a horse trailer. It was early, not quite seven, but the sun was heavy on him, sensuous, a good spring morning.

By the time she came he had almost finished drinking his breakfast and smoked a cigarette and was idly watching cars pass in the street. Birds called aloft on the trees above him, children bicycled past on their way to school. She had just got off the midnight shift and had not even bothered to change out of her uniform. MEMPHIS POLICE DEPT., the emblem on her shoulder said, she had a badge to prove it. She was a meter maid.

Claire eased the car to the curb and shoved it into park and left it idling. She wore a scarf over her dirtyblond hair and an air vaguely theatrical and, when she pushed her sunglasses up with a scarlet fingernail, her eyes were the color of irises.

What are you doing in this part of town, sailor?

Just waiting for someone like you to come along, he said.

You ready to roll?

He got in and slammed the door and looked out the window at the houses sliding by. Ready as I'll ever be.

Where were you last night?

Here and there, he said. Around and about.

You weren't anywhere you were supposed to be, that's for sure. I asked where you were.

I've got an alibi, honest, he said. Get that light out of my eyes, will you officer?

If you were as funny as you think you are you'd be something else. If you were as anything as you think you are you'd be a worldshaker.

He was silent. He drank the rest of the orange juice and slid the carton into the floorboard. He glanced covertly at her when she stopped for a redlight. The car had a straight shift that was awkward for her. She missed low gear when the light changed, the car jumped and died. Well shit, she said. A wisp of ash hair had straggled from beneath her scarf, curled onto her forehead, she blew it away. She looked angry.

I was at the library, he said. For a while. Then I just wandered around. I was in that bar awhile, the one on Central.

She did not reply, showed no evidence of placation.

They were in an older section of town, driving past mansions of splendid opulence, immaculate lawns where the grass looked as if it had been trained to grow some precise height and then cease. Rococo statuary arrogantly watched their covert passage, the battered old car did not linger long midst this splendor. The old mansions fell away, the houses grew ever smaller, tackier, as if they adhered to some abstract rule of diminishment that would render them infinitesimal should they continue long down this way. They drove on, like water that sought its own level.

This was Memphis, Tennessee, the middle of April in 1955, washed-out sunlight running on the storefront glass like luminous water. She was driving down a series of sidestreets in these steadily degenerating neighborhoods. What winos and such streetfolk were as yet about seemed stunned by this regenerative sun and so unaccustomed to such an abundance of light that they drifted alleyward as if extended exposure might scorch them or sear away their clothing. Bars and liquor stores contested for space on these narrow streets and both seemed well represented. They had a stunned vacuous look to them and their scroll-works of dead neon waited for nightfall.

She glanced across at him.

God, I hate the way you dress, she said. I'm going to have to buy you some clothes.

Edgewater was wearing a Navy dungaree shirt and jeans held up by a webbed belt the buckle of which proclaimed US NAVY. I'm all right, he said. I'm waiting for the loincloth to come back into fashion.

Listen. You're going to have to bear with me on this. Just hang in there no matter what happens, okay?

Wait a minute. What does that mean, no matter what happens? I thought we were just picking up your motorcycle.

Well, you know. They were my in-laws, after all. There might be a few hard feelings.

Here were paintlorn Victorian mansions where nothing remained of opulence save a faint memory. Rattletrap cars convalescing or dying beneath lowering elms. Shadetree mechanics stared into their motors as if they'd resuscitate them by sheer will or raise them from the dead with the electric hands of faithhealers. There were unkempt grassless yards with dump-replevied lawn chairs blown askew by spring winds and derelict automobiles entombed, parts-robbed, on cinder blocks. They drove by people with no trade save porchsitting who watched them go by with no interest and meanlooking dogs hopeless on knotted chain tethers anchored to old car casings. There was everywhere a sooty despairing dreariness. Edgewater grew restless, he felt an embryonic need to be elsewhere.

What do you think it'll bring?

I don't know, he said. Four or five hundred maybe.

What'll we do with it?

Whatever you think. We might buy a vinecovered cottage in the wildwood.

Elves to do our menials, she said, smiling for the first time, scanning the houses abstractedly, looking for the one she knew so well, had no need to search for at all. Past a rotting blue mansion with a red-tiled roof, she halted the car and, peering backward with a cigarette cocked in the corner of her mouth, she cut the wheel and backed the trailer expertly over the sidewalk and down a driveway bowered by lowhanging willows. A motorcycle was parked in the driveway, a faded tarpaulin crumpled on the ground beside it.

Showtime, she said.

The house was no better or worse than its brothers, replete with garish abandoned attempts at improvement, the side had been painted a hot electric pink and the front had been homebricked. The brick started at the corner and as if drawn by an aberration of gravity began a wavering descent, tended straighter, rising then, as if the house had been set upon by a band of drunken bricklayers with not a level among them.

Edgewater got out and let down the tailgate, stood watching the house with some apprehension. He had not wanted to come, had pled other commitments. All polished chrome and sleek black leather the motorcycle seemed waiting and coiled to spring, sitting alien and futuristic. Claire got out and slammed the door, climbing slowly out of the car like someone cautiously easing into deep cold waters. There were a couple of two-by-eights in the bed of the trailer and Edgewater aligned them into a makeshift ramp and turned to the Harley-Davidson leaning on its kickstand.

He stood regarding the motorcycle. The big ugly Harley had every kind of chrome that could be bought locally or mailordered out of anywhere appended to it and it had a distinctly heavy look about it.

She stood looking the scene over narrowly, her in her cop uniform, her cop eyes, what's the trouble here?

They goddamn, Edgewater said. They could hardly roll it. Eight hundred pounds of shittin chrome, he said. Why didn't he just gold plate it?

She did not reply. Her face was red with exertion, throat puffed and splotchy.

Come after it, I see, a voice said.

Yes, I come after it. It's mine, Claire said. I got the paper from the judge in my pocketbook.

A screen door slapped loosely against its frame. A short heavyset woman had come onto the back porch and she was crossing the porch rapidly in no-nonsense strides and she was rubbing her hands together in an anticipatory way.

Put one whore's hand on that motorcycle and you'll pull back a bloody stub, she said.

It's mine, Claire said, I got the paper from the judge.

You know what you can do with your judge's paper, she said. She spat toward Claire. Trash, she shouted. You slut, I didn't think you'd have the brass. Lie on the stand about my boy the way you done and then have the spit about you to come in my very yard and bring him with you.

I didn't lie, Claire said. But it doesn't matter. It's over.

Let's go, Edgewater said.

He'd no more than raised the kickstand and angled the front wheel toward the ramp when the woman began to scream, You slut, you ruined my son's life, you bitch. She was coming down the steps two at a time and Claire turned and took a tentative step away but the woman closed on her remorseless and implacable as a stormfront and slapped her face hard then laid a hand to each of Claire's shoulders and flung her onto the grass.

Shit, Edgewater said, walking around the trailer. He grabbed the fat woman around the neck and began to tug her roughly off Claire. The woman whirled on him. He could smell sweat and perfume and stale deodorant and an unclassifiable smell of anger, musky, he thought of an enraged boar. He could feel her hot breath and hear her grunt and something hit him at the base of the skull so hard bile rose bitter in his mouth and he fell beneath their combined weight.

The driveway was little blue granite pebbles. He lay on it studying them as though they contained some great knowledge, could he but decipher it. There was a roaring in his ears, there was an unbearable weight on him, lights flickered on and off at random.

Billy, Claire called. He hit the woman in her stomach with his elbow as hard as he could and felt her slacken. He shook her off and got up. He grabbed the motorcycle in a haze of half delirium, he had the motorcycle halfway up the ramp when the screen door slapped again and a middleaged man with a torn gray undershirt came out with a doublebarreled shotgun unbreached. He was unshaven, bald, hirsute chest and arms, a looping belly like a half inflated inner tube about his waist. He was fumbling waxed red cylinders into it. He dropped one and felt wildly about for it.

By the time Edgewater heard the gun barrel slap up he'd rolled the cycle off the ramp and straddled it and kickstarted it and he was already rolling when the concussion came like a slap to the head. He went through shredded greenery that spun like windy green snow, skidding blindly onto the street then across it and through a hedge before he could get the motorcycle under control and out onto the street again, leaning into the wind, houses kaleidoscoping past on either side like the walls of a gaudy tunnel he was catapulted through.

The street rolled in and out of the rearview mirror then the white Ford appeared and followed at a sedate pace. Edgewater slowed and turned the motorcycle into the parking lot of a liquor store and she turned in beside it. The Harley idled like some fierce beast that wasn't even breathing hard.

Hard feelings my ass, Edgewater said.

Do you believe this? He shot the shit out of that tree, did you see that?

I rode through it, Edgewater said.

Ahh baby you got it all in your hair, she said, brushing it away with a hand.

What'd she hit me with, anyway?

I don't know. I didn't see anything.

She had to hit me with something.

Claire shook her head. I'm just glad it's over.

They had to manhandle the cycle onto the trailer because she hadn't thought it wise to stop for the boards. Edgewater lashed it upright to a support with the rope she'd brought.

That's twice I've wrestled this heavy son of a bitch up here, he said. My first time and my last.

You're in a good mood, she said, grinning, getting into the car.

I'm not real fond of getting shot at, Edgewater said.

She eased the car out into the street and headed north, glancing in the rearview mirror to check was the cycle secure. You'll feel better tonight, she said. We'll get you a sport coat somewhere and go out to a really good restaurant. Italian maybe, we'll get a nice bottle of wine. Okay?

Okay, Edgewater said.

He stared out at the streets. Businesses were fleeing past the car like buoys in treacherous waters. Pawnshops, bars. A multitude of liquor stores that must sell one to the other.

Who needs this shit? he asked no one. I don't.

The prospective motorcycle buyer lived in a town called Leighton east of Memphis. They drove toward it past tract houses and apartment complexes and onto a flat countryside of housetrailers and farmland beset by tractors that Edgewater watched move silent down cottonfields that seemed endless.

He turned to study her against the slipsliding landscape. There was a faint blue bruise at the corner of her right eye and a scratch on her cheek but with the wind blowing her hair and the silk scarf strung out in the breeze she looked rakish and well satisfied with herself. In the brief time he'd known her she seemed always to be playing some role. Seldom the same one twice. Just the star of whatever movie today was. He'd had the impulse to glance about and see were cinecameras whirring away, a makeup man with his potions at the ready.

Then as he watched her profile seemed to alter. The flesh itself to sear and melt and run off the skull and cascade down the linen blouse she wore and the linen itself blackened and rotted and the wind sucked tatters of it away and when she turned to grin at him, bone hand clutching the steering wheel, the hollow eyesockets of her skull smoked like a charred landscape beyond which a faint yellow light flickered and died. Her grinning teeth had loosened in their sockets and there was a blackened cavity where the right canine joined the jawbone.

They were coming up on a white stucco building with a Falstaff beer sign framed by a rectangle of light bulbs. CAROLYN'S SHADY GROVE, the sign said. A quiet bucolic name that conjured up images of deep woods, of the creekbanks of his childhood.

Pull in there, Edgewater said. He was determined not to accompany her to sell it, felt perhaps that he had done enough motorcycling for the day.

What?

Let me wait here for you. I have to make a phone call.

She'd already begun to slow but she turned to frown at him. This doesn't make any sense, she said. We're almost to Leighton. You can call from there. Besides, who would you call? You don't know anybody. How'll I get it out?

Sell it as is, he told her. Sell the son of a bitch on the hoof.

He was out almost before the car stopped rolling. Pick me up after you get your business transacted. I'll be in there drinking a beer.

She glanced toward the sign. Just make damn sure you keep your hands off Carolyn, she said.

Edgewater crossed a glaring white parking lot of crushed mussel shells. The bar was set on earth absolutely bare of tree and shrub that belied its name. The stuccoed honkytonk seemed to have sucked up all the nourishment for miles around. DANCING SATURDAY NIGHT TO LIVE MUSIC, a placard in the window promised, but Edgewater was already touched by a rising desperation and he promised himself that by Saturday night he'd be dancing somewhere else.

He went into a cool gloom that smelled of hops and cigarette smoke and all seemed touched by a silence so dense it was almost cloistral. A man seated at the bar watched him cross the room. Edgewater's eyes were still full of the April light from outside and the room seemed a cave he was walking into, the drinkers seated at the tables troglodytes who'd laid aside momentarily their picks and were taking respite from their labors.

Let me have a draft, he told the barkeep. He withdrew a worn and folded five-dollar bill from the watchpocket of his jeans. The barkeep filled a frosted mug from a tap and raked the foam into a slotted trough and slid the beer across the counter. The barkeep had Vaselined red hair parted in the middle and a red freckled face and brownspotted fingers like sausages.

Edgewater took a long pull from the beer and lit a cigarette and sat just enjoying the silence. Even the drinkers at the tables were quiet, as if still contemplative of whatever had befallen them the night before. He could feel the silence like a comforter he'd drawn about him and he was glad that Claire and the motorcycle were rolling somewhere away from him.

There was something jittery about Claire that precluded calm. She was always in motion and always talking. He'd watched her sleep and even then her life went on, her face jerking in nervous tics at the side of her mouth, her iriscolored eyes moving beneath nightranslucent lids like swift blue waters. Her limbs stirred restlessly and he'd decided even her dreams were brighter and louder and faster than those allotted the rest of the world. Watching her sleep he felt he'd stolen something he did not want but nevertheless could not return.

He felt eyes upon him and looked up. The man two stools down the bar was watching him. He was a heavyset man in overalls whose tiny piglike eyes studied Edgewater in drunken fixation. He seemed to be trying to remember where he'd seen Edgewater or perhaps someone like him. He made some gesture near indecipherable to the barkeep and the barkeep brought up from the cooler a dripping brown bottle and opened it and set it before the man then refilled his shotglass with something akin to ceremony. There was a drunken, belligerent look to him. Seedy, dissolute, as if he had tried respectability and had not cared for it.

What are you lookin at? the man asked Edgewater.

Nothing, Edgewater said. He looked away, into the mirror behind the aligned green bottles. His reflection dark and thin and twisted in the wonky glass.

He took up three of the dollar bills and slid them across the bar. Let me have some change for the telephone, he said.

Was you in the war? the man downbar asked him.

Edgewater thought of the concussion of the shotgun, the drifting shreds of willow leaves. Not in one of the official ones, he said.

Change rattled on the bar.

What the hell's that supposed to mean?

Edgewater raked the change and cupping it in a palm went past a silent jukebox to the rear wall where a telephone hung. He stood watching it for a time as if puzzled by its function or manner of operation, the fisted change heavy in his hand, and he could feel sweat in his armpits tracking coldly down his ribcage. He turned and went through a door marked MEN and urinated in a discolored trough and washed his hands and face at the sink and toweled dry on a length of fabric he unreeled from its metal container. His cheek had been scratched by the gravel and he felt a raw scrape under his jawbone. Above the sink there was no mirror, just four brackets where a mirror had been. On the spackled plaster some wag with a black marker had written: YOU LOOK JUST FINE.

He went out and used the phone, heard it ring in what by now seemed some other world entire. Yet the room where the phone rang and rang was real in his mind and he wondered idly was anything missing, anything added, had they painted the living room walls.

Finally a young woman answered the phone. Edgewater's sister.

I'd about given up on you, Edgewater said.

Billy? Is that you? Where in the world are you at?

How is he?

He's how I said he was the last time you called. He's dying. Why ain't you here?

I'm on the way, he said. I'll be there. I ran into a little bad luck.

She knew him, she didn't even want details. You'd better get here, she said. He has to see you. Has to. He wants to make it right. He's tryin to hang on until you get here.

He said that? He said he's trying to hang on until I get there?

You know some things without them bein said, she told him. Or ought to. Would you want to go before your Maker carryin all that?

I'm not looking forward to it carrying it or emptyhanded either, Edgewater said.

Well. You and your smart mouth.

I've got to go, Edgewater said.

There's something wrong with you, she said. If you weren't so—

He quietly broke the connection and cradled the phone. Then he took it up again and held it to his ear and it seemed a wonder that there was only the dialtone. No news good or bad, just a monotonous onenote electrical drone, sourceless yet all around him, the eternal hum of the world slowly diminishing. He recradled the phone.

The man at the bar had swiveled his stool to watch Edgewater and Edgewater had seen the look on his face on other faces and he thought: Fuck this. He picked up his beer and what remained of his change and moved to the corner of the bar.

You're out of uniform, the man called after him. Where's your neckerchief?

I'm discharged, Edgewater said. I'm not in the service.

What?

I'm out. I'm a civilian.

The man had a red face, mauve with burst capillaries, cratered with enlarged pores. Don't you know it's against the law to wear that uniform? The man struggled off the stool and drained the shotglass and turned up his chaser and drank, Adam's apple pumping spasmodically. He set the bottle back and lumbered heavily toward Edgewater like a gracelorn dancing bear. Edgewater wished for a pool cue, magic winged shoes. A motorcycle.

You disrespectin that uniform whether you in or out. Them's Navy workclothes, don't think I don't recognize them. What I wore all durin the war. You got on them clothes and you're not even covered.

I never thought much about it. Edgewater fumbled through his change, got up and went to the cigarette machine, deposited a quarter and made his selection. When he got back to his stool the man had scooted four spaces down and had moved all his paraphernalia of swizzle sticks and napkins and cigarettes and change and was awaiting Edgewater's arrival.

You're a disgrace to the uniform, he informed Edgewater.

I probably am, Edgewater agreed, drank his beer. He sat as if undecided whether to move or remain.

I retired out of the Navy. Chief boatswain's mate. Twenty years. I saw a lot of little chickenshit fuckups like you.

I don't doubt it a bit, Edgewater said. I saw a few of them myself.

The fat man searched his face for guile, then stared into the depths of his drink. What'd they kick you out for? he asked craftily.

I got discharged, Edgewater said carefully, straining for clarity. In Long Beach, California. I'm out. I served four years and I'm on my way home.

Bullshit. What was you?

Radarman.

I might have known it was some pussy rank, the ex-boatswain's mate said disgustedly.

Behind the bar was a sign that said, AROUND HERE WE'RE JUST ONE BIG HAPPY FAMILY. IT'S GOT TO STOP. The barkeep had sensed dissention, approached them, began industriously to polish the bar in front of them. His face was smooth, expressionless, professional.

What do you think about that, Charlie? Man says he's out of the Navy and wearin them puked-on whites.

Edgewater ordered another beer. The bartender set the bottle before him, deftly picked up the change. His eyes avoided Edgewater's. It's nothin to me what he wears, he said.

The fat man began to mumble to himself. World War Two, he was saying. Then more, wet with spit, indecipherable. It sounded like he had fought and died for his country. Edgewater felt a wire pull taut, hum with ominous tension, vibrate, the pitch rise. He laughed softly to himself.

What?

Nothing.

What was you laughing about?

Nothing to you.

Was you laughing at me, shitface?

No, Edgewater said. To his amazement the man had taken on an uncanny resemblance to Claire's ex-father-in-law. There was the same beefy face, slack middle, mean little animal eyes. Some doppelganger, occult double bent on revenge. Queer out-of-body projection seeking him out by arcane divination here in the Shady Grove.

I was laughing at something I just thought of. It had nothing to do with you.

What?

Why hellfire. Nothing. Everything. What does it matter?

You silly son of a bitch.

Edgewater picked up his mug and cigarettes. He pocketed the Luckies and moved farther up the bar. Let me have another draft, he said.

Maybe you ought to drink up and move on, the barkeep told Edgewater.

Move on where?

Move on wherever you want. It's a wide world out there.

I'm waiting on somebody.

The barkeeper's cloth made little circles, there were black hairs on the barkeep's fingers, the bar gleamed with his industry. Maybe you ought to wait somewheres else.

The hell with that. Let him wait somewheres else. He started this mess, not me. All I'm doing is drinking a beer.

Don't fuck with Ed, the barkeep said. He's bad news.

He damn sure is, Edgewater said. But I'm hoping it's for somebody else. He arose, slid the bottle back across the bar, began to gather his change. This is the damnest place I've ever been in.

The fat man had gotten up too, some grotesque host seeing his guest to the door.

How about you fuckers? Ed asked. He was leaning forward into Edgewater's face. Edgewater could smell him, see the cratered pores of his skin, veins like tiny exploded faultlines in his nose, feel his angry pyorrheac breath.

While I was over there across the waters fightin and dyin you fuckers was over here drinkin all our whiskey and screwin our wives. What about that?

Hellfire, Edgewater said. I wasn't even old enough for that war. How about leavin me the hell alone?

Fought and died for you fuckers. Got medals to prove it. You was probably one of them, one of them conscious objectors, Ed said.

Edgewater drained the mug and set it gently atop the bar. He slid his cigarettes into the top of his socks and turned to go. I don't want any trouble.

Trouble wants you, the big man said. Nobody sets on their dead ass and sniggers at me.

Before Edgewater'd taken the first step a heavy hand fixed on his shirt collar and jerked hard and he felt the buttons pop away and the shirt rip down the back. It all happened very quickly. He whirled and grasped the mug and slammed Ed in the side of the head with it. It didn't even break and while he was looking at it in a sort of wonder the barkeep disdaining normal means of approach vaulted the bar with a weighted length of sawnoff pool cue and slapped Edgewater hard above the left ear. Edgewater's knees went to water and he pooled on the floor. The world went light then dark. Somebody kicked him in the side and a wave of nausea rocked him. His vision darkened gray to black and after a while when he came to he could hear sirens. The old man is finally dead and here comes the ambulance, he thought. He looked about. Ed was at the bar downing a shot and the barkeep was at his station and the troglodytes seemed not to have glanced up. Whoop whoop whoop the siren went. A wave of vomit lapped at his feet. Edgewater spat blood and pillowed his head on his arm and closed his eyes.

He slept. He awoke once in an empty cell and in some halflight like twilight or dusk and there was an old man with ferret eyes watching him from the cot across. He dreamed he felt probing hands at his pockets but he rested easy, there was nothing of moment there anyway.

He woke once in the night and the old man was crying, Help me, Jesus, the house is afire. Help me get her out.

Hush, Edgewater told him. There's no fire.

The house is afire and Lucindy's in there, the old man persisted.

She's out, she's all right, Edgewater said.

The old man whimpered to himself for a time while Edgewater watched what he could see of the still night beyond the high grilled window.

Then Edgewater dreamed he was a pallbearer. There were six of them, Edgewater at the left rear of the bronze casket. It was a huge coffin, leaden, a weight not to be borne, he felt he could not go on. They crossed a wooden bridge through whose slats Edgewater could see the lapping of yellow water far below them and ahead of them a hill rising up, domed and stark and symmetrical, cedars at its crest bowed black and mournful. The horizon was spiked with crosses and spires and graven angels. There were mourners winding ahead ascending the hill, he could hear their cries. The way was so long night fell on them and torches were lit, a winding procession of wavering light. Stop and rest a minute, he dreamed he said. Let's set it down a while before we go on. They ignored him and trudged on, ragged and out of step. He stole a look at one smarting hand, found blisters already broken on the palm, droplets of blood beginning to form. He swapped hands, peered at his right, it was bleeding as well.

He awoke and above the window rode a high remote moon, pale light that fell oblique and frangible upon his palms, the shadows of the bars running horizontal and vertical and infinite, latticing the sleeping old man where he lay. Before he was awake and at himself Edgewater had already examined his hands, but they were healed, it had all been long ago.

It was ten the next morning before she got him out, they came out of the City Hall in Leighton and down the steps into the sunlight. People going in and out of the courthouse glanced at him with interest, with no envy. She had on her sunglasses, seeking anonymity perhaps, a respectable woman bailing miscreants out of the drunk tank, followed by this curious hatless sailor lost so far inland. She was not happy. The Crown Victoria waited at a parking meter and he got in and closed the door. It was a while before Claire followed. She stood by the car peering in at him, studying him as if he was something malignant, bad news on a glass slide. Finally she got in. Her jaws were tightened and muscles worked there and she clutched the purse as if it were some weapon she might fall upon him with.

But the sun was warm and Edgewater closed his eyes and turned his bruised face to it and just absorbed that and the heat from the hot plastic behind his head.

He could hear her fumbling out the keys. The engine cranked and they were in motion. She squalled the tires savagely, spun smoking into the street, not looking at him. They rode for a time in silence. He lowered his hand, watched her clean profile against the shifting pattern of traffic, pedestrians moiling like ants. He studied her intently, as if he had never seen her before, some unwary stranger who had lowered her guard and permitted him trespass to her very soul. He saw for the first time the faint cobwebbing of lines fanning out from the corners of her eyes, the grainy skin magnified by the merciless sun. He looked past her eyes into her and found there imperfections as well. Cold vapors swirling off the River Styx. We grow old, we grow old.

She did not speak all the way to his motel. The Starlight Motorcourt, the sign corrected. Edgewater had no motor but he'd had four dollars a night, they let him stay anyway.

He went in and showered and shaved and brushed his teeth. He put on a clean T-shirt and a pair of khakis and peered out the window. She was still parked outside, waiting. You've got to have your say, he said. He took the blade out of the razor and put the razor and toothbrush and a sliver of soap into his pocket. He put on a longsleeve shirt and looked about the room to see what of him remained: a dropped paperback by the bed, a couple of magazines. The room seemed to be fading, losing its reality, a poorly executed backdrop for whatever had transpired here. He looked out the window then sat in a chair by the sill and watched her blonde head beyond the neat green lawn.

When he came up to the car she had her eyes closed, the glasses made them dark and enigmatic. Drive around awhile, he told her. Out of town somewhere. I've got to have some air.

They were not out of town before she commenced on him, as if it had taken her some time to gather her forces. She had many things to tell him. He listened absentmindedly, watched out the glass.

What do you have to say for yourself? she finally asked.

He opened his eyes. Not much, he said.

You son of a bitch. How do you plan on paying this money back? That was a big chunk of my motorcycle money.

He didn't say anything.

You beat anything I ever saw.

Edgewater dug out the crumpled pack of Lucky Strikes the jailer had returned to him. He pulled one out and straightened it and lit it from the dash lighter. He turned and watched the sliding landscape. Houses thinning out, Memphis falling away at last, a weight lifted from his shoulders. He didn't know where they were going but the countryside was slipping past, field and stone and fence, cows like tiny painted cows in a proletariat mural. A dreadful flat sameness to this western world. It went rolling away to where the blue horizon and bluer sky were demarcated by windrowed reefs of salmoncolored clouds.

She had never been so humiliated, she told him. She would never have treated him in such a fashion. She would not have done a rotten dog that way. She'd had no sleep, her job was in jeopardy, he was ruining her life.

They rode in silence for a time, getting into the country now.

You wouldn't even have called me. I had to go looking for you in that terrible bar and hear about you picking a fight with some war veteran. What's the matter with you? I should have just let you rot there.

He seemed not to have heard. Beyond the windowglass a man clutching the handles of a turning plow went down a black field so distant he seemed in some illusory manner to be pushing plow and mules before him. Edgewater wondered what his life was like. What his wife said to him when he came in from the fields, what they talked about across the supper table. He would have two children, a boy and a girl. Later he would tell them a story as their eyelids grew heavy and sleep eddied about them like encroaching waters. A flock of blackbirds tilted and cartwheeled and spun like random debris the wind drove before it.

I never sent for you, he finally said.

I know as well as anything you did it deliberately. Set this whole thing up. You couldn't just walk away like anybody else. You have to get yourself locked up and ruin the nice dinner plans I had made and waste all that money.

Is there much more of this? he asked.

I've just about had it with you. And on top of everything else you're the coldest human being I've ever seen. And I've seen some cold ones.

Well, I guess I could have left you a note. But people kept coming at me with blackjacks.

You invite it. You drive them to it. What's the matter with you? All that money thrown away. Besides having to go up there and sign your bond for assault and battery with them making fun of me behind my back. They wouldn't have let you out at all if I hadn't been on the police force.

He had no words to say.

What do you have to say about all my motorcycle money gone?

I guess there goes the vinecovered cottage.

Goddamn you, she shouted. Do you think I'll put up with this shit forever? Do you think I'm going to let this mess start all over again with you the way it was with Clifford? Hell no I'm not. Let's me and you get some things straight right now.

Stop the car. I'll get out anywhere along here, Edgewater said.

What?

Let me out of the car.

She locked the brakes and the car slid to the shoulder of the road and sat rocking on its shocks. Edgewater was out and perhaps thirty feet down the road before she realized he was gone. She sat as if undecided what to do.

A car was approaching behind them. He turned and stuck out a thumb. In the sun the car seemed to be warping up out of the blacktop road itself, swift and gleaming and shifting through transient stages as if it had not yet assumed its true form. It shot by without slowing in a wake of dust and roadside paper that rose and subsided gently to earth. He went on. After a time she put the Ford in gear and followed along beside him until he went down the embankment and climbed through a barbedwire fence and started across the field. She stopped the car then and shouted at him then gathered stones and began to hurl them at him. But her arm was poor and the stones fell wide, as did the curses she cast that in the end were just words and he had heard them all so often they had become powerless.

Billy, she shouted.

He looked back as she was getting in the car, the sun on her hair.

He waved her away onehanded without turning. He went on.

He got two rides that put him farther down the line. Just before dark clouds blew in. Ominous lightning flickered briefly luminescent in the southwest, flickered as if in set relay up and down layered clouds. Then thunder rolled hollowly, a premature dusk fell on the land.

Sometime back he had come onto the highway and now he angled toward the woods, gazing about for shelter, scanning the sky for rain. A bleak drizzle displaced out of November began to fall, and in a few minutes he was sodden.

In a bare area near the road he came upon the site of a burned house, blackened rocks and rubble and smoked tin twisted like crumpled and discarded tinfoil. Lightning pointed out a log smokehouse beyond two foundation rocks. Its door hung impotent on strips of rotted leather. Kicking about him he went in, rested on a cardboard box of fruitjars and watched the lightning flash staccato and fierce through the unchinked walls. Cracks showed him a world in tumult, lightning-rendered trees bent and tortured in the wind. It rained harder, pounding on the tin, lulling him soporific. He half dozed.

He dreamed again of his sister, could hear her voice faint with distance, across the miles, Tennessee to California. It had been his sister. The old man had not deigned speak to him.

How is she?

Lord God, Billy. Mama's dead. We buried her Thursday.

She fell silent, there was static in the receiver, trouble along the wires.

Where was you, Billy? She wanted you there at the last.

I don't know. The brig. When was it you tried to get me?

Lord we been tryin. You knowed she was bad.

The operator told him when three minutes were up, charged for time passed, not for words, mostly there'd been silence.

Her hair had done come out and everything. From them treatments. God, it was awful, Billy.

Yeah. Well.

Are you comin?

Yeah.

When?

I'm on my way now.

What'll I tell Cathy?

Tell her I had trouble. Tell her I'm coming. I'll have to hitchhike.

There was silence again, he could hear the voices at the other end, dim, indecipherable. She back on. The brig or a beerjoint one, she said all in a rush. Goddamn you, Billy. Why do you do like you do?

He hung up. His hand ached, he had not known he held the phone so tightly.

He awoke. He heard thunder and came to. The rain had stopped, there was a deep and lingering stillness. Then fieldmice moved softly about the joists, keeping their furtive rounds. Something conspiring perhaps against the interloper from the night beyond the walls.

And what is the height of your arrogance, the geography of your righteousness? Oh sister, you've changed, you change still. You who squatted and pissed in the road in front of a carload of boys who dared you. All your drunken laughter in the moonlight. He told me so, in the alley behind the poolroom. It caused me great pain, sister, not the least of which was the arm he broke with the tire spud. When the weather is just so it pains me still. At sea it did, perhaps the damp.

What are you now, where have you gone these years? You were a little girl, there was a dirty stuffed lamb you would not be shut of. Now factory floorwalkers berate you, and, undone, you weep against limegreen walls. We are all changed, time cheapens us all.

He entered the outside. The night was clearing and there were patches of sky almost silver. Frogs called from some near pond, nightbirds took up the chorus. Whippoorwills from some deep hollow. He walked through the rubble, momentarily lost from the way he had come. The moon came partway out, Rorschach shards of clouds stringing over it medusalike, in the keep of some high wind unimaginable.

Starting out he went the wrong way at first and was drawn to a lightning-struck tree burning away in the night. He approached it and stood in wonder, as if he expected admonishment, absolution. There was only the pop and snap of burning timber.

He went on. He shambled down a hill to the highway, went on east as if there were some compass in him that would draw him home. His shadow trudged behind, a squat caricature of the man it joined at first one foot and then the other.

Few cars passed. He thumbed them from force of habit, to no avail. No compassion for this hard traveler. In the small hours of the morning there was something sinister about him, he would not tire, the deep timber beckoned him to rest but he would not heed it. They watched from the womblike warmth of their cars as they passed him, felt perhaps a momentary quirk, a stirring of unease. Garbed in white, he was a wraith in their headlights, a spectral revenant reenacting some old highway carnage, a warning rising up in their headlights to encompass them. They went on, they wanted no truck with him. He was the phone that rang deep in the night, a death in the family, bad news at journey's end.

The next night. Cold vapors swirled the earth like groundfog. Midnight maybe, perhaps later, it scarcely seemed to matter. The last ride had let him out on this road hours ago and he walked through a country which in these shuttered hours seemed uninhabited. Not even a dog barked. Just a steady cacophony of insects from the woods that fell silent at his approach and rose again with his passage, an owl from some timbered hollow so distant he might have dreamed it. Nothing on this road and he thought he'd taken a wrong turn but then it occurred to him that on a journey such as this there were no wrong turns. If all destinations are one it matters little which road you take. The pale road was awash with moonlight as far as he could see and in these clockless hours when the edges of things blur and the mind tugs gently at its moorings it seemed to him that the road had never been traversed before and once his footfalls honed away faint and fainter to nothingness it would never be used again.

The moon rose, ascended through curdled clouds of silver and violet. His shadow appeared, long and ungainly, jerked along on invisible wires, a misbegotten familiar he was following.

It had grown cold with the fall of night and he thought with regret of his coat and blanket but there was nothing for that. He looked both up and down the empty road but source and destination faded into the same still silver mist. He left the road and angled cautiously through branches and blackberry briars into the woods.

The passage of an hour had him before a huge bonfire, the piles of leached stumps and deadfall branches and uprooted cedar fenceposts with stubs of wire still appended roaring like a freight train and sparks and flaming leaves cascading upward in a funnel of pure heat.

He warmed awhile then seated himself on a length of log and unpocketed and unwrapped a candy bar and ate it in tiny bites, forcing himself to chew slowly, making it last. There were two cigarettes remaining in the pack and he lit one and tucked the other carefully aside for the morning. When he'd finished the cigarette he built up the fire and lay down with the log for a pillow.

Out of the dark a whippoorwill called three times and ceased, whippoorwill, whippoorwill, whippoorwill. After a time another called from a distant part of the wood but the first remained silent, as if he'd said all there was to say. Edgewater closed his eyes and images of the day lost drifted through his mind like a disjointed film he was watching. Slowly he settled into sleep.

His dreams were troubled and he tried to wake but could not. In the dream he was in a Mexican hotel room. There was a bed, a basin, a chest of drawers. From rooms up and down the hall came shouts and raucous laughter but no one was laughing here. Here something had gone awry.

The girl on the bed was leaking. Spreadeagled on spreading scarlet as if her white body lay on an enormous American Beauty rose that grew as malign and ill-formed as cancer. The old woman and her smocked assistant were preparing to flee. Rats who'd choose any ship but this one. The woman said something in Spanish he didn't understand and the man mimicked her hasty exit and left the door ajar and before he fled himself he leaned close into her face and watched the fluttering of her eyelids and cupped his hand hard between her legs as if he'd contain her and Don't, he said, Don't, as if dying was a matter you had any say in.

He wanted out of the room and out of this dream and he went down the hall opening doors upon startled participants in their various couplings and a girl on hands and knees being mounted by her lover like a dog turned and studied him calmly over her shoulder with breasts pendulumed between her distended arms and her hair falling like a black waterfall and as her lover slid into her she looked away and Edgewater closed the door. In the room next a sailor was emptying a bottle of rose hair oil into the graythatched vagina of an old woman and in the next a man turned to blow out the match he'd lit the window curtains with and he grinned at Edgewater and winked while behind him the gauzy curtains climbed the walls like flaming morning glories and the rosedappled wallpaper curled and smoked and stank like burning flesh.

His father and his sister were in the next room, the old man abed and the sister attendant. His caved face, his deathroom smell. The eyes of some old predator who's crawled into his den to die. She turned from her ministering with a damp cloth in her hand and Edgewater saw that the old man had been berating her and she was crying. She dropped the cloth, turned away and leaned against the plaster. Finally she turned upon her brother such a look of sadness and loss that he wept despite himself. If you weren't so…she said, and he closed the door in her face.

Before the last door he stood holding the doorknob. It was hot to the touch and seemed to vibrate beneath his fingers. Something was holding it on the other side of the door. He realized that beyond this door lay whatever the other rooms had been preparing him for. He steeled his nerve and took a deep breath of the smoky air and twisted the doorknob hard and shoved the door open and fell into the room.

He woke shaking and appalled and for a moment he didn't know where he was, where he'd been. He wiped a hand across his mouth. He held his face in his palms. God, he said. God. He raised his face and hugged himself against the cold. The fire had burned to a feathery white ash that rose and drifted in what breeze there was and there was a steely quality to the bluegray light that stood between the trees.

Objects were softly emergent, tree and stump and mossgrown stone, and to Edgewater these objects seemed to be attaining not mere visibility but existence, things that were being born into the world for the first time before his eyes and he studied these things in a kind of bemused wonder.

He had a thought toward rebuilding the fire but more than warmth he wanted quit of this glade of dreams. He paused only long enough to rake the ash away until he found a glowing coal to light his cigarette.

When he came out of the woods onto the roadbed there was already a faint roseate glow in the east and he went on toward it through the first tentative birdsongs. The world was awakening. All sounds were clear and equidistant, somewhere a cock heralded the dawn, on some unseen road a laboring truck shifted gears. A red rim of sun crept above the trees and consumed the horizon with gold and silver light.

Hunger lay in his stomach like a fistsize chunk of teeth and claws and broken bones but his heart was lifting and his feet felt fleet and light. The day was new and unused and this day was one that had never existed before and he saw it as a footpath that led into a world that was sensual and manyfaceted and complex beyond his understanding, but for the moment he was comfortable in it and roofs and shelter and ill weathers were things of no moment. He thought the only dwelling he needed was the unconfined and unwalled world itself.

———

Once more on the road, Edgewater came upon a store that was deserted and empty. Its shelves shelved only rat dung and dead roaches. He had some time back passed through a scrubby settlement where there was a building marked POST OFFICE with peeling paint and there was a deserted-looking church but there had been no store at all. The land he passed now seemed deserted, fallow fields without even grazing cows to watch his passage.

His shadow was long before him and he feared that all the stores, should there be any down this way, would be long closed before he reached them. He had two candy bars and he ate the melting chocolate as he walked and when he came upon a concrete culvert that carried a stream beneath the road he angled off and followed the branch through bottles and scrap paper past these signs of habitation to where the water passed clear and cold over mossy rocks. He drank deeply from the stream and washed his face and hands. He arose and started back the way he had come through swarming gnats that fogged about his eyes and when he came back onto the road, there was a slack dissolute look about him.

Roosterfish judged it about quitting time but the day's labors had gone well and he thought he'd try one more service station. He'd lost count, this would be the tenth or maybe the twelfth, pickings were good here. He figured there must be a good market for gasoline in this part of Tennessee. Sinclair, Direct Oil, the dinosaur sign. He eased the Studebaker into the Direct station and cut the switch.

The Studebaker was something to see, a one-of-a-kind limited edition. It was a green 1947 sedan, the model that looks the same coming or going, but its designer would have been appalled to see the grievous changes that had been manifested upon it. Half the cab had been cut away with a welding torch and the trunklid removed and a camper of plywood cobbled up behind it. A rolling shack, a sharecropper's shanty on wheels.

Roosterfish got out and surveyed the service station. The day was waning and the glass front of the building was awash with liquid fire. He went through the screen door. No one seemed about save a man in greasy coveralls behind a long counter. Behind the man a sign said NO CHECKS, NO CREDIT, but it didn't impress Roosterfish. He was accustomed to a world marked POSTED, KEEP OUT, VIOLATORS WILL BE

PROSECUTED TO THE FULLEST EXTENT OF THE LAW. A world in which
most every move he made was illegal in some form or other.

The man set his Coca-Cola on the countertop and stood regarding
Roosterfish. What he saw was a tall thin man with a missing arm. The
left arm appeared gone from just above the elbow and the sleeve of the
blue workshirt neatly safetypinned to the shoulder. The man wore carpenter's overalls, worn but clean, and his neatly trimmed black hair was
covered by a carpenter's cap of striped blue ticking. He had pale blue
eyes that looked benevolently and directly into the world's own eyes and
his hatchetlike face with its slightly famished cheeks was freshly shaven
and gleamed with aftershave and there was about him a faint odor of
Sen-Sen and Lilac Vegetal. He'd converted part of the greasy coin of his
realm to a more digestible medium. Counting out nickel after nickel,
dime after dime.

What'd you do, the storekeep asked. Rob a paperboy?

It's money ain't it? Still counting, never losing count.

Well, yeah, it's money.

Says so right on it.

Just count it out.

Okay then. The coins mounded on the linoleum covered counter.

They've got all this new stuff now, the storekeep said. Looks like
green paper. Foldin money, they call it. You can bend it and carry it
around in a pocketbook. It's the damnest thing.

I'll have to try it, Roosterfish said.

Then Roosterfish hung his head a bit and leaned over the counter. I
need a favor, he said. I don't know who else to ask.

The man shrugged. You don't know me, he pointed out.

I know. Of course I don't. I'm passing through, a stranger here. I
don't like askin for help but I'm up against it. Pretty bad shape. I've
gone about as far as I can go. I'm buttin my head against the wall and
the wall won't move.

The man had taken from the breast pocket of his overalls a bag of
Country Gentleman smoking tobacco and was constructing a cigarette.
When he'd finished he fished up a Zippo and lit it.

You wouldn't let a man bum a smoke would you?

The man silently handed the tobacco over and Roosterfish singled
out a paper and laid it atop the counter. He tipped tobacco onto it

and took it up and expertly twirled onehanded a professional-looking cigarette, thumbnailed a match to life and lit it.

Ain't had one all day, he said through the smoke.

Just what is it you want from me? the man asked.

I got a promise of job in a town east of here called Ackerman's Field, Roosterfish said. Workin for my brother, he's a carpenter up there. He's goin to let me do trim work. I was on my way and last night down in Lake County, a motel in a place called Tiptonville—here Roosterfish looked about as if to see were ladies present—some son of a bitch stole every tool I had right out of my truck. Tools and what money I had.

I still don't see why you're tellin me, the man said. This ain't a bus station.

Some of these old boys are a little dense, Roosterfish was thinking. Goodhearted but a trifle dense. I just need a little help, he said. A couple gallons of gas, a buck or two. Hell, half a dollar, anything.

The man was silent. I don't even see what a onearmed man could do as a carpenter, he said at length.

It'd surprise you what a onearmed man can do when he's up against it, Roosterfish said.

Well. I'm sorry about your tools and all, but this ain't no gravytrain I'm ridin here.

I know. That's fine, I appreciate you takin the time to listen to me. Sometimes it helps just talkin about your troubles.

He turned to go, paused to crush the cigarette out in an ashtray by the door. He paused for a moment as if awaiting something. The cash register chinged behind him.

Hell, hold up a minute, the man said. Roosterfish turned. The man was proffering a bill. A five, Roosterfish's expert eye discerned. I been down and out myself, the attendant said. If this'll help, take it on.

God bless you brother, Roosterfish said, making a mental note to include the Direct Oil Company in his prayers that night.

Just don't piss it away on whiskey, the man said.

Roosterfish was going through the doorway. I don't much hold with spirits, he said.

His radar was infallible when applied to the presence of police cars and he saw the one parked across the street immediately, though he didn't acknowledge it. He got into the Studebaker and closed the door, the five-dollar bill exuding a subtle and reassuring warmth against his thigh. When he pulled into the street the cruiser cranked too and eased along behind him. He glanced up once to the rearview mirror then ignored the cop. He'd been just a shape behind the wheel, stolid and inevitable as the rest, and Roosterfish figured he'd come in a box stamped: one Southern smalltown cop. Nightstick and gun and attitude included. Red lights flashed and sirens sounded. Roosterfish pulled over.

He heard the cruiser door open and looked right toward a brick schoolhouse beyond an expanse of green lawn. Children were swinging on playground gymsets and laughter rolled toward him bright as unstrung beads. Laugh it up, he told them. Wait'll you see what's around the next bend in the road. He took a deck of Camels out of his bib pocket and began to peel away the narrow strip of cellophane with his teeth.

License and registration.

Roosterfish dealt them up.

The cop was scrutinizing the license. You a long way from Ackerman's Field. What are you doing down here?

Passin through, lookin for work.

You a mechanic?

No.

You seem to have been patronizing all our garages and service stations. Was you looking for work at all of them?

Roosterfish didn't answer.

That's against the law. It's called soliciting.

I didn't know soliciting was against the law.

It is here.

I really wasn't doing that anyway. I was just askin for a favor. Is that against the law?

It damn sure is.

There seemed no fitting response to this. Roosterfish at length began his wellworn tale of Lake County tool thieves, the purloined money, the carpenter job, but he was interrupted.

Get out of your vehicle, the cop said. Open up that back end and let's see what all's back there. We've had a string of burglaries around here.

Roosterfish felt on firmer ground. I wouldn't steal a nickel from the richest man on Nob Hill, he said, climbing out of the Studebaker.

The interior revealed a battered suitcase, five or six fivegallon buckets, two wire cages with fighting cocks in them. Over all a rich smell of raw gasoline. Roosterfish's worldly goods revealed to their essence.

What's them chickens for?

Roosterfish pondered this. Finally he said: They're not for anything. Whatever chickens are for. They're just chickens.

They look like fighting cocks to me. Cockfighting is a felony in the state of Tennessee.

Well. That's why I got them in separate cages there. So they won't tie up and fight. Won't break the law.

Goddamn it you know what I mean. It's against the law to fight roosters and bet money on it. Are you that dumb?

I'm pretty dumb, Roosterfish said.

I could arrest you, the cop said. He closed the camper door, opened it and slammed it so that the latch caught. I could vag you, but I'll bet you've got money in your pocket, don't you?

A little, Roosterfish said. He dealt up his hole card. Listen, he said, I'm just doin the best I can. Life's hard for a onearmed man.

Life's hard for one and all, the cop told him.

Roosterfish was silent. He thought about bringing up hearth and home, old grayhaired tearstained mothers, but a man needs to know when to quit.

I could lock you up but the county'd have to feed you and if you're clean the judge'd just turn you loose. I think the simplest thing is you just get the hell out of my county. I'm going to follow you to the county line and I don't ever want to see that rollin piece of scrapiron around here again. Are we right clear on that?

Yes, Roosterfish said. Which way do you want me to go?

Any way that suits you, the cop said. Let's pretend that right here is the center of everything and that any way you go in a straight line will get you somewhere else. Just pick a direction and head out.

Roosterfish drove eastward at a sedate pace. The cruiser followed, red light pulsing. We look like a goddamned parade, Roosterfish thought, grinning at himself in the rearview mirror, but he had always had a great fondness for parades and he did not let it bother him.

Roosterfish drove past the last grocery store late in the afternoon, surveyed it carefully as he passed. They were all beginning to look alike. Double Cola signs, Bull of the Woods chewing tobacco, 666 Tonic. Even the same whittlers lollygagging on upended Coke crates. He turned into the graveled yard of an old church and leafed through his notebook to see had he been there before. He had not. He backed onto the chert road and drove slowly back, easing up to the gaspump. He adjusted his striped painter's cap, his expression of hangdog humility, assumed the air of a man cruelly put upon by the world, but who will not acknowledge defeat. Hard times on the land.

How many?

The man was heavyset, stolid. Cold little eyes as compassionless as a hog's. A hard sell for sure.

Good buddy, I'm in trouble, Roosterfish told him.

The man looked up and down the road as though there might be prowl cars, bloodhounds, pursuit.

My name's Lipscomb. I'm a housepainter by my trade, and I got promise of a job over by Clifton, if I could just get there. I've had sickness and the loss of a loved one. I've pawned most of my tools just to get this far and I ain't got a red cent left. Not a cryin dime. You my last hope.

Dubious of this honor he still stood stolid, scratching his head.

Roosterfish had intended asking for three dollars, automatically compensated down. Two dollars would get me way down the line. I'd stop on my way back and settle up with you.

I give gas to everbody comes through here I wouldn't even be here when you come back. If you did. Now would I?

Well how about just a dollar to get me somewhere else? She's settin right on the peg. He waggled his stump. Life's hard for a onearm man.

Life's hard for one and all, the man said. He was peering into the Studebaker. I might swap them chickens.

Lord them ain't eatin chickens. Them's fightin cocks.

They'd still sweeten up a pot of dumplins.

That Allen Roundhead there's won upwards of two thousand dollars.

Maybe you could get him to spring for the gas, the man told him.

Just move ye foot back. I got to get on.

There was a logroad that came up before the blacktop did and he turned in here and turned off the motor and got out. He opened the back, drug out one of the five-gallon cans and walked bent onesided with its weight and with wrist and elbow hoisted it onto the top of the hood. He unscrewed the gas cap and got out his siphoning hose.

While the gas ran he checked the sun, called it quitting time, the self-employed keep hours of their choosing. He did a quick account-ing of the worn wadded bills in his pockets. When he was through he shook the can to see how much gas remained and went back and rested against the open front door. Some of these McNairy County folks is rockhearted sons of bitches, he told the chickens.

Roosterfish, in more congenial surroundings, had taken for his dwelling an abandoned fishing cottage on a cliff above the Tennessee River. No one knew he was here, the wrong season for fishing and no one stumbled across him. No fishermen had come and probably no one cared anyway. The road up here was long and winding, the Studebaker would barely negotiate its steeper turnings. Wind or the slow accretions of time had tilted the cabin on its axis of foundation stones and when Roosterfish first found it it had been the keep of raccoons and foxes. Now it was swept and scrubbed and cozy as a badger's den. He'd furnished it with recycled window curtains over the one window and the broken table he replevied was covered by a new oil cloth lithographed with coffee grinders and spice bottles.

But he thought he'd take dinner on the veranda tonight. The evening air was pleasant if a little windy and he built a fire in a brick grill covered with an oven rack he found in a dump. When the fire was burning well he set two castiron skillets atop the rack. Waited a bit. Spooned in lard, watched its slick oily slide across the warming black surface.

Fish tonight. Catfish done up in white butcher's paper and tied with string. He rolled the fillets in a bowl of seasoned cornmeal, checked the temperature of the grease, laid the breaded fish aside and began peeling potatoes.

The grease sizzled when he laid in the pale catfish. Rich smell of seared cornmeal, bright crinkling odor of black pepper. He sliced pota-toes into the other skillet, wary of the popping grease.

While things cooked he took a pint of whiskey from beneath the seat of the malformed truck. Sipped it slowly with one eye on his din-ner, holding the whiskey on the back of his tongue and diluting it then swallowing. Good bonded whiskey. I.W. Harper bourbon, no popskull crazyman's potion here. Taking the whiskey like a sacrament, like the distillation of all his past, while the river moved below the steep bluff like the comforting murmur of days out of the lost country of his youth and the light slowly went down in the world.

When the food cooked he ate from a blue enameled plate, catfish crisped and browned and greasy potatoes and lightbread fresh from its cellophane wrappings. Done, he mounded the plate with potato peelings and scraps and raked everything over the bluff into the river and scoured the plate clean with sand and stowed it away. The night drew on, the farther trees like textured fabric against the deepening twilight and the river louder. He set out the caged cocks before the fire and filled the trays with water and the feedbins with cracked corn. The wind was rising, you could hear it in the leaves, in the soft clash of branches. Ain't you a meanlookin son of a bitch, he asked one of the roosters. The cocks just watched him with eyes like bits of black glass. The wind guttered in the grill and the light running across the cocks looked every shade in the spectrum, gold and red and indigo and gradations of deep seagreen.

The level fell in the bottle. Roosterfish felt comfortable and warm, at peace with the world, squire of all he surveyed. He set the bottle carefully on a stump and rose and took from the truck a fiddlecase, from the case a fiddle and a bow.

How about a tune? he asked the roosters, and clasped the fiddle with his chin and the stub of his left arm, bowing with his right, the strings opentuned to accommodate the way he has to play since he can't note anymore. He wasn't drunk but he did a crazy little jig just the same, the demented fiddle evoking kilted highland dancers and whiskey flowing like water and longlashed eyes cutting at you in the smoky firelight.

Then after awhile he recased the violin and just smoked and drank and listened to the river. A lone whippoorwill called out of the timber, another, and he asked the rooster, Ain't that a lonesome sound? I bet you can't do that.

More of them, a chorus of them, a choir, he's camping in Whip-poorwill City here.

He took a drink. We goin to get Harkness, he told the fighting cock. Him and his rooster too. We're just bidin our time, gettin us a grubstake. Buildin up the kitty. Me and you. You take the little one and

I'll take the big one. He sipped. Or if that don't suit you, you take the big one and I'll take the little one.

The cock fixed him with an arrogant black eye. Firelight ran like quicksilver on its iridescent metallic feathers. It looked like caged lightning, like some gaudy killing machine from an alien world.

When full night came he carried the cages into the cabin and while they made querulous complaints he lit a kerosene lamp and when he reglobed it the yellowlit room sprang fullformed out of the dark with its comforting familiar features and he lay down on an old Salvation Army cot leveled with bricks and took up from beneath it a wellworn truecrime magazine he found here, and sipping from time to time he read these dispatches like a diary the world kept of its heinous and bloody doings.

After a time there was a murmur like distant thunder and he went out to see. Sure enough, far downriver, a staccato flickering between and above the trees, the sky flaring electrically and subsiding and flaring again. Just a murmur of thunder, a realm of thunder, an almost lost memory of thunder. The wind was at the trees again, they whispered and clashed in liquid disquiet and the air smelled like rain and the wind on his face was warm and damp.

Some time in the night he woke and the rain was pounding on the tin roof in a downpour without variation, but he'd retarred the roof weeks ago and he didn't worry about leaks. He listened to it rain for a time and then he eased back down into dreamless sleep.

There were days when Edgewater's desire to be home was near manic, when he pushed himself with ferocity and recalled, with self-loathing, money he had in times past thrown so carelessly away. There was idle time to repent, but he repented small things, a guitar pawned and not redeemed, drinks bought for buddies, for whores with only first names. Greyhound buses passed him, the blue smell of diesel fiercely nostalgic, faces looming down strange as if they inhabited some other world. Then it was gone and the land it moved across was as green and flat as a pool table.

These days all the demons of deeds done and deeds imagined seemed to coalesce into one, some gaunt outrider of the fates whose footfalls coincided with his, who while he lay in troubled sleep pressed on untired, came implacably on with a vague and timeless inevitability: then it would seem that the family he moved toward were no better, surcease had flown when he did. Death had enlisted them in its cause and scattered them wherever its winds decreed them, left them with seeds of their own to sow, small plagues of their own to spread. He did not know what drew him on. The girl was no more than a name and a packet of abandoned letters, a ring a shyster jeweler had unloaded on him in San Diego, a face he could no longer call to mind even in half-sleep.

He moved across country of dreary sameness, he wished for mountains, hills, anything that would break the featureless monotony of flatlands. On a map he picked up at a service station Highway 70 lay like a spoke in a wheel that had Nashville as its hub. Another spoke led away east to Chattanooga. There were rides to be had in Nashville. It loomed like a goal on the horizon he moved toward.

There were few rides here. He rode in rattletrap pickups with wizened old men and he crouched in the cabs of flatbed trucks trapped in small malignant whirlwinds of bits of straw, dust, fertilizer. Country moved away and there was yet more of the same, as if he were lost, they were all lost, going in circles. It was as if they moved through some area where the process of creation had been set in motion long ago, and, demented, it continued to produce a country new and yet eternally the same.

The newlooking cars with out-of-state tags would not stop for him and he came to believe that no one was going anywhere. Just down the road is all. To the grocery store, to town on Saturday. Town was never far away. Sunday there were carloads of people bound for church, stiff and straight in old highbacked cars lacquered with dust. Little girls like cut flowers. Boys with grim visages who turned to stare at him with envy down this dusty roadway.

He strayed off Highway 70 with a garrulous peddler of Watkins products and rode all day with him, watching with interest as he dispensed from the loaded backseat nostrums and tins of pie filling and vanilla extract and boxes of exotic-smelling spices. He sat idly in the spicy heat amidst this merchandise outside a tarpapered shack while the peddler screwed a gaunt old woman with snuffjuice at the corner of her mouth and lank strands of dead irongray hair she smoothed coyly away. The peddler came out buttoning his fly and gave Edgewater a knowing wink.

He thought vaguely of San Francisco.

Where'd you find her?

Find her hell. She found us. Me and Tubbs was both broke and lookin for somebody off the ship to hit for five bucks when she hollered at us. She was standin outside this apartment building, Lord, she was seventy if she was a day. She said she bet we was lonesome so far from home on Christmas and she said she had a whole turkey and trimmins cooked up and nobody to eat it but her. We was broke and who knows, she might have had a bottle up there. So we went up and Tubbs screwed her first.

Jesus. I thought I was bad but I can't hold you a light. You sons of bitches are perverted.

Hell, MacPherson said. She wanted it. I didn't know they wanted it that old.

They don't in Huntsville, huh?

Not that I know of. Tubbs was screwin her and it didn't suit him some-how and he had the bottle of Fitch's Rose Hair Oil in his ditty bag. He upended her and poured it in her and went back at it.

Hellfire, Edgewater said, then sarcastically, Did she come?

Like a Winchester repeatin rifle, MacPherson assured him solemnly.

Edgewater riding with a talkative sewing machine salesman. The car the salesman drove was comfortable and the flat country had slipped away with deceptive ease. The salesman was generous with his cigarettes and he was glad of an audience for his tales and it did not bother him that Edgewater mostly rode in silence. His tales all seemed to concern his various escapades with housewives. Most of them had him with clothing in hand escaping from windows, back doors, or hiding under beds and in closets. His narrow escapes were many and his virility had entered into female folklore, and under the cumulative weight of all his evidence Edgewater was forced to conclude that sewing and machine were the two most powerful words in the English language and that when combined they produced an aphrodisiac of irresistible and unreckonable potency.

For a time he was torn between the comfort of the upholstery and the tedium of these tales and the indecision was his undoing. By the time he disembarked he was as far north as you can go in Tennessee without wading into the Mississippi River and he was far off any major highway that led east.

There were cotton fields unimaginable, cotton fields that seemed to go on as far as the eye could see, look out the window it was cotton, look out the door it was cotton, he imagined they must see cotton in their sleep. There were little gray clapboard shacks that seemed to be receding back into the earth and the cottonfields came up to their very porches, there were paths wending to the road. As if whoever owned these lands demanded that every foot of it be employed to productive purpose.

He passed these shanties and here and there a country store owned by the selfsame man who owned the land and who paid his hands on Friday and took it back on Saturday for overpriced groceries, as if he had pulled money from his left pocket and placed it in the right, money which had marvelously reproduced itself, the ultimate alchemist. He passed shanties with naked children playing in the dirt and shanties with wilted flowers growing in dissected car casings and Maxwell House coffee cans and once in a while a woman came and threw dishwater into the yard and leant a minute and watched him go.

The people he saw looked to him like survivors of some great natural cataclysm, had not yet come to terms with the way their world had changed. But most of the shanties were empty, choppers were in the field strung out like foraging birds. They moved across the field in a great staggered line and their hoes rose and fell in some vast unconcerted motion that ultimately took on a rhythm of its own.

He set out afoot now the way he'd come, on some nameless back road in Lake County. On his right some sloughs of brackish yellow water sometimes seemed to threaten the road itself and he wondered if the river flooded or if these were just the backwaters of the Mississippi. The sun stood at its zenith and the day had grown progressively hotter and after a while he began to notice how thirsty he was becoming.

There didn't seem to be any water to drink in this country. To the left of the road stretched vast cornfields of a uniform arsenical green and they went as far as the eye could see and did not end but simply faded out with distance.

He left the road where turgid yellow water had eaten a chunk out of the red chert and went through coarse tall sawgrass following the shore of the slough. Perhaps there was clean water, a spring bleeding in. He gave up after a while and rested beneath the shade of a water oak and studied the opaque yellow surface where water spiders darted and checked and the surface rimpled with arcane life and worked with soft gaseous expulsions of something decayed or some hidden commerce. Crayfish had a veritable community worked into the banks with their gray mud houses, a cottonmouth dropped from a low branch with scarcely a sound and vanished in a diminishing series of esses and the child he'd been shivered within him and his imagination envisioned huge crocodiles broad in the dark hours dragging entire cows sloughward for a midnight feast and he dreamed of legged monsters that clambered up the muddy banks and staggered after him in the wake of his flight.

An old grandfather turtle drowsed on a halfsubmerged cypress. Seven kinds of meat the old folks say. Hunger had dogged him for days, he imagined the turtle alchemized, mutated into a thin hot broth that steamed fragrantly in an enameled kettle, the broth sweetened with baby carrots and tiny green sweet peas and white chunks of potato.

I should go, I should go, but the dying will die unassisted, it's a skill they're mastering, even the most inept grow proficient, it's what the dying do best. And there are worse things to dread than that.

The water he uplifted in his cupped palms stank of dead fish and tiny black hardshell bugs swam in it and he flung it away and wiped his hands on his jeans and spat dryly into the tepid water and went back through the rough grass to the road.

He went past weathered sharecroppers shacks that seemed to sit on the earth without benefit of foundation with rot creeping upward like some malignant fungus and the houses stood like the dried husks of some cultural metamorphosis from other seasons that had cast them off and gone on to better things. He saw no soul about save an old sepia woman who sat unmoving in a willow rocker from the purple shadows of a porch and who gave no recognition that he'd passed. He raised an arm in greeting and let it fall and thought to ask for water but something in her stillness gave him pause. As if he'd gone invisible in the world, become a ghost still haunting a land he could not quit. She sat still as some mockery of sticks and hair and castoff clothing and she looked like nothing so much as some mummified old grandmother swiped from an undertaker's wares, sitting here as a posting to warn off whatever had decimated this blighted waste. War, plague, madness. He looked once and she hadn't moved.

He saw brick columns that bookended a porch and a drive that wound through a stand of older trees. A gently rising slope where in a grove of cypress sat a house of improbable size and grandeur, white through a blur of green, brick chimneys rising past a red-tiled roof, but the house had the shimmering quality of a projected image and he perhaps suspected it was a mirage. He went on.

Soon he came upon signs of commerce. The cotton fields had begun to be populated. Workers were strung out with hoes chopping toward the end of the field, childsized workers in straw hats, the more vigorous pulling ahead like contestants in some curious race and the oldfolk bringing up the rear.

A red Diamond T truck was parked in the shade of a cottonwood at the border of the field. There was an enormous watercooler aligned on its edge, a short swarthy man stood before the cooler filling a tin cup.

How about a shot of that water?

Help yourself, good buddy. The man drank and tossed the remainder of the water onto the earth and proffered the cup. He had a broad pleasant face and a nose so miniature it seemed to have been stuck on as an afterthought.

Edgewater filled it and drank. The water was cold and good and he filled the cup twice more before he was through.

Thirsty work, walking, the man said. You looking for somethin else to do?

I'm just passing through.

The man looked comically around, scanned the four points of the compass. Where the hell from?

I got turned around.

You damn sure did if you wound up here. Say, you aint got a cigarette have you?

Edgewater had two the salesman had given him. He handed one to the man and lit his own and passed the matches across. The wail of a distant ambulance sounded like a dream of someone screaming.

Name's Pugman, the man said through the smoke, Paul, but everybody calls me Pug. I'm no strawboss but I could get you on if you needed a few days' work.

Two other choppers had come up with their hoes and leaned them against the truckbed. An old crone in black bonnet and long dress like garments of mourning and a young darkhaired girl whose clothes seemed from seasons past so tightly did she fit them. The girl gestured for the crone to drink first and the woman rinsed her mouth from the communal cup and spat a dark amber of snuff and filled the cup to drink her fill, the girl gave Edgewater a cornereyed look of covert interest then glanced abruptly away when he met her eyes. Edgewater hunkered in the shade of the truck.

What's your name?

She didn't answer. The crone turned upon Edgewater a sharp vicious look and placed the cup in the girl's hands. Get it and let's go, she said.

What's your name?

Iva Mae, the girl said.

When she'd finished drinking she turned toward him. A small gossamer face, long dark hair parted in the middle. Her eyes had a look that was both shy and at the same time bold and impudent.

What's yours? she said but the old woman—grandmother, keeper, who knew, fairy godmother—had her by the elbows and was hastening her away.

Edgewater crushed his cigarette out on the earth. What does it pay? he asked.

That old woman watches her like a hawk, Pug grinned. Touch that biddy and Grandmama'll flog you to death.

Sometimes you just make the wrong move. There's a moment when something dreadful is going to happen and maybe half a moment when you can do something to stop it. But if you don't the dreadful thing happens and once it's done it's done forever. She's dead and there's no bringing her back, the fingers trail, sliding from your grasp and the waters tear her away and everything has to be paid for, all accounts have to be settled. There is no free lunch and no one gets out alive.

He took a row adjoining them but they pulled easily ahead of him, hoes flashing in the sun, grass and weeds flying and the young cotton thinned and the earth pulled to it just so. Iva Mae had looked back once as they worked down the endless green rows and grinned at him and Edgewater simply abandoned the row and caught up one over and began hoeing alongside them.

The girl was laughing. You can't do that, the girl laughed.

You skipped ahead, the old woman said. That'll get you fired.

I'm just trying to be sociable. Where do you all live?

In a house with a top on it, the old woman said viciously. Just do your job and let us be.

Late in the day they broke from the field with the sky already reddening in the west. The choppers who had the farthest to go climbed aboard the bed of the truck their legs dangling over the sides and set off homeward and the folk within walking distance strung out purposefully along the road. Folks forever shortchanged for the night will not replace what the day has stolen. Edgewater had lost sight of the girl and her keeper and was looking about for them when Pug hailed him.

Pug was standing by the roadside with a young woman shorter even than he was. She had a guileless open face with hair coarse as a horse's mane pulled back in a knot behind her head and she was looking Edgewater up and down, sizing him up as if judging his suitability for some unstated purpose.

I reckon they mean you to bunk tonight with us, she said. That's what Hobart said and he's the big dick around here. There ain't no more empty houses. We eat pretty good when we're working. Not much on variety but there's plenty of it. Hobart said they'd make it up to me, slip me a few bucks. Likely what they'll do is take it out of yourn and pay me with it. They don't never give nobody an extra nickel here, they take it away from somebody else first.

I don't want to put you out, Edgewater said.

Hell, don't worry about it. We got an extra room, we'll get by.

The woman's name was Pearl and she was Pug's wife. She told Edgewater she was from Alabama and she and Pug had met in a cottonfield.

They had started westward along the road. Edgewater wondered where they were going and how far it was but he didn't ask. His shoulders ached and the palms of his hands felt as if he'd held them to the surface of a hot stove and he was almost too tired to be hungry. He felt vaguely disoriented. Here in the vast flat world a man used to hills and mountains lost all sense of distances, the landscape seemed to be shrinking, drowning in upon itself. Above the western horizon the sky gleamed like polished brass and the clouds shifted through shades of ultramarine to a deep blue and the edges where the sun flared looked hardedged and seemed composed of some curious metal unknown to this world, arcing out of the light like some brimstone byproduct of the conflagration itself. Against the light such trees as there were appeared charred, abruptly tarnished and black and depthless as inklined likenesses of trees, like a paper silhouette with its flat illusion of depth. When the sun finally went it burned beyond the flat horizon like the smoldering remnants of some rumored holocaust.

The house was a mile or so the way Edgewater had been going. It crouched near the road on a treeless and grassless plot of land that Edgewater judged useless of agriculture or anything save tenanting these folks where lives were so marginal they seemed scarcely to exist at all, everything that passed between the paper that proved their birth and the paper that proved their death just rumormongering and hearsay. There was no bathroom, not even an outhouse. But when he saw Pearl come from behind the house unplucking her dress tail from her underwear he guessed calls of nature were to be handled on a case by case basis and depending on where and on circumstances and opportunity.

Edgewater went with a borrowed towel to a longhandled pump in the back yard and filled a blue enamel washpan with water. The water came up slick as if already soaped in the earth and there was a reek to it and when he drank from a cupped hand he swallowed a time or two then spat it onto the dry earth. Goddamn, what's the matter with this water?

Nothing the matter with it, Pug said. It's limestone water, sulfur water, somethin, medical water. They say it's good for you. It ain't hurt us none.

It does have a mediciny taste to it, Edgewater said. Reckon what it cures?

Whatever you got, what I heard. Shit, we'll probably come away from this place cured of stuff we hadn't even had a chance to get yet.

He watched Edgewater at his crude and sorry bath. You travel about as light as any feller I ever seen, he said. I've heard about them old bindlestaff hobos they had back in the thirties, but hell you ain't even got a bindlestaff.

Edgewater was washing his hair, toweling it dry. My bindlestaff was stolen out of a Greyhound bus station in California, Edgewater said. Along with everything else I had.

Money and papers and such?

Everything. A seabag full of clothes. What little money I had left. Luckily I'd already pissed most of it away.

You get done with your toilet there we can walk down to the store. I got a ticket you can use. Get you some dinner and stuff and we'll settle up Saturday.

Edgewater in a land of novelties. Aisles of tinned foodstuffs, pork and beans already marvelously studded with sliced wieners, sardines in exotic foreign oils, red devil cans with their lithographed salmon that evoked in Edgewater a response so Pavlovian his mouth watered. He bought a quart of milk and drank from that while he scanned the shelves. Binned eggs, crated apples with their smell of childhood past. A cakeroll of cellophaned pastries which he gave a wide berth, a meatcase so bloody and septic-looking and flyspecked and bedecked with unidentifiable cuts of meat so outré they might have been hacked from the bleeding flanks of mythological beasts or carved clandestinely from the roadside dead.

You ain't got a little drink hid away back there nowhere have ye? Pug asked the storekeep.

Might have, the storekeep said. It's agin the law to sell it but I might give one away.

Pug drank from the bottle and offered it to Edgewater who moved it away.

I'm drinking this milk, he said, raising it aloft, showing the bottle.

My runnin mate here had all his clothes stole in California, Pug said.

If the storekeep wondered that there were no available clothes between the California coast and the backwaters of west Tennessee he had the grace not to say so. I always heard that was a rough place, he said. I heard them Mexicans out there would just as soon cut a man's throat as look at him.

A man don't have to go all the way to California to have that done, Pug said. Or find a Mexican to do it, either.

Edgewater stacked his selections on the worn countertop while the storekeep totaled them up. Tinned Vienna sausages, crackers, the beans and franks. A package of cigarettes, a candy bar, a bar of soap, a razor and a toothbrush. He had an eye for a tube of toothpaste but the price was dear and he was running on Pug's paper here and guessed the soap would suffice. Edgewater looked at the largess, his holdings in the world had increased marvelously.

The storekeeper's pencil was busy. You hear about old lady Joplin dyin?

Hell no, said Pug. When'd she die?

Today sometime. They left her all right this morning and come in from the field and found her dead on the front porch in a rockin chair. Had shirt she was patching on her lap nearly finished.

Edgewater thought of the busy needle in the cloth, the halfstitch taken, the still needle, oblivion.

What killed her?

Nobody knows, the storekeep said. Hell, she was old, old. She just run out.

She just run out, Edgewater thought, taking up his paper poke, the sand run out.

Pug was an expansive and generous host and he gestured Edgewater toward the steaming food on the kitchen table. There was fried beef liver and onions and fried potatoes and biscuits and Edgewater needed no urging. He piled his plate and fell to eating. Moths kept guttering with a sizzling sound in the kerosene lamp and Edgewater fended the survivors away onehanded from his plate.

Later they went out into the cool of the evening. Full dark had fallen now and the sky lowered itself onto the resting earth and stars shown so generously and haphazardly you could have walked by their light and the earth itself richly suspirious with vapors and the nightcries of birds and the night so quiet and weary Edgewater imagined he could hear the Mississippi River wearing away the channeled earth and bearing it to the gulf. Sitting in the yard smoking he looked up at the sound of wings and watched a white owl pass low and enormous, the stars winding with its passage and reappearing in its wake like some great bird of myth and folklore that could control stars and diminish the heavens themselves.

They sat for a time in a companionable silence. Letting weariness ease away, the cells rebuild themselves. Edgewater's hands still throbbed and he kept flaring his fingers as if to see would they still bend. After a time Pug arose and walked around the corner of the house. He was gone a time and Edgewater felt the weight of Pearl's eyes and looked at her. She was grinning at him from the doorstoop where she sat, her dress had ridden up and she'd pulled it up as if to accommodate his eyes and here was a long expanse of starlit thigh and the pale crotch of her underwear.

You might pull that dress down, he said mildly. I reckon we've all seen one. We all know what one looks like.

Speak for yourself, Pearl said, but she tugged her skirt down.

He looked away.

Looky here, looky here, Pug said.

He had a streaming water bucket from which he dealt up three dripping brown bottles of beer, one to each.

Well now, Edgewater said.

I had em down in that old cistern, Pug said. They ort to be cool enough to drink.

The evocative power of the beer caused Pug to reminisce. He'd been in the invasion of Normandy and so luckless he'd made the Battle of the Bulge as well and he recounted to Edgewater such strange and bloody carnage and on a scale so confusing and mindnumbing that Edgewater had a thought for the outward limits of human endurance. He wondered if he would have been capable of these things and without meaning to he wondered it aloud.

I guess by God if it was the only thing to do you'd do it.

Edgewater remained silent. He'd known at one time the only thing to do was go home but he hadn't done that. Start looking for a scrap of lumber to rebuild burned bridges. He'd come already most of the distance, it was the last mile that was turning out to be hard. Once it had seemed easy to undo things, to unsay things. To forgive things said and done to him. But deeds and words had a permanence he hadn't been aware of and it was easy to become distracted by life in its infinite and beguiling variety.

Pug set his empty bottle aside. Well that's it for me, he said. I'm wore out and mornin comes early around here.

How wore out are you? Pearl said.

I'm pretty wore out. Bindlestaff, there's a blanket there in the front room. Just go on back when you're ready.

Wore out, wore out, Pearl said softly to no one.

There was the creak of bedsprings inside the house then silence. Edgewater became conscious of the rasping wall of frogs from the slough, as if they'd all thousands of them suddenly thought of something to say.

He's always too wore out to do anything, Pearl said.

Edgewater didn't say anything. She smoked one and studied the worn leather of his shoes.

He's mean to me too.

How's he mean to you?

One night he got drunk and throwed the only good pair of shoes I had in the slough.

After she'd gone in he sat for a time just listening, the croaking of the frogs diminished by the enormous silence of the night. A pale sliver of moon had risen, the bottom edge poised to cup water, a dry barren moon. By its meager light the fields of cotton looked silver, a vast expanse faintly luminous, like St. Elmo's fire at sea. Earlier there were lights from other shanties but they had gone down to darkness now, and he could see the moment it happened, the face leaned to the lampglobe and the harsh expulsion of breath and the sudden darkness that smells of kerosene and the slow creak of the bedsprings, and the murmurs, the whispers, all over the sleeping land, demurred, passions spent and passions spurned in the temporary dark while the earth tilts inexorably toward the waiting sun. As if he'd be clarified in the crucible of crazed austerity, made whole by the innocence of love, or at least cauterized wherever the bleeding was coming from. The nights were never long enough, the night would not replace what the day had stolen. In all their beds in all their shotgun shacks they lay burled against the quilts in agonized crucifixion, their troubled dreams biased by the enormous tug of gravity from the invisible and lost country they had come from.

He awoke deep in the night and dreamed he heard some sounds beyond the normal sounds, the call of the nightbirds, the incessant cheep of frogs from the vast water. Goddamn mosquitoes, he said, slapping. They were all about his ears. The voice came again, Pug's, a murmurous chorus from Pearl, wheedling, placating.

I'll kill him, Pug said. Edgewater felt a disquiet, wondered if the threat was general or specific. He fancied other voices, up and down the levee, faint and faraway, from the coal oil scented yellow shacks. Voices seeking entry, seeking egress. Seeking excitement, seeking peace of mind. Seeking anything to make the night rock easier by.

I ever catch you with another son of a bitch like I done that time I'll cut his fucking throat with this very knife, Pug said.

I won't do it no more, Daddy, came her voice pleading faint from the outskirts of death.

He pulled the blanket about him, felt the cool wood of the porch, watched pale stars through a rent in the tin.

At last he slept.

The day in abeyance, the troubled waters of sleep lapping at the improvised bedposts, trying to belong he felt at once a kinship and a distance. In his counterfeit sackcloth, his imitation ashes. This respite from the dumbshow a wary pageant where inept actors can never remember their lines, cannot improvise or even remember their motivation. And Edgewater the worst of them, the worst of the lot. Easing through like a sneak thief, an agent provocateur, taking things that would not even be missed. A glance, a word, a memory, a moment that no one else notices. It might have been lost save that I have replevied it as salvaged raw material, to build myself. What do you want me to be? I'll construct a self from all these plundered lives, a prism from this broken glass, I'll be you but not quite, a distorted replica of what you see when you lean toward the mirror, when your reflection leans toward you in the glass. I'll steal your shadow and reflection and warp it to my purpose and steal away under cover of darkness and move on unnoticed with only the spurious credentials of my blistered palms, even your gatekeeper was sleeping at the watch. I passed her blind eyes unnoticed, she was dead with her patching in her lap.

When he went in he could hear their coarse heavy breathing. He took up the blanket and went with it toward a doorway that was just a rectangle opening onto Stygian blackness. A struck match showed him a floor of bare earth, a few rotten planks laid across it like a wooden pallet. The match glittered red in the eyes of a huge rat regarding him from the corner. Gray and scaly-tailed and avaricious-looking, the rat seemed determined, even outraged at this intrusion and appeared intent on contesting him for territorial rights of this domain. Edgewater blew out the match and threw it at the rat and went with his blanket back to the porch.

He slept cold and woke before daylight with the blanket wrapped around himself like a shroud. There was no going back to sleep and he rose and built a fire in the kitchen range and put on a pot of water and rummaged around until he found the coffee. When it was done he sat on the edge of the porch sipping a cup of it and watched the skies incrementally lighten. The stars beginning to vanish, winking out one by one as if they were streaking away into remoter corners of the known universe, disappearing into unknowable distances.

In midweek the rain began and it settled in with an air of permanence as if it would never cease. At noon on Saturday the Diamond T equipped with wooden sideboards and roofed with tarpaulin made its way along the backroads and wagon lanes, stopping before each of the sharecropper shanties. Family by family they clambered aboard until at length they were crowded in like upright sardines or refugees packed for some uncertain but dire destination. The adults had a restrained air about them, they wore their Sunday best, clean shirt and overalls and even a necktie or two and the felt fedoras old farmers affect. They nodded with an unaccustomed dignity to their neighbors, saying, Hidy, looks like it may blow up a little rain here after a while.

The children were in a more festive mood of barely contained glee as if bound for a carnival and already in, then hearing a distant calliope, they had to be constantly called down by their mothers. When the truck was finally loaded it climbed the levee and headed east toward Tiptonville, with a trail of smoke rising behind it.

The truck parked by the tie yard below the railroad track and they clambered off, the men assisting the children and the ladies down from the high truck bed. They stood for a moment wordless, the men pulling their hats lower, brushing dust from clothes, the women running last-minute combs through their hair, damp handkerchiefs to the faces of their children.

I'll be leavin at nine thirty sharp, rain or shine, Hobart said. Hobart was the driver and there was an air of authority about him. If you ain't here at nine thirty I'll figure you ain't goin or you got another way back. Just remember it's bettern fifteen mile to the farm.

Hot damn, Bindlestaff, Pug said. Let's see if we can find us a dry place and get up a pill game. Drink us a cold one or three.

They played pool at a place called Dixie Billiards for an hour or so but Edgewater kept glancing through the rainblurred glass at such commerce as was passing in the street and at length he drained his beer bottle and hung his cue in the wooden rack.

I'm going to walk around a bit, he said. See what this place has got in it.

I know what you're up to, Pug said.

Edgewater just grinned and shook his head.

Be a killin, Pug called as he was opening the door. That old woman totes a little snubnosed pistol in her drawers.

Edgewater just waved onehanded and let the door fall to behind him.

He crossed the aisles of the five and dime, eyeing the binned merchandise. Eyed himself by sober girls in cool green lisle. The old woman was fingering bolted rolls of cloth with her back to him and at first he didn't see the girl. Then passing up another aisle he saw her studying costume jewelry, cheap corded earrings and gaudy bracelets of plastic and colored glass. A salesgirl was watching as if Iva Mae might be planning a major jewelry heist.

Hey, Edgewater said.

The girl turned. Hey. I wondered where you'd got off to.

Looking for you for the last hour. I've been in every café in town. You want to go get a hamburger or something?

I don't know.

Let me pay for that thing you're holding and let's go.

You want to buy it for me?

Sure.

I'd have to ask Grandma about going to eat with you. She don't like you.

She doesn't know me. Let's leave before she does.

She knows you well enough. She thinks you're trying to get me off to myself.

I guess I sort of am.

And, you know, do things to me. Are you?

What kind of things?

You know.

Right now I'm just trying to buy you a bracelet and a hamburger, Edgewater said.

I'll have to tell Grandma. She'll think I'm lost.

Hellfire. This town isn't big enough to get lost in.

But the old woman had some arcane sense perhaps subconsciously attuned to Edgewater and his ilk and she'd approached silent as a plague. She seemed not to move in the customary manner but to glide as if her feet did not quite touch the floor or if she were equipped with tiny ballbearinged wheels that propelled her about.

He just wanted to buy me a hamburger, Iva Mae said.

Hamburger nothin, the old woman said. I'll just bet he did.

As she hustled the girl toward the cash register the girl looked back over her shoulder. We'll be at the show after a while, she called.

No we won't, Grandmother said.

Edgewater bought a hamburger and fries in a place called the Eatmore Café and put them in a grease-splattered bag and a sixpack of Falstaff he picked up at the pool hall and went below the railroad track where the truck was parked. He climbed up inside and sat with his feet hanging over the tailgate then clambered up and adjusted the tarpaulin forward and reseated himself in the dry and ate listening to the mesmeric patter of rain on the canvas, eyes looking at nothing, thinking no thoughts at all.

When he was full, a lean smokecolored hound appeared below Edgewater's feet. The dog looked at him expectantly as if he'd had news there was to be food left over and Edgewater tossed him half the hamburger. The dog caught it in its razorous jaws and swallowed twice and waited to see if more was forthcoming. That's it, Edgewater said. The dog eased beneath the truck and vanished.

Edgewater drank beer and leaned against the wooden frame of the tailgate. He closed his eyes. He could hear nothing from the town but he guessed later there would be reveling, confrontations in the alleys, honor would be impugned, honor defended. Southern women would be drunkenly insulted, brass knuckles would rattle on the barroom floor, the red lights of the police.

As if in rehearsal an ambulance crossed the railroad tracks briefly airborne and lit rocking on its shocks and streaked eastward lights winding, siren already beginning to wail, speedometer in a fast steady climb into the red. Trouble in the hinterlands, the citizenry are restless, there is disquiet on the land. Something is amongst us and must be contained. Almost immediately a black and white cruiser followed, the revolving dome light pulsing arterial red into the blowing rain. He thought this the strangest of trades, this laying on of order onto chaos. To sweep up the broken glass, hose away the blood. Haul away the smoking wreck whose speed had altered its shape to accommodate the shape to that of the concrete bridge abutment. To saw into warped and jammed car doors, sparks flying beyond the safety glasses, watch his arm there. Take stealing peeks into hell, eavesdropping on their telephone lines. A little preparatory licensed course and they can move through nightmares with impunity, nothing is posted to them, there is no such things as trespass. Sewing up the wounded, closing the eyes of the dead. Reassembling the scattered and bloody pieces of the puzzle, does this go here or here?

Once long ago his father had shaken him awake in the night. Get up. The unfeatured black shape looming over him, the face shown in his mind rather than his eyes told by familiarity, by the countless times he had seen it, every day of his life, the black shape just a widebrimmed silhouette.

Where are we going?

Just shut up. Don't wake your momma.

They went through the woods. The woods silver as in a dream. Ebony where the moonlight didn't fall, the light streaking away like chrome, like electric on the dewy upturned leaves, the world turned down until reduced to its elemental black and silver, the trees dim and ancient engravings. His feet were wet, his jeans soaked to the knees.

After what seemed hours they stopped to rest. They were on a hillside overlooking the farm of a man named Crouch. They were very close. Wet tin roof, a barn, windows dark with sleep. Edgewater could see the German Shepherd chained to the clothesline. Hear the chain shirling as the dog walked back and forth the length of the line like a sentry at his post.

Son of a bitch beat me, the father said. Eight days work clearing new ground and the son of a bitch refused to pay me. Not couldn't pay me, just flat out refused.

Then law him, Edgewater said.

He carries the law folded up in his pocketbook. I was goin to take it out in hide and his old woman called the law on me. On me. I got a little hide but nowhere near eight days' worth.

Edgewater could smell his father. The smell of sweet chewing tobacco, the vaguely wetanimal smell of the hat, the smell of his anger like the smell of metal heated bluewhite in a forge, dipped in water to set the temper.

That dog, Edgewater said but his father brushed him with contempt.

That dog won't even bark.

Why?

Because it don't want its throat cut, his father said.

They came down the slope into the barnlot. The slope below the house was littered with tins of food. Crouch went with women other than his wife and she used to go into rages. He'd attempt placation with largess, exotic things to tempt her, bags and boxes of food from the grocery store. She'd stand on the back porch and hurl it can after can down the hillside, where the weather unlabeled it and then it lay gleaming like jewels, the older cans already rusting. Reckon any of it's fit to eat? he'd asked once, and thought for a moment his father was going to hit him. But the hand upraised to slap finally lowered like a weapon that moved of its own weary volition. Likely it's all tinpoisoned, he said.

What he was after was a turning plow. I priced one of these at Grimes's Hardware, he said. It's about the same as what he owes me.

What do you want with a turning plow?

You may have to help me here. This son of a bitch is like lifting the world.

At last he had it hoisted, the crook of the plow on his shoulder, the point over his chest, the handle upraised into the air. Goddamn, he said.

We'll have to double up on it, Edgewater said.

I can do it.

Back into the woods. They wound back the way they'd come, turned down a fading road grown kneehigh in brush to an old houseplace the father knew about. They came out in an old plum orchard grown rank and mutant and stopped to rest, the father squatting beneath the weight of the plow as if afraid he'd never get it hoisted again, the enormous point resting against his heart, a rat squatting there in the halfdark with the plowhandles rising above his head like huge curving horns he looked like some weary beast so aberrant he was outside the world's dominion, beyond the pale, forced to haunt the very perimeters of a land that would not have him.

You want me to help you with it?

You may have to brace me when I get up.

There was a well covered over with halfrotted chestnut boards. He lowered the plow and stood breathing hard. This is rougher than clearing the goddamn new ground, he said.

He cleared away the debris. Edgewater looked down the handhewn sides. Slick wet earth, glistening rock around the throat. A moon trapped at its bottom, the water gleaming like quicksilver.

Help me line her up here.

The plow went skittering down the sides, there was an enormous splash when it struck bottom.

Well now, the father said. That's better. I'm even with him now.

I believe I was goin to steal something I'd pick something a little easier to carry, Edgewater said.

His father was in a better mood now. I priced all that junk. This was the only thing that balanced it out. Evening up always takes a big weight off you.

Edgewater hadn't known he slept but someone had him by the foot shaking him awake. He opened his eyes to a cop, a police car beyond him gleaming in the rain, lights flashing, garbled electronic voices from the scanner.

You can't drink that beer here. Did you not know that?

No.

You can only drink it where you bought it at or outside the city limits. You are well inside the city limits. You with Hobart's bunch?

Yes.

You want to drink beer, set in the pool hall and drink it or take it home with you.

All right.

Where you from?

Not here, Edgewater said.

I don't want to see you again with one opened.

All right.

When the cop had gone he finished the rest of the beer and slid off the truck and followed the railroad tracks back toward town. He didn't know what time it was but the light was dimming down and there was still no sign of a sun anywhere. The rain still fell. Two men were arguing in the alley beside the poolhall. Just hit me you son of a bitch, one of them said. You hit me, the other said, and you'll think a boxcar fell on you.

They stopped to watch Edgewater's passage.

You want some of this? one of them called out.

Fuck you, Edgewater said.

Lights were on at the Dreamland Theater. The grandmother and her charge were scrutinizing the posters. A whitehatted cowboy with a guitar in one hand and a smoking pistol in the other. They bought tickets and went in. When the side doors opened Edgewater could smell popcorn, hear the sound of gunfire.

Outside the movie, three boys sat on the curb solemn and silent.

What goes on here on Saturday night, he asked them.

Both smaller boys looked toward the biggest. He chewed and swallowed. Oncet in a while they's a fight or a cuttin, he said.

Edgewater said that was about what he expected.

Briefly that night he took in a dance. The Rambling Mountaineers were playing at a converted roller rink near the outskirts of town. He could hear the fiddles and the stomping and the raucous laughter and it drew him on to where cars ringed the old building and drunks staggered up and down the high steps.

He decided it was not worth seventy-five cents to see if the old woman and girl were inside. He doubted it. Anyway he could hear from outside: the song changed, became plaintive, mournful. *When the warship left Manila, headin to deep blue sea, deep blue sea. She's my Filipino baby.*

A drunk woman swung onto his arm, pressed a bottle into his hand. Hello, sweetie, she said. A smell of perfume, splo whiskey, then worse. She staggered, fell to the ground, began to vomit. We've got to stop meeting like this, Edgewater told her, began to wipe vomit off his shoes. A man came up and helped her rise, gave Edgewater a malevolent look. Edgewater pocketed the bottle, moved on.

He did not know how he had failed to think of the movie theater. When the show let out they spilled out with the rest, onto the sidewalk, attended by moths, eyes blinking in the unaccustomed light. They moved toward the waiting truck, Edgewater straggling along behind. They were among the first. A few women. Children, eyes still numb from the vision they had seen. A far land of red sunsets and purple mountains, heroines with unimpeachable virtue, lawmen who shot pistols that invariably inflicted only flesh wounds. Then a few drunks began to stagger up to the truck. Looking about to see was there anybody needed whipping.

The old woman and the girl and Edgewater sat on a bench formed by a plank inserted between the slats of the sideboards, some curious family portrait, harridan with progeny, perhaps.

You going to church tomorrow?

No, the old woman said.

I may, the girl told him.

Where's the church?

She began to tell him. He hardly listened. He was devising a plan for getting her out that night. Perhaps in the dewy cotton rows. His blanket. So sweet. So sweet.

Let's get it loaded, the driver called. Edgewater turned to look. It was not his employer but a new driver, bigger, a hefty man with muscled arms and a length of leaded broomstick cocked out of the back pocket of his overalls. People began to climb onto the truck. A fat man half made it, toppled backward to stare openeyed at the sky. He was hefted and slid into the back of the truck.

Edgewater had never seen such an outstanding and rich variety of drunks, even in the Navy. There were mean drunks, happy drunks, crying drunks, drunks with jokes that needed telling, drunks with puke on their clothes and their flies unzipped, drunks trying to seduce other men's wives and other drunks trying to hold onto what they had. He began to believe everyone on the truck was drunk save the old woman and the girl. He had a foreboding of disaster and considered walking but remained where he was. Then the old woman arose and pulled the girl erect and wended her toward the back where the women and children were, Edgewater following. He was standing against the girl and he could feel her breast against his arm, a scarcely perceptible weight. She turned slightly, increased the pressure, he fancied he felt the nipple erect through her blouse.

It took some time to get a headcount.

Clyde ain't come, a woman said.

We'll wait a minute, the driver said. They waited awhile and then they left without Clyde.

They eased out of town, a cattle truck of Saturday night revelers drifting toward Sunday morning. They were scarcely past the city limits when a scuffle broke out near the front of the truck. There were squeals, curses, feet struggling for balance in the slewing truck bed. Someone began to pound on the cab of the truck, bong, bong, bong. The truck pulled over to the side of the road and ceased and the driver got out into the moonlight.

All right, what's the matter?

Fightin, a woman said.

Who is it?

Pug, another said.

Pug what's your trouble?

There was silence.

Family trouble, the first woman said.

Pug, can you hold it in till you get home? Cause if you can't I'm comin up there and pitch you over the side. Now what's it goin to be?

There was a pause. Go ahead on, Pug said.

They moved on. Edgewater was standing against the girl, felt her hip leant into his thigh.

Angry voices arose. Goddamn good for nothin slut, Pug screamed. There were sounds of blows and the thick press of bodies leaned away from the fight like water filling in an overturned bottle and he felt her close and electric against him. Someone banged on the cab with a fist.

This time the driver did not inquire as to what the problems there might be. He slammed the door and climbed up the tailgate. The people parted for his easy passage. He grabbed Pug and shoved.

You son of a bitch, Pug said. He had his hand in his pocket.

The driver had the stick out. Come ahead. It's some people want to go to bed, he said.

Pug had lit on hands and knees and now arose covered with dust. Pearl, you get your ass off of there.

It's a long way home, she said from the dark of the front. I reckon I'll just ride.

Anybody else want to walk? the driver asked. This is the last call, the next bunch won't be able. He waited. No volunteers? All right then.

As the truck commenced to pick up speed Edgewater felt someone shove him and looked down for a brief moment into the face of the old woman then he was fighting for balance leaning horrified out over the fleeing road. There was white billowing dust, patches of grass dark as deep waters. He lit running and felt his knees dig into his chest and felt his arms flailing wildly and he fell face forward into the dust. He ran a few steps after it. Hey, he yelled. Hey. He ceased running and went over to the side of the road and rolled his pants up and began to inspect himself for injuries. His knees were scraped and raw and his right elbow was cut and had a trickle of black blood welling from it.

After a minute or two he saw Pug beside the road, dragging his feet in the dust and talking to himself. Goddamn slut, he was saying. He fetched up short when he saw Edgewater. Where the hell'd you come from?

That old woman pushed me off.

Pug sat down in the road and held his sides and began to laugh.

After a time Edgewater said, What was the fight about?

Pug stopped laughing abruptly. What's it to you?

Not one goddamned thing, Edgewater said. Just forget I asked, all right?

Well. Since you got to know. I reached down to grab Pearl's pussy and it was a man's hand already there. I'm headed right now to kill em where they lay. Pug grew silent for a time. Then he asked, You ain't got ary drink have ye?

No, Edgewater said, then he remembered. Yes I have. He pulled the bottle out and handed it to Pug. Pug drank deeply and then sat clasping the bottle between his knees. He was sitting hunkered in the road like some grass bird perched atop a wire. After a while Edgewater noticed that he was watching him.

It wadn't you, was it?

What?

Was it you had his hand on Pearl's pussy?

Son of a bitch, Edgewater said. I was way in the back.

Let me see your hand. Whoever it was had a ring on. Pug had his knife out.

Edgewater arose and held his hand out in the moonlight and showed him no ring. Pug sat back down and sat holding the knife in one hand and the bottle in the other. I'm gonna rest a minute and then I'm goin on, he said. To hell with em.

Edgewater had turned and began to walk up the moonlit road. In the pale light the dust looked like trackless snow.

Hey buddy, wait up.

I got to get on, Edgewater said without turning.

Get on where?

No reply.

Hey don't you tell em I'm comin, Pug called across the widening distance.

Soon Pug was lost to his sight. The road wound, fenced and walled in by brush. It dipped, bordered by trees, into a wood. He trudged on. His footfalls became loud to his ears. He feared there were eyes on him, beasts about, footfalls coinciding with his, noises aloft at his scent. Nightmare beasts of fearful myth moving malign and hydrophobic just beyond his sight. Then at last the bowering trees fell away and he followed the road into open country, silver in the summer, starlit, the road bound on he knew not where.

A bewenned hand pulled aside the curtains, goldrimmed glasses leaned to see what fresh hell this was. Beyond the rainwashed glass she saw a green Studebaker parked beneath the chinaberry tree in the front yard, a thin man already coming purposefully up the brick walk. He was carrying a white oblong box.

She let him knock several times before she opened the door. When she did she opened it a bare crack, she could see the man in a white shirt and a blue suitcoat standing there leaned toward the door to get his head out of the rain but all Roosterfish saw was one myopic goldrimmed eye. She could see that he looked harmless and that he only had the one hand that clutched the cardboard box.

Who are you? She opened the door a little wider.

I'm Robert Goforth, ma'am. Reverend Goforth. I'm here with good news for you.

I could use it, she said, stepping aside to let him enter. He eased into the room, eyes scanning so swiftly it seemed only a glance, but he'd catalogued everything of value in it and he'd ascertained that there was no son or son-in-law about.

All right bring your good news on in here, she said. I'll let you know ahead of time if it's something you're selling and the good news is it's marked half off, I tell you I don't want it.

You're a right tart-tongued grandma ain't you? Roosterfish thought. No ma'am, I'm not a salesman, he said. Except that we're all salesmen in the spread of God's word. I'm with the Unified Church of the Aftermath of God's Righteous Wrath.

He sometimes became bored with the same churches all the time and allowed himself to be a little creative. Sometimes he tried to see how outrageous he could become without being called on it. He had never been called previous and he wasn't called on it now.

That looks like a book. Is that a book?

Just so there's no confusion, he said. Are you Mrs. Clarence Ashton? I'm Bertha Ashton.

If we could sit down we'll see, he began, looking about the room.

I don't see any better sitting down, she said. Does pressure on your backside affect your eyesight?

He didn't even have the Bible unboxed. Roosterfish could feel it all falling apart. He'd had a feel for these things and this one had disintegrated before she'd fully opened the door, it just wasn't working, and it wasn't going to suddenly start working. Just turn and go, he told himself. He remembered some old song, *Hand me down my walkin cane, hand me down my watch and chain, ride that midnight train,* and thought to himself, just get the fuck out of here, tip your hat and walk out the door and get in the goddamn car and stamp another Bible and roll down the line.

Instead he set the box on a chifferobe and worked onehanded, raised the lid and took up the box and tipped out a white leatherette Bible. He opened it to the frontispiece where an inscription had been stamped in gold leaf. He reached the book toward her.

She didn't take it. What is it? she asked.

It's from your loving Clarence, he said.

My loving Clarence is dead and in the ground, she said. What is it?

It's a Bible personally inscribed to you, the Reverend Goforth said, and I'm aware that he's passed on. But before he did he had the foresight to order this token of love, an especially designated Bible for you from the Standard Bible Company.

What does it say?

It says, for Bertha, my beloved wife of thirty years. Narrow is the path but bright is the way. Your loving husband, Clarence.

You may as well sit down a moment, she told him. I've got to think this over. Roosterfish laid the Bible on the chifferobe and crossed to a sofa with its arms covered with doilies.

She seated herself in an armchair facing across from him. There was a gilt sprinkled card on the wall behind her that said CHRIST IS THE INVITED GUEST AT EVERY MEAL.

You're not from here, are you?

No ma'am, he said. I'm from back east of here. He was thinking she might offer him a cup of coffee, a cup of tea. Homebaked cookies. What he was actually thinking about was the bottle under the carseat and its unbroken seal but there was no hope of that. There was just something about Bertha Ashton that made him want a drink.

And you're with this Standard Bible Company?

Yes ma'am.

I thought you were with the Unified Church of whatever it was.

Well, I'm on a sabbatical, getting out in the field, out with the lambs, so to speak.

I imagine you've sheared a lamb or two in your time, she said. If you were from around here you'd know more about Clarence. The way was never bright for him, or anyway he griped all the time, and he strayed from that narrow path more times than a few. But say that Bible's mine free and clear.

Roosterfish was fumbling out the order form. Well, not exactly free and clear, he said. He scrutinized the ticket. There's the matter of the balance, twenty-seven dollars and sixty-eight cents. He proffered her the ticket, she glanced at it in a cursory manner.

So what it amounts to is I'm paying twenty-eight dollars for a Bible for myself but I'm signing it from Clarence who's been dead going on a year now.

Roosterfish couldn't fathom how that happened. He'd read back issues of the county paper in the newspaper office and didn't see how an obituary going on a year old had appeared in the paper with accounts of the newly dead. He'd made a list and inscribed the Bibles accordingly and here Clarence was already rotting in the ground, his Bible was just now being delivered. It didn't say much for the efficiency of the Standard Bible Company, of which Roosterfish was sole owner and proprietor.

It took us a while to find you, he said. There was some misunderstanding about the address. It only just got straightened out.

She didn't answer. She laid the invoice aside and opened the Bible and read the inscription. Roosterfish took heart. Her lips moved as she read. She hadn't taken the book with the relish he'd anticipated but at least she was nibbling around it.

Maybe he had a change of heart, saw the error of his ways, Roosterfish said tentatively. Maybe in his last days he had a premonition that the end was near and he wanted to make amends.

Clarence wasn't much on premonitions, she said, or he'd be here today for that matter. And he was even worse at making amends.

He studied her. She wasn't as old as he'd first thought, the gray hair had deceived him. He saw now that she had dyed it silver gray, had it done in ringlets so alike they appeared to have been stamped from sheet metal at a ringlet factory. She was in her late fifties, maybe, and not unattractive from a more intimate angle, if slightly dumpy. The Reverend Goforth wondered if he ought to approach the business transaction in a more intimate fashion. But twenty-seven dollars and sixty-eight cents was a lot of money. He wouldn't have kicked her out of bed, but then again he wouldn't have expended much effort to drag her into one either.

I don't feel right about not taking it if he wanted me to have it, she said at length. But I really can't afford it. What'll happen to it if I don't pay the twenty-eight dollars?

I'll have to send it back to the Bible company to be shredded, Roosterfish said. Grindin up God's holy word is a sin and it don't look good for a Bible company to be a party to it.

That's the solution, she said. You just give me Clarence's Bible and tell the company you shredded it.

It seemed to Roosterfish that in the last few minutes their conversation had gotten stranger and stranger. He studied her blond features as if he'd judge the depth of her guile. Something did not feel right. It was as if he'd gone along a wall tapping for solidity and tap it was solid here, then tap tap and there was the unmistakable sound of a hollow place. He wondered what was in the hollow place and he wondered whose leg was being pulled here and unless he was badly mistaken, and he didn't think he was, he thought he'd felt a tentative tug or two on his own.

The hell with it, he thought. Sometimes you just have to go with the craziness. Just lay back and look at the ceiling and wait until it's over. Let it roll.

Maybe you could just tear out the page with Clarence on it, she said craftily. And let them shred the rest of it?

I'm not an official shredder, ma'am, Roosterfish said. That has to be done by a licensed official of the Standard Bible Company. They won't allow just anyone around the shredder.

Jesus, he thought. How much deeper is it going to get around here?

That's the first page they shred when they get them back, he finally said.

Well. Let me think. Maybe we can trade it out some way. I've got a car I need to get rid of. The truth is I was noticing your car out there in the yard. It don't seem a fitting car for a representative of the Standard Bible Company, much less a preacher of the Unified whatever it was. What was it?

Roosterfish couldn't remember himself. He was thinking a twenty–eight-dollar car wouldn't be much of an improvement.

If you'll excuse me a few minutes I'll show it to you, she said. I've got something in it I need to move. You sit right here and wait on me.

I believe I'll step outside while you do that and go through my tickets, Roosterfish said. Kindly catch up on my paperwork.

She went through a curtained doorway into another room and he heard what he guessed was the back door open and close. He went out the front door and fumbled under the front seat for the bottle. He held the bottle, broke the seal, put it under the stump of his arm and twisted the cap righthanded and tilted the bottle and drank. Past the bottle he could see just the flat gray sky and when he lowered it there was the red road winding through the wet rampart greenery, rolling mist blowing off the fields like smoke, and there was an enormous temptation to get in the car and just drive away, leave her the Bible with its spurious goldleaf salutation from the dead and just forget her, mark her account closed, get on to something else, feed her to the shredder.

Mr. Goforth?

She'd been standing at the corner of the house watching him drink. He capped the bottle and slid it into his coat pocket. He crossed the yard and followed her around the corner of the house to the back yard.

I knew you for a Christian gentleman right away, she said. Even them old prophets in the Bible would take a drink. What happened to your arm, did a lion tear it off?

I lost it in the sawmill, Roosterfish said.

There's the car, she said.

The car sat gleaming in the rain and it looked as if it had just come off the assembly line. It was a green and white DeSoto no more than three or four years old. He walked all the way around it. It didn't have any dirt on it, even the tires looked new.

I couldn't afford no car nothin like that, he said.

I'm prepared to make you a good deal on it, she said. The keys are in it. Just get in there and start it and listen to it run. Then tell me you can't afford it. It's not as new as it looks, but Clarence kept it up and it's in fine shape.

He opened the door. He was instantly assaulted by an almost suffocating odor of flowers, sickeningly sweet, honeysuckle, gardenia, the odor of roses, something.

What's that smell? he asked.

It's been sitting here shut up for a good while, with the windows rolled up, she said. I sprayed it down good with air freshner while you was doing your paperwork.

He fanned the floral stench out of the air. That's some highoctane air freshener, he told her. He cranked the car and the engine seemed to catch before it had fully turned over and it sat idling smoothly with no ping to the motor. He put it in gear and he rocked it forward and the transmission caught instantly. He put it in reverse and that worked too. He got out and walked back to see if any smoke was coming out of the tailpipe. There wasn't.

What's the matter with it?

There's not a thing in this round world the matter with it.

Then why do you want to sell it?

It's a personal matter, she said. But I don't mind telling you. It's painful seeing it set out here every day. It reminds me of Clarence.

What would you take?

I might take two fifty if you'd throw in the Bible.

Oh Lord, I couldn't afford that. Can you come off that figure a little bit?

I know it's worth more than that, she replied. You've got a pretty good mark up on those two-dollar Bibles. I imagine you could come up with it.

You wouldn't take about a case of them Bibles would you?

She just looked at him.

He got back into the car and cut the switch. The odor was as over-powering as it had been before. The smell reminded him of something but he couldn't think what. There's a hole here in the front seat, he said.

I imagine Clarence got in with a screwdriver in his pocket, she said. You could darn that right up.

In truth he wanted the car. He'd had an intense vision of himself driving it down the main street of Ackerman's Field, past the house where the wife who'd cuckolded him still lived. Parking it in front of the Snowwhite Café, de Vries cabstand. He saw himself pulling up in front of the Swiss Colony cockpit, Here comes a highroller, some old farmer would call out.

You in the tall cotton ain't ye, Roosterfish? he thought to himself.

He went back around to his car. He leaned against it thinking. He took a drink and thought some more. He took out a worn billfold and leafed through the contents. Two hundred and fifty dollars would about clean him out, but the car was worth it. Besides, he could always earn it back. There might not be a sucker born every minute, but they come along often enough to suit him.

He left a few minutes later in the DeSoto. He was towing the Studebaker with a length of chain he'd found in the barn and that she'd charged him five dollars extra for. He drove off with her standing on the front doorstep with a sheaf of greenbacks in one hand and the inscribed Bible in the other and he had all four windows rolled down in the hope that the rainy wind would blow the smell of perfume out of the car.

You could run a French whorehouse out of the back seat of this son of a bitch, he said aloud, and then it hit him that what the car smelled like was not a whorehouse at all but a funeral parlor, the tenanted casket on the catafalque and the banked wall of gardenias with their sickening reek fanning outward bound like a miasmic cloud of radiation.

It was three miles back to the crossroads grocery where he'd planned on stopping to get a drink and before he'd made it a good deal of the floral smell was blowing into the atmosphere and he was ruefully imag-ining it settling visibly in crevasses and sinkholes and stinking up the countryside for miles about when he became aware of another smell that was asserting itself, a scent that was even worse: a dark charnel house scent of corruption and death, as if the car had come not from a Detroit auto plant but a reeking slaughterhouse, as if the car was not metal and chrome and rubber but something organic, something that had been alive and wasn't anymore, and hadn't been for some time and he glanced in the rearview mirror nervously as if half expecting clouds of vultures descending and he slammed the brake pedal and got out and just stood looking at the car.

What the fuck is that? he wondered.

At the service station he stood and smoked one, just breathed in the cool damp air that smelled of clean woods and brushcut grass and the distant river.

Say you ain't got no kind of air freshener or deodorant in there have you?

The storekeep looked at the DeSoto and made some noise in his throat that might have been a laugh and might not.

What the hell's that supposed to mean?

You ain't from here, are you?

No.

I see you met the widow Ashton, he said.

She sold me this here car.

The storekeep didn't seem surprised. She's tried to sell it all over two counties, he said. Nobody'll have it.

Why? What's the matter with it? It seems to run all right.

It does run, it runs fine. You just can't get the smell out of it and folks around here all knows the story.

The story, what story?

That DeSoto got something of a history, he said. It's the car that Clarence Ashton died in. You sure you want to hear this? Yeah, just go on and maybe you can drive it when you got a bad cold or somethin.

So he died in it, Roosterfish said. I've lived in houses folks died in. Folks die all over the place. What's the big deal?

He was shot in it, the storekeep said. Two folks was shot in it. He had that oldest Potts girl out on a logroad and they was in there naked and somebody shot and killed em both. They wasn't found for a month. For a month, and that was in July and part of August. When some hunter run across that DeSoto and opened the door you can't imagine what it was like. Her head was in his lap and she'd been shot through the head and whoever it was shot Clarence in the head as well.

Godamighty, they Lord God, Roosterfish said.

Damn right. Folks around knowned Bertha done it but she had a daughter over by Milan swore up and down Bertha'd spent the night there. Folks says they was in it together. But nothing ever came of it. They never even found the gun. She had a wrecker haul it home and washed it out good and kept on washing it. Trying to get the smell out. Can you imagine washing up after a mess like that?

I can barely imagine driving the son of a bitch, Roosterfish said. Maybe she'll give me my money back.

And maybe when Clarence went through the gates of hell they issued him a set of ice skates, the storekeep said.

He was a mile or so down the road when he decided to stop and get out a minute just to breathe deeper. He figured maybe he'd try driving with his head outside the window for the breeze but the blowing rain complicated it and he drank from the bottle and repocketed it and without thinking and for no good reason he stuck a finger into the hole and probed in the seat. Something hard there, hard as concrete at the tip of his finger. His forefinger came out with black grains and a black dried substance caked under his fingernail. He stood studying it a meditative moment. Then he went hastily holding the finger before him down an embankment and scraped it clean in the grass. He thought a time and then poured whiskey over the finger and scraped it again.

He pocketed the bottle and climbed back up the embankment and went back and unhooked the towing chain and just stood there, feeling the weighted iron links. He slowly walked up to the DeSoto and reached in the open window and cranked the wheel all the way to the right, then pulled the gear shift into neutral. He climbed in the Studebaker and eased it up till the front bumper engaged the rear bumper of the DeSoto and then pushed till the front wheels of the DeSoto were over the incline and watched as the car disappeared down the embankment.

Edgewater made his way back into town and took the main road south. The next evening about dusk he thought he heard music. It was distant, faint, a cappella. There were no words he could decipher, or even melody, just a delicate piety inlaid on the fragile dusk. He soon came upon a camp meeting. Now he could hear the singing, they were girls' voices, ethereal and pure. *Oh why not tonight?* they asked. *You must be saved…oh, why not tonight?*

There was a tent and dark shapes and a preacher ranting salvation, an electric hum that hung over them all like a revelation. There were forms writhing about the ground in apparent ecstasy at promise of imminent and eternal torment, random movements went to and fro in the beleaguered woods.

Edgewater crossed to the far side of the road, but a dog had barked sharply at his passage, two men had spied him and separated themselves from the thronging dark and loped toward him through the dust and entreated him to hold up. Edgewater increased his pace. They came up to him on either side and caught his arm. Hold on brother. Come on in to the meetin and let salvation into ye soul. We got the devil on the run tonight.

He did not speak but turned on the man and something in his face or eyes gave the entreator pause for his arm was dropped instantly and the two men stopped uncertainly in the middle of the road. They did not call him, but he could feel their eyes on his back and he could hear the singing for a long time. Far off there was a stand of cypress he moved toward, it seemed assuring in falling dark.

But a third man had come up. He was older than the other two, beefy with pouched freshly shaven jowls and a slack, dissolute look about him. His black hair was shot with gray and slicked down with grease. He had on a white shirt with a dirty collar and wool slacks and work shoes.

Where you headed in such a hurry, brother?

I got a long way to go, Edgewater told him. Clear across the state.

Well, the man said, beaming at him and rocking back and forth on his heels. You didn't plan on makin all of it tonight, did you?

I need to make as much of it as I can. Edgewater was peering down the white road. In the vague distance blue dusk was shimmering and the dark trees were merging one with the sky as if the coming night was dissolving them, they lost form, seemed afflicted by some curious motion.

Which way you tryin to go?

I need to get back on 70. They told me up the road if I kept on this way I couldn't miss it.

Well, it's this way all right but it's fifteen or twenty miles and you liable to get turned around in the night. Now you just come on in and let Jesus show you your way.

I know my way, Edgewater told him. I just need to be on it.

No you don't. They's lots think they know, but mighty few that does. You may think all the where you're goin is Highway 70, but, brother, you're wrong.

Praise Jesus, the two flanking him said. Edgewater glanced at them with some misgivings. Their faces were blank as still water and he had begun to fear that the trio was not going to allow him to pass on his way, would fall upon him and beat him with their mercy until he repented some vague, undetermined sins. He looked again down the road. The man had leaned close into his face, his eyes narrowed in accusation.

Is that a half-pint bottle I see through your britches there?

· It may be, Edgewater told him. What about it?

What about it? The man peered upward to the sky gathering night. Jesus. Everthing about it. I fought moonshine whiskey all my life and it won ever battle but one. I just this week got shut of it. Monday night at this meetin God laid a hand on me and picked me up and shook me the way you've seen a dog shake a snake to pop its head off. I knowed it would either kill me or cure me. Well sir, I been a drunkard all my life and run over as good a woman ever drawed breath. I lost grocer money to crooked dice and I gone with whores talked out of both sides of their mouths and laughed behind my back. Well bless Jesus, no more. No more. I'm saved.

During this tirade Edgewater had taken two or three steps backward but the man had followed him. What are you, some kind of preacher? Edgewater asked.

No, I ain't a preacher. But I'm full of the Lord, running over with Him. We all soldiers in the army of the Lord.

I didn't know he had armies, Edgewater said inanely.

The man grasped his arm. Now you just come on in here, brother. Forget that whiskey, forget whatever worries ye. I won't ask ye to do nothin ye don't want to do. Now if you want the Lord, you'll know it, and if He wants you, He'll know it. All I want you to do is come on up to the camp. Then after the meetin me and my wife's gonna give you a bed to sleep in and as good a meal as ever you ate. And tomorrow I'll sit you down on Highway 70. Now is that fair or not?

Edgewater allowed himself to be pressed toward the crowd at the tent. Lanterns had been lit, hung aloft on poles that supported the canvas and moths and bugs dove impotently at their yellow globes.

The congregation was singing, their eyes glazed, their bodies swaying as though some occult wind moved them. There seemed to be forty or fifty people in the tent, old and young, Edgewater moved by the steel hand clamping his bicep into the realm of the maimed and crazed. An old man on hands and knees shook in some queer palsy, afflicted perhaps deeper by whatever mercy moved here tonight. There was an invisible current of tension, an inaudible hum like high-voltage electricity. Arm in arm courting couples passed with autistic eyes toward the brush drawing close to the tent.

A thin little man in a black frock coat ranted about the devil. He seemed possessed, his eyes feverish. Oh, I have seen him, he told them. His voice rose and fell. I know his guises, I have seen the other side of his face. I have seen him moving through my sleeping house, going through my pockets in the dark like a sneakthief. The old man's sparse hair was plastered with sweat, there was a yellow sheen on his skull. I have seen him in the dregs of a whiskey bottle, seen him reflected in the eyes of a harlot. The devil is here among us tonight.

He went on at some length about the devil and all his works. Edgewater fell to studying his teeth. He had the falsest-looking set of false teeth Edgewater had ever seen and they looked for all the world like the wax teeth he had bought in childhood ten-cent stores.

After the preaching there was a call for souls and they began to sing softly again. Four or five leapt eagerly forward to be first and the man pushed Edgewater toward the center of the tent. Edgewater stiffened his knees and staggered a step or two and whirled. You keep your hands to yourself.

There were several to be healed. Various afflictions: all the ills man is heir to. A cancerous old man, throat half eaten away, a woman goitered and swollen, the crippled, the eviscerated and flayed by life. This preacher healed them all.

Then a man began to pass among them with a coffee can, Edgewater could hear the clink of coins all down the line. The man carried a stack of tracts, giving one to each donor. The can stopped expectantly in front of Edgewater, waited. I need it worse than you do, Edgewater told it. The eyes above the can were almost pitying. At last the man gave him a tract anyway. Before the can passed on, the man behind Edgewater threw a dollar into the can. For him, he said. Edgewater folded the tract and slid it into his pocket. You read that, the man told him.

They spilled finally into the warm mothflecked night, moving toward their vehicles. There was an air of camaraderie. Yins come see us, they called to each other.

The man saved from alcohol was Lester Batts and his wife was Jesse. He was a pig farmer from down on Little Creek and he shepherded Edgewater and the woman toward his battered pickup. The woman seemed to be still in an ecstatic state of bliss. She hung onto her husband's arm and she urged Edgewater to praise Jesus. They got into the truck and backed around in the clearing, cut toward the road. Their lights briefly lit the preacher and the man holding the coffee can. As they disappeared from sight the preacher had one arm raised in farewell or dismissal and the other was reaching into the depths of the can.

Compared to the shanties Edgewater had been passing, the house Batts lived in was relatively prosperous. It was just a square box of a house with a hipped roof like a pyramid set atop but there were electric lights and the best he could tell the yard seemed neat and clean.

The woman made him two ham sandwiches with thick slices of homebaked bread and poured him a tumbler of buttermilk and he ate at the oilcloth-covered table while they watched. The man paced nervously about the room, as if whatever had laid hands on him would not let him be.

There'll be another meeting tomorrow night, he told Edgewater. It goes on all this week.

Edgewater did not reply, his mouth was full of ham. He ate hurriedly. There was a demented look in the man's eyes and Edgewater feared that he was going to begin preaching. The woman watched him with pride. Perhaps she could not yet believe the miracle that had happened, the transformation that had occurred.

Edgewater went to bed in the loft room they showed him. There was a musty, unused smell to the room and Edgewater raised the window to the night. He lay back with the cries of the whippoorwills about him and pondered the road that had brought him here. He marveled that he slept warm and dry and that he had come to Little Creek and wondered where its place in the universe might be.

They all arose early and breakfast the next morning was a steaming pot of oatmeal with butter melting on top of it and the smell of cinnamon rising off it. There was fried ham again, redeye gravy and fried eggs and a pan of biscuits browning in the oven. The kitchen was rich with the aromatic smell of brewing coffee.

Batts was already eating when Edgewater sat down among all these varied smells and began to help himself.

I got a little harrowin to do this morning. Lord willin I'll finish it by dinner and then I'll take time to run you out to Highway 70. Unless you been thinkin about the meetin tonight. It'd do me a world of good to see you admit your sin and be cleared of it.

Edgewater was watching the slow slide of melted butter down the side of a hot biscuit. He reached for the honey jar. I've not decided yet, he said.

I'd take it as a personal favor if you'd think about it.

After breakfast Batts found Edgewater a five-gallon bucket of viscous tar and a paddle whittled from a piece of pine planking and set him to patching leaks on the roof. He went toward the barn and as Edgewater was climbing the ladder to the roof he saw Batts come out with the geared mules and lead them across a plowed field.

The sun began to climb, the day to warm up. The roofing was warm through his shoes. Birds called to Edgewater from the trees in the yard. He began to search for leaks. He got a paddleful of the pliable tar and began to spot nailheads with it. The roof steepened near the top and he did most of his patching on the lower roof. He patched everything that looked like a leak and anything that looked as if it might be a leak in the future and after a time the sun made him languished and drowsy and he crossed over to the shady side and lay down on his back. The sky was a clear deep blue, there was not even a wisp of cloud and so high above him he did not see them at first hawks or buzzards wheeled and tilted in aerial ballet. There was no sound save the birds calling from the woods and he lay still, completely relaxed, feeling the warmth of the roofing through his clothes. He pretended he was at sea, he had remembered the sea this color. As flat and slick and smooth as glass and it went on forever.

After a while he heard the woman calling him and he got up and was around the roof and began to descend the ladder. She was standing in the shade of a cottonwood with a half gallon of iced tea in one hand and a glass in the other.

I thought you might be gettin hot up there.

I'm about through, he told her. He was peering across the field to where the mules pulled the harrow in a rising plume of white dust that dissipated behind them and the form of Batts to the side with the lines in his hands and occasionally he could hear his cries to the mules, staccato and indistinct, harrying them to slow or make haste.

She followed his eyes, he heard her sigh. That's a different man now since he quit that old whiskey, she said. She shook her head. You'd just never know, she said, what we went through. It was the Lord's guidance helped me get him to that tent meetin.

Edgewater took the tea she offered and hunkered in the grass.

Lester said you had sick folks, she said. Who is it if you mind me askin?

Well, Edgewater said, peering at her, gauging. What did she want to hear? Who did she want it to be? I'll be what you want me. You create me, whole out of yourself. She was looking at him out of a bland, friendly face, the eyes that fixed his were dull and almost stupid.

Well, it's my mama, he began. She's bad sick havin an operation and I'm tryin to get there. I just got discharged out of the service and got all my stuff stolen.

Lord have mercy. You mean money and everything?

Edgewater was shaking his head slowly from side to side, expressing his disillusionment in his fellow man, eyes wide and hurt by misplaced trust. Hard to accept people would do one in his shape so gross a wrong.

Money and orders and discharge papers, and bus tickets and all my clothes. I wired home but they must not have got it. I waited awhile and then I just struck out.

No wonder you got a lot on your mind, the woman said. Here, get you some more tea. She refilled his glass, peered at him expectantly. Was there more?

You know how it is, he told her. Wantin to get there bad and at the same time dreading it. Not knowing what to expect, but expectin the worse all the same.

The woman set the tea down beside him carefully in the grass and walked into the house. She was gone for some time and when she came back out she was carrying a pocketbook. She opened it and withdrew a bill, stood smoothing it with her fingers. It was a five, he noticed.

Here, she said. You take this and I don't want to hear a word about it. It's my money. My daddy died a long way from here and I never got to go see him when he was so bad. Lester was bad on the whiskey then and he never let me. I know how you feel.

He folded the bill and slid it into his shirt pocket.

I'll see that when Lester drops you off it's somewhere you can catch you a bus. You buy you a ticket with that and get on home.

I thank you, Edgewater said.

You just see you get on home.

Batts came in from the field about ten o'clock and came into the house and looked all about the kitchen. Is they not any tea made? he wanted to know. She looked to see. I reckon it's all drunk, she said. I'll make you some more.

He was drinking water at the sink. Let it go, he said shortly. I ain't got time. Me and that boy's takin a load of pigs into Selmer this evenin.

Pigs? She turned from where she was slicing meat into a pan. You never said nothin bout sellin no pigs.

I reckon it slipped my mind. I got to ungear and feed them mules. You get through?

Just about, he said, already out the door.

Edgewater stood around awhile and then he thought he'd walk out and see could he help feed the mules.

Batts was in the loft throwing hay down with a pitchfork. He climbed down the ladder and stood regarding Edgewater.

I'm through with the roof.

Well. I need you to help me load them pigs.

All right.

Edgewater started walking toward the house.

Say, Batts began.

What?

Batts seemed abstracted and nervous. What was it you done with that old whiskey you had last night?

I poured it out.

Oh. Good, good, he said, although he did not appear especially pleased.

They did not even wait for dinner but drove down below the barn where the hogpens were and Batts backed up to the chute. They loaded the hogs and drove to the stockbarn in Selmer and sold them without incident. After getting a few items in town they started back. Batts said since they had made such good time he figured he might take another load. They could get in and sell them and still be back in plenty of time for the meeting.

They drove back through Selmer and through a seemingly endless string of beer joints and gambling houses and achromatic-looking housetrailers set on shadeless graveled lots. They drove further still and a mile or so out of town, Batts slowed down and looked toward a weatherbeaten shack forty or fifty feet off the road. The house was set in the middle of a motley of car tires and old ragged bedsprings and old motors and transmissions, behind it sloping junkmountains of immeasureable richness.

Lester Batts did not say anything. He drove on until they reached the first side road and he turned in and still wordlessly backed out and went slowly back up the road the way they had come. When he was even with the shack he stopped and peered at the house with his hands clasped on the steering wheel. And many a dollar I throwed away here, he said.

Edgewater had broken the five-dollar bill in Selmer and bought a pack of cigarettes and now he took them out and began to open them.

A nigger bootlegger lives here, Batts said. A man bound for hell if one ever was. It come on me like a revelation that it's one thing to resist whiskey I ain't even got. It'd be something else again to have it right in front of me. To just look at it and hold the jar and then set it down and just say, no thank ye. I don't use it no more.

Edgewater did not reply. He had lit his cigarette and sat peering out across the junkstrewn yard and house and as he looked a black girl of six or seven years came onto the porch and sat down in the swing and began to rock listlessly to and fro.

Wouldn't it?

Wouldn't it what?

Wouldn't it be something else again?

I guess it would.

Batts fumbled in his pocket and selected a bill and reached it to Edgewater. You go get us a quart of that stuff.

A quart? Looks like half a pint would be sufficient for resisting purposes.

Any half-saved fool can resist a halfpint, Batts said. You get us a quart.

Edgewater got out and walked across the yard and up the broken cinderblock doorstep. He peeked at the screen door. The child in the swing stared at him or through him as if he were not there at all.

Yeah? A thin dark face crosshatched by the screen door.

Give me a quart.

The black turned away, returned with the fruit jar. He peered up the bank to where the pickup idled.

Ain't that Lester Batts's pickup truck?

Yeah.

You tell him I said get on away from here fore he opens it up. You tell him I said the law is givin me a hard enough time without him messin me up again like he done last time.

He's not goin to drink it, Edgewater said. He's saved. He's going to resist it.

The black handed him the jar. Sho he is, he said. You tell him what I said.

Edgewater wended his way back to the road through wrecked and accordioned cars that the falling sun invested with an unreal, almost pastoral beauty.

He got in and handed the jar to Batts. Here you go, he said. You goin to resist it here or take it on down the road.

Batts did not reply. He sat the jar between his legs and put the truck in gear and they drove back down the road. After a mile or so the presence of the whiskey seemed to make Batts voluble, as if he in some manner absorbed the essence of it by convection through his thighs.

He began to regale Edgewater with the stories from his life. Lessons learned the hard way. Good money thrown endlessly after bad. Time cast to the winds and lost forever. You're young, he told Edgewater. Got your whole life ahead of you. Repent ye sins now and none of this has to happen to you. Why that woman has whipped me right down to the ground with a stick of stovewood and me blind drunk as a mole and no more sense about me than a yeller dog. I've been beat bloody time and again over the same mess sloshin right now in this fruitjar.

They drove for four or five miles and a log road came up and they turned off into scrubby cutover timber and Batts stopped the truck and cut the switch off. There was a deep silence in the woods.

He took up the jar, his hands caressing, unscrewed the lid and smelled. He set the jar on the dash and sat staring at it in disdain, as if it were a thing of no import. And there you sit, he told it. They sat for what seemed to Edgewater two or three hours and at the end of this time three quarters of the whiskey was gone, almost all of it drunk by Batts. He was sodden drunk, had fallen to favoring Edgewater with sidling glances of suspicion, as if he could not remember who Edgewater was or where he had appeared from.

It's getting late. You still plan on taking me out to 70? Edgewater asked.

Batts was surly. In a while. Help me load them other hogs and I'll let you out in Selmer.

Well.

On the way back to Batts's farm, he raked a mailbox and then slowed down to a cautious ten or fifteen miles an hour. He drove past the house and the woman came out onto the porch and watched them pass with some interest. She raised a tentative hand and called once but Batts ignored her and drove on down toward the hogpen. It took several attempts before he was backed up to the chute to his satisfaction.

Edgewater was looking toward the house. Jesse came out and started toward them. Behind her came the faint slap of the screen door. Batts saw her too. You go head her off. See what she wants.

Halfway there the woman called to him. Is he loadin up more hogs?

Yes, ma'am.

Why Lord, he ain't got time. You tell him I said start washin up for the meetin.

I'll tell him.

Edgewater went back and told him.

I ain't studyin no meetin right now, he said. He had the jar out and cocked aloft and he was eyeing the bead. Me and you in the hog haulin business right now. He drank off the rest of the whiskey and threw the jar into the tangle of honeysuckle and stood unsteadily in the mud of the hoglot. There's the very one I been dreadin all day long, he said, pointing at a huge spotted sow that stood watching him with wary distrust.

He had the hog halfway up the chute when for some reason or other she stopped dead still. There was not sufficient space for her to turn and she began to back down the chute. Batts's face grew apoplectic with exertion. He could not force her back up. He grasped her tail and twisted it and hit her on the rump with his fist. You get up there you hussy, he said. The hog leapt backward and knocked Batts off balance and he fell in the slick black mud. The railing off the chute caught him a glancing blow above the eye and he lay dazed a moment before he arose. He sat up in the mud and looked all about wildly and rubbed his head and left a streak of mud in the wake of his hand. A drop of blood welled, zigzagged down to join the mud at the corner of his mouth. He tasted it tentatively with his tongue. How about you gettin off your butt and helpin? he said thickly.

Edgewater arose and climbed over the fence. The sow had retreated to a far corner of the pen and stood with feet apart and head lowered regarding them with malice.

Spread out and help me herd her, Batts said.

Edgewater kept to the cleanest part of the lot and stepped gingerly through the mud and offal. Batts plunged ahead slipping and sliding.

At the end of a few minutes they still did not have the hog loaded. Batts had fallen two or three times on his own and once the hog had bolted past and knocked him down. His head was bleeding worse and he was crazed from head to toe with blood and pigshit.

Goddamnit, will you get your thumb out of your ass and help?

I hated to interfere. It looked like something personal between you and the hog. Edgewater stepped gingerly through the shallowest of the muddy offal and Batts plunged in ankle-deep, slipping and sliding.

Batts began to chase the hog around and around the pen. The sow's eyes were wild and mad as if she were in flight from some reeking demon of lecherous intent and Batts went slewing through the mud windmilling his arms for balance. Then he launched himself onto the hog's slick back and locked his arms about her neck in some lascivious parody of lust and part of the time Batts was riding the sow and part of the time she was riding him and when at length they ceased the sow's jaws were slathered with foam and her sides heaved spasmodically and Batts was struggling for breath.

He and the hog stood regarding each other without affection and Batts lowered his face down eye to eye with the hog and began to curse it as if it were some human opponent who had taken unfair advantage. You chickenshit mullyfucker, he told it. You worthless whorin slut.

Edgewater glanced toward the house and the woman was striding toward them at a purposeful pace. Hey, he called to Batts. Hey. Batts kicked at the hog and fell on his back in the black mud and lay staring at the sky. Edgewater climbed the fence on the far side of the pen and dropped to the ground. When he looked back this time Jesse had increased her pace and somewhere she had found a stick. Edgewater moved on. Batts had arisen now and seen the woman and was trying to call to Edgewater on his hands and knees. He was calling at the top of his voice but Edgewater stoppered his ears, did not know whether it was rage or entreaty, pleas to wait. He did not wait to see. He looked back once and the woman was astride the fence and he looked forward at the field he was running through and heard the stick fall and a startled yell. Then they were cursing each other as loudly as they could as he ran through the creek where it shoaled shallowest, and as he climbed the bank and went on through the willows on the other side he could not hear them anymore.

Roosterfish awoke with the first auguries of dawn, the chattering of birds above the bluff that formed his ceiling, the crowing of the cocks in their wooden cages. He lay for a time cocooned in his musty blanket for the night had turned chill after the storm. He lay peering up to where sunlight spread along the span of bluff seeking out the shadows and destroying them, acid eating away remnants of the night. He could smell the river that flowed beyond him and hear it lapping and its suck among the ironwoods and willows depending into it. He lay still, at peace. The sun was already warming the dark blanket. He could feel the slow spread of its heat. At length he arose.

With the stub of his left arm pinning the blanket about him he fumbled in a cardboard box and brought out a charred and handleless coffeepot, started toward the river. He appeared some crippled monk or hermit of simpler times, the old brown blanket episcopal vestments of some arcane order. He approached the river and descended the bank with some caution, for after the torrent fallen in the night he had detected sometime before first light a subtle change in its tone, a deeper, swifter pitch to the language it spoke, entreaty forsaken for threat. He dipped the pot into the roiling yellow water and climbed back up the incline and dropped the blanket, revealing himself already dressed, marvelously prepared for whatever honest toil this day might offer up for a man with one good hand.

He had ringed old purloined cinderblocks and atop them he set the grill from the abandoned cookstove. He crumbled tinder, bits of dry sticks and leaves from beneath the bluff. Soon a wisp of white smoke arose, fragrant in the morning air.

While he waited for his coffee water to boil he got a cup of cracked corn from a lard bucket and fed the two gamecocks. They watched him from their slotted cages with their fierce, arrogant eyes. He came back and from a Styrofoam icechest laid out two eggs and a round cut of bologna still in its white butcher paper and a half-loaf of bread. He set a skillet on the fire and poured in half-congealed bacon grease from an old jelly jar. He watched its slow spread across the bottom of the warming pan and then he unpocketed his knife and took up the round of bologna. He sliced wedges off it into the pan, peering intently at its texture, its grain, white chunks of fat, here and there a porcelain shard of tooth or bone laid like a pearl. Who knew what curious beasts had fallen so that he might have this meal. He threw a good handful of coffee into the roiling water.

After he had cooked and eaten his breakfast he immediately busied himself about the camp. He washed his meager utensils and put them away in the icechest with the food and carried chest and all around the bluff to where the incline decreased and hid it and the blanket behind the uprooted stump of a windfall poplar.

He got the crated cocks on his shoulder and started across a narrow peninsula thick with willows. He came out in a field sown in fescue and skirted it, keeping in the old wagon road that followed the course of the river. Below him he could see the skeletal trestle spanning the river where the bridge crossed.

It was some distance to his car. By experience he had learned that the wagon road was passable only in dry weather and at the first drops of rain he had driven back to higher ground and pulled off the shoulder into a sideroad. When he came upon the Studebaker, he set the cocks down and unlocked some panel windows on the plywood camper. Already a smell of hot plastic hung about the interior. He gave a cursory examination of the oddments of equipment in the back: compressors and pumps and coiled hoses like sleeping serpents and signs proclaiming various trades, none his, but he expected no discrepancies, these were honest folk about. He stood still for a time, just listening to the sounds of the morning: jays quarreling in the trees, the chattering of a squirrel, a cock crowing from some misty farmhouse. The sun slowly warmed him, he drew strength from it like a soothing balm. The sun rose steadily, seemed not to be shining through the sheltering branches but annihilating them, scorching them away. He judged it near work time, checked the sun against his pocketwatch. He stowed the crate of chickens in the back and got in the car. He had high hopes for this day, as he had for all days, each day no worse than the best of them.

Roosterfish was a man of many guises. He would paint your barn, spray your roof for leaks, exterminate your termites, sell you what he called a magazine prescription. The exterminating business was the most profitable, but he had been thinking about retiring this line. It entailed too much crawling around. The customers expected at least a modicum of show. Even if what he sprayed foundations with was no more potent than river water, he still had to crawl under musty floors expecting to be snakebit at any time and ruining his clothes.

So when he saw the hitchhiker ahead he already knew he was going to stop, knew what he was going to say. The man alongside the road did not even thumb him, appeared to consider it a waste of effort, plodded on with eyes fixed on the wavering treeline. Roosterfish stopped anyway, leaned across to unlock the door then peered back once to where the empty highway lay flat and straight.

The door Edgewater reached for had a magnetized sign affixed to it: WEST TENNESSEE EXTERMINATORS, INC. Perhaps it afforded Edgewater grim amusement; if the fates had a sense of humor they might come for him in such a fashion. But he opened the door anyway.

Get in, get in, if ye don't mind ridin with the chickens. Ye'll have to set em in the back there. I'm a chicken with one wing myself.

Edgewater put the coop into the back atop the motley of cans and sprayers and hoses. When the door was closed and they were rolling he said, Where you heading?

Just down the road apiece. Where are you?

Further than that.

Wherebouts you comin from?

San Diego.

They Lord. Out in California? How long's it took you?

I lost track. But I made a stop or two along the way. I stayed a while in Memphis.

Where's home?

Up around Monteagle.

A long way come and a long way still to go.

I guess so.

You in a hurry?

Not anymore.

How you fixed for money? It ain't none of my business but I guess if you were rollin in money you'd be drivin or ridin a bus one.

I'm a walking depression. I got discharged from the Navy and my mustering-out pay lasted awhile, but it finally all got away. I don't worry about it.

Least you don't have to worry bout gettin robbed. Way this country's goin to hell even the highways ain't safe no more. Folks won't stop to pick ye up and ye can't blame em. Why they found a feller over in Decaturville in a ditch had his throat cut from ear to ear. Decked out in a tailormade suit and a silk shirt with snap-on ruffles on the front. Car gone and wallet gone and a money belt around his belly with fourteen hundred dollars in it. Roosterfish's voice sounded rueful, subtle comment perhaps on man's inhumanity to man, or regret that he had not been first on the scene. You can't trust nobody no more, he finished.

Edgewater rode in silence, he might have been asleep.

You short of money, me and you might work up a deal, Roosterfish said. You ever done any sterminatin?

Any what? Edgewater wanted to know.

Edgewater decked out in a twin of Roosterfish's cap, becoming knowledgeable in the termite business. Already a vice president, mentor and protégé, craftsman and apprentice at their work. An old man watched, held somnolent from the shade of a chinaberry tree while they strung hoses, wire, pumped air into the portable sprayers. Roosterfish at his potions like some alchemist of old.

Edgewater crawled under the house, dragging the electric drill along with him. The house was built close to the ground and the nearness of the floor joists oppressed him. There was no finished floor above and as he crawled on his back Edgewater could see slatted light flicker through the cracks and hear heavy footsteps in the rooms above.

From time to time he would hammer on the sills, turn the drill on and let it run a few minutes as Roosterfish had told him. Sounds of work being done, money being earned. He lay on his back listening to the whine of the drill, smoking. Scraps of old newspaper were stuck to the planks. He read disjointed accounts of old doings, juxtaposed bits of people's lives. Social recounting of folks long dead. Among the guests at Mrs. Lamson's reception were Forrest and Retha White, now deceased. The old papers were foxed and yellowed with age. Sepia faces trapped in time smirked at him with spurious goodwill.

There was a musty, claustrophobic smell under the floor, dryrotted lumber, graveyard earth the sun had perhaps never shone on. Then more. Feeling watched he looked behind him and saw near his shoulder the mummified remains of a dog leering at him from out empty eyesockets. The dog was on its belly with forepaws extended as if inviting petting, a kind word. But its teeth were bared in a snarl of eternal ferocity.

Edgewater fled in a curious crablike motion using elbows and heels, forgot the drill and had to haul it in by the cord. He crawled into the sun. The sky was as blue as any sky he had ever seen and the sun falling through the greenery was hot and bright. He breathed deeply, then rolled the cord around the drill and put it in the toolbox in the back of the Studebaker.

I'm through in under there, he told Roosterfish.

Roosterfish was engaged in spraying some sort of oily liquid around the foundation of the house. Well. We still got to spray a little bit in under there.

I'm through in under there.

The old man paid Roosterfish, wetting his thumb with his tongue, rubbing each bill with care to see it practiced no deception on him. He asked for a receipt and Roosterfish wrote him one in the name of Clyde Turnbow, principal stockholder in West Tennessee Exterminators.

We don't usually fool with these little jobs, Roosterfish told him, pocketing the money. I done it mainly for accommodation. Had a little spray left from a schoolhouse job over at Selmer.

I preciate it, the old man told him.

Back in the Studebaker Edgewater took the proffered money and without counting it slid it into the pocket of his jeans. What'd make an old man termite a shack like that?

I don't know.

Don't you feel funny about taking his money?

No. I give him what he paid for. You think he could get that house sterminated for what he paid me? Hell no he couldn't. How funny'd you feel about what of it I give you?

A termite would curl his lip at that old shack.

I don't know. I guess maybe it makes em feel important. He can tell folks he got his house sterminated. Hell, he can prove it. He's got a receipt in the bib pocket of his overalls.

I doubt if you could drown a termite in that shit we sprayed if you dropped one in and laid a rock on it, Edgewater persisted.

Hell, don't lose no sleep over it, Roosterfish grinned. We hadn't got his money he'd just piss it away on grocers or somethin. You a likely sort. You hang around me awhile and you'll have somethin in ye pockets besides ye hands.

They rode in silence for a time. Then Edgewater said: There was a rotten dog under that floor. Just laying there. No tellin how long he'd been dead.

Roosterfish looked at him curiously. A dead dog never bit nobody I ever heard tell of, he said.

Out of an ingrained sense of caution Roosterfish did no termiting close to home so it was a long drive back to the river. They did two more jobs and then stopped at a restaurant outside Selmer called The Golden Saddle and ate there. Roosterfish and Edgewater confidently among the country club set. Flush times. Roosterfish inquiring solicitously after Edgewater's steak. Was it rare enough? Tender? Edgewater slowly chewed bites of the red meat savoring each mouthful. There was a garden salad, a baked potato with cheese atop. Tender mushrooms he rationed out to himself. He'd forgotten such pleasures were still extant in the world.

We ort to do this more often, Roosterfish said. He folded his napkin when he was through. Edgewater was still eating, he was eyeing the apple pie on the table across. Now I got some places to show ye, Roosterfish told him.

It's a bootlegger down by camp there, Roosterfish said. Edgewater would come to believe that Roosterfish had committed to memory some esoteric traveler's guide of whores and bootleggers not procurable in service stations.

Edgewater climbed the steps to the bootlegger's, knocked on a glassless door. There was a little door within a door that opened inward on soundless hinges, a hard pallid face that looked out without recognition or interest. Beyond it against the far wall stacks of pint bottles of wine, halfpints of whiskey, cases of beer stacked to the ceiling. A hoarder's dream.

What do you want?

Four pints of wine.

Who are you?

He said tell you Roosterfish wants it.

Oh. What kind, then?

He said Gypsy Rose.

The man turned, shuffled goutily away.

Edgewater stood looking into the room. On an old carseat against the wall sat an old, old woman staring at nothing with rheumy, unfocused eyes. Her clawed hands clasped each other in her lap and she sat decorous, patient, as if she awaited something a long time coming. A sorrow, a nameless dread, lay on him like a plague.

Here you go. Was it anything else?

No. He handed over the two dollars.

All right. Come back.

The next day they stopped at a country store and bought a chicken and a loaf of bread and two onions. Get something to drink, Edgewater said. That evening the fighting cocks watched expressionlessly the demise and cleaning of their storebought brother, the dignity of their own doom foreordained. Roosterfish roasted the chicken on his improvised grill while they sipped wine, treacly, a burning aftertaste, extract of no fruit Edgewater could call to mind.

A long cool summer dusk lay on the river, a sleepy humid tranquility. When the light was gone bullbats darted among the trees, fed among the gnats and bugs thronging the river.

How about this place? Roosterfish asked him.

Well. It sure beats sleeping in smokehouses and living on candy bars.

I reckon a man's always wonderin what's on down the road. But if you ain't in no hurry you ort a hang around awhile and get ye a stake. Find ye a girl and settle somers around here. If a man ain't got to be no place in particular one place is good as another. Ast me. I been all over and they ain't thirty cents difference in none of it. Besides, they's lots of things I can't work by myself, on account of my arm.

What happened to it?

Roosterfish looked at his arm, made a fist. The tendons tightened, flared like drawn wire beneath the flesh.

Nothing happened to it.

I meant the other one.

There ain't no other one. This is all I got.

Roosterfish thought of saying he had lost the arm at Anzio, Normandy, wherever advantageous it might have fallen, but somehow he knew Edgewater would not believe him. I got it tore off in a sawmill, he finally said.

Edgewater winced. How come they call you Roosterfish?

Lord, I been Roosterfish all my life, nearly. Started when I'se just a kid. Course, Roosterfish ain't nothin but a fancy way of sayin cocksucker. I forgot who it was called me that first, you know how boys is always cussin one another. It was one of my buddies, and it was all in fun. If I'd a just let it pass that'd been all of it, but I didn't see it that way. I raised hell, we fought and I lost, and I was Roosterfish from then on.

He turned the chicken, basted it delicately with grease. I reckon you hear a word over and over it stops meanin anything, or changes. I've had women call me that. Mr. Roosterfish this, Mr. Roosterfish that. Old ladies call me that and I hardly ever even think about it meanin cocksucker.

How'd you get into your line of work?

Like everything else, a little at a time. I started out straight. I'd really termite em, but hell, folks didn't know the difference. One time I'se out of spray and I just went ahead and done it anyway. Money spent just the same, and I got to thinkin. After that I'd just mix up a mess of whatever I had and shoot it on.

One of these nights they'll all band together and tar and feather your ass. Or lynch you.

I'm a student of human nature, Roosterfish said. I'm going to school, you might say.

Seems to me you're putting other folks through school, Edgewater said. The school of hard knocks.

Shit. You ain't dealin with no amateur. This here is an old established firm. I know these people. Hell, they ain't like rich people. They don't think like em. I steer clear of folks with money, I ain't that ambitious. Poor folks is my customers.

Never heard of Robin Hood, huh?

That's a crock of horseshit. Robbin from the rich and all. You're old enough to know about the law. You've heard of the law? Well, they in the rich man's pocket. He loses fifty or sixty dollars, all kinds of folks want to jump bad. Yes sir, they say. We'll get that back for ye in the mornin. Poor man loses it, they say, Well, we'll do what we can. Here's some papers for ye to fill out. Don't you know better'n to trust folks passin through like that? Besides, a rich man gets madder'n hell. A poor man is so used to things goin wrong, he thinks he's got it comin to him. He halfway expects it. He'll cuss a little or pray a little, dependin on his beliefs, and that's the end of it.

Maybe, Edgewater said. He drank wine and watched the river going indistinct until its near invisible motion grew murky and mysterious. All the sounds of the woods were the sounds out of his childhood, they became more real than Roosterfish's voice.

Sides, I know when to quit, and I spread myself pretty thin. I work the backroads and steer clear of town. Hell, hardly any of these folks got cars. Time word gets around I'm somers else, doin somethin different.

Or in the penitentiary one.

Maybe. Not so far. The work's light and the money's good. I don't worry much about orphans and widderwomen. I guess I been screwed so much in so many different ways my first reaction's just to whirl around and pop it to somebody else. Besides, I got troubles of my own, ain't you?

I guess every man's got his demons.

Do ye? Roosterfish judged the chicken done, began to carve portions onto paper plates. What's yourn?

Everybody but me, Edgewater grinned. So it doesn't ever bother you conning folks like that? Taking their money or chickens or trade or whatever.

I don't know. I don't think about it much. I guess when you get fucked over past a certain point you turn it on other folks ever chance you get. A man's got to live. The Bible tells you that even the lilies of the field got to eat.

Even the lilies of the field got to eat?

Yeah.

What the shit does that mean?

I don't know. Hellfire, Edgewater. I'm drunk. I heard a preacher say that one time. That or something like it.

Edgewater rose and glanced at Roosterfish. He began ostentatiously to roll up his pants legs.

What? Roosterfish said.

Drowning in bullshit is one of the sorriest ways to go I can think of, Edgewater said, and I think I'm in danger of it. I'm moving to higher ground.

Sometime deep in the night he awoke. The sky was overcast and there was a soft mist of rain falling on his face. It had just begun, his blanket was not yet wet. He woke Roosterfish and they moved to the shelter of the bluff. Roosterfish had barely awakened, went almost immediately back to sleep.

Edgewater sat wrapped in his blanket, peering beyond the bluff across the water. The rain intensified, he could hear it falling in the river, a steadily increasing hiss. The coals of their cookfire guttered soundlessly, vanished. He sat in a vast timeless silence that was only deepened by the rain and the river, the world was in a hush, even the nightbirds held their cries in abeyance. A shifting curtain of rain swung off the shelf of limestone.

Far upriver where the bridge spanned the water, carlights crossed and arched briefly upward scanning the beleaguered heavens. The rain in their beams was silver, slanting, roiling the water where it struck like hot stones. Then the lights went out, the trestle was an inkblack skeleton whose image flared white on his retina and died, was perversely resurrected by a faint and soundless flicker of summer lightning. As the storm approached him, following the course of the river, the lightning became more frequent, there were faroff reverberations of thunder vaguely sinister. Then lightning quaked in one continuous arc as if some curious chain reaction had begun that if unabated would incandesce all it illuminated: slick rainglossed cars on the trestle, two doll-like figures peering toward the river. The world vanished, they would not share with him their darkness. Who were these wayfarers, would he know them? Was the world that wide, time that long? All up and down this river lay people in troubled sleep, what things done or not done would not let them rest? He would never know, the present was too infinitesimal to factor, all there was was past and future. Regret like a stab twisted in him that he could never live even a fraction of their lives. Their daughters tossed in chaste beds, he would never comfort them, their hot secrets would never fall on his ears.

Where he was going or not going, there was a girl who waited or did not wait. He had said what he was expected to say, did he mean it? It was in the past, dead, but even then it had rung false in his ears like lines from a castoff magazine, and what had her face been like? Perhaps she slept this night, serene in the faroff mountains. Did she dream of her sailor on bottleglass seas? Or was she fast in the seize of love, did another's body move above hers in the fecund sweaty night?

He had no way of knowing, nor did he care. He pulled the blanket tighter about him. He would go, or he would not go. He felt rootless now, uncompelled. The dread to come no worse than that behind.

After a time he slept fitfully. What woke him before daybreak was a boat going downstream, disembodied voices above the murmur of the river, sealbeamed lights flashing across the lapping water. Then laughter and the slap of oars.

In the morning the rain had ceased and the sun rose on a world that seemed to have become lush and green overnight. After breakfast Roosterfish exercised his fighting cocks while Edgewater washed the dishes in the river. Each cock was fitted with diminutive boxing gloves that padded their spurs. Roosterfish set them on the rocky floor of the bluff, stepped aside to watch them circle each other warily, light on their feet, stepping high, heads ducked like boxers.

Watch that blue one, Roosterfish said.

The cocks feinted and dodged, stalking each other, their eyes intent as if their concentration excluded all save the enemy. The blue rooster leapt into the air, in one graceful motion pared of the extraneous and stabbed at his opponent's head.

Roosterfish knelt and separated them, soothed them with strokes and soft words. He'd had a cockheel he'd a hooked him right through the eye. That's his style of fightin. Goes right for the brain. You ever seen a cockfight?

No.

That's a Allen Roundhead rooster. He's got royal blood in his veins. If he was a man he'd be a prince or a king. I got him out of Cullman, Alabama, and I been bringin him right along. Look at his eyes, Roosterfish said. He's a mean son of a bitch, I've fought him a couple of times. He goes for the kill, he don't take no prisoners. There's a cockfighter up in Lewis County gonna be sorry he ever laid eyes on me.

Where?

Up between here and where you're headin. They have cockfights up there and I aim to clean em out. They got highrollers drive all the way from Texas in Cadillacs just to go out in them woods and drink whiskey and bet chickens.

Sure they do.

It's a fact. I'se raised up there and lived there most of my life. For the last year I been workin my way back, takin my time, just enjoyin it, bringin my chicken along. The only thing on my mind's that cockfight. I got my money laid back and one morning I'll ease in there with my rooster under my arm, and when I walk out I'll be even with D.L. Harkness and I'll have money in ever pocket and money in my shoes.

Or a dead rooster.

Bet me. Not this rooster, son. Puttin him up again them chickens they got is like putting a thoroughbred in a mule race.

There were green meadows kept bound by rows of chestnut trees where somnolent cows grazed and the sound of their bells tolled faint like bells of a long time ago. There were white houses set atop declivitous closecrop lawns with fruit trees in careful rows and they seemed remote, foreign as if they had been built out of the reach of the aching poverty besetting the lower regions. Roosterfish spurned with contempt these mansions where country squires sat at their counting tables for the wonky little shacks at the mouths of hollows, tilted askew and looking as if they had been hastily constructed of whatever oddments of material fell to hand. Curious oblique little shanties somehow imbued with menace, sinister with years of misfortune, nights of death, stillbirth and hunger, hard words and deeds harder still.

Gray clapboard tenant shacks in bare earth yards, unglassed home-made doors opened noiselessly on leather hinges to reveal Roosterfish and Edgewater, once again mentor and protégé, father and son. Roosterfish with his rolled-up copy of the *Saturday Evening Post*, hat aloft, his foolish dimestore spectacles slid down on this nose to make him more—what? Scholarly? Benign? Spectacles lensed with window glass and even that suspect, spectacles as spurious as the rest of him.

Shuttered gloom. Fetid air, miasmic with tinned mackerel, with the residue the years deposit in their wake. His smile innocent, benevolent. They watched him as if he were some traveling wizard awaited with intense patience. Whatever legerdemain he might perform. Edgewater looking about the sparse furnishing, seeing mirrored the enforced austerity of his youth.

You get one of these a week, he would be saying, right here in ye mailbox. Nothin you'd have to hide did the preacher drop by.

Good Christian readin matter, too, not like these here trashy dime detectives and true story books. Come over here where the light's better and look at these receipts. Sign this receipt and you'll get this here magazine delivered to your house for one year. These here kids needs this magazine. Man could grow up cultured if he never read nothin but the Good Book and *The Saturday Evening Post*.

His pencil at work, tablet on his knees, alert eyes scanning for something to trade should no money be forthcoming. Preferably something readily convertible to cash.

At the end of the day the old Studebaker would be cocked on her springs with the day's accumulation of largess, bags of garden stuff, scrapiron, curious old pieces of farm equipment, car batteries he could sell for the zinc. Odd bits of copper, canned goods, perhaps a chicken or two. His receipt book thick with names, a perverse census of the region's unwary.

 Stopping past a covered bridge where a spring boiled out of limestone rock and a tin cup hung by a lichened pipe they drank cold water, rested in the deep shade of liveoak, the air drugged with the rampant growth of spearmint. Roosterfish drank from his halfpint, chased it with water, sighed with the weariness of a man at the end of a long day, bonetired but satisfied with himself. Bemusedly he shredded the receipts, tossed them like confetti into the stream. They listed amidst the watercress, fanned out. Edgewater stood watching the creek take them.

The highway yielded up strange treasures.

 One Sunday morning they passed what looked like a slack and lifeless body thrown into the weeds. Some luckless casualty of Saturday night.

 I couldn't tell what it was.

 Hell, it was a dead man.

 We don't need to be foolin with any dead man.

 That's for damn sure.

 Roosterfish drove on a mile or so in troubled silence and when they came upon a church thronged with cars and wagons he stopped and cut off the switch and sat listening to the pious voices wafting out across the scrubby pines. Hell, I'm goin back, Roosterfish said. That son of a bitch might have been wearin a wristwatch.

 They drove back cautiously. Miscreants returning to the scene of the crime. They stopped and walked along the dusty roadbed bright with bursts of chiggerweed like orange flames. But it was not a body after all. It was a canvas sack filled with something lumpy and very heavy and secured at the top with a thong. Edgewater cut it with his knife. The top pulled open to reveal a cornucopia of green painted mallards, duck decoys carved by some loving hand.

 Well, shitfire, Edgewater said.

 Help me load em.

 I'm not interested in any sack of wooden ducks.

 Will you just help me tote the damn thing.

 Ever a man to pare a thing to the usefulness at its core, Roosterfish, when he could not sell them, gave them away as premiums with lifetime subscriptions to the *Progressive Farmer*. Left them sown like seeds along the creeks and hollows of McNairy County, curious souvenirs of his duplicity nesting among bricabrac on backwoods whatnots, set down with care amidst china dogs and Cheshire cats with painted smiles.

Down off the blacktops another world lay sleeping. Down cherted hills passing hollows deep and breathtaking and down to narrow barriered hardpan roads where raincrows called to them and scarecrows watched them over crops already passed with maudlin stares like Roosterfish's own.

His people, he told Edgewater. His heart warmed to sharecroppers and cordwood cutters, to all congenitally disenfranchised stairstepped children that came out and looked with faces that showed you nothing at all, not expectation at their arrival or disappointment at their departure, washed out dried up women with lank hair, nothing much left to say. Their nubile daughters who giggled at Edgewater and hid behind their hands and their eyes said that whatever had befallen their mothers would never in a thousand years happen to them.

A few years back I happened on a good thing, Roosterfish told him. Traded for a few old battery radios and I'd carry em out to some of these here shacks like that and hook em up and turn em on. I ain't got no money they'd say. Don't even turn that thing on. Don't worry about no money, I'd tell em. I'll just leave it here a week and then I'll come back around and if you don't want it just say so. If you do you can pay me, if you don't I'll take it on with me. I'd tune it up, and show em where the dials were. Well sir, I'd go back in a week's time late Saturday evening when they was looking forward to the Grand Ole Opry and hopin I wouldn't come. I don't know where they got it but they'd have it. Stole it or borrowed it or sold the cow or what but once they got a taste of Roy Acuff they had to have that radio. You couldn't have prised it out of their hands with a wreckin bar.

Roosterfish waxed nostalgic, mellowed in the homey flickering firelight. They sat wrapped with blankets against the damp of the night, there was strong chicory in tin cups.

You've heard people talk about their old women, he told Edgewater. I've heard many a man say, I had the best little woman in the world and

I done her wrong. Not me. I had one I thought the sun rose and set between her legs and she managed to shit on me ever which way I turned.

Edgewater grinned into the firelight, said nothing, listened to the rush of the water, to owls that called lonesome from some forlorn wood.

Her and D.L. Harkness, Roosterfish went on. Between em they put me where I am today. My arm wound up in a loose belt in his sawmill and she wound up in his bed.

Edgewater's eyes glanced at Roosterfish, then back to the fire.

Well. I lost my arm and I felt he owed me for it. I couldn't get no compensation and I couldn't work. We had a hearin and he got up in court and swore I was drunk and fell into that belt. Course it wasn't so, a lie. I got no reason to lie about it now. But him and the judge had to go dove huntin that evenin so the hearin didn't take too long. He was just a lowlife son of a bitch. Pushy and overbearin. Got a little money and a sawmill he won in a crap game and things started fallin right the way they will. Always a knife in his pocket, not perty by a damn sight. Ugly as a look into hell, you wouldn't think a woman'd look at him. A man thinks with his peter instead of his head. The only women he wanted was always somebody else's.

How'd he get your old lady?

Well, it was a matter of time before he got around to her. Like I said, she was a fine-lookin woman and seems like she'd started screwin everbody from the paper boy on up and everbody knew it but me. I guess they say the husband's the last one to know, Roosterfish continued. I had a feelin. I thought she's fuckin the light man, you know comes around and reads ye meter? On the morning he's supposed to I went off like I'se goin to work and then slipped back in and hid in the bedroom closet and just waited. Time just crawled by. That's the longest morning I ever put under and as hard a work as ever I done.

What happened?

Nothin happened. I set there and I set there and I heard the dog barkin and the pickup come up but he didn't even cut the switch off. Turned out I guess the light man was the only one she wadn't fuckin. Just got back in and drove off. I'se afraid to come out, fraid she'd see me and about to die for a smoke. I lit one up finally and was faggin away when she come in and seen smoke rollin out from under the door. They Lord, she thought the house was afire. She flung open the closet and there I set.

I bet that was hard to explain.

Yeah. But by then I'se half crazy. She's a pretty woman, the prettiest I ever saw. Bout ten year youngern me. And a woman couldn't be satisfied no matter what she had. I don't mean screwin, though it might have been that too. I mean everthing. She could see a couch in a store that was the prettiest God ever allowed upholstered and I'd buy it and time I got it home it was a piece of shit a dumpkeeper wouldn't have. She was like tryin to fill up a hole didn't have no bottom. You'd throw in ever-thing fell to hand, all you could get, but it was never enough, more, more, more, and she had a cruel mouth. She could twist the heart out of ye.

It looks to me like you ought to be glad she's gone, Edgewater told Roosterfish.

I guess that's one way of lookin at it. Course I thought a lot of her, never could get over that. But the main thing is that Harkness took her and he didn't have no right to do that. When one person does that to another one it throws the scales out of balance. All I'm lookin to do is set somethin about the same weight on the other side of em.

He fell silent, was quiet for some time. By the wavering light his face was abstracted, perhaps he attended hills and fields of his youth.

She took to workin in one of these here garment factories, he finally said. Worked all hours, you'd think the place'd shut down without her to look after things. Like I said, long about then I'se half crazy. I took to going through her pocketbook like a sneakthief. Lookin for overtime on her checkstubs. They wadn't none. Then one time I found one of these lil old plastic boxes holds three rubbers and one of em was gone. I can't tell you how I felt when I studied on the fate of that missin rubber.

What'd you do?

I took me a needle and punched me a little bitty hole in the ends of the two that was left and put em back like they was.

Good God. Why'd you do that?

I don't know, I told you I'se crazy. Why? What's the matter with that?

It just seems a little inadequate to me.

I always thought if she ever done me like that I'd shotgun em both on the spot, but you never know what you'll do till it looks you in the face. I guess that ain't my style. I can wait as long as it takes, just as long as I can see the end of the road. That cock in that coop yonder is a born champion, bred for generations back to do just what it's fixin to. When the time's right.

I guess there's a certain amount of poetic justice in you getting back at him with a fighting cock.

What?

Nevermind. Go ahead.

I'll ease in there early some Sunday morning with its feathers all wooled up and it lookin like somethin I jerked out of a fox's mouth and I'll act about half drunk and pull out my roll and the suckers'll wink at one another and line up on ever side.

If you say so.

Hell yes I say so. I know these people, son, I been among em all my life. I know Harkness. He can't let a sure thing slide by. And when I walk away he won't have a pot to piss in or a winder to throw it out of. I'll win enough to buy that son of a bitch and sell him, if they's any taker left.

What about her?

I don't know. She may be tired of him by now. He may be tired of her. I been gone a long time; she may be dead, she may be in a whorehouse. But I expect by now he's dumped her and she's tendin bar in a honkytonk somewheres, sleepin wherever night falls on her. And with whoever it catches her with. I maybe could get her back. Or maybe not. I don't even know if I want her. I guess I'm better off like I am. You can't own a living thing, Roosterfish said. I can say that rooster belongs to me but he don't. He belongs to his own self.

He arose and set the coop nearer the fire. I hope this damp air don't give em somethin, he fretted. The firelight flickered in their inscrutable eyes, black gems of arrogance, generations old. As if they held themselves above whatever tawdry uses might be found for them.

She could be the softest woman, Roosterfish said after a long time, as if he had forgotten Edgewater's existence and was talking to himself, the night, no one. She'd fly mad about somethin and after a while she'd be like it never happened. You could just reach for her and she'd lean towards ye and she was just the softest woman I ever seen.

A yellow light came on somewhere far across the bottomland, the only sign of humans in this lonesome night. What woke them, what roused them about at this hour? Death, sickness, childbirth? Arrival, departure?

———

I need to be moving on east, he told Roosterfish the next morning.

Hell, I thought we had a deal.

Edgewater shrugged. I stayed awhile. I've got the money now to make it home. I need to be getting that way.

Son, we are gettin that way. We're goin on east pretty quick. We'll wind this county up and move on down the line. You stick with me and I'll have ye in silk an satin. I'll have ye eatin steak and drinkin wine got corks in it stead of screw-on caps. Just trust old Roosterfish.

Raincrows calling from a nearby cornfield warned them off, but he had no ears for them. Nor for the frogs calling from the pond across the way. A thunderhead lay like a tumor on the southwestern horizon but Roosterfish was blind to it, was giddy with triumph. He had money everywhere except his shoes.

It was not yet three o'clock and they had painted three barn roofs in the final phase of Roosterfish's sweep before moving on east. They had taken in a hundred and forty-five dollars and enough of what Roosterfish called paint remained to finish another. It was not paint. It was a mixture of cheap re-refined motor oil and enough pigment to give it color; when sprayed onto a hot tin roof it immediately dried and healed over into something that looked like paint, but it was not wise to use it when rain threatened. It did not weather well.

It's goin to rain.

Hell, it won't rain the way our luck's runnin. It's goin around, you can tell.

I can't tell.

Just take old Roosterfish's word for it. Tomorrow night we'll be eatin steak in the best restaurant in Savannah.

Edgewater looked at the horizon, scanned the heavens. Save for the thunderhead far in the distance there was not a trace of cloud in all that blue and nothing to threaten the serenity of this day in early June. There was a somnolent murmur of insects from the tranquil woods and the air was thick with honeysuckle.

The farmer stood with his thumbs hooked in his overall galluses and conversed with Roosterfish and a transparent look of craft came into his eyes.

You said how much?

Fifty dollars.

That's highern a cat's back.

We do good work. Go down the road and look at Escue's barn if you got any doubts.

I ain't callin you a liar. You said had just enough to do one more barn and it looks to me like you ort to give me a break on it.

Fifty dollars for a barn that size is a break. You try to get it done anywhere else for that.

The man did not reply. The barn loomed behind him, the roof rusted to a dull umber. The farmer's two sons came silently and flanked him, freckled and sunburnt. One with a dished face watched Edgewater with vacant mindless eyes like the eyes of an old sepia photograph, a face with no name to put to it, just a displaced face out of a long time ago. The trio somehow fit together to form an implicit threat.

Paint ain't milk, Roosterfish said. It won't clabber if I don't use it all today.

I'll give you forty dollars.

Roosterfish turned to Edgewater. What about it, son? Can we come out like that?

If we're going to do it then let's do it. We need to be in Savannah.

My partner says forty then.

They drove down as close as they could get to the barn and began to unload the equipment, the three standing alongside the house and watching them.

Watch what I tell you about that old man, Roosterfish said, uncoiling the sprayer hose. I said fifty and he argued me down to forty, and when we get through he'll come up with maybe thirty dollars. I've seen a thousand of that same son of a bitch.

You watch him. He's got a mean set to his eyes.

Hell, let him think he beats us. I got maybe fifteen cents a quart in that stuff at the outside.

That's not what I mean. I got a bad feeling about him. And it's going to rain, too.

Rain hell. By the time the first drops come pitter-pattering down we'll be in Wayne County with our feet propped up and somethin cold in our hands.

The sprayer was powered by an old kerosene-fueled compressor and Edgewater dragged it through waisthigh burdock and pokeweed to the edge of the barn, peering warily about constantly for copperheads. There was a hot still smell of baking tin and sere hay and the moted light fell white and oblique through the slats in the walls. An unseen woodpecker hammered staccato from the woods beyond the barn.

He cranked the compressor until it started and when it hit barn swallows and starlings rose aloft with protesting cries. The throb of the compressor seemed out of place in this pastoral setting, this bucolic countryside that looked like a sentimental painting of a peaceful landscape that never was.

Roosterfish tended the machine and kept the hoses strung and untangled and Edgewater started at the ridgepole and worked his way down, umber beneath him changing to a pale verdigris. After half the roof was painted they shut off the compressor and drug it around to the other side of the barn and started it again. Edgewater clambered up the ladder and turned on the sprayer and when he glanced southwestward he was amazed by what he saw. The thunderhead had arisen until it loomed almost to the sun and even as he watched the sun was swallowed, hung like a rind of gleaming disc against the black cloud like an eclipse. The air turned to smoked glass, thickened, his squat shadow faded transparent and then disappeared. The thunderhead seethed at its base as if feeding on all it passed across and forked prongs of lightning walked stilted about the horizon. There was a faint rumble of thunder, a mere suggestion of sound. There was already wind in the highest branches and there was a disquiet in the air. He swore and bent to his work, spraying a thin skim of oil on the hot tin.

At another time Roosterfish would be acting with importance, pointing out features of the equipment to the old farmer, but now he was silent and there were weightier things on his mind. Hey, Roosterfish called. We got to hurry.

The three men ambled slowly down toward the barn, the elder occasionally glancing toward the darkening heavens. There was a yellow-green cast to the clouds now and the thunder was clearly audible. All the world had darkened and lightning quaked constantly from one side of the gleaming metallic base to the other.

Hey. It's goin to rain like a cow pissin on a slate rock.

If you can spray this son of a bitch any faster than I can then drag your dead ass up here.

The three had come down into the lot and stood all alike like clones of varying sizes with hands pocketed watching Roosterfish with interest. He was pouring the last of the paint into the sprayer and Edgewater moved over the hot tin like a man demented, spraying a poison green film over anything that moved in front of the nozzle and raising aloft to peer toward the approaching storm. The air was filling with flying bits of windtorn leaves whirling like chaff from a thresher and birds before it cried its dire intent. The wind ballooned Edgewater's shirt and trouser legs and tilted him askew with its weight.

When he finished the last lower corner he slid the sprayer off the edge of the roof and did not even descend the ladder but leapt from the lip of the tin and landed in the weeds simultaneous with the first drops of rain. Roosterfish was coiling the hose before the sprayer even reached the ground.

Let's get the hell out of Dodge, Edgewater said.

Roosterfish had the plywood rear door of the Studebaker open and he was hurling gear inside. Huge glycerinous beads of rain were falling and behind these scattered drops an almost silver wall of rain was moving slanted across the field toward them with wind-tilted grass portending its coming.

The three men aligned themselves beneath the eaves of the barn and watched Edgewater hauling the compressor through the weeds. The rain began singing on the tin and he was instantly sodden. Roosterfish grasped a side of the compressor with his one arm and they hoisted it into the back and latched the camper door.

They ran for the shelter of the tin and Roosterfish wiped the rain out of his eyes. We need to get on, he told the man. We got a job in Wayne County in the morning.

The man had his wallet out and he was counting laboriously. The wallet had a plaited leather fob on it like a pocketwatch and the cord wended somewhere back into the folds of his clothing.

Roosterfish kept glancing at his wrist though he wore no watch there. Gettin late, he said.

You reckon it got good and dry? the man asked.

Hell yes it's dry. You could of fried sidemeat on that tin.

The old man was counting still. One of you boys been in my pocketbook?

One of them snickered and rolled his eyes upward to the rain shin-
gling off the eaves.

I can't find but twenty-seven dollars here, the man complained.

Edgewater had a cigarette in his mouth and all his matches were
wet. He was going through all his pockets. The old man was counting
aloud now, licking his thumb between bills. Twenty-six, twenty-seven.
Edgewater threw the cigarette into the rain and glanced upward and
saw with an inward sinking that the film of oil was loosening. The
rain had penetrated beneath it and it had slid perceptibly, perhaps
a quarter inch of it extended below the rim of tin. Take it, he told
Roosterfish.

Roosterfish was shaking his head. I don't know, that's way short. I
couldn't of come out even at forty dollars.

Hell, I thought I had morn that. Tell ye what I'll do. Gimme ye
address and I'll send ye a money order for the balance. Less see. What'd
that be, thirteen dollars?

Roosterfish had seen the paint. He calmly took the scrap of paper
the man proffered and dug out stub of pencil. He was writing down a
nonexistent company at some nonexistent location. He took the twenty-seven dollars. The farmer now exuded goodwill. He seemed well
pleased with himself. Yins come in and have some hot coffee with us.

Go, goddamn it, Edgewater thought. The paint slid an inch this
time, then further still, surely they would see but they stood dumbly
watching the rain froth bits of straw.

Thank ye anyway but we got people waitin on us, Roosterfish said.

The man nodded as if that was right too. Suit yourself. Boys, best get
in fore the wind gets any worse.

The three walked into the rain, walked like cattle with lowered heads.
Roosterfish and Edgewater ran to the Studebaker. As they wheeled
around and the men were not yet halfway to the house, the paint lifted
with a great near-liquid ripple and draped itself along the rim of tin, a
vast green gelatinous fabric like a curtain closing some curious show,
behind it the roof marvelously umber again, a reptile shedding its skin.
The entire front section of membrane had separated itself delicately
from the tin roof and risen like some enormous creature spreading

gossamer wings in tentative flight then came abruptly unbound by the winds. Then the wind caught in it and it lifted, hung swaying, rose briefly intact and then shredded, great shards of it settling in trees and over the country like kites of ash, Fortean curiosities for the next day's travelers.

They were far down the road when Roosterfish said, That is some closer than I like to see em played.

That bunch ain't going to forget this.

They can tell their descendants about it for all of me, long as I ain't around to hear it. Sides, I told you I've seen a thousand like him. Brain like a shittin chicken. If he's constipated all he'd know to do be swaller a rat and sit on a hoop of cheese.

The night was heady with limitless possibilities. Heading back on the Jackson Highway they passed a seemingly endless string of honkytonks bathed in bright neon, intense as if the highway itself was consumed with garish fire. Headlamps blurred yellow in the falling rain, the rhythmic slap of the windshield wipers vaguely comforting. It was good to be warm and dry and setting out in the world of pleasure.

This looks like a good un, Roosterfish said, choosing a parking lot at seeming random. We'll check out the women in this un.

Inside a huge bar curved like a horseshoe, a country band on a plywood stage singing plaintively of adultery as if a Greek chorus to the throng of men and women lining the bar. They drank beer for a while and after a time the barkeep sold Roosterfish a bottle of bonded in a paper bag and they began to drink boilermakers. Roosterfish checking out all the women, apparently dissatisfied, they moved on.

Edgewater began to get a little drunk. He lost track of the boilermakers and then he lost track of the places he drank them in, the bars became stagesets held for his approval and then discarded, ever renewed, ever the same. He did not know where the night went. The night began to come and go in scenes like snapshots, isolated frames with no continuity.

Roosterfish became enamored at last with a hefty blonde who had a blacked and swollen eye and strove to hide it with a black eyepatch like some debauched pirate. She had a coarse and ribald laugh, a scarlet cavernous mouth.

A young blackhaired girl, who told Edgewater she was a displaced Eskimo, led him across a graveled parking lot toward an aluminum housetrailer. He was fascinated with an Eskimo here in this land of so much sun. He fell and lay in the driving rain and she helped him arise. Looking up in a moment of terrible lucidity he saw on her face contempt, anger, impatience to have it over with and done. It's not like that, he wanted to tell her. Her face looked older, disapproving. Faces out of his past shuttled there like a series of rippled photographs. He wanted to be in her favor, to impress her as he once had teachers, but he could not find the words. She did not want words anyway. All he had she wanted was money, and he needed that himself.

Another snapshot: eyes closed to a slit and feigning sleep he saw past his black-socked feet on the bed her going through his pockets one by one, casting garments aside, naked, breasts pointing and bobbing with her movements, the glossy thatch of her pubic hair. The mounded belly some-how erotic, but her face was bemused by her work, her dark eyes avaricious.

He lay supine and watched her. His money was in his sock, he could feel it comfortable against the sole of his foot.

Bedlam drew him out to the parking lot. Roosterfish had fallen afoul of the management. Feeling displeased or cheated he'd set afire the curtains in the trailer. Half-undressed he was hurled into the rain, lay on his back reclining in the mud. Slick healed weal of scar tissue covering the end of his stub. Displeased voices were reprimanding him, a threatening figure pointing to the slick rainwet highway with a black-jack. Roosterfish kept calling for Edgewater. He had a shoe on one foot, a sock on the other.

Rolling again. Other articles of clothing misplaced, lost forever. Sobriety only a vague memory. The Studebaker careening through the night. Fear of the law long gone, a thing of the past. Edgewater went to sleep to the strobic flash of headlights, the sound of Roosterfish hum-ming to himself.

He awoke at first to sounds and sensations he could not at first identify. Reality was amorphous and sly, he could not lay hands on it. Slewing wheels, the splat of mud slathering the sides of the Studebaker. The whine of spinning tires, the stench of smoking rubber.

He looked out into a vast field that seemed inundated with water. He could not fathom where he was. The fields seemed endless, trackless on every side, he could not imagine how they'd come to be there or where they were.

He got out into the sucking quagmire of the fescue field and then he could hear the angry roar of the river off his right side. He looked up into black and weeping night. He knew where they were.

Roosterfish would try to go forward and when that would not work he would slam the car into reverse and spin backward. He beat on the horn angrily but that did not help either. Edgewater rested his forehead against the cold metal of the top, it throbbed fiercely beneath him.

He opened the door. You might as well quit. It's stuck.

Tell me somethin I don't know.

What the shit are we doing out in the middle of the field?

We're tryin to get to the goddamn camp, what do you think? Pickin blackberries?

How come you didn't leave it on the highway?

I ain't walkin through no such shit as this. Besides you was passed out.

I was asleep, Edgewater said.

I believe it's goin a little.

Straight down, maybe.

Well fuck you, Edgewater. You ain't got no right to bitch. Pass out on a man and leave him to do everthing hisself. I can't do everthing.

Edgewater looked back toward the highroad where lights passed swift and distant and he could not imagine how they'd come so far in a sea of mud. You're not even pointed the right way, he said.

Well, I was a while ago.

We may as well get out and forget it tonight. You're going to blow the motor up.

Stand back and let the son of a bitch blow. They still makin em up in Detroit. I hate a goddamn vehicle won't do right.

Hell, this whole field looks like a rice paddy. You ought to known better than to drive off in a mess like this. We need to be gone.

Don't I know it.

They started out toward the camp, reeling drunkenly through the gummy mud. Roosterfish left the car running and had to go back and shut it off. He kicked the door panel. Trade you off in the morning, he told it. You son of a bitch. I knowed when I seen you on that carlot you'd bring me bad luck.

He had to go back one last time; he'd forgotten the cocks. He found a scrap of tarpaulin and covered the coop with it. The cocks made disquieting noises to themselves as the coop bobbed on Roosterfish's shoulder, their small and fetid world borne drunkenly across a tilting landscape turned to water.

They woke to a grim and sodden world. Mist from the river shrouded the banks like fog and everything in their sight dripped with leaden rain. There was unseasonal coolness to the air. Even the crowing of the cocks sounded tentative and unconvinced. The two men moved sluggishly about their morning chores as if the air itself rendered all motion slow and difficult. They did not even speak until they had managed to build a fire and brew a pot of coffee. Then they perched before the fire like a brace of herons, coffee cups clutched in their hands.

I wish you'd woke me up when it started rainin hard. We can't even get the damn car out now.

It was that damn wine. Sick tastin shit. I drunk mine and I reckon I must of yours too. Did you not like it?

I can't drink that sweet stuff. Taste like Log Cabin syrup or something.

Roosterfish arose. Well. I guess we might as well walk down and see what it looks like.

It did not look encouraging. There was pooled water in the lowlands shoemouth deep and the earth beneath it was soft and sucking. They went on to the fescue field, halted at its edge; the field was a vast expanse of muddy water, the Studebaker at its center forlorn, derelict, some vessel cut adrift and abandoned. Water was up almost to the hubcaps and still rising. Roosterfish kicked at the spongy loam disgustedly. Well shitfire. I guess we're just by God stuck.

How bout tryin it around the edge?

Naw. We'd just get stuck worser. Sink down in the damn mess and it'd take a tractor or a team of mules to pull us out and the fewer knows where I hang my hat the better it suits me. I had in mind to sell some prescriptions today.

Some what?

Magazine prescriptions. All I know is to wait till it goes down. Which it's bound to sooner or later.

They returned to the bluff in a deepening drizzle and wind stiff off the water. The day did not warm as it should. Edgewater dragged to the shelter of the bluff old stumps leached pale as driftwood, sections of windfall cedar, fencepost still adorned with spikes of rusted wire as if he divined some reversal of the seasons, a winter's tale only the prepared would survive.

Old promises and old liaisons haunted him, old obligations shunted aside. They came in the night like succubi that would not let him be; nothing was ever really lost, he could not forget anything. But there was nothing he could do. How can I roll, he asked them, when the wheels won't go.

The second day the rain fell undiminished and they moved to a higher ledge and built a fire there. They moved all their blankets and the crated bedraggled cocks and sat against the limestone wall of the bluff staring down into an unreal world, a mad swirl of water advancing far into the bottomland.

The river inched upward, you could see it rising. Edgewater fixed a mark on a stump with his eyes, watched the river lap upward and coat it with foam, recede, return to it and draw it into turbulent darkness. The nether bank of the river was not steep and the water broke through here and seethed foaming and implacable into the flat spread of cornfields, leaving the woven-wire fences clotted with leaves and debris.

The main body of the river was a shifting pattern of treelimbs and stumps and as he watched an entire tree went by, its branches turning slow and stately. There was a motley of rotted planking and ruined household artifacts and once the intact wall of a shanty riding the waves flat and slick, a deserted windowed raft, and he would not have been surprised to have seen tattered survivors clinging to its decks and watching the rapid shift of passing greenery with stoic eyes. A mule had been caught up in the torrent, it passed with eyes rolling white and wild, its head bobbing from sight then reappearing like some gross fishing float, its threshing impotent against the greater threshing of the current that bore it on.

The river fascinated him, he'd not seen one so close before. It came to seem some lost highway of the undone, accommodating not wayfarers like themselves but debris and artifacts jettisoned by souls lost upon it, empty gestures of appeasement, offerings to a god not listening anymore.

There were no storms now but a dull and remorseless rain from an invisible sky, a gunmetal firmament melting and falling as if the earth were some vessel it was intent on filling. Along the river's edge and as far as the eye could see the world was misty green, a lush fecundity glutting on the rain and growing, softening the ridges, hazing the far blue treeline. Seen through the driving rain and the mist the landscape seemed to merge, field and road and woods bleeding together to form some cessation of clarity, vision from dream or madness, possessed of a weird and unreal beauty.

They skirted the fescue field and ascended the sloping bank through a near impenetrable wall of dripping rushes and came out on the blacktop. They looked about them. In faded gray distance farmhouses set pastoral and unreal, dreamlike in the mist, so intangible they might vanish. The highway lay empty, finite, vanishing in a white wall of vapor at either end. The world was soundless, deserted, as if they alone had survived the flood. They crossed the trestle and paused to peer down, Edgewater momentarily dizzy at the movement of swift yellow water.

The blacktop wound high past alluvial bottomland already planted in corn half underwater, water seeping silent and threatening, some demented irrigation system berserk and out of control. The road forked past there and the roar of the river began to fade. In the fork set a country store. Ancient gaspumps like relics of better days, or yet artifacts the race who dwelt here had progressed past and forgotten, or remnants of some more advanced culture, purposeless, monuments to some god proved false.

They moved among the merchandise, careless Sunday shoppers seeking bargains. Few to be found here under the wary and jaundiced eye of the storekeep. There was tinned food and mounded harness and a tray of pocketknives enshrined beneath flyspecked glass. A rack of rakes and hoes and scythes that stood like a stack of weaponry Edgewater felt might ultimately be used to arm the agrarian populace against them should they not flee. Boxes of tissued utilitarian shoes open for inspection, shelves of Duckhead overalls, a smell of denim, dye, leather.

I bet she's rollin, the storekeep said. You still camped out over there?

Yeah. Yeah, she's walkin and talkin, all right.

You liable to wake up some mornin someplace you never went to sleep.

Roosterfish had approached the drink box, selected a bottle from the icewater. Nah. I'm on a ledge over there and the bluff's steep. It ever gets up there they'll be more souls than me huntin a higher roost.

They's a lot huntin it today, the storekeep said. Them in the bottom's comin out by boat, if they comin at all. She still risin?

Anybody about today?

If they are they'll be up at Simmons's. Bad weather don't hurt a bootlegger's business.

Edgewater sat on a drink crate and ate an enormous ice cream cone the storekeep built up from the freezer behind the counter. The taste and smell of vanilla was almost hallucinogenic, sensuous, Edgewater was reminded of drugstores long ago: there was a slow hypnotic ceiling fan he stared upward at and a clean composite of drugstore smells and racks of books he might have looked at had there been more money.

The cone was handed down, the nickel paid, he could hear the flat clink on the glass counter. He was holding to the leg of his father's trousers. Leaning down to lift him, the face was abstracted, a face with other, less pleasant duties to perform.

Then back through the hot streets to a store much like this one and a storekeep much like this one, their eyes are all the same, like blackjack dealers.

Till Saturday? This is Saturday, if I'm not mistaken.

Till next Saturday.

Oh, next Saturday, then. I reckon you owe about everbody on that other side of the street. What'd you do, bring ye trade over to spread ye business around?

No reply. Then: you people always want it till Saturday. What's Satur-day, the end of the rainbow?

I got some money comin Saturday.

And you people always got some money comin Saturday. I guess if ever-day was Saturday you'd have the store and I'd be over there astin for credit. You reckon?

They had turned and taken a step when the storekeep said: Well get it gathered up then.

There had been a moment when the hand holding his tensed and he could almost see the flinty eyes, hear the words forming: You keep your god-

*damn groceries. Yet there were mouths to feed, eyes that even now watched
the road for their return. There were empty pots and pans, a cookstove dormant and waiting. They turned, already eyeing the binned merchandise.*

*The storekeep had his ticketbook out, waiting with an air of exaggerated
patience.*

Slice us about a pound of that round steak there, Roosterfish said,
pointing to a cut of bologna in the meatcase. The grocer took it out,
began carefully to slice it onto white butcher paper.

You know that Simmons is a peculiar feller, he said, eyeing the meat
wafered atop the scale. He leaned confidingly toward Roosterfish. He
come down here late one evenin when they wadn't nobody around and
wanted to know did I want to make forty dollars. Naw, I told him. I figured he wanted whiskey hauled or somethin. Turned out all he wanted
me to do was turn in at his driveway at exactly ten o'clock that night.
Well sir, he laid two twenty-dollar bills right on that counter there and I
done it just like he said. I turned in at ten on the money and shone my
headlights in his window and backed out and left. I've wondered many
a time what made my headlights on them windows worth forty dollars.

There were signs portending Simmons's before they got there. They
could hear the flat slap of a small caliber pistol interspersed with
purposeful pause as if some invisible assassin fired, took plenty of time
and careful aim, fired again. There was a distasteful tinge of smoke in
the air now, a smell of burning rags.

Then they began to pass the wrecked cars that marked the bound-
aries of the property. There were innumerable cars, arcane makes and
models, all crushed, an unclassified collection of highway disasters.
The old man had used cars for every purpose imaginable. Three were
tilted atop each other in the mouth of a deep gully, dirt half hiding
the bottom one, as if flung there by some petulant giant. Chickens
roosted and nested in them, eggs rotted there ungathered, guano
mounded the seats. A dog chained to one and perhaps forgotten
watched them down the road with surly eyes. A vast sea of cars, until
it somehow seemed perverse, as if all civilization funneled its crumpled and bloody waste down to Simmons, who drew death from the
broken cartons in some erotic gratification, experienced vicariously
and from safety the split second in eternity when they changed from

sleek machines knifing away the night to junk, the moment of no return when all control had been cast to the winds, the breathless hush of flight, metal on metal, the last rattle of falling glass.

There was a thick greasy coil of smoke from the stovepipe lowering along the ground and there were four men in the yard and a fifth Edgewater first took for a child. They were gathered about a fifty-gallon oil drum and one of them was reloading a pistol.

Hey Rooster, one of them called. You late for the ratkillin.

I been late all my life, Roosterfish told him. And most of the time glad of it.

Old Simmons had corn in this barrel and went down there this morning and it'd about all turned to rats. They's thirty or forty caught in there fightin over one little ear of corn. We brung it out here and Pulley there's about finished em off.

Edgewater peered into the depths of the barrel. There were a dozen or more dead rats in attitudes of repose and others cowering spattered with blood in the bottom. They were gray rats almost as big as housecats and their tails were scaled, as big as his forefinger. They watched him with their little calculating eyes. He turned away with something akin to scorn.

You might at least of turned the barrel over and let em run, Roosterfish said. Give em a sportin chance.

I could of got em all a little bitty pistol and let em shoot back, too, Pulley said. But I decided against it.

Pulley was tall and broad, an overalled barrel with appendages stuck on like afterthoughts. His face was hot and florid, flushed with blood. He had fierce little eyes not unlike the eyes that had stared at Edgewater from the depths of the barrel. He appeared to be drunk, the neck of a pint bottle protruded from a side pocket.

What's that smell? Roosterfish wanted to know. That's the stinkinest smoke I ever smelt. The house ain't on fire, is it?

Pulley shoved a magazine into the butt of the automatic and gestured toward the house with his head. That damn Simmons, he said. He's cold. He burnt all his wood back in the winter and he's too stingy to buy more and too shittin lazy to cut it hisself. He's burnin whatever he lays his hands on. Mostly clothes and rags. He's burnt two three boxes of rags that old woman saved and nigh ever rag of clothes she's got.

Is he drunk?

You might say that, Pulley told him. Pulley had on a short sleeve shirt, his arms were huge and freckled. He walked back to the barrel. But no drunker than a hog that fell in a salt barrel.

The man Edgewater had judged a child was in reality a man of middle age, though he stood no taller than a ten-year-old boy. His back was hunched, a great misshapen lump of flesh rode between his shoulders. He was impeccably dressed. He had on a white shirt with a button-down collar and a pale blue tie that matched his powder-blue jacket and diminutive trousers. His shoes were glossy, as if they had been spitshined. He was watching all that transpired as if it were beneath him. There was a dignity to him, a kind of contempt, as if he carried himself above the joys common folk found in rat killing. The men seemed to subtly defer to him, as if he possessed the last word on everything.

Been a game today?

Nah. Tyler here come out to play but him and Simmons the only ones got any money.

I might set in a hand or two, Roosterfish said.

Simmons is too drunk, Tyler said. Tyler was the hunchback. He had a distinctive, almost cultured way of speaking. Simmons can't tell the kings from the deuces today.

Let's go in, Roosterfish said. They's sights I'd stand around in the rain to see, but Pulley shootin unarmed rats in a oildrum ain't one of em.

I'd about as soon walk on back, Edgewater said.

And do what? Come on in and get a drink of whiskey.

The air inside was close and hot and fetid. The one-eyed bootlegger was crouched by the side of the sheetiron heater and its sides were cherried with heat. The stove door was open and Simmons held before it poised some lank rag of castoff clothing like a tidbit for some curious beast still in the act of chewing. The old woman still sat on the carseat as she had before and there was another woman in a canebottom chair studying her hands as intently as if all the world's knowledge was imprinted there.

Goddamn, old Roosterfish, Simmons said jovially. I figured you was astraddle of ye mattress polin for the Mississippi.

I'm still high and dry, Roosterfish said. You got any whiskey fit to drink?

Simmons stuffed the rag into the stove and closed the door. He arose. He swayed gently, as if he moved to some music unreeling in his head. Got Bobwhite.

Is that whiskey?

Course to hell it's whiskey. Ain't you never heard of Bobwhite?

How much is it?

Dollar and a half.

Seems like I have somers. Give us a halfpint apiece. Roosterfish was counting out quarters.

Simmons left the room complaining about the weather. Blackberry winter came later every year. He could not take it like he used to. He came back with the whiskey and handed it to Roosterfish. Who's ye runnin mate here?

Why this here's my boy. Got discharged out of the Navy and come home to the family business.

The family business you run from under a bluff. He squinted his one rheumy eye in Edgewater's face. He don't favor ye much.

Roosterfish had cracked the bottle, drank. I reckon he taken after his mama, he said. I hope he amounts to morn she did. She cut a trail with a drummer one morning when this chap was barely crawlin around.

Women will do ye like they will do ye, Simmons said philosophically.

The younger woman had arisen, stood holding the window curtain aside, peering into the yard. The old woman sat motionless. Perhaps she has died, Edgewater thought. He studied her covertly. She was dressed in some old black garment like mourning and there was a cameo brooch at her throat. She looked like an ancient, desiccated bird. She sat very still as if she were listening for the beginning of some faint, faroff sound. But when the flat slap of the pistol came she did not flinch.

Edgewater opened the bottle of whiskey and drank. It was cheap whiskey, raw in his throat. A blossom of fire spread outward from his stomach. He looked about for a chair, but there was none. Perhaps Simmons had burned them. He hunkered on his knees, staring at the watermarked wallpaper. Roses of some faded and unlikely hue climbed here. He wondered had she been young here. Perhaps Simmons had been born here, played about these floors while she watched him and dreamed the dreams you dream.

The young woman turned from the window. There was a vacant, stupid look about her, as if she did not know where she was. Nor did she care. Her eyes were child's eyes, a sly, lazy child. She sat and fell to staring at Edgewater.

Tyler thought he'd get me drunk and clean me out, Simmons was telling Roosterfish. Son of a bitch. Scuse me, Mrs. Tyler, he said drunkenly, but she appeared not to have heard, was again lost in scrutiny of her hands. I drink and I gamble, Simmons finished. But not at the same time.

We just thought they might be a game.

Tyler's a county court clerk or somethin. Smart son of a bitch. If he could keep his mouth off whiskey and his mind off pussy he could be president of the United States.

Edgewater glanced at the old woman, Simmons intercepted the look. She's deaf and blind, he said. She can talk but I reckon she's about talked out. She don't have much to say anymore.

Well, I wisht he'd come on, the girl suddenly said.

The pistol came again, there was a yelp of laughter.

Hey, Edgewater said. Perhaps he shouted. Everyone turned to look at him save the old woman.

What is it?

What'll you take for the rest of those rats?

What? Simmons was looking at him in disbelief.

The rats. Are they for sale?

Hell, everthing I ever owned is for sale. But I never heard tell of sellin no rats.

What'll you take?

Shit, I don't know. Reckon how many's left?

It don't matter. Just give me a price for the lot.

Hmm. Is a dollar and a half too high?

It sounds fair to me. Edgewater had arisen, was digging in his pockets, uncrumpling a dollar bill, finding dimes.

Just for my own information, what did you plan on doing with em?

I don't know yet, Edgewater said. The notion just struck me I wanted some. He dropped the money into Simmons's outstretched hand.

I lost the papers I had on em, Simmons said. He stood drunkenly looking about the room. I know I had them pedigrees here somewhere.

I better see about my stock, Edgewater told Roosterfish. Roosterfish had almost finished the bottle. He drained it, studied the painting of the bird on the label. He stood the bottle against the wall. He was shaking his head from side to side. He was laughing. You crazy little son of a bitch, he said.

It was cool and damp in the yard. It was still raining. Pulley was aiming, steadying the pistol with his left hand, the barrel resting on the rim of the drum. He fired just as Edgewater approached the group.

Edgewater looked into the oil drum. There were two rats left, crazed and slick with blood. Roosterfish was coming out the door grinning, a fresh bottle in his hands. Pulley was aiming again.

You about to shoot my property, Edgewater told him. I bought these rats from their owner.

Done what?

They're my rats. I gave seventy-five cents apiece for them.

You're so full of shit it's comin out your ears. How come you want to start somethin up with me?

I can get a receipt if you want to see it.

He told me I could shoot these rats.

They were his rats when he told you that. They're not his rats anymore. They're my rats.

Why that's the craziest goddamned thing I ever heard. What do you aim to do with em?

I may have a market for them.

Tyler was grinning to himself. I knew it, he told Pulley. I had that boy figured for a livestock dealer all along.

Why they ain't nothin but goddamned gopher rats.

These are special rats, Edgewater said. Royal blood runs in their veins. If they were people they'd be princes, kings.

They about to be dethroned, Pulley said, aiming.

Hold it just a minute, Tyler said, grinning. He turned to Edgewater. You say you can produce a receipt for these animals?

You could holler at Simmons.

Hey Simmons.

Simmons appeared in the door.

You sell a pair of rats to this boy?

Hell yeah, Simmons said. Is he not satisfied with em? I sold em as is. If he ain't satisfied he's just stuck. They wadn't no garntee on em.

It was more a question of ownership.

Oh, he owns em all right.

It looks like they're sure enough his rats, Tyler told Pulley commiseratively. He can law ye if ye shoot them.

I guess you'd be his lawyer, Pulley said disgustedly. You bench-legged little shit you.

That was either the whiskey or the pistol talking, Tyler said. I can't tell which. Put the gun in your pocket and we'll see what he has to say.

Pulley stood uncertainly holding the lowered gun. Edgewater pondering what to do with his rats.

Just start to point it at me, Tyler said. I'll open you up like a can of peas.

This is between me and him. I ain't gettin straight-razor'd over some fuckin rats.

Edgewater found a burlap bag in the crib. Help me get my rats rounded up, he told Roosterfish. He held the sack while Roosterfish tilted the drum. The rats scurried about inside and at last scampered into the bag. He stood holding the bag, swinging it lightly. He could feel the frantic movement of the rats straining against the burlap.

Tyler winked at him. They look like good breedin stock, he said.

The others had fallen back, stood awkwardly watching Pulley and the gun.

You as crazy a son of a bitch as I ever come across, Pulley told Edgewater.

Edgewater had started wending his way among the cars. Roosterfish got his sack of bologna and bread and followed along behind.

Chickenshit, Pulley called.

That was the notorious rat king of the Chicago stockyards, Tyler said.

When they reached the top of the hill Edgewater dropped the bag by the side of the road and nudged it with his foot. After a moment a rat peered out whiskerfaced and sniffed all around him, scurried into the brush. The other followed.

I don't know about you, Roosterfish told him. Did you ever fall a long way and light on your head?

———

The day was long and monotonous but when night finally did fall without the setting of any visible sun but some mere incremental darkening of the world and an almost perceptible compensatory increase in the pitch of the water below them Edgewater wrapped himself in the blanket and lay on his back watching the play of shadows, the flicker of firelight teasing about the stone ceiling.

A vague peace would come over him, not yet resolution but a feeling of uncontrollable postponement, fateful decisions the elements had wrested from his hands. He came to think of time not as some amalgamation of scenery and people and voices and deeds that rushed overwhelmingly over him, but as a flat winding ribbon of asphalt he moved along. There were sideroads and alleys branching off it and logroads bowered by dripping rushes and empty houses abandoned to progress: gaptoothed treeline and people hidden with secret lives he would never know. But all the time that counted was the serpentine road, slick and black with rain or dazzling bright under a high tracking sun. His advance along it was a measurement of his allotted time and he could delay it on the sideroads, while he stumbled down alleys crept with lichens, time stopped, all the world that he mattered to held its breath and waited.

In some perverse way he could bend time to his will: time had curious warps in it and pockets of elasticity and he was at its center and he could move it to his whim.

Yet in the night there were voices that bespoke him out of a past recent but already lost, out of faces dimming and remote, faces he would never see again. In the unsleeping dark out of a night alive and vibratory with voices he might recognize the timbre and cadence of one he had known, old acquaintances lost and gone that returned like familiars or revenants to carry forth in ghostly enactment liaisons long terminated, incubi and succubi that would not let him go. He could not forget anything, nothing was ever ended, ever really lost.

Once with something akin to fear he heard Jenny speak, but there were no voices beyond the grave, casket lids close gently on silence inviolate.

Sometimes past dusk and downriver carlights would arch upward toward the high bridge trestle. In search of what? Who were these interlopers in the night? Lovers, revelers, gamblers on the lost highway? Could he but share their musky dark his own dread would be assuaged, shards of it pressed onto unwary strangers as if he were some salesman dispensing under pretext these evil and unnameable wares, until all the dread that accrued to him was shuttled away, weight shifted to other shoulders, and, with his own lightened, he could move on.

In the morning the rain had ceased but the sky looked dark and sullen. By midmorning a streak of metallic rose appeared in the east where the sun broke briefly through and they took heart. They walked down to see what sort of shape the car was in and debated between them how long it would take the field to dry out. But before they were back to the shelter of the bluff the sky smoothed over seamlessly and rain began to fall anew. It rained for three more days.

There was a disquiet to the river this rainy night. Lights hovered about the trestle, looped like fireflies above the curving highway in something like desperation, as if they were trapped in some asphalt maze. There were sounds the night brought to them where they sat like an encampment of eavesdroppers, unwilling conspirators in the passing of the night. Car doors slammed, voices from the bridge reached them disembodied and robbed of identity, an incoherent dialogue composed of the voices and the roar of the river and the eternal dripping of the trees that Edgewater felt he had listened to always. An occasional squad car passed, red light diastolic, fishers of men.

Just look at em, Roosterfish said, gesturing vaguely toward the lights, uncapping a bottle of Gypsy Rose. The young uns runnin after pussy and the old uns from it. And ever one of em drunk as a fiddler's bitch. Tomorrow they'll wash up in jail or the hospital or across from the old lady and wonder what they done. People around here get squirrelly as hell of a Saturday.

Perhaps they heard the ticking of death's clock, Edgewater thought. Would try by any means to slow or speed it according to their preferences. To drown the metronomic precision of it.

You may notice I keep to myself a lot, Roosterfish went on. That's because I'm leery of them crazy fuckers. I've seen too many cuttins and shootin scrapes and I know where the line's at.

What line?

The line between bein here and expectin to get up tomorrow mornin with my life still in one piece on one side and wakin up in a cell knowin I killed somebody, or not wakin up at all, on the other. One minute you're arguin with somebody and the next one somebody's dead. You don't know where the line's at ever minute you in a world of trouble.

Seem to me you take a lot of chances.

That's because I know where it's at. A man knows that can get closer than one that don't.

Edgewater squinted his eyes. I never figured you for a philosopher.

A man by his self a lot gets to studyin.

I guess so.

What about you?

What about me? I'm not much of a philosopher.

Roosterfish paused with a drink from the bottle. I had a lot of time to think when I'se in prison.

What were you in for?

I was framed. Ah, hell, I know what ye thinkin. Everbody I ever met was framed cept a feller that they had in there for fuckin dead women. You talk about a son of a bitch with a mainspring busted. A undertaker. He never said if he did or he didn't but I guess that'd be kind of a hard frame to set up. I've often wondered what kind of a look he had on his face when whoever caught him walked in on him. It'd be hard explainin a thing like that.

Considering you met him in prison I guess it must have been impossible.

Anyway, my uncle set me up. He had a barn the insurance was gettin hot on and he talked me into burnin it. Hell, I'se a kid, I didn't know no better. I'se accommodatin. They caught me and I kept waitin for him to come down and say it was all a mistake. I'm still waitin. That was the first in a long line of valuable lessons I learned.

Wouldn't they believe you?

Hell, I never told them. I'se young then. I'd read too many story-books, I thought everthing had a happy endin.

What was prison like?

It was like hell. That's exactly what it was like. They had ever kind of crazy son of a bitch in there you could imagine. They had people in there for rapin and killin. They had people in there for fuckin babies and people in there for fuckin ninety-year-old women. They was a boy in there raped and killed his old black mammy. Got up about seventeen and raped her and smothered her to death with a pillow.

At least they were locked up, Edgewater considered.

It ain't nothin wasted, nothin you don't learn from. It learnt me two things. By and large people ain't worth a shit and I never want to be back inside them walls again.

They fell silent, listening to the river. Edgewater tentatively sipped at his wine. A motor ceased, a car door slammed up on the highway. Roosterfish could not let the subject go.

Hell, even the goddamned guards got squirrelly. They had one used to put on his uniform off duty and go out and direct traffic and arrest people. Thought he was a damn law. And them guards was cold, cruel people. They ever got ahold of one by accident that had any human about him he didn't last twenty-four hours.

Down through the scraggly woods on the upper side of the fescue field flashlights appeared, descending the grade. They came out of the woods and skirted the field, intent as purposeful fireflies, side by side, maintaining their distance like malevolent eyes.

Reckon who that is?

Lord, I don't know. Coonhunters, maybe, seen the fire. I hope they're sober. Failin that I hope they're peaceful. Lot of these highrollers think Saturday's wasted if they don't kick the shit out of somebody.

Maybe somebody swore out a warrant.

And they found us this quick and waded out here tonight to serve it? Not likely, I never seen one with that much energy about him. Them ain't hasslin drunks or tryin to catch somebody screwin is settin on their butts somers drinkin coffee.

The paper boy, mused Edgewater. A preacher. Census taker.

They fell silent and watched the company drawing nearer. You got anything in the nature of a weapon?

I got me a twelve gauge with the barrel sawed off and the stock cut down to a pistol, but the barrel's loose and I ain't never shot it. Lord knows what sort of damage it'd do to them and me both. And whoever else happened to be in the neighborhood.

Through the misty rain two apparitions drawn up like moths, they came on to the fire dressed alike in dress pants slathered to the knees with mud and white shirts open at the front and with the collar turned up. Their shoes were layered with sticky clay so that they looked like outsized clown shoes, and one of the men, when they went into the flickering half-sphere of light, began to kick his feet against a ledge, first one and then the other, dislodging the gummy mud.

Roosterfish turned his head aside in annoyance when the light struck him in the face and the man turned it aside.

Hidy.

What say?

We seen ye fire and thought you was somebody else.

I reckon not. Just us.

The men hunkered before the fire and extended their hands to its warmth as if the night were cold. Edgewater did not know them but he had seen hundreds like them. He had seen them in beerjoints and cafés on Saturdays and outside locked poolroom doors before daylight, as dispossessed as any tenants evicted from their homes. The light flickered about their faces and their hard eyes and there seemed to be an inherent violence to them, arrogance and defiance as much a part of their genetic makeup as the color of eyes and hair. Their eyes were remote and studied and Edgewater wondered idly why all the faces he saw in this vast land seemed to allow for no middle ground between arrogance and servility.

We seen ye light and thought you might be a feller we're lookin for. You ain't seen nobody around here tonight have ye?

No, Roosterfish said. Just lights and cars up on the road there.

Poindexter's our name. Our little brother Willard's down here on the river somewhere. You know that little sawed-off feller Tyler?

I know of him.

Tyler's huntin Willard too and we got to find him first.

We ain't seen a soul. Yins care for a drink of wine?

They took the bottle with dignity and drank and passed it one to the other. Lord, ain't that old river rollin, one of them said.

I reckon so. We got off in here drunk and got our car stuck and stranded ourselves. When you reckon she'll go down?

They Lord, they ain't no tellin. I ain't never seen her on a stem-winder like this. Ever time it quits and the clouds break up she just clouds back up and sets in again. Feller was down by where them

Mennonites live and he said they was two or three feet of water in some of their houses and cows standin around belly-deep. Said they was drownded-lookin chickens ridin planks and buckets and whatever wouldn't sink. No tellin at the crops it's ruint. Is they any way we could help you get ye car out?

Couldn't no cattypillar get it out now, Roosterfish said. I'se drunk like I said and I just kept settin her down. I thank ye for offerin.

Roosterfish laid a piece of cedar on the fire, gnarled and gray, worn by the weather as smooth as driftwood. Watched it catch, the rich aromatic gasses flared blue.

The men arose. I guess we better get on. We got to find Willard.

He may be up at Simmons's place. It's usually a crowd up there.

We was headed up there next. And say you don't know Tyler?

Just when I see him.

Pound for pound he's the meanest son of a bitch ever wore out shoe leather. He'll cut ye if he can and if he can't he'll lay for ye. He's got a little pull with the law around here and he's as overbearin as they come. I reckon somebody'll just have to kill him.

The other one spoke. Willard's out with a whore Tyler thinks he owns and Tyler's huntin him. We out tryin to stop a killin or at least see it falls on the right side.

They started back toward the field and coincident with their going a soft drizzle commenced. Through it they watched the lights swing misty like something vaguely sinister seen underwater.

There goes an accident fixin to happen, Roosterfish said. And I damn sure hope it happens somewhere else.

They were already in their blankets and the fire waning when next they entertained company. They were abed but not asleep, for there were voices from the road, tones threatening but words indecipherable.

I thought you said you had privacy down here, Edgewater complained. Hell I slept in quieter bus stations than this.

Well, it was back in the winter. Hell, I don't know what's the matter with these crazy sons of bitches. Man finds hisself a quiet little place and ever goddamn drunk in the world tries to move in on him.

I guess the neighborhood's going to hell, all right.

I'll be glad when all this water's gone. If you ever catch me in Mc-Nairy County again you can mark it down I'm either drunk or crazy.

Roosterfish arose to his elbow, listened to the beleaguered night. The rain fell still and it lent an unreal air to the sounds, they came now vague and sourceless, now with knifelike clarity, like vestiges of some ancient and spectral violence, as if the Poindexters had been harbingers of some dark pageant of mythic transpiration from when the trains labored phosphorous-laden through just such nights as this one, through the slow moth-flecked summer darkness, the curses of tired miners, the easy laughter of the whores who plied their craft from cardboard river shanties.

Sounds like they're comin closer.

It damn sure does.

The sounds had separated themselves into male and female, assailed and assailant. There were bitter curses, threats of dire harm, cries of protestation.

Do you reckon they seen the fire and are headed over here?

Looks like it.

Goddamn it. Help me find that old brown tackle box. That's where my piece is. I've put up with about all this old crazy shit I aim to.

You want me to throw a bucket of water on the fire?

I guess they done seen the porchlight, no need in turning it out. They don't seem that interested in us noway. Roosterfish was dumping out the contents of the tackle box, looking for shells. He broke the gun and loaded it, stuffed a handful of shells into his pocket.

Light that lantern will you? I hear somebody running.

Up out of the fog a figure appeared with only the sound of its approach to warn them and as though it gained visibility all in a rush or had stumbled half-dressed and instantaneous through some curtain separating reality from fantasy: it leapt upon them fully realized, a crazed man or boy wearing only a shirt and it unbuttoned and distended cap-elike behind him. His pedaling feet were unmindful of rocks and roots but leapt unshod through what Roosterfish had always thought of as his bedroom and out the other side, hands clutching a pair of trousers as though he intended dressing up for whatever fate held in store.

His eyes were wild and his greased hair rose and fell all in a sheet and rode his head like a flat skillful cap and there was a bleeding cut tending from his jawline down his throat. When he came upon Roosterfish and his enormous pistol his eyes rolled and he ran sidewise like a shying horse with his hands making clawing gestures at the air as if for purchase: as if the honeysuckle air was some medium he swam or flew through and he made a whimpering sound in his throat but he did not slow his pace but ran fulltilt into the darkness with bracken crashing in diminishing series as if whatever lay before him could not possibly equal whatever it was he fled.

Lord God, Roosterfish said. Who do you reckon that was?

I guess it was Willard.

Well he was in a shitfired hurry.

A girl was crying in a harsh and animal-like yelp and earlier there had been the sounds of blows, a stick or strap falling on flesh but they did not hear this anymore, as if their source had grown satiated or perhaps just fallen behind. What they did hear was running steps and rocks and shale falling into the river in continuous and steadily approaching splashes. Then ragged breathing and a girl too sprang past the near-opaque wall of fog and was amidst them all in disarray, some woodsprite or nymph the disciples of Pan had ill used. She was naked except for a pair of panties still wound miraculously round one ankle and a brassiere twisted so that one breast bobbed above it and the other below.

She fetched up short near Roosterfish and gestured mute and desperate toward the still-fallow dark that had expunged her and stood panting hard for a moment. Rape, she said at last. Stop him. She stood breathing deeply and then stooped to untangle her panties, pausing before rolling them up to pick offending bits of twig and honeysuckle from her pubic hair and she stood with breasts unplumbed peering apprehensively into the fog as if it was the already rippling surface of some vast water she expected something dread to surface from. There had arrived imminent with her a hush of all sound as if the night quieted to hear what transpired. The river alone moved implacably on, disinterested, above this tawdry tableau.

Who is it? Who's after you?

She did not reply save to gesture again toward the dark. She drew near Edgewater, as if she might hide behind him, and Edgewater himself felt an unreasoning fear, uncertain what beast or predator might next spring upon them.

When Tyler strode into the circle of yellow light he came casually as if he had been strolling along the river when all this madness erupted around him. He was swinging a walking stick jauntily along and the hand-shaded face peering myopically at them was bland as still water.

My man, Roosterfish, he said, not bowing exactly but performing an abrupt inclination of the head and neck, an acknowledgement. And the Rat King himself, I believe it is.

Then he ignored them and started toward the girl. She had swung onto Edgewater's arm and begun a whistling expulsion of breath. Don't let him take me, she said.

You trifling little slut, Tyler said. I'll learn you when to run. She was behind Edgewater as though whatever small shadow he threw might hide her, might swallow her up.

Roosterfish was sitting on a rock with the tackle box in his lap and the pistol athwart his knees, and he kept cocking it and holding tension on the hammer and letting it fall gently to.

When Tyler was directly in front of Edgewater, he ceased. Rat King, I believe you're standing between me and something I've already bought and paid for.

Edgewater stood staring down at him. At this gross parody of a man cast in miniature from some faulted and misshapen mold: shoulders humped as if God had freighted him with more weight than a man should bear, childsized legs encased in boots of patent leather, the wide maroon tie painted with the likeness of a rearing palomino that glowed as if it might have batteries concealed about its person. The straw boater adorned with a cockfeather. He could smell him. Cheap perfume, Sen-Sen, whiskey, dissolution: all the sweet smells of deliberate ruin, the carrion smell then of slow and self-inflicted death.

He looked down into the glossy little eyes as depthless as a stuffed animal's or the result of some inexpert taxidermist's art and saw there for one moment pain, a quick flash of outraged dignity; then perhaps they read on Edgewater's face not fear, but pity, for they went instantly malevolent, a loathsome doll's eyes.

I'd hate to cut through you to get her, but cut through you I will.

You do whatever suits you.

Have a drink of wine, Tyler, Roosterfish said.

Another time, Tyler said without turning his head. I'm not here socially. I've got a little unfinished business with Miss Ware.

Funny the way folks describe a thing. You call it unfinished business. Rape was what she hollered.

Tyler turned then. She's down to the bottom of the barrel. She *is* the
bottom of the barrel. Rape's all she's got left to holler. He gestured with
his arm and hand, fingers together, thumb extended, a curious stagy
gesture like an actor playing to the balconies, to a vast audience beyond
the lanternlight. Now I don't feel called upon to share my business with
any man. But since we broke in on you here and disturbed you, I'll
tell you. I gave her twenty dollars. That's a lot of money. When I give
twenty dollars for a fucking, I want it in the biological sense. She gets
the hots for some sawmill hand or poolshark and they give me the slip.
Anybody planning to lay up and fuck and drink on my twenty dollars
is living in a dream world.

You can't buy me with twenty dollars, the girl said. I'm not a whore.

You might not have been up till you took my twenty dollars.

Roosterfish sighed. Well. I don't know. In a world of inequity
yours is not the least of them. But all I know is I'm tryin to sleep and
I got naked people trompin over me and you with that stick and no
tellin what in your pocket. I don't give a goddamn what you do, as
long as you do it somewhere else. But nobody's gettin beat to death
tonight. Not here.

I've already apologized for interrupting your sleep. I apologize for
Miss Ware, since she seems uninclined to. I apologize for the boy. Did
he come through here?

He damn sure did. And you can write him off. Nothin short of a
bloodhound could even pick up that feller's scent.

Tyler smiled. He thought for a minute I was going to cut his throat.

He thought it longer than that.

Well, that's neither here nor there. You show me a deed to this place
and I'll be on my way.

I got it right here in my lap.

Tyler sighed. So you have, he said. He turned to Edgewater. And
what does Rat King have to say about it?

I've already said it.

I see everything in black and white, Tyler told him. He who is not
with me is against me.

Ever how you want it.

That's right. How I want it. And you're lining up with them?

We're not linin up with nobody, Roosterfish said. But you ain't killin nobody or whuppin no girl here tonight. Not while I got a scattergun in my lap.

You think that's the only gun in the world.

It's the only one I see.

Fireflies drifted over the river, winked in and out of sight in the fog, gleamed like plankton in the eerie medium, otherworldly creatures earthbound.

Edgewater stood watching Tyler. Tyler was not paying him any attention but was peering past him at the girl as if to see was she worth dying over. She was adjusting her breasts back into the pockets of her brassiere and her face was lowered, her eyes half-closed to her work. In the wan light she looked young; save for the breasts she could have been a child at her toilet teleported here by some dark communal magic, object of these old men's winter dreams.

I want my twenty dollars.

I ain't got it. I give it to Willard.

Willard owes me more than money. What Willard owes me money wouldn't pay the interest on.

Willard's gonna kill you.

Willard's took to the deep pineys. Willard's never killed anything except a halfpint of whiskey and his mama's dreams.

Can you drive? Roosterfish asked the girl.

Yeah.

You better get up on the road and start drivin then. Tyler ain't leavin for a few minutes yet. He's goin to visit awhile and drink some wine with us.

I come and go as I please, Tyler said. I won't bother her tonight. I've got plenty of time and I don't mind waitin till the cards fall my way.

I want him to walk up there with me, the girl said. I'm scared of the dark. She had her hand on Edgewater's arm.

It didn't bother you a while ago.

Tyler turned his head and spat into the darkness. I think she's got you picked to finish what Poindexter started, he said. Poindexter kindly got interrupted.

You go to hell, the girl said.

I don't have twenty dollars, Edgewater said.

Come on, she told him.

They walked all the way without speaking but he could feel her beside him, once in the dark her hip bumped him, he could hear her breathing. They skirted past the river where half-immersed trees loomed dark bulks through silver fog and walked around the fescue field on the upper side where it was driest through shadows darker even than themselves and she took his hand beneath where unseen owls watched yelloweyed and silent from the keep of the trees of the night.

Then out of the woods and into the field at once limitless and finite where the world lightened incrementally and the fog was corporeal, a moist wall they moved through, solid through solid, to where the embankment loomed and elderberries and sumacs became opaque presences of the night, shrouded cedars were denizens of some unreal world gathering out of the mist to harry them on.

The car was in a sideroad, the door still open, a yellow glow from the domelight tending away to nothing. When they came into the circle of light Edgewater looked about him, the car in disarray and evidential of violence and sudden departures. Willard's missing shoes, so placed as if he had leapt out of them and fled: a dress crumpled in a silken ball, a purse upended and contents strewn as if from some moving vehicle. The scant remains of a halfpint of whiskey propped against a stump. The radio played on, sang the mindless virtues of barn paint.

Edgewater picked up the whiskey and sat on the stump. He drank, lowered the bottle. Bobwhite again, he said to nobody. She was sliding the dress over her head, he glimpsed detachedly the moonwhite expanse of her belly, the rounded mons veneris of her panties. Her face appeared, hair disarranged by her dress, beaded with water from the fog.

It wasn't true what Tyler said. He's crazy.

What?

About why I wanted you to walk up here. I really was scared. I guess I didn't have time to think about runnin down there. I just seen the fire and figured it was somebody campin out. It was the only place to run.

It doesn't matter.

I guess not. She began to pick up scattered coins, photographs. He wondered idly was there one of Willard. She studied her face in the mirror of a tortoiseshell compact, kneeling, rapt as if in prayer, knees rounded and brown below the hem of the white dress. She applied lipstick, pressed it smooth with her mouth. Her eyes cut to him on the stump watching her.

What are you lookin at?

Nothing. He arose, drank again. You better get that stuff arranged and get out of here. He won't stay down there forever. Roosterfish won't shoot him and likely he knows it. He's got you boxed in here with his car.

Can you back it out of the way so I can get out?

I can if the key's in it.

It was. He cranked the car and wheeled it back onto the blacktop. When the girl had Willard's car turned he pulled it back in and cut the switch off.

She was waiting on him. Want to ride around awhile? she wanted to know.

I guess not.

Why?

I'm heading out in the morning. I need to get to sleep.

Head out tonight and I'll give you a lift. Come on, I don't bite.

What the hell. All right.

Going across the trestle the bridge swayed, steel on steel protested their passage, warned them back. Edgewater had only crossed it on foot: it might have lain in wait like a deadfall, might yaw apart like a rising drawbridge, twisting I-beams warp like foil, cars skidding lockwheeled down a rusted plane to the river.

She turned left at the crossroads and stopped at Simmons's. There was no light on. She got out without speaking and he watched her walk to the door and knock and after a time the door opened. Still no light came on. The staggered ranks of Simmons's derelict cars were softened and rounded by the fog, their crushed contours smoothed. Roses and hollyhocks grew among them, wild roses might take them yet. Debris of denouement.

He closed his eyes and felt the cool plastic upholstery and the healing balm of the summer night scented alike with pigsty and roses. He listened to the silence, to the untroubled dark. He opened his eyes and drank the last of the whiskey and reached down and turned on the radio. Now a country comedian was on, Edgewater listened soberfaced to him, to the audience that would draw him into their laughter.

Somewhere outside there were voices, a door's closing cut off short, and wraithlike she came down the muddy walk and got in. She had a halfpint of whiskey with her and a bottle of Seven-Up to chase it with.

Underway again. The road twisted and shifted, a spinning skein of yarn, a madman's shuttle reeled off as they used it. She drove slowly until they topped out on higher ground and the headlights abruptly broke through the fog, a world of icy clarity he'd forgotten. Once rounding a curve they came upon pedestrians, an old man and a bent old woman clutching a shawl. Edgewater had her stop the car and back up and he offered them a ride but they would have none of him. The old woman shook her head mutely and clasped the shawl tighter and the old man kept walking down the road staring at its litterstrewn shoulder as if he had lost something among the baubles of bottlecaps and cellophane and expected to come upon it. They went strolling along beside the car until at last he rolled up the glass and they fell behind.

He did not ask where they were going, perhaps felt it did not matter. They drove on through a defoliated area bleak as if it were being prepared as a sanctuary for the mad or damned: a birdless forest where trees rose black amid stark branches of telephone poles. A road led off through it and she turned, a chert road tending downward again, crossing a stockgap and wending up through rainbowed cedars the color of copper within whose branches sodden birds roosted like black and mutated fruit.

Where she finally stopped there was a rock quarry like an enormous amphitheater, shapes of machinery vaguely saurian, hazy in the tangible air, cliffs rising dizzy and plumb.

Why did you come here?

Tyler wouldn't ever think to come here.

Nobody would think to come here. Besides, he's probably forgotten you by now.

Not Tyler.

He stared through the windshield, and when she cut off the wipers silent rain blurred the scene. It ran like watered ink, and when she turned off the lights the darkness was absolute. He began to hear the rain.

Hand me that light out of the glove compartment and I'll show you where we swim.

They got out and walked cautiously to the shelf of rock. The batteries were weak in the flashlight and its beam barely penetrated the fog.

It caved in a long time ago here. Folks say there's a steamshovel down there deep, Willard's seen it. It's two or three men down there they never did get out. I've heard old folks that was here then tell about it and they said it was like a earthquake or somethin.

He shined the light toward the dark abyss. Where the limestone ceased there was only fog. The ledge fell away below, a great misty wall of stone scored by drillbits and hammers, and across there was nothing, the light did not reach the other side and when he dropped a stone it vanished before he heard the splash.

You mean people swim in this place?

Sure.

How do they get out?

Here. She took his hand and guided the light toward a roll of woven wire fencing strung out down the precipice. It was secured around metal stakes in drillholes. It's like a ladder, see? You can climb right up it. The beam of light followed it over the edge and down to where the fog took it.

Edgewater stared at it. It vanished in the haze and he wondered how far it went on before the water began, what waited there. A curious primitive stairwell to the waterlogged chasms of the earth. Life there mutant and strange. Life is adaptable, he thought, will not be undone. Pale slugs thrive in sewage, flesh so loathsome it belies the name. What mutations here. A beast from the land of counterpane lies dreaming among marrow-sucked bones of divers past. He arose and when he did she took his arm, swinging the light along. They got back into the car.

What's your name, anyway?

Billy Edgewater. What's yours?

Faye Ware. Did Willard look bad hurt when he come through down there?

He was moving a little fast to tell.

Me and Willard aim to get married, she told him.

You do?

Yeah. But we won't live in this hick place. We're goin to Chicago. Willard's been there and he knows the ropes. He got him a tattoo there.

Curious place for a tattoo, Edgewater said.

He says up there folks mind their own business. Down here everbody meddles. Folks got it in for Willard.

Why?

The damn law. They got it in for him because Willard don't take no shit off nobody.

Oh. Nobody except Tyler?

He was goin to kill Willard. He's so jealous. He did cut him. I'm kindly worried about him.

He wasn't hurt bad enough to slow him down any.

There did not seem to be much to say. They fell silent and Edgewater settled himself comfortably in the seat and drank whiskey. The radio played on: unseen dancers whirled and clogged to some fiddle tune unreeling far away.

Where you goin?

Home. Up east in the mountains.

You got a girl there?

Not anymore. He lit a cigarette, threw the match in the rain. He halfturned in the seat to face her, but he could not see her: she was just a presence he could sense, a warmth he could feel. Then her face loomed near his, wide-eyed and without definition.

Her mouth tasted sweetly of whiskey. She made an incoherent sound and it opened under his, her hands rose whitely to his face, pulled him tighter, as if she would merge with him, absorb him into herself, feed off him. Without releasing him she slid down in the seat, her skirt rode up, there was the white expanse of her thighs. He tossed the cigarette into the dark and propped the bottle against the gearbox. When he cupped her breast she gasped, a sharp intake of breath. Then she took his hand and guided it between her legs. She was already wet, he could feel the warm moisture through her panties. When he rubbed her with the heel of his hand her hips moved against him. He could feel her hands at his zipper.

Her head slid backward beneath the steering wheel. He could smell perfume, sweat, soap in her hair. You want to get in the back? She did not reply. He could see her eyes, the whites of them, her vague and harried face almost against his own. She opened her legs, pulled him onto her, reaching under him with her other hand to pull the crotch of her panties aside and guide him in. She was locked to him, heat and the hot musky smell of her but mainly the heat, a moist torrid warmth he thought he must drown in.

Beneath him her face was shadowed, lost to him. Where did his thrusts take her? Who rocked her on these waters, he wondered, did the face of Willard burn beneath her eyes? He thought of what Tyler had said, smiled twisted into the dark. The congenitally disaffected. He tried to call forth the lines of her face but he could not. She could have been anybody. He tried idly to recall a face from the past to bestow upon her but none came to mind.

Roosterfish must have been half awake already because when Edgewater came into the camp he was sitting cowled in his blankets watching him approach as if the dark held worse than Edgewater and he had been expecting it. He still had the pistol laid out and he had allowed the fire to die and only coals throbbed there faintly orange in their white cauls of ash.

All the company gone?

It left right after you did. It was by God mad, too. Did you have to rub his nose in it?

She's no more Tyler's than she is anybody else's. If she's anybody's I guess she's Willard's.

Well, Tyler would dispute you, but he ain't here. Nobody here but me and old Gypsy Rose. The least you could of done was bring me some back on a stick. I'da done the same for you.

The least you could do would be to use a little respect towards the girl I aim to marry. She's coming after me in the morning and we're going to Chicago and get us a tattoo, Edgewater said sarcastically.

Roosterfish did not reply. He lay back and drew the blanket about him but his eyes stayed open. He lay for a long time in silence like a man awaiting sleep the night owes him but will not pay.

You got to watch a son of a bitch like that got an in with the law, he said at last. A man like that won't even shoot less his dice is loaded. I member when I'se little it was a county court clerk killed my mama. Him drunk as a bicycle and run a stop sign and run right over her and never even stopped till he come up agin a light pole. I'd just stepped off the curb watchin and I seen it all. I'se about six year old. I stood there watchin and

I remember I could still feel her hand on my arm even if I knowed she was gone the way a cat or dog or anything else is that's run over.

What'd they do to him?

Nothin to speak of. He got out of it. Bought his way out. I'se too little to know much about it. I reckon Daddy did finally catch him out and whup his ass but a thing like that don't even tip the scales.

He lay still and quiet until Edgewater thought he slept and then he said: Daddy never liked me much, I never knowed why. He died of cancer in 1932 and I went to see him when he was bad off and he run me out of the room. I never knowed why that was either; a man ort to know how a thing like that can be. I stayed outside there and I kept thinking he'd call for me when he was dyin but he never did. They said he was breathin and then half a breath is all he took. That was it. I went to his funeral, but he didn't have nothin to say to me there either.

His wineblurred voice sounded far away like some voice of accusation, of remonstrance that bespoke Edgewater with hindsight out of his own more recent past so he did not reply. He rolled his own blanket out and lay down on his back and saw beyond the bluffs and the shapes of cedars a break in the clouds where a three-quarter moon was haloed with golden rings and three stars were set within like jewels. Weariness lay on him like a coverlet. Too weary for words he lay conscious of the faint buzz of the alcohol and aware of himself miasmic with the smell of her lipstick and the sticky musk of her sex. A softer bed there than this. The path there less thorny than through this sylvan bottomland. The dreams less troubled there. Would my own father call my name? Time cheats us all. A face as hard and shorn of give as the rock where I lay my head. Yet I seem to recall other days. I recall the warmth of his flesh, the feel of his shoulders, the way the world looked from up there. The way the horizon bobbed and tilted when his feet struck the ground as though the very earth shook when he walked. Time is the enemy, time is the acid God pours on events to etch and change them, real and unreal are no more than words and interchangeable at best.

Did Willard ever come back through? he asked aloud.

If he did he tiptoed through, Roosterfish said. Willard's gone. Willard is a lost ball in the high weeds.

He slept a little before dawn and he dreamed he moved across a homaloidal waste peopled only with the snags of trees scorched by ancient fire and the world was covered with white ash that rose and shifted with what breeze there was. There was a verdant blue horizon so far away it lay dreaming in haze and he knew without knowing why there was something dread about it. Something awaited him there and a fear of it lay in him heavy as a stone but it did not turn him back.

He grew weary and searched for shade to rest in but it was a surreal world of sourceless light that cast no shadows. He sat beside a hollowed treetrunk and felt terror at the pristine land of feathery ash he'd crossed and left no tracks. He sat numbly and he dreamt he slept, dreamt dreams of the mountains, of winter snows.

He awoke thirsty and tried to go back to sleep, dozed once, half-dreams of cool dark mountain water.

When they did come it was night again and there were ten or twelve of them and they left their cars at the ruins of an old warehouse behind the river. Save a lack of frivolity you might have taken them for hunters or revelers but there was an intent air of high purpose about them that precluded this. Then some of them donned pillowcase masks with eyeholes cut out and like a convention of specters they filed past the caved wall of the warehouse and on past old machinery rusted and purposeless with years and through a thin grove of sumac. Sawbriars pulled at their shoes and the dew-wet cuffs of their overalls and then they came upon a low brick wall weathered pale in the moonlight and crested with a scrollwork of honeysuckle.

There was an old fallow hillside field they went across, angling toward the woods and the woods did not look like anything identifiable at all in the world of form but simply a concentration of the cool blue dark.

They were overalled men of indeterminate and myriad size and even one dwarfed among them, short legs scissoring to keep up, as if to prove the parable that a little child should lead them.

Then in a straggling line formless and without rank they reached the woods and one by one were swallowed up until the moonlit field lay dewed and silver and pristine and there was no sign at all that they were about.

Then from the deeper woods one called to another in a travesty of a whippoorwill and another answered, charting their progress into the disquieted woods.

———————

There were approaching cries of nightbirds spurious and blatant but they slept on through them. When the men regrouped themselves and moved into the diminishing circle of light from the waning fire they came instantly and violently as if man's darker side had been given brief corporeality and they embodied it.

Edgewater came awake to the sound of crockery and cookware kicked about and to a foot in his side. He arose blearyeyed with surprise to see Roosterfish being hauled from his fetid quilts, halfclothed and wildlooking, hand still clutching his covers, his eyes those of one in the seize of halfmen or demons of the night, some vast tribunal that had tried them and found them wanting.

Two of them drug Roosterfish erect and struggling, one hanging onto his arm, the other behind him, a constricting arm about his neck. But he wrenched free. He leapt barefooted toward the crated chickens and grasped up the coop with his one arm and tilted with its weight peered all about for an opening in the well of men.

There was none. He ran blindly toward the curving line and came up against two farmers without give or mercy. He was knocked back and fell and the coop dropped and one of the men fetched it a broganed kick that left it upended, the cocks disoriented and protesting with muted threat, their world spun off its orbit into the dark. Then it toppled from the ledge, scraped through brush, bounced, splashed in the water below.

Edgewater found himself held erect between a brace of them and facing a third, unflinching eyes dark in the expanse of pillowcase mask that rose and fell rhythmically with the man's calm breathing.

I guess you didn't figure on this, did you?

No reply.

I said did you?

If I had I wouldn't have been here.

I'll just bet you wouldn't. Are you ready for your punishment?

The hands on his arms tightened, urged him forward, as if to better view some cowled judge peering down with eyeholes blind from oaken bench.

Punishment for what?

The man laughed and turned toward the woods. Is he cuttin them hickories?

He's supposed to be.

I guess he's pickin among em to get good stout ones.

These two drownded rats look like any'd be stout enough for them. They look too faintified to last till the hickories get here.

These were voices Edgewater recognized like voices the past expunged to exacerbate him. There was the farmer with the shed barn roof and others of his ilk and he had no doubt that Roosterfish knew them all. Then up from the troubled dark came the dwarf, himself perversely masked as if a pillowcase alone rendered him unidentifiable or yet he was some child apprentice learning his craft on the job.

One of you find that tackle box he's got. Who's got the ropes? Get them tied to a couple of these trees.

You want em together or one at a time?

One at a time'll last longer; let's make each of them watch the other.

You ready to confess?

Confess what?

Now you'd be the only one to know that, wouldn't ye? Ain't that what a confession is.

Goddamn what a pistol.

All right I confess.

That's better. Confess what.

Whatever you got. You just fix the sins in your mind and I'll confess to them.

I think we got the makins of a smartass here. He's a two-hickory case if there ever was one.

Well, a man don't have to stop with hickories does he? Nobody within miles and that river right down there. Trash like this nobody'd miss and there'd never be a word said about it.

I doubt the river'd have em.

The river was below them, invisible, an unseen movement through the dark. A screech owl cried fierce and feline from across the bottoms.

That boy ain't got nothin to do with this. He's just a hitchhiker I picked up. Just a feller I was helpin out.

The men laughed and one of them said, If this is helpin ye out I reckon you're proud he didn't set out to do ye wrong.

Where you come from, anyway? What all you done before you even got here?

I didn't do anything, Edgewater said.

I guess you just fell into bad company.

Edgewater was silent.

Well, bad company ain't jackshit to me. A man's what he is no matter who he's with and you got the look to me of somebody that don't cull much.

You said that about bad company. I never said a goddamned word.

Now he's cussin us. Give a man a chance to own up and all he does is cuss ye.

No tellin what he's done and got away with.

He may be wanted somers.

He don't look to me like he's wanted nowheres, by nobody.

He damn sure ain't wanted in McNairy County.

Drag him over to that sapling.

Less get the onewinged un first and save this un for last.

Let him tell what all he's done first.

What all have you done?

Edgewater looked about him as if he had somehow fallen upon a merger of the crazed and vengeful. The worst thing I ever did was wind up with all you crazy sons of bitches, he said.

Someone slapped him hard and openhanded and he would have fallen had he not been held on his feet. They thrust him forward for another blow and Roosterfish said, Let me tell you cocksuckers somethin. Whatever you got planned better be fatal because I know ever goddamned one of ye. And I won't rest till I've hunted the last one down. I'll burn ye houses in the night. If I can't catch ye out somers I'll poison ye livestock. If I catch ye asleep I'll cut ye throat and keep on goin. And the son of a bitch that kicked my roosters in the river is a dead man already and ain't even heard the news.

You mighty loud chicken to be nestin in a den of foxes, the dwarf said. I think this one first. Head my man Roosterfish toward that sycamore.

The men holding Edgewater turned abstracted to watch and he wrenched his arms free and struck blindly and as hard as he could. There was a surprised grunt through the expanse of mask and almost instantly blood blossomed at its center and spread outward and a stick knocked him down and laid a line of fire across his shoulder blades.

He arose scrambling and bent, feet running before he was even off
the ground and all about him were shapes crouching with hands outstretched, weaving in the firelight. He could hear the stick whistling
before it caught him again and this time it did not knock him down. It
propelled him faster and uncontrolled toward the dim shapes of men
and he dove past them into the beckoning dark. He lit rolling and trying to shield his head from the outcropping of limestone that seemed
to be revolving beneath it. He was up and climbing, hands and feet
clawing for purchase in the shale, he seemed to be going straight up in
the dark, rocks falling soundless away to nothing behind him.

He attained another ledge with shapes struggling after him. Run,
he called out to Roosterfish, but Roosterfish appeared stunned, stood
unencumbered but peering into the depths that had taken his roosters.

The men were calling to one another from below and now even
from the sides, the darkness thronged with them. They came implacably upward, misty forms clambering over the slick wet rock and hoist-
ing themselves by the slender trunks of alders and a blind panic seized
him, a realization that they did not intend to let him be. They were
determined that whatever they were fated to mete out should befall him
and they seemed vested with some higher purpose beyond vengeance.
He plunged blindly upward and at right angles to ease the incline with
hands thrust forward into the dark as if beckoning for whatever solace
it might offer him and fending aside with them scrub brush coming
at him in a rush as if it too were attacking him. Until he was on the
topmost ledge and the moon came from behind the clouds and showed
him the world below with silver clarity.

There he is. Who's got the pistol?

The river was below him and he could hear voices all about him, a
necklace of men with the string drawing taut. There was an explosion and
a bright bloom of fire and somebody screamed and kept on screaming.
He closed his eyes and launched himself over the tops of cedars into the
void and there was a suspension of all sound. He drew his knees up to his
chest and clasped them with his arms and it seemed an eternity down.

He plunged deep into swift darkness and he went down for a long
time, he could feel the bottom, felt himself drug end over end over
snags and embedded sticks like hands that would restrain him, he felt
himself a scrap of paper in the wind.

When he broke the surface his face broke it first and he was on his back so that the first thing he saw was the moon looking down on him, remote, unforgiving. He was downriver and the cries of rage and invective were faint and shrill. He peered toward the bluffs and there were shapes aligned there like spectators but he could discern no motion so did not know if they were men or dwarfed cedars. Then he was borne on past other bluffs and other shapes that could not have been men but he imagined them there as well.

Delicate light fanning out from the east brought him awake as the night slackened its weary hold. A first faint unreal illumination called to him with the daylight's warm balmy breeze, thick with the blossoms of honeysuckle, and disparate odors from the river, musky and rank. He rose from the creek bank and wandered across a field. A stiff wind high above him drove the white clouds ahead, their shadows moved like the tracks of behemoths across the field. He came upon a near abandoned road.

The sun in ascension. Edgewater's clothes began to steam as if they burned with some curious singeless fire. Or he was some refugee newly up from the nether regions, a touch of brimstone hovering about him yet. Far on his left hand and across a stream like molten silver in the sun, a farmhouse and barn lay and, as he watched, pigeons rose above the barn in a diffuse cloud. Caught so in the sun they glittered like shards of tinfoil spinning in the wind. The road wound through unkept greenery wet with dew and burdened with grass blossoms of caterpillar cocoons, silver and near translucent in the sun.

Further around a bend in this green-thronged road he came upon a house with windows stoned blind and door a yawning emptiness. A chimney half-fallen, yawing away from the house, so that at the eaves there was a hand's span of daylight between. A cur dog went deeper into the weeds, watched him with surly eyes. Perhaps he kept some vigil, awaited some long-gone master. A return of child's laughter, some refusal to accept abandonment that would persevere against all odds. Does force not move mountains? The yard was littered with wind-driven shakes, weeds in promiscuous abandon. No one hailed him from these unglassed windows, called from the tilted porch. Whatever revenants dwelt here expected no company down this weary road.

Further still there was a church and a grassgrown graveyard and he began to feel that he had come ashore in some land beset so with plague or violence that all its inhabitants had dropped their tiresome lives and fled for other climes leaving only their dead and their castoff dwellings.

He sat for a time and rested among weathered stones and marble spires so old all traces of their manufacture had been erased and they seemed some anomaly of nature. A concrete crypt shifted by forgotten tremors. Old out-of-date resplendence. A fallen stone angel with a broken wing. Earthcaught, her face against the rampant weed looked up at him serene and untouched and so remote it looked worlds removed from the mawkish tawdriness of his life. And from these other lives already spent, old stories long told, teller and listener alike perished to the shifting seasons. Who learned by their telling, who profited? While they lay with clasped hands and sewn eyes, the world spun with its cargo of dead through a black and trackless space unfathomable, beyond comprehension. His mariner's mind fell to pondering on its command. Who kept the lookouts, whose hand steadied the helm? Or was it a ghost ship looming soundless out of fog and St. Elmo's fire in a night as black as only a night in the China Sea can be?

The cries of doves from some far hollow reached his ears more mournful than the voices of these old lives enshrined here, and thoughts of his own more recent dead brought him erect and back onto the road. There was a momentary vision of her behind a steam table, hairnetted, ladling food out to strangers, weary, weary beyond words. Earning the money for his graduation ring. In a wild nonstop orgy of abandonment, he'd drunk it up to the last drop at a string of roadhouses that went as far off into the night as a man had the will and resources to travel. A goodly part spent on a willowy blonde who ended up getting sick. Graduating ringless and remorseless, but are there not circumstances extenuating beyond control?

Goddamn you, Billy, why do you do like you do?

He put it from his mind. It was a good warm morning in June with the dew drying and money in his pocket and the world might lie in wait past any curve in this strange road.

There was a store set down in a crossroads amidst all this desolation, weathered board and batten behind its RC and Bruton snuff signs, built high off the ground as if whoever built it had been wary of rising waters.

He prowled its gloomy aisles, gathering his purchases, carrying them on one arm. A good solid pair of shoes, a complete change of clothing, him squinting to determine sizes in this poor light.

An old woman sat by a cold heater and rocked and darned or knitted and he wondered about the light and then saw she was blind and past all concern with light. Her hands moved at the construction of some grotesque garment and she rocked on unmindful as if she were a resident of some land that lay between this world and whatever waited beyond.

Would they be anything else now?

Edgewater selected razorblades and cigarettes and matches and turned momentarily toward the meatcase where specimens lay in state or like museum pieces in flyspeckled glass.

But the storekeeper was afflicted with some malady, his face was inflamed and pustulate with open sores, something dread in riotous final stages. His eyes looked one step beyond dementia and as if he were not there at all, he had no curiosity about this unshod and unshirted wayfarer, perhaps his own misery precluded any commiseration, even any knowledge of what passed before him and everything was done now by rote. Leprous or cancerous perhaps, goitered and misshapen and proclaiming its malignancy to whatever of the world chanced here. Edgewater suspected the existence of other strains, dread strains.

Just take out a cold drink.

He paid and went out, the screendoor slapped to by its keeperspring. He was halfway down the steps cradling his purchases when he went back and opened the door.

How do I get on the highway?

The storekeep pointed wordlessly on down the road.

Thanks.

Come back.

He passed from sight of the store and wondered for a fey moment had it been some alchemical conjurement of the fates or had it been real. Perhaps it was even now being dissembled and drug from off the stage, crated in numbered crates to be stored in some alcove of limbo, watched and guarded by whatever stagehands moved in divine stealth in the wings of his world, to be patiently kept for reassembly in the chance he passed this way again.

Marvelously altered and respectable, Edgewater appeared through the curtains of elderberries shrouding the road and continued on his way. A few cars passed him now. A convertible with two girls slowed and the brake lights came on and they turned to watch his approach, one a pale blonde with a hand to her hair. He must have failed some esoteric test for the brake lights went off and they sped away.

An old hopped-up Ford full of boys full of beer slewed in the gravel and rocked on faulty shocks and slid to a stop several yards ahead of him. A wild red face peered back down the road to Edgewater. Hey, you tired of walkin?

No, Edgewater said.

The driver appeared momentarily confused. He had been going to say, Well, run awhile. Well fuck you, he finally said inadequately, and sped away.

Later he got a ride in a pickup truck with a vacuum cleaner salesman. The truck was filled with vacuum cleaners, wares and an upright model even rode in the seat beside Edgewater. The salesman kept up a running wane flow of conversation across it and Edgewater began to think of it as a silent third passenger. He wondered did the salesman talk to it when there was no one else to talk to and in their private moments did it answer him back? He studied the country's slide away from him in a shifting green frieze and after a time they hit the blacktop and there was a different sound to the wheels.

The salesman fell into a grim awed silence when they came over a rise and suddenly onto a scene of carnage. There were revolving lights of varied hue and an ambulance that looked poised to spring, its businesslike rear doors open, attendants sliding stretcherburdened down a clay bank into a cotton field, wreckage strewn about the highway. When they stopped the first thing Edgewater heard was the crackles of the radio in one of the police cars, disembodied voices, detached and calm and hard on that a low wailing. Somebody has shore played hell, the salesman said.

The convertible with the two girls had come head on into a Mennonite wagon. Far down the road he could see pieces of it, a seat, an axle and two wheels intact with tongue between them set cattycornered in the road and there was a horse lying there that did not stir. The car had continued on into a lightline pole and the pole had been severed and lay in the cotton field fouled in its wires. Sunlight winked off a blue glass insulator. The road was treacherous with broken glass and curving smears of scorched rubber showed where the car had been.

The man got out and Edgewater sat where he was. The salesman in his rumpled suitpants and white shirt Edgewater could see sweatstains in the back approaching a highway patrolman scrawling on a pad. Edgewater pondering what horrors written into the notebook. How they were made coherent. How could order be formed from this chaos? Even then the two attendants half straightened alike with the girl limp between them and laid her onto the stretcher and immediately seized it up and bore it toward the road. The slack form resembled nothing that had ever housed life. Nothing that had ever raised a soft hand to windtossed hair.

An old Mennonite couple all in their pious black lay broken. The bonneted woman was sitting, legs at an unreal angle. She seemed to be trying to crawl toward a bareheaded man lying on his back and staring at the high silent press of clouds borne south. As if locked in a deep study to unriddle the mysteries of the universe, what sped them in the keep of the heavens, and all the while steadfastly ignoring the keening of the old woman.

There were details he did not want pressed on Edgewater, not through effort to see but as if his mind were being forcefed harsh electronic bits of knowledge. A vague wind stirred and cooled the sweat at his throat and it ruffled the dead man's hair and rolled his flatbrimmed hat teasingly against the dewberry briars. A broken bottle of suntan oil lay spreading on the hot asphalt. Down the glass-strewn road lay the Mennonite's goad, there were attendants arriving to see to the second girl.

The highway patrolman seemed vexed with the salesman. He pointed at the truck Edgewater sat in and then down the highway where the horizon undulated with heat and the salesman shrugged and turned. As he returned to the truck he veered off his path and stared wonderfaced into the wrecked convertible. When the policeman said something in a harsh voice he went on.

She was froze on the peg, he told Edgewater in awe when they were cautiously passing around the wagon wheels. He said it as if being frozen on the peg was result and not cause, just another casualty of this wreck on the highway. Some curious chastisement.

She was froze at one-twenty. Lord, they must have been movin. It was blonde hair and blood all over that dashboard.

Edgewater said nothing. They passed over the pool of suntan oil and
there was a shoe in the grass at the road's edge. The old man's goad twisted
beneath their wheels and something wrenched in Edgewater when he
felt it. Something stirred in him akin to fear. He had always suspected
something of control in the world, some relationship between cause and
effect. It all seemed random, careless, slipshod. It was as if the past and
present had come explosively together, had tried for a breathless moment
to occupy the same space in time. Matter and antimatter meeting head-on
through some misplotting of their course, some unfactored error. Yesterday
and today greedy for the same abstract instant, each annihilating the other.

Dawn came but it did not awaken him. Then light from a sun tracking
high above the treeline was on his face but Roosterfish slept on through
it. He was lying across a log, left cheek in the sand, arm beneath him.
His shirt was ripped from tail to collar and his back was lacerated with
welts and encrusted with dried blood. A ragged line down his cheek
where blood had tracked from above the hairline. About him the camp
was a shambles, cookware scattered, plates and cups broken, blankets
muddy and trodden upon.

Perhaps the cock crowing below him awoke him, for he soon stirred
and tried to rise. He rose by degrees, as if every motion pained him.
When he was sitting he cradled his head for a time on his arm and
appeared to be oblivious of the world he tenanted.

Later he climbed down the bluff following the sound of the cock
but it was not the blue after all, only the red cock he used for a sparring
partner for the Allen Roundhead. One end of the coop had splintered
on an outcropping of limestone and the blue was gone; he looked down
but all he saw was rolling water.

He opened the door at the end of the coop where the red cock was
but it would not come out. It huddled in a corner, watched him with
distrustful eyes, wary of this freedom held like bait.

Ye might as well come on out in the world, he told it. This travelin
life ain't for you. Find ye a nice hen somers and settle down.

He looked back once and the cock was watching him go, peering
through the slats in the cage.

The money was gone and camp held nothing worth salvaging. Nor
did he tarry long at the Studebaker. The field was still too muddy to at-

tempt rescue even had he felt like worrying with it. He threw gear out the back until he found a change of clothes and the shotgun hidden under the piled hoses. He worked hurriedly, feared other repercussions, did not plan on being here when the other shoe fell. His eye flickered often to the road and back, every car a threat. The first thing he did when he found the shells was load the gun and then he felt a little better.

He looked back as he crossed the field but he was not losing anything he regretted losing. He felt somehow different, as if all that was extraneous had been cut from him leaving only the essential: he had arrived at some curious destination. He was the core of his being. Divide him or multiply him times himself and it would all be the same. All there was left was purpose.

A fortuitous ride and a strange vehicle became Roosterfish's windfall. He got the ride at a truckstop at Adams with a crewcut young Alabama man on his way to the Sunday races at Lawrenceburg.

The car was a wonder to Roosterfish. It had a primer spotted Chevrolet body with a twelve-cylinder Cadillac engine so huge that the fenderwells had been cut out with a torch to house it.

You have to jack it up and pull the front wheels off fore you can even change the spark plugs, the boy told Roosterfish with pride. It had a Lincoln transmission and rearend and it had sections of railroad rail welded beneath the chassis for stability. You ort to see it corner, he said. You'd have to have a bulldozer to turn er over.

This farmboy who had come into his own in the age of the internal combustion engine drove him from Adams to Savannah. He told Roosterfish more than he had ever wanted to know about engines, transmissions, and carburetors. His voice was evangelical, he was a prophet of some new gospel, baptized in highoctane holy water. He accepted with blind good faith Roosterfish's story of stolen vehicles and tools, a job on a vague horizon. What do you think about this car, he had asked.

Well…it seems like it might be idling a little rough.

The boy laughed. Watch this, he said. He pulled a switch in the floorboard and immediately the motor smoothed out with a hum like a Singer sewing machine. I got a cutout in here, he explained. I can let her hit on part of the cylinders and when I want to I can throw the rest of em in like this. Listen at it purr. You could balance a quarter on that motor.

They were sitting parked in a drive-in restaurant in Savannah eating hamburgers when opportunity presented itself. He had the cutout open and the motor loped and missed and wheezed like a detuned tractor so that the entire carbody jumped and vibrated and was a great source of interest to a man in the car across.

The car was a new Oldsmobile lacquered a deep metallic blue and its owner kept favoring Roosterfish and the automobile with looks of amused contempt. Finally he could contain himself no longer. He threw his Coke cup out and glanced at the crewcut boy.

You better get this junkpile home before she flies apart on you, he said. I believe there's a city ordinance about leavin scrapiron like this on the street anyhow.

The boy was picking shredded onions out of his hamburger and dropping them one by one out the window. He did not even look at the Oldsmobile. She generally runs pretty good, he said. Just got a little miss in her. She gets away from the lights pretty good.

I hope to shit you got a miss. What you runnin, a Massey Ferguson? Say she gets away pretty good? You want to run her? Lay five on her and roll her out and I'll just blow you away.

The boy had finished his hamburger. He wadded the waxed paper into a ball and threw it out. He seemed very businesslike now. He looked the man level in the eye and he smiled a small smile. I've got fifty goddamn dollars says you won't blow me nowhere, he said.

The man in the Olds grinned in disbelief. He cranked the car and sat listening to the stroke of the engine and the reassuring lick the car was hitting. Roll her out, he said.

The Chevy died twice before he was backed out but he was finally turned to his satisfaction. They gave the money to Roosterfish to hold. The man in the Olds came up with two twenties and a ten and Roosterfish's friend gave him a crisp fifty so new Roosterfish looked to see was the ink dry. They let him out at the corner and he stood watching with the bills clutched in his fist. He seemed to detect some heat from them, a warm cheery glow that crept up his arm and throbbed comfortably at his elbow.

When the boy hit the cutout the man in the Olds jerked his head around limbernecked to see what transpired and there was a curiously stricken look on his face. Its shape seemed to elongate and lose defini-

tion. When the light went green the Chevy was gone so fast even Roosterfish was amazed. The hybrid leapt and was gone in a long undulation
wail of rubber and was almost at the next light before the Oldsmobile's
spinning wheels caught traction.

People on the street turned openmouthed to watch and a prowl car
coming out an alley was interested as well. Its red light began to revolve
and its siren gave one brief squall as it spun onto the main drag. When
the boy saw it he had the signal blinker on for a right turn but decided
not and the Chevy seemed to squat on its springs for a millisecond and
then it was gone in a full throated roar on across the Savannah bridge
with the prowl car in its wake.

Roosterfish turned to run. He turned at a jeweler's and ran down an
alley past a shop where a giant's eyeglasses hung suspended and past the
smells of cooking from cafés and on where the alley narrowed and the
surface became cobblestone or weathered brick. He slowed his pace to a
dignified purposeful stride past little white shanties, their porches adorned
with blacks in rocking chairs and gliders who turned to watch him listlessly
on his way. He had the money wadded in his fist and his fist shoved deep
into his overall pocket and his feet were weightless with elation.

He walked past hedgetrimmed yards replete with car casing plant-
ers that seemed to have been halved with gigantic pinking shears. He
seemed to be regaining his assurance, undergoing a curious metamorphosis. He became a figure of dignity nodding gravely to whoever he
met on his way, a returned veteran perhaps, arm lost at Anzio, Normandy. Perhaps he had sensed some minute shifting of the weights,
a delicate compensatory adjustment to the scales. A change in the
tempers of the times.

He passed a used car lot where the old cars sat in neat rows like some
curious crop awaiting harvest and he paused for a time and studied
them with the appraising eye of one who had the wherewithal to make
his choice did he care to. He went on and after a time he passed a filling
station where he paused long enough to buy himself a cold drink and
break one of the twenties. The next place he came upon was set on the
corner and the sign proclaimed it the Savannah Motor Court. There
was a sign of painted plywood hung by a chain and on the red wood,
VACANCY. Roosterfish stood staring bemusedly and then after a while he
started across the graveled yard toward the office.

Roosterfish was still and watchful a long time before he moved but when he did he was fluid and catlike, movements shorn of the extraneous, man and task welded seamlessly to one. It was an evening that suited him very well for settling a score with Tyler. He had waited for just such a one. The night was absolutely dark with no moon scheduled and you could not have told where the trees ended and the sky began. He came out of the scrubby pines and loped across the road and silently ran and stopped below the battlement of hedge to where the black Oldsmobile sat. He was carrying a homemade rope, rolls of strips of cloth torn from a bedsheet and tied together and the whole thing was soaked with gas. He spun off the gascap and began to feed this juryrigged fuse into the tank and turning ran back, uncoiling the strips like a man paying out line and he was back where the dark pooled on the pine needles.

He glanced at the house: it lay steeped in sleep, a vague bulk he could hardly discern. But he had seen it by daylight. A pleasant white frame with green trim and no neighbors within half a mile and time running out like the whirring hands of a clock.

He took off the gas-soaked glove and stuck it in his hip pocket and sniffed his hand then wiped it on his pants and sniffed again. Satisfied he fumbled for his matches.

When he touched the fuse a rope of fire blossomed instantaneous across the road and the yard was afire, then there was a loud *whump* from the Oldsmobile and it erupted in flames. The trunklid blew up and off and for a second seemed to lift and then settled back on its springs. It roared like a locomotive, burning fullthrottle away in the night. There was no wind and the flames tended straight and plumb twenty or thirty feet in the air and he could feel the heat from where he lay. The tires caught and oily black smoke began to rise and the rubber shot sparks off into the night like Roman candles and when they burned through the air hissed out. The windows went with dull thumps and began to melt, viscous flaming mass creeping down the quarterpanels.

He lay behind a clay embankment like a soldier in the trenches and he peered down the barrel of the secondhand shotgun at the picture window moiling orange with refracted light as if the interior of the house was in flames. He not with me is my enemy, Tyler had said. As if to remove all doubt as to this enmity Roosterfish steadied the barrel against a gnarled root and shot out the picture window and there were no flames at all but only a shaft of black emptiness like the opening of the mouth of a tunnel and the echo of the shot rolling back from the timbered hills and all the other myriad sounds of the night held in shocked abeyance. A last piece of glass fell like an afterthought.

He moved the aim of the gun smoothly from the window to the door and cocked the hammer of the other barrel. He waited. He could feel sweat creeping down his ribcage, an ant or mosquito on his arm. He willed Tyler to appear, the door to open and an image to materialize there like a slowly developing photographic plate.

There was no one. Then after a time a porchlight came on far down the roadbed and a little bit after that he heard a car crank and the headlamps came on. They yawed against the trees, wheeling back, spun into the road.

He uncocked the shotgun and turned and eased into the thickening umber following some trail of his own back into the darkness. He looked back once and the car was burning like a funeral pyre, an enormous candle flailing against the night.

Ropes of fog swirled near the ground, serpentine phantoms accompanying him like familiars down this road. A pale rose predawn light washed the east like light through tinted glass. Off his left hand must lay a river, for fog rose thickly here and opaquely immeasurable, walls of gray stone out of darker trees from which his mind built old lost cities of another time, bastioned walls fallen in by forgotten wars.

When the car came he thumbed it as soon as he could discern its lights. It came slow and dreamlike and near silent out of the fog, as if he were watching its creation rather than its arrival, saw it gather solidity and form and detail and saw too late the escutcheon on the door, family crest of some brotherhood aligned forever against him. He pocketed his hand, turned to walk on up the blacktop as if the fog might open to receive him then close behind him.

The car slowed, ceased a few feet past him. Edgewater walked on up the road, his eyes ahead.

Hey.

He stopped.

You stay right where you are and keep your hands where we can see em.

Edgewater stood waiting, watched the door open, the sheriff get out. The face close to his own, intent as if the eyes would call forth from memory some old lost unsolved crime to match the countenance they studied. They were haggard, tired, the face once handsome matinee idol of generations past resurrected dissolute and wasted. Water beaded on the polished visor and ran down the edge.

Put your hands up against the car here and spread them legs.

The door on the other side opened and a deputy got out. Polished leather and blued steel, all the trappings. Edgewater stared at the moist metal where water ran and dripped and at his vague ghostlike reflection, two eyes staring apparitionlike uncomprehendingly from underwater. There were hands busy at him, the radio said something unintelligible and official sounding, some language foreign to him.

The search ended. Get in, a voice told him. He got into the back seat. The two got back in and closed the doors. The motor was still running, the radio staticking as if trying to devise a signal from some station that no longer existed. The windshield wipers clipped on endlessly, water funneling down the sides of the glass.

The sheriff handed him the folded money across the seat. Edgewater took it wordlessly, pocketed it. The sheriff seemed to be studying Edgewater's other belongings.

That's it, Edgewater said lightly. No ransom note out of cutup newspaper. No bloody knife, no smoking gun.

Not much in the way of worldly goods, the sheriff said at length. A toothbrush, a razor, a mouthharp. Wherever you're going, you're travelin mighty light. But I don't see nothing here tells me who you are.

My name's Edgewater. I'm just passin on through.

I hear you sayin it. I would have liked seein it in print. You know it's against the law to hitchhike in this state?

No.

Well it is. He raised his face to study Edgewater, did not seem pleased with what he saw.

How come you ain't got any papers?

Papers?

Papers. ID card, driver's license, social security card. Don't get smart with me. You know what I'm talkin about.

Oh. All my stuff got stolen out of the bus station. I'm tryin to get home, up by Monteagle.

We'll find out who you are, the cop said.

Try to prove who I am, Edgewater thought. Rifle through the files, lookin at fingerprints, snapshotted likeness, mug shots, already charring to yellow, word of mouth, transcripts of a fugitive order, well he was here, but he went on. Now you see me, now you don't, like the flicker of shadows, like a face briefly glimpsed or imagined through the windowglass at night, already warped as to be unrecognizable. Take nothing with you and leave nothing behind and when you know who I am let me be the first one you tell.

Ask him did he detour over by Natural Bridge, the deputy said.

You been around the Natural Bridge Road?

I don't even know where it's at.

Then you couldn't rightly say whether you been around it or not.

No, I just come straight in from McNairy County.

Ask him does he remember cuttin that girl's throat and slicing her titties off and droppin what was left her off Natural Bridge, the deputy said.

Edgewater remained silent. Somewhere a door into darkness had opened, an icy wind blew on him. His mouth was dry.

Warren, the sheriff said. If you want to run this job you'll have to run for the office the way everybody else does. That's just the way it's always been done.

Well, he just looks like a smartass to me.

He may well be, the sheriff agreed. He turned back to Edgewater. Where'd you get that money?

Chopping cotton down in Lake County.

You workin now.

I said I was passin through.

A early riser like you are must surely find the world his oyster. Work oughtn't be hard to come by for a man on the road before daylight.

Edgewater remained silent.

If I didn't have a good notion of who I'm huntin for this morning I'd take you down, the sheriff said. I'd unbreech you and break you down like a shotgun and I'd come up with something. I can tell by the look of you. After twenty years I ought to. You just don't feel right to me. If I had time I'd do it anyway. Do you know why?

No.

Do you want to know why?

Not particularly, Edgewater said. He was staring out the window to where day was coming. He was intent on the bleak landscape as if he could draw himself into it, the grating noise ebb and fade from hearing. Trees looming like wet black monoliths out of misty fields, trunks half immersed in fog as if they were swimming in rising water. Blackbirds silent as phantoms foraged in a distant field.

Because I am sick of you. I am tired of turning over rocks and you son of a bitches crawlin out. No shave and no haircut and nothing to your name but a shittin French harp and a go to hell look on your face. No more ID than a newborn baby brings into the world. Hell, you can't live like vagrants. Always headed somewhere else. Well, mister, we work county prisoners in this part of the state. That's why the roads is kept up so good. So if you don't want to apply your talents to pickin up bloody Kotex and litter and shovelin dogshit you best be huntin you a Greyhound bus.

Edgewater looked him in the eyes for the first time. I told you as plain as I could I was passin through. If I had known a road around this place, whatever it is, I would damn sure have taken it.

Let's book the smart cocksucker for suspicion, the deputy said.

Suspicion of what? Edgewater asked.

Of bein a smart cocksucker, the deputy said and laughed.

Hell, we know he's that, the sheriff said. We don't suspect him of it.

Come in Unit Four, the radio said.

The sheriff took up the microphone. This is Parnell, he said. His eyes were on Edgewater all the while as if he were addressing him and not someone invisible and listening.

Sheriff, you need to get down on Sinkin. It's a bunch down there got somebody treed they say killed that girl and they liable to do away with him before you talk to him.

Where on Sinkin?

Up by the mouth where that old huntin lodge is.

I'm on my way. He released the button on the microphone. Get out, he said. Edgewater sat mute, looked about him, there were no door handles. The sheriff sat still and angry for a moment then he got out disgustedly and opened the door. Edgewater climbed out.

If I ever see your face again let's let it be through a bus window, Parnell said as he got back in, rolling the window up, the face behind it going pale and indistinct.

The tires spun on the blacktop, caught and hurled the cruiser into the morning breaking and from his sight.

There was no bus station in Waynesboro, only a sign behind the café counter and a cigar box of tickets the waitress took up when he asked. She studied a worn schedule.

The next bus to Chattanooga is one o'clock.

Well, thanks.

You want your ticket now?

I guess I'll just wait.

They won't be no cheaper at one o'clock, the woman told him. He grinned and went on out.

Noon found him ensconced with other Saturday idlers in the poolhall. He drank a beer at the bar, idly watched a pill game progress in the rear. A ceiling fan listlessly rotated the stale lethargic air. He listened to talk of the last night's horrors. Some mad vivisectionist abroad in the land. Men feared for their womenfolk while they drank, with each beer, each halfpint, each retelling the horrors grew worse. Unspeakable evil had passed through here under cover of darkness. He felt their eyes on him, appraising him, stranger, pariah.

In midafternoon, a diminutive and curious young man blew in. He kicked the door to and looked all about him. He raised a hand in expansive greeting to all present although no one save Edgewater had seemed to notice him. He looked half mad, harried, as if he must be in three places at once and could not decide where to go. He leaned against the counter next to Edgewater. He wore a pair of overalls too big for his skinny birdlike frame and no shirt. There was a smell of the woods about him.

Gimme two beers at once, he told the counterman. What say sport, he said to Edgewater. You think you can whip my ass or not?

The face was sharp, demented, beyond madness. The eyes were beset and wild.

I never give it any thought.

A wise move, the little man said. It would pay you not to. I'm so bad the undertakers in three counties gives me a kickback.

The counterman set two bottles of beer on the counter. The man tilted one up, his Adam's apple pumping the beer down in great chugging gulps. He sat the empty down and took up the full bottle. He winked at Edgewater.

I'm a bad son of a bitch, he said. He began on the second beer, peering all about him. No one paid him any attention.

He set the empty down and fumbled in his overall pocket, drew out a wadded bill. He unfolded it with care, laid it on the countertop. The fan moved it listlessly and he set the empty beer bottle on it.

I've got twenty dollars says I can kick any ass in the house, he announced loudly.

The game went on in the back. No one even looked up. The counterman rolled his eyes upward and went to wipe the bar somewhere else. Edgewater went back to his beer.

What about you, sport?

I been sick, Edgewater told him. Not me.

You're a wise man, a little chickenshit maybe but wise all the same. I've got twenty dollars says I can whip any son of a bitch in here, he screamed.

An enormous barrel-chested man arose from the bench with an air of weariness, of boredom. He racked his cue and came through the swinging door separating the rear and moved the man aside, saying no word. He picked up the twenty-dollar bill and pocketed it and stood with a patient air. Then after a moment he shrugged and went back to the pill game.

The glass on the door rattled when the little man stormed out. He stood on the sidewalk for a time shaking his fist, raving. Then Edgewater saw him peering in the window, his eyes shaded for the dark interior. He had a pocketknife open in his hand. He seemed to be talking to himself. After a while a fat woman came and drug him away.

In midafternoon a commotion on the square drew him out to see what transpired. The sidewalk had become thronged with people all staring toward the front of the courthouse, where two uniformed officers drug a manacled man from the backseat of a parked cruiser. The red light flared and died, flared and died all in silence. People struggled forward forcing Edgewater with them, surged slow and implacable as floodwaters toward the trio ascending the steps to the courtyard. They watched in awed silence as if the horrors of the transgressor's deeds had transcended some other world than this one, left them with no comment adequate to make.

It was an old man. He protested, hung back, he locked his legs and his feet went skittering, stabbed at the concrete as they drug him; for a moment he and his captors swayed almost motionless like some perverse and graceless dance, he fell, they seized him up and bore him on like some fallen comrade seared in battle.

Open a hole up there, Parnell ordered.

The old man's white whiskered face was twisted on his corded neck as if he were trying to see his tormentors, his unseeing eyes wild with rage or madness.

Edgewater was trying to back up but there was a wall of flesh and bone behind him, he could feel the heat from it, smell the sweat and musk of the crowd. A contagious madness touched him. The old man passed very near. Edgewater could hear his ragged breathing, see the tobacco juice stains in his beard, saw how his hands were stained to the wrists with something dark and dried halfmoons of this substance ringed his fingernails. He wore what appeared to be a dirty flannel nightshirt tucked into overall pants and as he passed his clawed hands seized Edgewater's shirt as if he were drowning and would drag him down with him as if Edgewater could halt his passage.

Parnell hit the old man's wrist with the flat of his hand and grasped it and forced it to the old man's side. The arm was thin, the hand was old, gnarled and ageless like weathered wood or the talon of a desiccated bird. Parnell's harried face looked for a moment at Edgewater's eyes but there was no remembrance or recognition. Then they passed and went up the courthouse steps.

Even when the crowd had dissipated Edgewater could feel the clawed hand against his ribcage, could see the mad and evil face, smell the carrion breath. It would not fade. It burned on the periphery of his memory as if madness were contagious, not as if it were some face he had seen in a crowd but his own, glimpsed out of the corner of his eyes, warped and heightened by the glass of some sideshow mirror.

The two had waited for some time and when the tall youth came through the poolroom door they turned and watched him stroll nonchalantly across the floor toward the pinball machine.

There's pretty boy now, one of them said to the other.

Edgewater turned to look as well. The newcomer was something to see. He had on pegged checked pants low on his hips and a pink shirt with a buttondown collar and a black necktie as narrow as a shoestring. He had on brown shoes with white explosions radiating out from the toes and he had sunglasses with mirrored lenses hiding his eyes. There was a rum-soaked Tennessee Crooks cigar clamped far back in his lean jaw and beneath the stingybrim hat his yellow hair was as smooth and shiny as a bird's wing. He looked like a farm boy's fantasy of what a cheap gigolo must be.

Hey, prettyface, one of the men called. Edgewater drank from his beer; in the bar's mirror the man's eyes briefly touched his own. They were black and tiny as a pig's eyes. They jerked away as if Edgewater might suspect he addressed him. Then he wiped his mouth and turned toward the pinball machine, in the wavering mirror there was the yellow of his hair, white cropped expanse of his neck.

Hello, P.D., the boy at the pinball machine said. He raised the sunglasses to his forehead as if the lenses were opaque. What could I do for you boys?

Wolf just got to wantin to see you, P.D. said. He stretched his feet out in the floor and fell to studying the scuffed leather of his shoes. He said if we seen you tell you to drop by the cabstand a minute.

If I get time, the boy said. He looked at his wrist, frowned as if he had absentmindedly forgotten his watch. I'm pretty tied up this evening.

Tell you what Bradshaw, P.D. said. Wolf said you might be busy. He said it was important we was to persuade you.

Bradshaw grinned. Behind him the pinball machine lights flickered in abeyance. I'm kind of a hard sell, he said. How did he say to persuade me?

P.D. grinned. He said tell you to jump and if you didn't ask how high he said kick the livin shit out of you.

Bradshaw flushed. He took off the glasses, held them in his hands as if absentmindedly studying his reflection.

You tell him I said if he wants his money he can by God whistle for it. Tell him my accounts is like the dust, the rain'll settle it.

The man shrugged. It's your lookout. He'll get it one way or another.

You think I just crawled out of some holler, come off Punkin Creek or somewhere? Hell, I been around. He think I don't know a marked card when I see one? He think I'd believe them cards come with little pinholes punched all in em like that? Shit, P.D.

If they was there it took you long enough to find em.

Hell, I was just playin him along.

Sure you was.

Tell you something else, P.D. You look just a cunthair light in the ass to be a hired gun.

You son of a bitch. I been lookin for an excuse to bust that face.

Watch him P.D. He's got that little switchblade. I seen him cut a nigger over by Clifton.

P.D. was already off the stool.

He better of brought one with a chocolate handle, he said. He crossed the floor in two or three huge steps and began to slap the blond boy's face. The stingybrim snapped off and the blond hair whipped from side to side with the methodical blows. The mirrored glasses fell, were kicked aside. The blond boy had one hand in his pocket but he could not seem to get it out. P.D. hit him in the face and he fell backwards, his elbows went through the pinball machine top with an explosion of breaking glass.

You a tough son of a bitch all right, P.D. said. He picked Bradshaw up and spun him around. There was blood running out of the corner of his mouth. He hit P.D. a glancing blow on the jaw and P.D. side-stepped easily and wrestled him to the floor. He rolled atop him; the face looking up from the floor was twisted, pale and wild. Then the mouth worked convulsively. He spat a mouthful of blood into P.D.'s face and began to laugh through broken teeth.

Crazy son of a bitch. He began to pound Bradshaw in the face. The man on the stool was watching Edgewater. Don't even think about it, he said.

What?

You looked for a minute there like you wanted to play too.

Hell, be nothing to me.

That's what I just told you.

Tell you what, Edgewater said after a time. I'm getting a little tired of everybody in this damned town tellin me what I think.

The counterman kept screaming at them to stop. All at once Edge-water found himself sliding across the floor on his back and shoulder with lights flashing on and off in his head, the counterman part of a receding vision, his face twisted with anger, phone to his head, finger busily dialing. He pitched up against the dope box. Then the man was running toward him across a slick and tilted floor, the door looked miles away. He saw the foot coming, rolled, felt the shock of pain run down his thigh. He grabbed the man's legs, felt a rain of blows on his head and shoulders, the man fell heavily alongside him. Somewhere sirens began. It couldn't be this quick, he thought. They grew louder in volume. Bradshaw and P.D. were on their feet circling. The counterman hit P.D. with a chair. His eyes went wide and white and he fell like a dropped stone. Goddamn hillbillies, the counterman was saying. He was advancing on Edgewater with the chair raised.

Let's go, good buddy, Bradshaw said. He done called the fuckin law. He wiped his mouth. His forearm came away streaked with blood. Hit the back door.

Bradshaw's car, a new Pontiac convertible, was in the back parking lot. Bradshaw did not even open the door. He leapt into the driver's seat and the motor caught on the first crank. Everbody's got to call the shittin law, he said, squalling and smoking before Edgewater had the door closed.

Son of a bitch, Bradshaw said. A black and white blocked the alley's mouth, its lights sinister and strobic. He looked the car down, lurched and swerved sideways and threw it into reverse and they went careening crazily backward into the parking lot. He spun forward toward the alley's nether end.

All we got to do is make the city limits.

Bradshaw had already run two red lights before the prowl car fell into pursuit. Bradshaw was intent on his driving. He narrowly missed a wagon full of pale and startled faces, cornered at the Baptist church and shot off a long hill. JESUS SAVES, a sign there said. Another: JESUS CHRIST IS COMING, BE READY. He went past the city limits sign at eighty.

So long, motherfucker, Bradshaw said.

Edgewater had turned in the seat, was peering back. I guess he never heard that about the city limits, he said. He's coming on.

He ain't supposed to do that, Bradshaw said. We got him by the balls now.

How you figure that?

Hell, just ain't supposed to do it. He's breaking the law his own self. He chuckled to himself, then he fell silent, uneasily studied the car in the rearview mirror. Hell, it don't matter. This is Mavis's car and it runs like a striped ass ape. We'll outrun the son of a bitch. She'll do one o five in a quarter.

They were in his country now, homes shot past, trees elastic and elongated, passersby frozen in motion, heads that turned slowly to watch their flight down the dusty roadbed. Telephone poles came like pickets in a fence.

A startled covey of berrypickers was their undoing. They came around a corner. Bradshaw was almost upon them before he saw them. They were crossing the road. He began to pound the horn, when he hit the brakes the back end slid around, they hustled broadside down the road, the steering wheel spinning crazily through Bradshaw's fingers, his face suffused with horror, a toothless old woman screaming imprecatory upon him, bonneted women hurtling berry buckets high into the air and fleeing blindly and arms akimbo into the briar thicket, faces frozen in mindless masks of impotent fear.

Lord have mercy, Bradshaw said. A rail fence broke with a sickening thump and the car jumped the shoulder of the road, veered through a bright field of bitterweed and squealing hogs, ceased on its side in a thicket of brush and its wheels spinning and the distant siren becoming strident and close.

Bradshaw and Edgewater crawled out, feeling for broken bones. Shit a brick, Bradshaw said. He was staring at the demolished car with something akin to fear. He got up and solicitously halted the spinning wheels one by one. He sat back down and his face looked as if he were about to cry. The new smell wasn't even wore off it, he said. The men began to climb down the brushy slope. The women still stood watching across the field. The patrol car had stopped on the road. Two men had gotten out and stood with the berrypickers. Other women straggled onto the roadbed, gathering their buckets. The group stood in silent and accusatory tableau, fingers pointing across the bitterweed.

Look at em. Bradshaw smirked. I bet if they had to come up with a dry pair of drawers between them they'd be shit out of luck.

———

Bradshaw took a rum-soaked Crook out of his pocket, unwrapped it, looked at it ruefully. He selected the longest piece, stuck it into his mouth, and struck a match on the cruiser door. He lit the cigar and inhaled deeply. He blew out the smoke and settled himself comfortably back against the upholstery. He crossed his legs. Uncrossed them, leaned forward, and spoke through the steel mesh.

You boys all set for the big lawsuit? he asked.

Parnell ignored him, turned off the dirt road onto the blacktop. The deputy turned and stared at Bradshaw through the grill, but not as if he was very interested. Which lawsuit is that?

The one I'm slappin on you, Bradshaw said. It's your fault Mavis's car is all busted up like that. She'll be at the courthouse with a slick-talkin Memphis lawyer and a stack of legal papers you couldn't put in a goddamned footlocker. If you don't think she'll shake things up you're livin in a dream world. When she gets through with that shittin courthouse bunch they won't be a picture left on the walls.

Who is this Mavis I keep hearin about? the deputy wondered.

Mavis Hodges runs the Starvue Drive-In and she pulls some weight in this county, Bradshaw says. Her taxes is morn you draw for a salary. Go ahead and lock me up and she'll have me on the sidewalk so fast your head'll spin.

She must be right fond of you, the deputy said.

She gets her money's worth, Bradshaw said. He gazed out the window. Edgewater stared past his profile to where Bradshaw watched freedom roll by, geometric rows of corn reeling past like spokes in a turnstile, a pastoral scene of grazing cows, with each revolution of the cruiser's wheels the landscape world became still more remote. For an agonizing moment the world outside became very dear to him, a real sense of loss twisted in him. If he were free he would do it all differently. Even now a bus he was not on rolled toward the serene blue mountains.

Rave on catshit, the deputy said contemptuously. Somebody'll cover you up. Side by side they sat on a hardened wood bench in an austere cubicle with other minions of the law. Their crackled names detached and ominous over the radio. Bradshaw listened rapt as if some curious fame or adulation had been bestowed upon him. A name in the public eye or ear bandied about by faceless and nameless officials in places far from this one. No prior convictions. Apparently nowhere by no one in all the world. The jawline hardened, the close-set eyes yellow and reptilian, a face to stare back at you from post office walls.

Okay, let's go upstairs, Parnell said. He arose, stood waiting. Bradshaw didn't move.

I get a phone call, he said.

You get exactly what I say you get and any more of that smart mouth and what you'll get is a blackjack alongside of the head.

You wait'll Mavis gets here.

I'm sick of hearin about Mavis, Parnell said. I don't care if Mavis is sleepin with Governor Gordon Browning, I don't care if she's got a inside track with God Almighty. You're goin on a public work gang or I'll know the answer why. He had approached Bradshaw, grasped the fabric of his shirt, slowly pulled him erect. Bradshaw hung slack and unprotesting. He might have been a bag of grain.

I warned you over a month ago to hunt you another roostin place. I warned your runnin mate there this mornin. Now move it. He shoved Bradshaw. Bradshaw staggered two or three steps, came up against the wall, caught his balance. A woman from a calendar smiled at him, her face unruffled and demure. Edgewater had arisen, started to the door. Bradshaw's hair was in his eyes. His cut mouth was beginning to bleed again. A trickle of pink welled on his chin. A hand came up to wipe it away. His eyes looked wild and congested. Listen to him, he told Edgewater. His face was trying to smile. Listen at him. Out of a job already and don't even know it.

Edgewater chose himself a cot and laid back, weary, his fingers latticed beneath his head. He closed his eyes. Bradshaw hunkered by the side of the bunk. His voice was a steady drone in Edgewater's ears. Edgewater opened his eyes. The walls were filthy cracked plaster. Graffiti composition aflare and transient. A roach watched possessively from a chink in a concrete block. His eyes flickered around to the five or six men who shared the bullpen.

If I had my hat on I wouldn't even by God take it off, Bradshaw said. I won't be here long enough to make myself at home. Not you neither. You saved my life, Billy. You think Mavis won't be tickled? I'll get you a job with her out there at the drive-in. Hell, you'll think you've died and gone to heaven. All the hamburgers and hot dogs you can eat and a pic-ture show every night and more women than you ever seen in one place.

It sounds nice. What do you do?

Just odd jobs, clean up. Kindly keep a eye on people, sort of like a bouncer, keep em from getting too rough. Sell stuff in the concession stand. He winked Edgewater a sly and enormous wink. I take care of whatever come up.

He fell silent, his face rueful, this involuntary refugee from the American dream.

Hell, Mavis can't get along without me out there. You can bet she missed me already. I was done supposed to be back. Lord, she got a temper. She'll blow in here in a minute like a scalded dog and you think the hair won't fly? Them sons of bitches. They'll be yessirrin and nosirrin and long remember the taste I'll leave in their mouth.

A barrel-shaped man in a dirty T-shirt winced and looked up with interest at Bradshaw from his worn copy of *Field and Stream*. He scruti-nized him with curiosity. Boys we got either a politician or one of them movie stars here, he announced. I ain't figured out which yet. He turned to his fellows with a broad smile as if to draw them into his joke.

Bradshaw gave a sharp look of contempt. The other men barely looked up. They seemed not to care, as if they had heard it all before. Or said it themselves.

Laugh if it makes you feel better, Bradshaw said. See how much you laugh when you're still settin here and I'm out somers blowin the foam off a cold one.

What are you in here for anyway, slick?

You figger it out.

The fat man took a pair of spectacles from his overall pocket, re-moved them from their case, and hooked them over his nose. The ways of human nature ain't unknown to me, he told the men. I ort to be able to figger it out for myself. Behind the glass his eyes were limpid and blue. He studied Bradshaw intently. Cowfuckin? he asked at length.

Income tax evasion, Bradshaw told him without batting an eye.

Suppertime. Meals fetched up here. The sullen jailer had aligned them on the floor above the stairs.

What is this shit? Edgewater kept asking. What is this mess anyway? Some kind of fried something of an indeterminate color and texture.

It exuded a strong fishy smell about it but it resembled no fish Edge-water had ever come into contact with. White beans and turnip salad. Atop the mounded greens a pale white worm nestled like some arcane garnish. He pushed the plate back. All about him the rattle of cutlery, the scraping of tin plates. Hungry eyes fell on his tray. Beyond the high barred windows a cool summer dusk had fallen on the land. The silent expanse of night.

You not eatin? the fat man asked solicitously. His hand already searching tentatively for the plate.

Take it on, Edgewater said. The man began to scrape it onto his own plate, raking the worm delicately to the side like some tidbit to save for last.

You'll develop a taste for it, he reassured Edgewater.

He slept adrift in the watches of the night. He could feel the high-way leaking back the day's heat through the soles of his shoes. Hear the warm wind in the darkening rushes. He dreamed his death and a velvet expanse of nothingness he was sliding down toward a corner of the world darker still where even light was imprisoned. Later he heard approaching voices, coarse, strident, the yelps of jackals calling one to another, mate to mate, the quarrelling asides of necromancers who fought bitterly over his flesh and bones. He awoke to the bright light of the cell and rubbed his eyes in wonder and looked about him.

His cellmates looked galvanized now with interest. They had arisen and were sitting up on their cots blinking their eyes, peering toward the stairwell as if some entertainment was being held there for their amusement. Above the lichencrept concrete of the stairs had arisen a middleaged woman's face like a disembodied and sinister idol or some mad priest's graven image from an older time. Her black hair was sprung out in medusalike ringlets and her eyes seemed to be afire. They were fixed with a fierce and palpable malevolence on Bradshaw who had arisen and made a tentative move to approach her. He had halted, there was a stunned and foolish look on his face as if he had been standing on something which had been suddenly jerked from beneath him.

You ignorant ungrateful turd, you backwoods cretin, the woman was saying. I knew you had shit for brains but I thought you could drive to the store and pick up a dozen eggs. What have you got to say for yourself?

Sugarbabe, Bradshaw said. He made shushing sounds with his mouth, his wild eyes indicated the presence of strangers. She's just all tore up because of the way they done me, he said aside to Edgewater.

I'm not tore up nothing to what you're gonna be, she told him. You slackmouth gapejawed son of a bitch. Send you for a dozen eggs and you wind up runnin over half the county with my lovely car and it not have a thousand miles on it. Oh, I ought to kept you on a leash, Oh, I ought to knowed you. You had to come into town and brag and show it off, didn't you? You had to bigshot around. Well, by God you ain't flyin so high now.

Honey, Bradshaw began.

You shut your mouth. Who's gonna pay for that car? Look at your clothes tore off you and your mouth all swelled up. Pick you up out of the gutter and buy you clothes and try to teach you to act like a human bein and this is how you repay me.

Honey, when we get by ourselves we can work all this out, he said all in a rush. You just sign them papers and …

Tell her how I saved your life, Edgewater put in.

We're as by ourselves as we'll ever be, she said. You lowdown shitass. If you ever get out of here and I see you sneakin around my drive-in I'll get a peace warrant on you and slap you so far back in jail they'll have to pipe the daylight in.

You're all wrought up, he told her, making curious deprecating gestures with his hands.

You're damn right I am but with any luck at all I'm lookin at your sneakin face for the last time. She turned, her black eyes shiny as buttons, and the head descended the stairs from sight. Bradshaw ran over to the edge of the cell steps but he could not get his head through the bars to see down the stairs. They could hear her purposeful steps growing faint.

Just forget it, by God, he screamed down the stairwell. I druther lay it out than have a slut like you on my bond. If I want out I'll do it my damn self. He choked, caught his breath. And I'm through with you too, he went on. Just don't come sneakin around tryin to apologize. He turned a harried face on his cellmates.

I guess you told her, Edgewater said.

Slick, you sure got a way with women, the fat man admired. How much would you charge me to learn your technique?

Bradshaw ran a hand through his blond hair. She'll be back, he said. His hands were fumbling for the other piece of his cigar.

Maybe she will, Edgewater told him. But I kindly hope I'm somewhere else when she does.

It won't do her a shittin bit of good. Any woman stands up and calls me everything from a chicken to a motherfucker in front of all my friends is walkin on my fightin side.

Welcome to Wayne County, the fat man said.

Where in the wide world you from, Billy?

Up in the mountains.

I bet you wish you was there.

I bet I wish I was anyplace but here.

Me too. Lord, I had as good a family as any man ever lived and I just let it all slide away.

Where's home?

Up towards Nashville. You got a family?

Everybody has. Edgewater was scraping caked mud from around the rims of his shoes with a wooden ice cream paddle.

You don't give up much, do you, Billy?

He grinned. I guess I don't have much to spare.

I got a mama and a sister; I ever get out I guess I'll head up that way and check on em. They get to wantin to see me. You ort to see my sister. Face like a cover on a movie book in a drugstore. Blonde hair and blue eyes.

Edgewater evinced his first interest here. What's her name?

Sudy.

How old is she?

Seventeen or eighteen. You got ere sister?

No.

Your folks back in the mountains?

Edgewater's eyes closed. His whole history plastic, reforming, a new world every day. People and events cut away and shuttled overboard. He thought of Roosterfish, wondered his fate. Continually discarding his past like so much weight he was unable to carry. He studied the shoe, laid it to the side.

My folks are both dead, he said. All I have is distant kin.

Bradshaw pondered this. I guess that's right. I guess you can't get much further off than dead.

Reckon when we'll get out?

Lord, Billy, I don't know. We ain't even had the hearin yet and can't make bond when we do. I'm good for a eleven twenty-nine. I don't know about you.

I had a little money but not enough to make bond, I don't guess I'll ever see it again.

Easy come easy go.

Sundays were interminable. He would have preferred the brush hook, the pick and shovel. They could hear somewhere a congregation in song. A backslid preacher was inspired to conduct a makeshift service, gave some drunken and rambling discourse on the gospels. He finally subsided tearfully in the face of obscenities and catcalls.

There were few visitors. Family ties apparently did not run deeply here. Bradshaw watched all the women eagerly but none met his exacting standards. Edgewater was learning that Bradshaw screwed no women save the prettiest, drove no car but the fastest, held no poker hand but the highest, escaped from no situation by anything wider than a hair's breadth. He fell to telling Edgewater of past exploits.

Best piece I ever had was in Arkansas, he said. I'se on my uppers and a feller picked me up in the poolroom to help him finish some concrete. Give me four dollars. We went out to where he lived and it was a porch he wanted me to help on. He done had it formed up and everything already and this big old truck come and dumped it full of concrete. We flew into levelin her down with rakes and shovels.

His old lady kept lookin at us out the window. She was about twenty and pretty as a picture. Had hair the color of a blackbird's wing. Little rosebud mouth.

It was in August and we was sweatin like mad. The concrete was about to get away from us, already startin to set up. I kept lookin at her and I took to wantin a drink of water. I laid my rake down and went in and she was in the kitchen. They had a bar across it and she was settin on one of these here stools spins around. Come here, she said. She pulled her skirt up and she didn't have on a goddamn sign of a drawer. I looked out the window while I had her backed up against the bar screwin her and he was in his rubber boots knee deep in that concrete rakin away. Ever now and then he'd look up towards the door real mad and then he hollered at me. I ortn't done it but I couldn't help it. I'm comin, I hollered back at him. We kept on and directly I seen him throw his rake and start toward the door. I went out the back as he come in the front and I never seen neither one of em again. I've wondered if he ever did get that concrete finished.

Monday morning. Harsh voices in the halflight behind the jail, the slap of shoeleather on asphalt. Eastward of the broken ranks of buildings a soft pastel rose, fanning outward spreading now, wrought of the scattered windows stained glass in the grimy alley. Pale exhaust from the idling flatbed truck. Rattle and clang of the tools they loaded aboard.

Under the watchful eye of the guards they climbed the ladder of welded water pipe to the bed of the truck, aligned themselves on benches in the canvas doghouse. The guard swung up. Roll it out, Bradshaw called. Let's get this show on the road. Everybody turned to look at him. Looked away. The guard came up and put his face very close to Bradshaw. Bradshaw fell to studying the handgun the guard wore.

I'se just helpin out.

You help out one more time and your mouth will have overloaded your ass. In a case like that bad things begin to happen to you. Are we all clear on that?

Yessir.

All right, roll it out, he called.

The sun at midday. A hot July sun pulsing in the vaulted heavens. Prisoners strung out along the highway carrying bags of gathered litter. Edgewater studying the passing cars with something like longing. A baldheaded man tossed him a half pack of Camels from a passing car. He covertly tucked them into the top of one of his socks. Turned to see the guard studying the wheeling of hawks in the distant throbbing blue.

Suddenly a fit seemed to take Bradshaw; he went to the ground and then began a curious ungaited dance. He wadded something, held it to his chest. He looked halfdemented. A fifty-dollar bill, he shrieked. Hot damn, I found me a fifty-dollar bill. He had it in his fists, throwing his arms, his feet shuffling in some gleeful dance.

Everyone turned to look. Efforts redoubled at scanning the ground. There might be more. Fleeing robbers. Perhaps a sackful. A wrecked Brinks truck.

Where? the guard said. He had a hand on Bradshaw's shoulder. Give it to me.

No, Bradshaw cried. It's mine, all mine, you'll take it away from me.

I said by God give it to me, prisoner. The guard shook Bradshaw tearing his shirt down the front.

It's mine, you can't have it.

Bradshaw fell on his knees. He had both hands locked together and clasped between his knees. His face turned up to the white light of the sun. He might have been praying. His eyes were closed. His eyes working. He looked possessed. I need it, he said. Please. I found it. It's mine.

I need it too, the guard said. He kicked Bradshaw, fell upon him. For a minute they rocked silent on the cropped ground and locked like lovers or madmen. The guard's fingers tore at Bradshaw's hands. At last tore them open, wrested from him a torn and grapestained popsicle wrapper. He threw it from him. He looked as if he might cry. You goddamn crazy bastard, he said. Bradshaw's face turned upward to accept the surreal white weight of the sun, he looked crazed, contorted with pain and glee.

Saturday night seemed a busy night in Wayne County. From four o'clock onward there was heavy traffic on the concrete stairs, a vast procession of the drunk and bloody and broke and luckless. A few familiar faces among the transients, regular customers perhaps. Until all the cots were taken, the air thick with the smell of whiskey, sweat, vomit. Edgewater began to contemplate vainly the possibility of escape. Wished himself elsewhere with an impassioned desperation. Were wishes animate he'd be thousands of miles away.

When dusk fell and the slotted window darkened, the revelers fell into a quarrelsome uneasy silence, contemplating perhaps their losses, a Saturday night that went on without them. Women that settled for second best, music others were hearing. They felt themselves cheated, wronged.

Sometime after midnight Edgewater came awake to yet another scuffle. There was fighting at the foot of the stairwell, sounds of blows, swearing, cries of pain. Little by little the fight progressed up the stairs until two deputies came into view dragging a third man between them. They opened the cell door and hurled him in. Edgewater immediately recognized the little man who had offered to whip anyone in the poolroom.

The deputies stood for a moment adjusting their clothing, breathing hard. One of them had lost a hat. The little man fell upon it in the cell. He stamped it viciously. Kicked it toward the corner of the bullpen. There, by God, he said. He turned a bladelike face toward the deputies, his eyes enraged.

You wormy little bastard.

Pick on a drunk, will ye? Hell, anybody can whip up on a drunk. What's your name, anyway?

Hodges. As you damn well know. Gimme my hat.

Hodges. I'll remember that. An eye closed in concentration. He turned to the other deputy. What's yourn?

Hinson.

Hinson and Hodges. Hodges and Hinson. He was feeling all through his pockets as if for paper and pencil. You goin way up on my shitlist now, he told them. You better be huntin you a high limb to roost on because when I get out I aim to be lookin you up.

You know where I live, Hodges said disgustedly. Morton, you want to hand me my hat.

The fat man in overalls got up from his bunk and made to approach the cap. It did not look like a cap at all. It looked like some luckless and shapeless animal elongated on the highway.

Go ahead, Morton, the little man said. If that's all life means to ye.

The big man paused and he stood regarding the little man quizzically as if what he was hearing must be through some defect in his hearing.

What? he asked.

I said pick that cap up and the undertaker'll be puttin ye Sunday best on for ye. I want my twenty-dollar bill, too.

Your twenty dollars is long gone, slick. I had twenty dollars I wouldn't be layin out a fine for a public drunk.

That's just tough shit. You pick up that cap and you're still a dead man.

What are you goin to do? Talk me to death? Morton bent down and picked up the cap, raised an obsequious grinning face to Hodges.

I'm a bad son of a bitch, the little man said. He jerked a snubnosed pistol out of his overall pocket and stood pointing it in Morton's face. Silent men faded back in staggered ranks. Edgewater himself drawing to the shadowed corner, the man with his pistol and the frozen deputies some unbelievable tableau from the vales of aberrance.

Get on your knees, Morton.

Pettijohn, you crazy fool, Hodges said. If a straitjacket's what you're huntin tonight you'll damn sure find it. You headed for a rubber room at Bolivar if you don't walk mighty soft.

I'll get to you in a minute. My mind ain't so bad I forgot them blackjacks. You just stay right where you're at and the first man even looks like he wants to pull a pistol on me goes down them steps on a stretcher.

Hell, it ain't but a shittin cap pistol.

Pettijohn whirled and fired. There was a flat report and the bullet sang off the concrete coping like an angry wasp and left in its wake a new-looking chink the size of a quarter. The deputies dropped from sight like retreating jacks-in-the-box and there was silence. The air smelled of cordite. The pistol swung back to Morton. His face was white and pastylooking, the face of a man to whom a doctor has just imparted dire news.

On them knees, Pettijohn said. He was leaning slightly forward, the pistol aimed directly into Morton's face. There was no tremor at all to the pistol.

Morton got down on his knees. He studied the concrete floor as if awaiting inspiration or searching for something he had lost.

Say, I'm sorry for the way I done Pettijohn all these years.

You better kill me, goddamn you. Cause if I live when I get through with you you'll need a magnifyin glass to find a greasy spot. Morton seemed to grow smaller, a more benign presence. I'm sorry for the way I done Pettijohn all these years, he said.

Say, Pettijohn ain't such a bad feller.

Oh goddamn.

Say it, by God.

Pettijohn ain't such a bad feller. Morton raised his eyes to the gun. He seemed to be looking straight down its barrel as if to divine something of eternity's pattern in the convolutions of its dark bore.

Pettijohn stood unsteadily, perhaps thinking of something else to make Morton say. He turned to study the crowd, swaying drunkenly from side to side. There's old Oneeye, he said. Accused me of stealin his shoat that time. Oneeye, say, I never stole that shoat. The pistol pivoted.

I knowed you never took that shoat that time, the man recited.

Edgewater could hear the deputies on the stairs. I thought you searched him, one said.

I thought you did. Hell, he never had no pistol before.

Morton yelled toward the stairs. You better do something about this crazy son of a bitch. You got a hell of a nerve puttin a crazy man with a pistol in with us. You better get Parnell up here.

He ain't here right now.

I wish to hell I wadn't.

Pettijohn, I'm giving you to the count of three to throw that pistol outside the cell. You don't, we're comin in after you. One.

Come on ahead then.

Two.

Pettijohn shot at the ceiling light. He missed the bulb and the bullet ricocheted off somewhere in the high ceiling.

Three.

There was silence. Pettijohn stood waiting, the pistol leveled at the top of the stairwell. He seemed not to breathe. Occasionally his eyes flickered to Morton still on his knees and back to where the deputies were going to come in after him.

Hey, Morton, Hodges called after a time.

What.

How about you and somebody else up there just jumping on him and overpowerin him? Take that pistol away from him.

Shit, Morton said in disbelief. He spat onto the concrete floor, knelt with his big hands spread on overalled knees.

Hey, Bradshaw?

I ain't qualified to do no overpowerin, Bradshaw said. You got the badge and the gun.

Hell, you're right on him there.

Forget it.

Goddamn chickenshit bunch. Hey, I could reduce ye sentence.

Not as much as this feller here with the pistol could reduce it.

Well, we can't just set here and let him wave a pistol around.

Get his old lady up here, Morton said. Maybe she can talk some sense into him.

Bring that bitch within a hundred yards of this courthouse and I start shootin whatever my eye falls on, Pettijohn said.

There was silence. Outside it had begun to rain. Concrete-muffled thunder came faintly and there was a fresh moist smell to the air. After a door clanged hollowly somewhere below and they heard voices at the foot of the stairs, undecipherable but with an undercurrent of anger. Then Hodges's voice: Lord, I don't know where he got it. He was clean when we brought him in.

Parnell's voice, authoritative, persuasive. Pettijohn, where'd you get that pistol?

It don't make no never mind where I got it, I got it.

Just what are you tryin to prove?

I ain't tryin to prove a goddamn thing. I'm just sick of you son of a bitches comin down there and draggin me out of my own house ever-time she gets a hair up her ass. She must be getting a fuckin kickback or somethin.

Well, what do you want? Parnell had not deigned show his face but his voice was resonant with assurance. A man well in command of the situation.

I want out of here and I want to see that old crazy man that cut that girl's titties off.

What?

I didn't stutter.

Lord, Pettijohn, he ain't here. They done took him on to Memphis. They givin him all kinds of tests.

Tests? What do you mean, tests?

Psychiatric tests. To see if he's crazy or not.

Crazy? You mean a son of a bitch cuts a woman's titties off and makes a pocketbook out of her snatch and you have to ship him all the way to Memphis to find out whether he's crazy or not? Shit. And lock me up for a public drunk. You son of a bitches is the one needs testin.

Pettijohn, you in enough trouble as it is. You want it worse?

That's the way I'm used to it.

Listen. If I give you my word I'll release you on your own recog-
nizance right here, tonight, will you give me that pistol and let these
fellers get some sleep?

I might think about it.

I don't want to hear about you thinking about it. I want to know if
you'll do it or not.

And you won't be right back down there after me?

I give you my word.

Well. All right then.

Parnell appeared. First his hand, then two agate eyes rising over the
railing. Satisfied he came on around the corner.

Keep your hands in sight.

There was a moment when he hesitated, you could see it in his eyes.
But he was already committed. More's the fool, he straightened his hero's shoulders and came on. He was bringing out a ring of keys the size
of a grapefruit, he was unlocking the cell door. He was not looking at
the gun, he seemed to be ignoring it in a studied kind of way. The door
was open and he was halfway across the floor when Pettijohn reneged.

Get down there beside Morton and say your prayers.

You gave me your word, Pettijohn.

It's worth about what yourn is. Don't you think I've heard you talk
out of both sides of your face? Now make your peace with God Almighty cause it's too late to do anything about this world.

Pettijohn, you'll live to regret this.

Don't you wish you would.

Hodges, you and Hinson draw his fire.

You want us to just start shootin, or what?

On them knees or I'll drop you where you stand.

You boys' badges is on the line.

Parnell got awkwardly on his knees. Some reluctant penitent. Everyone watched with interest, seemed to find a grim pleasure in Parnell's
predicament. Parnell seemed helpless. His rough-hewn face seemed
to go shapeless, the fine bone structure underpinning it to soften and
shrink. He seemed old, tired. His eyes were fixed on the floor beneath
him.

Say them.

He closed his eyes. No, he said. He seemed to be saying it to himself.

Pettijohn moved the barrel of the pistol a foot or so to the right of Parnell's head and fired. When the report slammed his ears Parnell's eyes opened wide and horrible and his entire body slackened as if the bones would not support it. His hands half arose then fluttered limberly back to the cell floor and lay there palm up, the fingers moving a little like the appendages of scorched spiders and there was a dark stain spreading out from the crotch of his knife-edge khakis.

Hell, you ain't so tough. I wisht I'd had a camera when I pulled that trigger. Ever man had a picture like that in his hip pocket he'd be a better man ever day of his life. He pulled the trigger again. This time there was a dry snap and he stood staring at the pistol in disbelief as if it had betrayed him. He snapped it four or five times in rapid succession and looked all about him nervously, his eyes slick and evasive.

Parnell was getting up dignified and ponderous and you could see life draining back into him like claret poured in crystal. There was a fierce glint to his eyes and he appeared not to notice when the two deputies crossed the cell floor taking out their blackjacks as they came.

Pettijohn threw the pistol at them and looked about for something to hide him. A rock, a church, sweet night itself. Jesus's love to appear incarnate and bathe these miscreants in its rosy glow. There was nothing. Oh, Jesus, he said.

Morton was upon him, for a moment he and Parnell stood swaying as if in dispute as to whose claim was valid. The deputies milled about them like dogs circling a fight. When Morton shoved Parnell aside Hinson hit Morton above the ear with his blackjack so that he staggered and went limberlegged for a moment but he did not let go. He stood swaying like some dancer struck deaf. The rest were closing on Pettijohn. They forced him to the darkest corner. He whimpered when his back reached the concrete. They were upon him.

Silent as sleep Edgewater and Bradshaw arose as one. Substanceless as shadow down the concrete stairwell, almost no sound down the dark steps. Two steps at a time, three. Chests tight with exhilaration. They were already out the heavy exterior door and on the street when they heard the sound of rushing feet above and behind them. A great uncoordinated stomping and running of what sounded like thousands of booted feet. The night they'd rushed into was harsh and mothflecked but when Edgewater looked up it had cleared and the sky was a great spill of stars.

Haul ass. Sounds like they all comin.

Down an alleyway Edgewater ran full tilt over a lean and startled hound foraging garbage cans and fell embracing the dog, scrambled up in a din of outraged yelping and garbage can lids clanging. And turned all about to see where was Bradshaw. A long shadow scissoring with no backward looks toward the alley's mouth. He ran after him.

They crossed an alley behind the pool hall and ran past sleeping dwellings awaking dogs from house to house in a great gamut of noise laid howl on howl until Bradshaw stopped his ears with his palms and veered through a backyard to where a scraggly stand of timber adorned a vacant lot. Slowed here where moonlight showed the way between the trees, peering back to the street where porchlights were coming on in random gradation, and somewhere, it seemed now far from them, what sounded like a scattering of pistol shots. They came out of the timber and crossed clotheslined yards and angled down a slope. There was a sawmill there, silent and still in the moonlight, a long covered shed and lumber stacked in neat piles.

Beyond the sawmill a spreading thicket of dark undergrowth drew them like a magnet. They plunged into it and ran for a long way, halted somewhere deep in the brush and lay breathing hard. Edgewater pillowed his face on the cool damp earth, felt the loam and moss against his cheek. He fancied he could hear from the core of the world spinning beneath him a heartbeat, renewed and sustained, the sound of life itself.

They came down a dry branch-run choked with shards of rotting lumber and castoff bedsprings and up a steep bank to a thin stand of sassafras through which showed pale and remote a sort of half light, a mere lessening of the dark. Caution edged them through the bracken, halted them where the timber ceased. It had clouded up again during the night and a soft drizzle fell, mute, as if the air about them was turning to liquid that misted their vision, pasted their hair lank and wet to their skulls.

The clearing opened up into a field like a pasture but there were curving ramps studded with metal speaker posts like truncated or dwarfed trees set out in soil that would not sustain them. Beyond them an enormous screen rising out of the mist on twin posts the size of telephone poles. A great blind rectangle dreaming in the fog, crystal eye sleeping

and awaiting colored visions to coalesce out of smoke and manifest themselves. In the foreground there was a stubby silver housetrailer shaped like
a cigar and a white stucco building low and square and boxlike. They sat
for a time in silence and waited. No cock crowed morning, no watchdog
announced these interlopers of the dawn.

She ain't here.

How do you know. You wrecked her car.

She had an old Chevy too. Besides, I knowed she wouldn't be here.
She's shacked up somers drunk, damn her. But I guess it's my fault. She
got used to it and now she can't do without it. You would have thought
she could of held out longer than this, though.

I don't give a shit about her sex life. Or yours either. If we're going
we ought to've been gone. I'm getting the hell out of here. You can do
whatever suits you.

Shit, Billy, now hold on a minute. I know we ort been across the
county line by daylight. But I ain't goin nowhere without my mad
money. You know what all I done for the bitch? Well, she wouldn't
hardly pay me, what I got in bed and at the table was about it. So I got
too slick for her. I sold tickets and evernown then I'd take their money
and not give em no ticket, just wave em on in. I'd pocket that. A dollar
here, five there. Change I'd squirrel away sellin hotdogs and such. A
man don't look out for hisself won't nobody else.

Where is it? She might have found it by now.

Wrapped up in meat paper in the bottom of the damn deepfreeze.
She wouldn't have thought to look there even if she'd knowed I had it.

Well, let's get it and get out of this son of a bitch. If I never see
Wayne County again it'll be a year or two too quick.

I'm about ready for a change of scenery myself.

Burst popcorn bags and crushed Coke cups. Spilt popcorn like a
patch of dirty snow. A condom draped limply across a speaker like some
arcane Piscean life, slick with the slime of primordial seas. This strange
specimen mounted here for approval. Kicking through halfpint bottles
and beercans. She's let this place go to hell already, Bradshaw said, looking about with a proprietary air.

The doors were locked but Bradshaw jimmied a window. You wait
here a minute, he told Edgewater. I know where everthing is and it'll be
quicker like that.

Quick's the way I want it. We don't know when somebody'll come
drivin up.

You can see the road good. We could make the woods.

I believe I've made the woods about my limit for this lifetime.

Bradshaw was climbing through the window. Edgewater stared toward the screen and below it to where the highway ran. He watched
with held breath a car pass from his sight. The road vacant again save
for swirling groundfog. Time passed. He wished for a cigarette, a drink,
for distance. Come on, he called into the dark interior.

Bradshaw threw out several bags of potato chips. A carton of cigarettes. Climbed out clutching under his arm a frozen package done up
in white butcher paper. Talk about ye cold cash, he snickered.

Are you ready now?

But Bradshaw was laying aside his parcels, reaching back inside the
building. With some difficulty he brought out a big black and yellow
chainsaw.

What the fuck now, Bradshaw?

Hold on now, Billy, Bradshaw said. He had set the saw down, knelt
beside and unscrewed the gas cap, inserted a finger to gauge the depth of
gas. I ain't stealin it. I just aim to borrow it a minute. He put the gas cap
back on, felt the chain for sharpness. How about totin the money?

Bradshaw arose, hefted the saw. Edgewater gathering up bags of potato chips, stuffing the carton of cigarettes inside his shirt. Nobody calls
me everthing from a chicken to a motherfucker and skates, Bradshaw
said. She's got it comin. He was striding off toward the screen.

Knowledge broke upon Edgewater like a wave of illumination. Oh
for sweet Jesus's sake, he said. He started out after Bradshaw. When he
was even with him he grabbed Bradshaw's arm. Come on, Bradshaw,
he pleaded.

Bradshaw did not pause. You just gonna have to humor me on this
one, Billy. Hell, you heard the way that slut talked to me. It won't take
but a minute.

Edgewater released him with a weary resignation and sat down on a
mounded ramp and leaned back against a speaker post. He opened a bag
of potato chips and began to eat. Bradshaw had knelt in the wet grass
near the screen and begun to crank the saw. When it started he arose
with the saw and studied the screen. Apprentice woodsman sighting

upward, studying angle of inclination, wind direction. After some de-
liberation he leant and began to saw the post, the whine of the saw loud
in the pastoral morning. Pigeons arose uncertainly from the summit
of the screen. Edgewater arose as well and retreated until he judged
himself safely out of range.

When the post was cut through the screen trembled, a great ripple
ran over the smooth white surface, the post a mainsail trembling in a
rising wind, it tilted, twisted with a great wrench of tortured wood.
Bradshaw was already hurrying toward the second post, the saw held
like a weapon. The raucous whine cutting through soft pine.

Edgewater was opening the package of money. Ripping aside the
white paper. Caught in the clear seize of ice were quarters, halfdollars,
bills of all denominations. A cornucopia of frozen money. Elation lifted
him. The world was wide, possibilities infinite for a man of means.

He looked up as the post split, running ten or twelve feet in the air,
splintering, Bradshaw leaping aside as the base kicked back. Even Edgewater was awed. The sky seemed to be shuddering. He began to gather
up his potato chips. The screen struck the ground with the force of
an explosion, crumpled, warped on itself like smoldering paper. Bradshaw was already coming at a lope, the saw abandoned, skirting the still
quivering expanse of rubble. Hot damn, he was saying. He rubbed his
hands together briskly. I wish she had two or three more. I'da made a
clean sweep.

Are you about ready?

Hell yes. Let's move it down the line.

They had run seventy-five or a hundred feet when Bradshaw suddenly stopped dead still and seemed to be considering something. I'll
be right back, he said.

What now? Edgewater wanted to know, but Bradshaw was already
in an ungainly lope back toward his pillage. Edgewater hunkered on
his knees. Weariness lay heavy on his shoulders. He lit a cigarette and
smoothed the wet hair out of his eyes. When he looked back he just
shook his head. Bradshaw had his shirtsleeve pulled down over his
hand like a mitten and he was wiping fingerprints off the chainsaw.

They came in on the back of a flatbed pickup truck, erect behind the
cab through a country of seemingly endless ascents over hills and down

a long steep grade with the old pickup's brakes smoking and slipping, as if the world was concave and they were speeding toward its center. Below them a winding creek or river cleft the landscape. When they crossed it and came out the covered bridge, the road wound up a sloping incline through scraggly pines where a rusted beer sign sprouted out of a tangled rot of kudzu. Bradshaw pointed and gestured toward the top of the hill. When Edgewater only shook his head in wordless incomprehension, he made gestures as if he were drinking an invisible bottle of something and when the rise leveled out he began to bang on the roof of the cab with his fist.

The truck eased over to the shoulder of the road and ceased across from a faded clapboard building with a high porch and they leapt unsteadily onto the roadbed. After the breeze from their motion, the air here seemed stifling. Edgewater could smell the pines, hot and astringent.

We thank ye til ye better paid, Bradshaw told the truck driver. You ort to come in and have a cold un with us.

The wizened old man just shook his head and raised one tentative hand in a gesture of goodbye, dismissal. The truck rolled away.

We ought to stayed with him as far as he was going.

Hell, Billy, we ain't ten mile from home. And I been spittin cotton across the last three counties.

They stood unsteadily, legs not adjusted to firm earth after the slewing truck bed. Sailor's legs so far from the sea. Squinting against a sun brutal off the white graveled parking lot and blinding off the decks of two cars parked there they crossed to the porch where canebottom chairs were aligned and inside to a cavernous coolness, to an amalgamation of smells. The sour winy smell of beer and the smell of old hot pine leaking from the floor and a residual smell of sweat and time.

The barkeep was a big scarred man who did not greet Bradshaw as if he were a long lost brother or a hero returning from the wars. In fact he stood regarding these two as if they might be the avatars of some bad news not yet in sight. He laid his magazine aside and watched them cross the marred dance floor, Bradshaw executing a little buck-and-wing as he came, solitary heel and toe to a silent jukebox.

I'm back, Swalls, he said. Get out the beer and lock up ye daughters.

Young Bradshaw, Swalls said, without affection or surprise. I thought maybe I'd never see your like again.

Give us two cold ones here.

Swalls was waiting to see was there money forthcoming. I believe I got a little ticket on you here from before you left.

Hell, I thought I paid that. He was digging in his pocket, dragging out a tortured-looking bill, spreading it flat on the bar, the reassuring face of U.S. Grant. Take it out of this and you still ain't give us them cold ones.

Swalls set out two cold bottles and took up the bill, studied it in better light as if to discover there marks of inept engraving.

Goblin's Knob's the meanest honkytonk in three counties, Bradshaw was saying. He drank down half his beer, sighed deeply. These old boys come off a Beech Creek and everwhere around here and you talk about tough. They bust each other with chairs just to warm up and then they set in about nine o'clock and just teetotally demolish this son of a bitch. Swalls had to get him a set of prints drawed up so he could get her back together on Sunday mornin.

Seems like I remember you sayin if you ever looked at this place again it'd be through the windshield of a Cadillac.

Well hell, Bradshaw said, taken aback for a moment. Well shit, I had to leave it out in the yard. You don't think I could drive a big thing like that through that pisspoor excuse for a door you got, do you?

Swalls made change from a sack with a drawstring top, aligning the money carefully on the bar, coins atop. Boxes of merchandise behind him cloned in the mirror where they hunched like revenants guarding their provender. Goody's headache powder. The cure may be bought where the disease contracted. In the mirror Bradshaw and Edgewater reflected darkly, washed up here like refugees or derelicts. In the lethargic air from a fan, a yardlong strip of flypaper black with flies rotated like some perverse carnival ride in miniature. A jar of pickled sausages, phalli in cloudy vitriolic fluid.

The day began to wane. The western window went red and then a pale rose, stained glass in this house of the unsaved. A cool blue shade lay on the east. They drank beer and Swalls went back to his magazine, abandoning it only for sorties to the beer cooler.

After a while a man came in looking all about him as if deadfalls lay in wait. A thin face shadowed by a greasy duckbill cap. A face curiously androgynous, aesthete. The eyes were skittish, nervous, as if something were continually in pursuit of him and he could not tarry long. He was carrying a crokersack bound with wire and when he perched on a stool he sat the bag by his side and stopped it with his foot as if it might escape or someone might take it from him and Edgewater thought he detected motion there, a convulsive movement of the burlap.

Give me a Sterlin, Swalls.

Swalls was not to be had so easily; he made no move toward the cooler. I might think about sellin you one, he said.

The man was going through his pockets one by one, as if he'd forgotten which contained his money. He was wearing an old outsize coat in this heat and he fetched up from the side pocket with triumph a handful of dried roots and blew the dust off them and laid them with care on the countertop. He began to separate them, fondling them, a miser at his coins. I got a little sang here.

Hellfire, Arnold. I told you time and again this ain't no tradin post. Next thing you'll be bringin in mayapple and scrapiron and God knows what all. What I wanted was just a little cash business here. You know, money. You've heard of money?

Arnold returned the ginseng reluctantly to his pockets. Shitfire, he said. Swalls seemed to forget him. He plugged the electric beer sign in and a rectangular vision of nature came on. Canoes on an electric river, blue water suggestive of depth. Mountains beyond, a harsh and fathomless sky. Arnold watched fascinated. A campfire flickered on the shore and fishermen oared the canoe toward the void at the picture's edge.

I'll pay you Saturday.

Swalls was solicitous. I'll tell you what I'll do, Arnold. I'm startin up what I call a layaway plan, I'll let you come around here to the cooler and pick out whichever one you want. I'll write your name on a little piece of tape and put it around the neck and set it off in the corner by itself. I won't sell it to nobody else, it'll be yourn. Then when you come in Saturday and pay me I'll give it to you. How does that sound to you?

Arnold took up his crokersack, came off the stool. It sounds like so much horseshit to me, he said. I reckon I'll take my business elsewhere.

Bradshaw had been taking all this in. What you got in the sack, Arnold?

A bullsnake.

A bullsnake? Let me see. What the hell are you doing with a bull-snake?

I just caught it. It was the biggest one I ever seen and I figured I might scout up some use for it. Maybe sell it to the fair when it comes through. He was unwiring the top, Bradshaw and Edgewater off their stools now, inside the bag they witnessed a vision offered up of ancient evil, scaly piebald skin dusted incongruously with meal or grain. Coils moving ceaselessly on themselves, lidless serpent's eyes implacable and old as time. Some medium other than flesh here perhaps, the means by which nightmares are made carnate.

Jesus. It looks just like a copperhead.

They favor some but it's a bullsnake all right. It blowed and swole up big as the calf of ye leg when I'se catchin im. I like to never got him in that sack.

How big is he?

Lord, I don't know. He was longern a hoe handle but I didn't have nothin to measure the hoe handle with.

By now Bradshaw had drunk five or six beers and perhaps he had divined a use for the snake. What'll you take for him?

I don't know. What'd you give?

Bradshaw was figuring. I might give a sixpack.

A case?

Shit. A case? I may be drunk but I ain't crazy yet.

I'll take twelve beer and you can do what you want with him.

Swalls, set him up twelve beers there.

Swalls was separating one poke from a stack. Did you want to take them with you? he asked hopefully.

I ain't goin nowhere just yet. Open em and set em up on the counter where I can reach em easy and we won't lose count of em.

Swalls began to open bottles and align them before Arnold. Arnold's eyes had a dreamy, faraway look to them. His dry lips moved as he counted the bottles. Swalls was at subtracting from the dwindling pile of money. You let that son of a bitch loose in here and me and you goin round and round, he told Bradshaw.

Bradshaw looked at him innocently. Hell, I wadn't goin to turn him loose. I just aim to have some fun with it. You never can tell when a situation'll turn up where a snake'll come in handy. He was rewiring the crokersack, stowing it between his feet. Possessive about it, a pet perhaps. He might teach it tricks.

Lord that's good all the way down, Arnold said, wiping a mustache of foam off his upper lip. I do believe Swalls sets out the best beer in this part of the country.

I just get it off the beer truck, Swalls said disgustedly. I don't bottle it myself in the backroom. I ain't got the recipe for it.

Edgewater went out back. There was an outhouse but he walked past it into the pines over a carpet of copper needles. He looked up. The pines moved gracefully in some wind that never touched the surface of the earth. Beyond their dark tops the sky was deep and limitless and he felt momentarily alone. More akin to the hawks that wheeled against the blue void as if determined to leave there marks of their passage, he felt adrift in distance, all destinations awash in a sea of miles. All points of the compass equidistant, himself slightly drunk at the exact center of the world. He buttoned his pants and went back out of the pines.

There was a man and a woman ascending the steps to the Knob and a pickup with an enormous set of bullhorns mounted on the hood sitting in the parking lot. Edgewater followed the pair in. The man was heavyset and unshaven and he wore shapeless dirty overalls. His face was florid as if he dwelt perpetually in some state of banked rage. His eyes were shrewd and small and not unlike holes chiseled into some chaotic darkness that seethed behind the mask he wore for the world to see. He moved with an inherent arrogance as if whatever was in his way would move before he reached it. The woman clutched his arm as if he were holding her afloat in perilous waters. She was younger than he was and heavily made up, eyebrows shaved off and then penciled back on in an expression of arch surprise, as if the world was constantly coming up with new toys to amuse her. She stood unsteadily, swaying slightly as if drunk or deranged with the heat.

The man took a leather billfold out of his hip pocket and extracted a bill from it. Sack us up about half a case, he told Swalls. He looked all about, small eyes blinking in the gloom. What say, Bradshaw?

What do ye know.

I thought you's out west somers shittin in tall cotton.

Bradshaw did not reply. He returned to his beer, stared into the mirror past the upraised amber of his bottle. The mirror gave the room an illusion of spaciousness, himself reflected small and blond at its center.

Take it out of this here. Me and Freda headin down to Lexington tonight.

We goin all the way to Lexington just to eat fish, Freda told Swalls.

You may start out eatin fish, the man said and winked at Swalls. You liable to wind up with something else in your mouth, you don't watch me.

She laughed, a sound harsh as splintered glass. She smiled at Edgewater and Bradshaw, a scarlet vacuous smile such as a celebrity might bestow upon an adoring public or flashing cameras. Hush your nasty mouth, she said, swinging on his arm.

Hold my change for me, Swalls. I got to step out back a minute. He disengaged himself from the woman and took up one of the beers and went out. She stood for a moment as if lost or set adrift. She looked around and crossed the floor to the jukebox and leaned against it as if she drew sustenance from the cool blue neon within. She fumbled coins from out a purse, dropped them, punched buttons.

That's as lowbred a son of a bitch as ever shit between shoeleather, Bradshaw said into Edgewater's ear.

The jukebox began to sing to them, a country blues. Lessons learned the hard way. *Just a deck of cards and a jug of wine,* it cautioned, *and a woman's lies make a life like mine.*

Who? That man with her?

Yeah. D.L. Harkness.

Well I'm a son of a bitch.

What? Do you know him?

No, but I run up with a feller that did. Roosterfish Lipscomb.

Goddamn, old Roosterfish. I didn't know you knowed him. What's that crazy old shit up to?

It's been a while since I've seen him.

That cocksucker Harkness and me got into it one time. Right after my uncle died. Son of a bitch can't leave a widderwoman alone. Come suckin around there and I finally had to run him off. Some man dies and he beats the shittin hearse to the house. Bradshaw fell to studying the crokersack. Goddamn, he said. Wait here a minute, Billy. I'll be right back. He arose with the sack.

Swalls stayed him with his voice. Bradshaw, you start him up to where I have to whup him and I'll fall right in on you.

Bradshaw was all injured innocence. Arnold and Edgewater turned to watch him go. The woman was lost in deep study of the jukebox. Bradshaw raised a disparaging hand to Swalls in dismissal. The screen door slapped and Swalls shook his head disgustedly.

Bradshaw was back in and seated before Harkness returned. Harkness drained his bottle and set it on the bar and pocketed his change without counting it and took up the sacked beer. Let's go, he called to the woman.

Edgewater studied him. He could see nothing about Harkness that would cause women to cast aside home and hearth and follow him. Yet there seemed something elemental about him, as if all the layers of convention had been peeled away leaving nothing save the need for procreation and violence.

When they were outside and their footfalls fading Bradshaw arose. Billy, you and Arnold come out here a minute. I want you to see this here.

They went out and seated themselves in the canebottom chairs. In the parking lot Harkness had the woman by the arm and seemed to be helping her into the truck. They seemed to be doing some curious dance, feet shuffling on the little white gravel.

A deep blue dusk lay slanted on the land. Beyond the high porches, a descending wall of pines fell away and across their tops. Edgewater could see distant hollows where shadows accrued mauve and still and from them mist rose like smoke from faults in the earth. He wondered if people dwelt in these hollows. What secrets troubled their pillowed heads. A long and empty road wound in and out of his vision.

The truck cranked and wheeled around to turn. It started forward and went fifteen or twenty feet and suddenly the brake lights came on and it abruptly rocked to a halt and the door on the driver's side sprang open. Harkness leapt out with the woman clinging to his back as if she were riding him. He had her arms wrapped about his neck and her legs entwining his waist like some succubus he was fleeing and she was babbling incoherently. Harkness ran a few steps then halted, dancing jerkily trying to shake her off. She slid down and set spraddlelegged in the gravel holding him by his feet and Harkness was jerking an enormous pistol from the shapeless fold of his overalls. She was crying and pointing at the truck and she turned a wild face on Edgewater and Bradshaw. Snake snake snake, she seemed to be saying. Big goddamned snake in there. Harkness fired into the interior of the truck and they could hear glass break.

Jesus, Edgewater said. He arose and seemed to be seeking some sort of shelter.

The snake came writhing out and dropped from the running board, moved in smooth undulations toward the pinewoods. Harkness shot at it three or four times and they could hear the bullets whining off the rocks and see little puffs of dust and gravel rising as if the ground the snake fled across was mined. Harkness ceased and began peering cautiously into the truck should the serpent have brothers there or reinforcements.

Bradshaw had slid out of his chair and he lay on his back on the rough board floor. He was holding his sides and his face was congested with laughter. Harkness had the gun aloft and he ran up the steps to where he lay as if to see had a stray bullet struck him.

Who put that fuckin snake in my truck? His face was enraged and his eyes rolling wildly and there was no slack at all left in the trigger of the pistol. Did you do it?

Bradshaw was shaking his head wordlessly from side to side and he seemed to be trying to stop laughing. He brought his face under momentary control but when he saw Freda crawling drunkenly about the ground his face twisted and he lay back weakly and went back to shaking his head.

Crazy hillbilly son of a bitch, Harkness said. Couldn't get any sense out of ye with a can opener. If I knowed you done it I'd shoot off ever one of your toes. He raised the gun and glanced one sharp glance at Edgewater and at Swalls's dark bulk behind the screen.

Bradshaw stopped laughing. Hell, she was in there with us. Ask her if I done it.

Harkness pocketed the gun. I doubt she knows she's in the world, he said. He turned and descended the steps. When he was in the parking lot he leaned down and jerked her to her feet. They got into the truck without looking again toward the Knob and drove away.

Fine lot of friends I got, Bradshaw said. You'da stood right there and watched that big son of a bitch rip off my arms and legs and not lifted a finger to help me.

When Swalls made no reply Bradshaw continued. Edgewater here's my buddy. I run up with him in Wayne County and he saved my life. Or my ass. We been traveling together since then.

Swalls glanced once at Edgewater who was staring at the bar as if in distraction. Edgewater's eyes were blank and black as onyx and nothing showed there but his glare. Swalls evinced no other interest in Bradshaw's life, or ass, saved or otherwise.

Bradshaw finished his beer, slid the bottle back as if in some gesture of finality and arose. Well, drink up and let's get on. We might catch a ride on home.

I'll just wait. I got to get on.

Git on where? Bradshaw mocked him. Hell, you promised you'd stay awhile on the farm. I want you to meet my folks.

After a time Edgewater shrugged and arose, as if one choice were the same as another, all roads the same in the end. He followed Bradshaw toward the door. Halfway there Swalls cleared his throat.

I guess you heard they buried your daddy last fall.

For an instant Bradshaw's face went blank as if he had momentarily forgotten where he was and his face faltered, a step left half completed. Then he grinned tightly, eyes slick as muddy stones.

I heard it on the radio.

Late of any afternoon you might see him at his rounds. Down off the curving declensions of Rocky Hill in the pickup with the bullhorns, some gross and boastful advertisement for himself, as if the truck itself was resultant from some mythical coupling of flesh and chrome. Down Three Mile Pike and across the river to the Knob or perhaps to Early McKnight's for a halfpint or a quart of homebrew and a laugh or two with the boys. He might rock awhile on Early's porch with miscreants of lesser light than himself while dusk fell and tell his lies and listen with scant attention to theirs but he was always abstracted, seemed as if he were straining toward some sound he could not quite hear.

Then down the line with the quart of homebrew between his legs and the miles of graveled road slewing away and the night coming as if the truck had left some land of daylight and was nearing regions perpetually in darkness.

From their porches men might watch the truck pass and spit and say, There the son of a bitch goes.

Harkness was wedgeshaped from the shoulder down but was an inverted wedge as if he'd momentarily softened and gravity had reshaped him with a wider stomach and hips.

McKnight mused, His ass got built up that way from totin that heavy pocketbook. He likes to shoot folks but what he likes bettern than that is cuttin em with a pocketknife and what he likes best of all is screwin them. He one of those fellers that gets away with everything, nothing don't touch him. He could slide through hell and never even singe his hair.

And another: Yeah. D.L. thinks ever night is Saturday night.

There was about him the proportion of myth, legend. This was told on McKnight's front porch: Talkin about D.L., you member that airplane he had? It's the only plane ever was around this town. He got it somers when he come back here after the war. Mighta gambled and got it like he did that sawmill. He was always wild. Anyhow, he could fly it. He had all that ground dozed off there behind his house where he could take off in it and if he come in at night his old lady used to go out there and park and shine the car lights cross that field so he could land.

Him and two more was up there one day drinkin and foolin around. You know how crazy he is. They was down on the Tennessee River flying under bridges and such foolishness as that and just kept getting drunker all the time. Come night they headed back. They got nearly home and D.L. radioed his old lady to get out there and get them lights on. He got where he thought he was home and seen a pair of car lights shinin. All it was, some coonhunters or somebody courting out in the woods but D.L. was drunk and he said, There she is, boys. Less set her down. Well sir, he set her down right out in the damn woods and they was tree limbs warpin em and all that and Bellwether, he was the sheriff then, he went out and investigated and he said they wadn't a piece of that airplane you couldn't have toted off in a shoebox and he said Harkness and them was a hanging in the trees like varmints. You know it tore that airplane into scrapiron and never killed a one of them drunk sons of bitches.

He owned a warren of mudcrept houses in Sycamore Center and his destination might lie there. The rents might be due, some were better collected at night. A bathrobed housewife might meet him at the door, a door opening out of musty darkness, onto another kind of darkness, a balmy summer dusk studded with porch lights and fireflies. A husband on the nightshift perhaps, who knew. She on the nightshift herself. Come in, Mr. Harkness. He owned the house, he needed no invitation, he was already in.

Watching the blackness roll by the windshield, the night would become a corporeal medium he moved through, the bullhorns splitting it into quadrants that sped below, above, to the right and left, a swimming amalgamation of trees and houses and empty stretches of silent pinewoods where a deer might whirl and vanish or buzzards rise reluctantly from their feeding and wheel away into the dark but all the while the wheels kept turning, the horns kept separating the night, he drove toward a point where the last of the eventide might go by in tattered shards like windtorn crepepaper and hot incandescence break upon him in a wave and consume him.

No less a predator than the foxes that turned away from his head-lamps, eyes orange as firecoals, no less an endangered species.

Behind the windshield his face, latticed by the night, and in the lights of cars he met his face was devoid of expression, the mouth slack and wet, glossy satyr's eyes slightly protuberant, the face changing only when he smoked and drank from the bottle he clasped loosely with his right hand while he drove.

Perhaps he had some subliminal instinct, vestige of other cultures, other times. He seemed to scent out availability in a woman the way a dog can scent impending death. Availability seemed his only criterion. They all fell his way, the young, the old, the maimed. The pretty, the disfigured alike. Pussy's pussy if it's hung on a dog, he liked to say in those days. There was about him a quality of true democracy, the dusky sisters below the railroad tracks were not deprived of his favors. Some compulsion moved him. Something that put him down these roads at dusk toward whoever waited, whether he knew it or not. As if the entering of another's body gave him renewal, some power over others, replenished whatever wells of arrogance he drew upon, the swagger that propelled him from one point to the other.

He seemed to know when a rift appeared in a marriage, was not averse to putting it there himself. It was said in half believing wonder that he could tell when a woman was going to be widowed, before she knew it or the doctor knew it or the undertaker even suspected. That when the event transpired he would be there cap in hand, offering his own peculiar brand of condolences to the bereft.

He was a backdoor man, a through the window in the dark man, a braggart, the man who crawled into your still-warm covers when you went to work in the morning.

It was told about Flatwoods what he did to Freda. The tone of discussion was awed disgust, save when Harkness did the telling; he did most of the talking himself.

I was on her screwin and she was just layin there like she'd dropped off to sleep or was tryin to remember the recipe for Aunt Myrtle's pickle relish and I said, Goddamn your soul to hell. Here I done laid out seventy-five cents for you a fish dinner and Christ hisself couldn't of kept a tally on the beer bottles, and you got the nerve to put such as this on me. I'se about drunk or I wouldn't of done it. But the pistol was layin right there in the floorboard and I thought, by God, no other man won't get stuck with no such sorry pussy as this is.

Two or three men straggled off in disgust but Harkness was oblivious. He went on with his tale.

I tried to shoot her right in the pussy but I missed and got her there in the leg. If they's ever anything done about it and I have to go to court about it I'll tell the judge, Hell, it was self defense. She had one of these here snappin pussies and it come at me in the dark and it was me or it.

People waited for father or brother to come out of the woodwork and annihilate Harkness but no such appeared. She had come from nowhere, to nowhere was relegated. When she got out of the hospital, she boarded a bus with her suitcase and the box she carried her blond wig in and she was gone.

People said: Somebody'll kill him one of these days. But nobody did. Everybody knew he carried a knife and that he did not mind using it. In time it came to seem that he was kept alive by sheer professionalism, by mastery of what everyone had come to think of as his craft.

The odors and sound of the dark were ordered senses of her existence and from where she lay on the screened-in back porch she isolated them one by one as if that would entice sleep. This summer she preferred the porch. Here the night was fecund with scents of summer; here was the antithesis of death, a steady and tireless wall of sound from cicadas and crickets, the heavy sounds of insects and bats thwarted by the screens, the lush sweetness of honeysuckle and hyacinth. This summer she felt kinship with a world rampant with life.

Inside, her mother slept in a chaste medicinal darkness, in a smothering claustrophobic room that she thought had taken on the characteristics of her mother, so much that it stifled her, she could not breathe there: or perhaps the person she had already begun to think of as a half-mad old woman lay in taut sweaty silence, awaiting the touch of murderers and rapists, straining to hear footfalls where no footfalls ought to be. Sudy herself bait, guarding the old woman's sanctity. Rapists might pause here on the porch first and, satiated, proceed no further.

After a time there was the first sound that broke the ordered pattern of her nights: a car engine that grew louder and coughed and ceased on the highroad. She half rose from the cot. It's Bobby, she thought, but it did not sound like his car. Perhaps he'd traded. Then voices came, disjointed and fragmented like voices in a dream or voices the mind conjures the ear into hearing. Raucous laughter the balmy wind brought down pointless and sourceless, the laughter of fools or drunks or both.

She arose and wrapped the sheet about herself and walked barefoot to the edge of the porch. Moonlight fell silvery and bright, the moon itself close and full, lowering itself onto the world, a sinister beauty. The night was a carved relief in black and silver, dark trees with their tenants of whippoorwills and owls seemed secretive and imbued with meaning she knew but could not articulate. Beyond them the rising hills and fields were a luminescent tapestry tending away to nothingness, a world profoundly of the night.

All soundless in virginal white she went nunlike, a wraith fleeing through high dewy grass. In the summertime she could not see the road from here. Had it been winter and the trees sere, there was a banked curve from which she could watch the road's traffic accomplish itself, but now lush greenery blocked from her vision even of the old road, which was below the highroad and was just a healing scar going to sumac and sassafras. She crossed the yard to the old springhouse and turned there following the branch tiptoeing delicately over slick rocks through watercress and mint with the babbling of the brook overlaying the unfocused voices. In the night her face was as ovoid and white and featureless as the moon, seemed touched as well by a refracted luminescence.

She crouched beneath the branches of a walnut tree, felt the rough bark of the bole through the sheet; she was naked beneath it. Above her something moved evasive and covert in the branches, she could smell the astringent odor of walnuts. The voices separated themselves, gained clarity.

She recognized with something of shock the voice of her brother. A bitter twist of disappointment, as if he had betrayed her, visited her with evil, or heard of wrongs done and come to avenge them.

The year she turned seventeen Sudy watched spring come with a feeling she'd never known, a heightened awareness of the world's awakening: trees budding and tiny wildflowers pushing through last winter's wind raked leaves and time seemed to slow and spring came so immutable and infinitesimally slow that she became aware of each unfolding leaf, aware simultaneously of life rising in her body like sap, so that it seemed she had never been alive, was being born now as well: all the life that preceded it was one vast uneventful day seventeen years long. All the things that mattered happened that spring; she had always been a good girl, quiet, they said, never a word out of her all these years and they did not know what to say to her, were completely unprepared. All they had for weapons were threats and silence and they were not enough.

You won't let him come to see me, she told her father. You let Buddy lay drunk and drive up in the yard with his whores and come in and get blankets and...

He'd slapped her hard and for the first time she tasted the blood from her burst lip and that had seemed slow and drawn out as well, the red face and the hand coming so slow she could have dodged but didn't and her hair sprang out and the incision of minute capillaries brought the warm salty rush of blood.

That spring Bobby Yates had an old black station wagon with the seats out of the back and he would get to the top of the hill and cut the switch and lights and coast off the main road to the old grownover skeleton of a trail left from when the wagonroad ran below the highroad and she would meet him.

All those balmy spring nights she'd come out soundless with her shoes in her hand and move fleet and spectral through the wall of awakening sounds and past the incessant call of frogs from the springhouse and sit beside the cracked faulted chert till he came. It was another world at night, a world she'd slept through, had never known existed. By moonlight the wildflowers looked fragile and of wondrous delicacy, tiny harebells and roosterfights and bluebells that looked as if they thrived as she did on the silver light of the moon, as if the merciless glare of the sun would sear them away.

He was above her and inside her when they'd heard the first sound and they'd thought it a dog or fox but it intensified and they looked just as the cudgel struck the side of the station wagon and the glass went. The door opened and her father's face was nigh unrecognizable, he could not find room to raise the stick and he was jabbing with it wildly as if it were a frog gig or a spear. Bobby was swearing and sliding across her body and then her face and out the back and around and for a moment father and swain stood locked and swaying with the stick clasped between them like figures from her nightmares given corporeality by some dark magic: then her father stopped and stood very still as if he'd heard someone speak his name and he was waiting to hear it again. He made some incoherent sound and fell and when they knelt beside him his face was already blue, a dead face watching up at them from the patch of violets he'd fallen in.

God Almighty damn, Bobby said. He was holding the stick. They'll say I done it, he said. He threw the stick as far as he could and climbed behind the wheel of the station wagon then had to get out and push with a shoulder to overcome its inertia and leap back in when it began to gain speed down the slope, going black and soundless and hearselike through and under the gray and silver branches overhanging it and it as well somehow spectral, a prop made carnate from a madman's dreams.

Bobby? She ran a few steps and the engine coughed and bucked and the lights came on and it seemed to vault into the night. She went back and stood there above her father and looking down she saw with horror that she was naked, that he had carried her clothes with him when he'd gone.

An old car lusterless even in the strong moonlight, a flat worn black that seemed to draw light to it rather than reflect it. The doors were sprung open but there was not light inside either. Then they got out. There were three of them, her brother and two men she did not know.

Drunk, she expected. Lacquered so with shadow they seemed somehow
sinister, a cabal of warlocks paused to plot some vague evil, fallen upon
the land under cover of darkness: a car passed and they all turned alike
to watch its lights and she thought, Oh no, it's Bobby, but it went on,
lights yawning among the willows, wheels sliding in the gravel, cutout
throbbing fullthroated when it reached the straight, the pitch of the
engine rising as if the night held something it was fleeing. As if the night
ahead was any better.

The tall boy walked toward her, paused at the road's edge, fumbled
with his trousers. A silent silver arc into the dark weeds. She shifted
her weight, turned into deeper shadows of the walnut as if to avoid
his eyes. Dew was soaking through the sheet, she came aware of her
nakedness beneath it. She opened the sheet to the night air, she could
feel it drying the perspiration, feel her skin tightening. She looked back
toward the road and the man had finished, turned back to where the
car was parked.

Oh Lord, they'll wake up Mama, she said to herself. For the one
with the cap had withdrawn a guitar from the backseat and had begun
beating on it, a tuneless frailing devoid of rhythm or melody or anything vaguely musical, just a dissonant and out-of-tune pounding he
began to sing over. It seemed curiously as if the song and its accompani-
ment were unrelated or were performed by different people to different
songs. It went on and on, a rambling obscene song that seemed to have
endless verses. Her brother Buddy began to sing with him; she only half
listened, for she was thinking, He died right over there, in the weeds,
and Buddy singing some nasty song right there where it happened.
Then she thought: Why he don't even know. It looked like somebody
would have told him, Buddy had his arm about the man's shoulder and
their voices grew louder and less restrained. She sat bemused listening
to the song's progression.

The third man was lying on the turtledeck of the car, an arm thrown
across his face. He did not appear to be listening to the song or to be
doing anything at all. He seemed apart from them. Perhaps a hitchhiker
they'd give a ride to, waiting with patience for them to take him wherever it was he was going. He was still, he might be sleeping.

The song ended on the socially redeeming note that V.D. inevitably
followed illicit dalliance and they began another but could not remem-

ber the words, trembled away, voices and guitar ceasing tremulously in dissonance.

The man in the longbilled cap was putting away the guitar, Buddy asking: You reckon Harkness got him any of that? And the man collapsing in laughter and saying, If he did I bet he'd found him a cherry. Settin on that snake probably drawed it up tightern a buttonhole, and she thought what on earth, are they crazy?

She sat so for a long time listening to their obscene banter, their pointless and drunken memories paraded for her, mute audience to a dumb show of the damned, as if they were familiars she'd conjured for her entertainment by occult rite: while the night slid its weary way homeward, while the moon hung poised over the Cimmerian horizon and then settled onto it, partly obscured as if the jagged branches were drawing off the light from it and leaving it in darkness, invisible, a thing of remembrance only. A dead and fabled world.

Bradshaw's face twisted momentarily, tears stung his eyes, his face ravaged by a grief Edgewater would not have thought him capable of. Perhaps some phantom out of his childhood had touched him, brief gentleness he'd forgotten or let pass unrecognized. He turned away from the table, wiped his eyes with his sleeve.

How come nobody got word to me?

The old woman turned from the stove where she was frying meat. How? she asked bitterly.

Bradshaw had no answer, just wordlessly shook his head.

There was a sliding window above the table and through its moted glass light fell on a worn oilcloth, a red and white checkered maze that shimmered hypnotically, a geometric pattern that would draw Edgewater into it. He looked away, past gauzy motionless curtains to where the yard ended not by any cessation of grass but by three strands of barbed wire beyond which a belled cow grazed, its bell echoing its movements like some encoded message for the blind. There were jays calling from somewhere past the perimeter of the visible world and the cries of crows from a near cornfield.

When did you get in? She was forking up bacon from popping grease.

We got off the bus in Ackerman's Field this morning. Run up with old Arnold in town and he brought us up to the road.

Edgewater smiled at his lies while studying the girl minutely, from long habit, as if to commit to memory every detail of her he might ever need: what might be used, what discarded. She sat across from him at the table, sipping coffee from a blue cup. Her face looked sleeprobbed, as if she had been instantly transposed from sleep to here. Her blond hair was tousled, she had an old white bathrobe wrapped about her. He thought her face a trifle too round, but the skin was smooth as fired pottery, a pale glaze unpored or blemished and the blue eyes looked serene, untouched. Innocent. Deep wells blue with distance, remote, fabled repositories for such innocence as remained in the world.

I kept hearin somebody up on that old roadbed last night, Sudy said. She stared into the steaming coffee.

Likely that Yates still sniffin around after you, Bradshaw said, unperturbed. Now that I'm back all that mess'll be straightened out.

It wasn't Bobby, I know his car.

I expect you do.

Whoever it was they was cussin and carryin on something awful. She stared out the window, the blue rim of the cup hiding her mouth. An orange butterfly fluttered against the window screen, a fragile and shimmering iridescence.

The woman dished up bacon and eggs, fried potatoes. Well, you're back anyhow. Say you got laid off?

He was slicing up his eggs. The company I worked for went out of business, he said. Me and Billy heard of this job down by Chattanooga. They hirin up there and payin good money. We headed that way. I didn't think about him bein dead.

Him? the girl asked. He was your daddy. Can't you call your father nothing but him?

Your place is here with us, the old woman said. Not traipsing up and down the highway. There's work enough on this place, and always has been, if you'd but do it.

Lord, it's been a long road back here. Nothin but trouble.

You can write, can't you? the girl asked. They're still deliverin the mail, anyway the last I heard.

He ignored her.

Edgewater ate abstractedly; he had heard it all before, in versions better than this one. It was taking on the fabric of myth, of fable. The woman was studying him, eyes limpid and pale behind the glasses, bitter, as if all the world's sorrows trickled down and pooled here. She glanced away as if she sensed in Edgewater things she did not want to know, sensed a predator in him, would have none of him.

As soon as he saw the old woman start across the field he began searching for the keys but he could not find them. She must have had them on her. Bradshaw did not let it deter him. There was an old rusty crowbar in the toolshed and he hooked it behind the hinges one after the other and just tore the door off.

Well ain't that sweet?

The Chevrolet gleamed richly with wax that had been buffed to a mirrorlike finish, the chrome had been cleaned and polished and even the white sidewalls had been scrubbed.

They walked into the shed, admiring the lustrous black car. The shed was barely big enough to accommodate it and they were scrouged between it and the walls. Bradshaw could not get over it. What'd make her do a thing like that? he kept asking. Why it looks like a brand new one. Even the inside was scrupulously clean and the upholstery smelled rich and pristine. Locked so in the shed the car had sat like a shrine, a monument. These two like covert desecrators ransacking the past, the fallen door some laboriously plundered tomb entrance.

Bradshaw checked the oil and held the dipstick to better light and squinted at it. Look at that. She's even had the oil changed. I bet she's had it greased and everthing. Won't we knock em dead, Billy? Is this transportation or not?

A shadow passed across them and Bradshaw started but it was only the girl standing there watching them. The sun was bright in her hair and her face was grieved and cynical.

You may as well get it out of your head, she told Bradshaw. She won't let nobody drive this car. I ain't even been to town since Daddy died.

Is she crazy? How do you get grocers and stuff brought out?

She calls and they send a cab. Mrs. Epley and them comes on Sunday and takes her to church. The girl had come in between them and from the polished trunkdeck their dwarfed reflections watched back at them, a triad of conspirators.

Bradshaw's eyes were thoughtful. A man's got to have a way to work, he said.

She sat rocking in silence while Bradshaw held forth, spinning lies, regaling her and Sudy with their exploits, his long legs cocked against a porch support, while crickets and whippoorwills called a dreamer's chorus from the honeysuckle dark.

I'se down in Lubbock. That's in Texas. I'se in a pool game there, shooting pill with two slickers that thought they had me boxed in. One of em was hooking me, or thought he was, and the other one was settin his buddy up ever time. I just smiled to myself. I was hustling them and they was hustling me. I let em win the first game and then I won four in a row.

The old woman, who had little if any idea what he was talking about, rocked with her eyes closed, and Edgewater divined that she was not hearing words, she was hearing just his voice, a chant, a litany, a murmur of water a long way off, a mariner gone long without water. The hard old eyes opened, glanced at him, then flickered into the dark beyond the porch past him as if he did not exist, as if there were something in the humid dark only she was privy to.

We's playin for twenty dollars and in the sixth game I had it sewed up and one of em raked the thirteen ball on me. I just happened to see him out of the corner of my eye. I throwed my stick down and told him to pay me. He got real innocent on me, said he made the thirteen ball and the other one backed him up. They was goodsized men and they knew they had me in a pinch. They was both laughin, they aimed to get my twenty and all I'd won besides. Then I seen this feller here sittin on a bench there watchin us, not sayin anything.

The girl's eyes, blue and wondering in her soft face, flickered from Bradshaw's face to Edgewater's. He felt that the girl worshiped her brother, wondered from force of habit if there was anything to play on, anything here to work to his advantage. He listened to the spurious animated story without interest.

Edgewater was just sittin there. I said, What about it, buddy? Did he make that ball or not? I fully figured he'd say he didn't know. Anybody would just say they weren't payin no attention or something. But not this feller. The fat one raked it in the side pocket, he said, and we all went at it. That was some fight. They finally called the law and me and Edgewater like to slept in the Crowbar Hotel that night.

The old woman might have been asleep. Her face in the moonlight was angular even in repose, Edgewater thought absently. The skin brown and wrinkled as old leather, the cheekbones high and flinty, not as old as she looked. Listening or not listening to this droning voice with an expression that old griefs had carved as infinitesimally weather carves stone. One grief more or less no more to her than one more rain was to granite.

They would of beat me to death if it hadn't been for Edgewater. Hell, they'da had to get my money.

The old woman roused herself, spat snuff into a coffee can. If you'd not been in such a place as that you wouldn'ta had it to worry about. Them that goes in there can just expect it and you wasn't raised to cuss like that, neither. Your daddy learnt you long ago Jesus saved you, she said to Bradshaw. You old enough to know that, whether you do or not.

I reckon he must have stepped out for a minute then, Bradshaw said. Edgewater was the only one come off the bench.

She pushed herself up by the arms of the rocker, went into the dark house.

Mama's getting old, the girl said softly after a time, as if this were some apology she offered Edgewater. She ain't the same since Daddy died.

Edgewater felt vaguely used, knew that Bradshaw felt no emotion with this knowledge and was using his presence to abate their emotions, knew if he had not been there there would have been a tearful reunion, a dredging up of buried griefs. He felt the sharp edge of old sorrows. That's all right, he thought. He studied her face, faintly pretty in the pale light. One hand washes the other. Like Bradshaw, the girl was pale, the facial flesh soft and vulnerable. But where his eyes were reckless and go to hell, hers were vulnerable, hesitant, as if she told the world: well, here I am. I'm not much but I'm the only one there is. Do with me what you will.

When she arose and went inside they sat drinking coffee. It had grown very quiet. The old house was so far from the highway that Edgewater could not even hear cars, could hear only insects and nightbirds, the faint sounds of the girl moving about inside the house. A light was clicked on inside.

They've sure let this place go to hell, Bradshaw said. Moths haloed against the square of yellow light fluttered impotently. I never seen a place go down so fast.

Edgewater did not reply, was not even listening. He was looking past Bradshaw toward the distant gap in the horizon, where the dark sky met still darker ink slashes of crazed trees. The highway was there somewhere. The highway was humming almost a silent counterpart to Bradshaw's complaining voice, it was an invitation he could accept anytime.

Financially she was better off with him dead for he had an insurance policy and times had sometimes been lean. Yet there had been a respectability about him that she could feel slipping away. The material signs of her respectability were still here: the neat brick house that was paid for, the shingles she'd insisted on over tin, the aluminum storm windows and doors. A lot of piepans of change had gone into the house, a lifetime of Sundays.

The day before he died they had had some bitter argument. She could not even remember what it had been about. He had been taking up hay and he came in at noon for lunch and there wasn't any. You're a grown man, she told him. You ought to be able to fix yourself some dinner. He'd cooked up some kind of mess and eaten it and gone back to the hayfield without washing the pans. She'd hurled them into the backyard. After they found him dead she went out and gathered them up one by one and sat senselessly among them and stared at whatever caked a skillet and it was proof that he had been alive, concrete, no less substantial than the daughter he had died and left at a bad age, or the son in Arkansas or wherever he'd drifted to like a steel bearing rolling downward in a maze.

Guilt assailed her. At first she'd carried his picture and his Bible every time she went anywhere, for fear the house would burn. The embodiment of guilt she must bear, the weight of stone. From the mantle where the picture rested when she was not carrying it, the eyes were complacent, guileless, staring out of a face with no regrets.

Then after a time it came to her how thoughtless he had been. Wherever he was he was not having to concern himself with saving a daughter's virginity or a son that seemed determined to drink himself to death. A virginity she could not help but assume: she'd never been let out with that Yates boy and there did not seem to be opportunity or time. Her own girlhood forgotten, perhaps, her generation's cleverness taken for granted.

She came to see this virtue as the last bastion of morality. Buddy might drink until his liver dissolved in alcohol and coursed through his veins but a girl's chastity was what counted anyway and she had come to see herself inextricably intertwined with her daughter's fate, had taken upon herself the thankless task of protecting this last grail of innocence—and recognized the moment her jaundiced eye fell on Edgewater a sworn enemy.

She loathed him. She saw in him a threat, sensed in him something old and evil. An unrepentant word, a misdeed awaiting atonement, for the ways of the world lay on him like clothes he had near outgrown.

She had made down the couch, turned back clean sheets, there was a pillow that smelled freshly of summer. But he lay wide-eyed, still, in the unfamiliar dark, staring at the ceiling, listening to the creaks of the old house, its complaints as it shielded these transients against the night. It was not the unfamiliarity of surroundings; Edgewater was long used to sleeping in other people's beds, using other people's belongings, to sifting through the rusty tin cans and castoff clothes of other people's lives. He was listening to the sounds the girl made. She was restless as well. The springs would creak when she turned over and yet that would not suit her. He felt himself waiting for her to turn again, holding his breath. Then it would come again. At last he heard her get up and the bathroom door open, her soft footsteps, the light click on. He heard water running.

He grinned into the darkness, as if to some invisible audience of familiars that applauded his actions, hung on his every word. He wondered if the old woman was restless, what she had been like when she was a girl. If she had ever had a drink of whiskey, if she had ever said a breathless yes a long time ago beneath the honeysuckle.

He stayed on a day at a time ignoring the old woman's bitter looks and remarks through a summer that day by day grew hotter and drier until the creeks dwindled to a trickle across fissured land and the earth seemed to bake in the sun and cornfields wilted in its pitiless glare with defeated stalks askew, as if some malign bird atop Edgewater's shoulder called down this indiscriminate retribution from a sky marvelously clear, a sky with absolutely no intimation of rain.

He followed Sudy across a plowed field, watched her disappear into the brush at the creek's edge, reappear a few minutes later ascending the hill on the other side, carrying flowers now, moving upward toward a thin stand of sassafras at the summit. He went on leisurely, as if they were merely strangers bound for the same destination.

The field was convex at its center and he guessed that long ago there had been an Indian mound there, the loam he walked across was littered with flint and shards of broken pottery and here and there a broken arrowhead among the silvered and leached-up cornstalks of summers past. Perhaps beneath his feet were the skulls of warriors of another day, bones scattered, scored by plowshares, careful ceremony and solemn rite come to nothing in the end. Destroyed as thoughtlessly as the careless wind might alter the pattern of driven leaves. Old gods left aghast and speechless and powerless at this desecration, sleeping, dreaming of simpler days.

Edgewater crossed on a footlog where the creek narrowed and deepened and went on up the sandbar through a stand of willows. Above the greenery the sun was tracking midmorning and there was no breeze and here in the lowland the willows were hot and still. He came out of them following a wellworn footpath and out onto the grassy base of the hill, cleared land here, the trees had been cut long ago and the brush burned. He angled up the hill, the grass worn away in a path like the padded trail that led to an animal's lair.

She had her back to him, kneeling, pouring red dirt from a bucket, smoothing it with her hands onto the grave. HERMAN P. BRADSHAW, the stone read. BORN AUG 1900. DIED JUNE 1954.

It was a double stone and the woman's name was *Emma*. Below the names, in script: HE LEADS THE WAY OTHERS FOLLOW. The grave was still red with the clay dug from the hill and it looked raw, bleeding, an unhealed wound. There was a fruitjar half buried in the earth of the grave and she had put wildflowers there, knelt arranging them.

She turned at his step, glanced at him, looked back to where her hands moved about the flowers. I thought you was Buddy. I don't reckon he's even comin up here.

He hunkered on the ground, looked out across the summit of the hill across other graves, a dozen or so of them, neat community of the dead. Are all these your people buried here?

Yeah. My grandparents on Daddy's side are here. But some of them are old, a long time ago. I don't even know who they all are. She gestured toward two rectangles of sunken earth, more diminutive than the others. I had two little sisters born dead and they're buried here.

I'm sorry.

She smiled wanly. I doubt there's anything you could have done about it, she said.

He tipped out a cigarette, offered her the pack, but she shook her head. He lit the cigarette, idly stuck the smoking match into the earth. What'd you say killed your daddy, a stroke?

That's what the doctor said. She absentmindedly drew a circlet in the red clay with her finger. The doctor said he didn't suffer, he died real quick.

Something of guilt here, he thought: something done or not done. Bitter words said and nothing to repent to but the vacuum a man leaves and this ochre clay staining her hands. Edgewater knew she was crying although he did not look at her, heard the faint tremor of her voice. There's always things you think of you ought to've said, she apologized, dabbing at her eyes with her sleeve. Above them sparrowhawks wheeled, dropped cries harsh as broken glass.

Why don't you let the grass grow up over it?

It would be like forgettin him, she said, faltering. It would be lettin him go. It was hard to give him up. You just don't know. Especially with Mama the way she was and nobody to do anything but me. Buddy gone again like he always is when you need him for somethin. Where's your folks live?

He paused, going through his lies like some old burntout actor sorting faded costumes in a trunk. Well. They're both dead. They had a carwreck when I was growing up and it killed both of them.

Oh, I didn't mean to pry.

You're not. It was a long time ago and we never got on so well anyway. My daddy was a preacher and he had a way of seeing things and that was the only way there was.

You mean your daddy was a preacher too?

On Sunday and every other day, Edgewater told her. Preachers sometimes run out of forgiveness before they get to their own house.

She nodded. They can be hard, she said. Mama's like that. They've got to have people the way they want them or they don't want em at all.

Edgewater began a mythical story of his youth. Improbable hard times, harsh words, harsh deeds. His eyes were pained, his voice sincere. You would have thought he believed it. Perhaps now he did. Perhaps he no longer knew. A part of him drew aside, a separate self that watched with weary cynicism while he sorted greedily among his lies and held them to the light like a miser counting coins.

I know what you mean. It's funny both our daddys bein preachers and both of them dead.

It is a coincidence.

She arose, smoothed her dress. I better be goin on back. Mama'll be throwin a fit if I don't.

Why?

She flushed. Well. You and me both gone at the same time. She's got an awful suspicious mind.

We're not doing anything wrong.

Try telling her that sometime at three o'clock in the morning, she smiled. She began to walk out of the spinney of sassafras, slim and graceful trees that did not shade the sun. He caught up with her. They began walking back toward the porch, their shadows close before them, already merged at the shoulders with noon's heat.

You got a boyfriend?

No. What in the world makes you think that?

I didn't mean anything by it. You're just a pretty girl and most pretty girls I've met had a boyfriend somewhere.

I bet you've met a lot of them.

Not prettier than you.

Not me. Well, there was this boy. But Daddy and Mama both hated him, couldn't stand the sight of him, he drank and all that.

What happened to him?

I don't know. A girl at church told me he went north.

The look was in her eyes, had been there all the time. A look Edgewater had long given up on analyzing, though he had seen it countless times before, would see countless times again. It was a curious look, part sensual, for a fleeting moment. Edgewater had seen the look in cafés and bars and streets. It said, All right. Do whatever you want to do. It was what Edgewater lived for. It was what got him down the road.

When they had crossed the creek and came out into the field he carelessly took her hand, swung it along. She did not pull it away until they came up the stone walk from the springhouse and saw the old woman standing on the porch, watching their approach with bitter eyes. When they came to the door she moved away, some ancient troll on a mythic road, permitting them grudging passage. She was fooled, defeated, as old women always are. She fired upon Edgewater a black and vindictive look, would looks kill he'd be six feet under. He paid her no mind, felt no need to influence her, win her over. She had nothing he needed. Her twisted face was a gargoyle left to guard some temple long ransacked and plundered, a sentry watching walls fallen long ago.

Seen through the kitchen window and washed by late afternoon light, the old woman was going with her milk bucket and men's shoes through the backyard toward the barn. Bent, stepping through the barbedwire fence and tiptoeing delicately through the lot's offal and on toward the stable, then out of sight. Just at this same moment and seen through the same window Bradshaw was moving through a field of cornstalks with a rifle on his shoulder, angling toward the big hickories at the wood's edge.

Edgewater came up behind Sudy where she stood facing the sink of dishwater and laced his arms about her, feeling the large soft breasts against his forearms, his weight laid against her, his face above the soap-scented blonde hair. He turned her to him and bent his face to hers. Her eyes were shut, her mouth already wet. Hands along his face slick with soapy water. She came tight against him as close as she could, a slack and unresisting weight, arms locked about his neck in a sort of dormant urgency he'd awakened.

Preferring the porch to the house, the girl gave over her bedroom to him. The old woman was already wishing him gone, glanced sharp suspicious looks at him but that did not bother him. Nothing much bothered him anymore; long used to being alone and to doing his will he took no more offense than if nature had decreed rain on a day when he would have preferred sun. It was all temporary anyway, tomorrow would change it. Tomorrow might find him down the line, head pillowed elsewhere.

The room was austere, utilitarian. It could have been a motel room, a furnished but untenanted apartment. There were no girlish stuffed animals, no movie star portraits adorning the walls. All there was to hint her occupancy was some floral scent, faint and somehow vestigial.

Long used to sifting through the artifacts and debris of other people's lives, he prowled through her dresser drawers. In the mirror his face was abstracted, intent on his work. A burglar stealing not valuables but knowledge, the minutiae of dull lives, a hunter familiarizing himself with the habits of his prey. Neat stacks of clean underwear, stockings, the familiar blue box of Kotex. A purse he emptied, glancing to see was the door locked, aligning the contents on the dresser top: seven dollars and odd change; a lipstick, unused, hidden in a zippered compartment. A bottle of scent, the same cologne the room smelled of. Something wrapped in a clean pair of panties. Curiosity piqued he unwrapped a halfpack of Camel cigarettes, laid them bemusedly on the dresser, his face absorbed, obscurely rewarded by this find. Some old dumpkeeper prowling through the garbage of the well-to-do.

He took up the cigarettes. A secret smoker, perhaps. What greater vices, more cleverly concealed? He tipped the cigarettes out one by one, felt them, smelt the tobacco. When all the cigarettes were aligned before him he picked up the package, peered into it, pecked out a snapshot rolled so that it would fit through the package opening. Each life no matter how small had its obligatory secret. No matter how insignificant the body, this was where it lay buried.

From the snapshot a young man regarded him, smiling, cocky, head a mass of light curls. In the background lay what appeared to be a stream of some sort and a tangle of brush and the boy was holding to the sun and the eye of the camera a string of fish. His other hand held a rod and reel. He was bare to the waist and there was what looked like a scar running the length of his breastbone, a narrow tapered scar like a spearpoint or arrowhead. The sun was in his face and he looked haloed with light, grinning, his teeth white and even.

Edgewater put everything back the way it had been and undressed to his shorts and lay atop the covers on the bed. After a time he got up and turned out the light and lay back down staring at the dark unperceived ceiling above him and listening to the sounds of the night beyond the window and thinking about nothing at all. He lay vaguely alert as if he did not allow himself to completely relax anymore. The world was wide for him but surprises few. Anything could happen, the inexplicable was commonplace. Scissors aloft and a mad harridan's face twisted, the old woman might break in on him, or even now the law might be rolling down the highway toward him, somewhere there were papers with his name affixed to them, needed only serving to alter his life forever. He lay awake listening but all he ever heard above the ordinary sound of the night was the back door open and close and the sounds of her footsteps approaching down the hall. Soft, clandestine. He raised up on his elbows, not so much in anticipation as curiosity; he'd not expected her so soon. But the bathroom door opened and after a moment he heard water running. It ceased and he heard her go back out.

He lay back down and thought of the old woman. He doubted she slept, expected that she as well heard the covert steps, the doors gently pulled to. Eavesdropped for the illicit intrigues of the summer night, suspicions honed razor sharp by the bits of knowledge the years pressed to her. He imagined her sleep troubled as well by the knowledge that the dark fox of her nightmares slept this night safe and dry within the henhouse walls.

Sudy came through the house carrying a clean dress and the iron. Set the board up and plugged the iron in. Her eyes already defiant although the old woman had said nothing at all.

When silent admonishment did not stop the ironing the old woman said, Just where do you think you're goin?

I'm goin to the show with Buddy and Billy.

The old woman snorted. Them going to a show? You go off with them and no tellin where you'll wind up.

Mama, he's my brother.

You still ain't agoin.

I set here on this creek day after day till I'm nearly crazy. I've got to where I can't tell one day from the next, and somebody hints that they don't mind—not ask me, mind, but just don't care if I go—and you think I'm not going?

You ain't agoin.

Try and stop me, Mama.

Bradshaw endured only the cartoon and a reel or so of the feature. Endless gunfights and bloodless denouncing held no charms for him. No black and white sunsets could hold his attention for long. He kept reaching across Sudy and punching Edgewater's shoulder. Hey, Billy. Let's go over to the poolroom and drink one. Pick Sudy up when the show's over.

Edgewater half arose but her hand was on his arm. Was there pressure there? He could not tell but he sat back down. It'll be over in a minute, he whispered. I want to see how this comes out.

Bradshaw was contemptuous of such smalltown pleasures. I don't see how anybody can watch a cheapjack movie like this. He done chased him by that same rock four times and shot at him forty times and never even reloaded.

I want to see how it comes out anyway.

Shit. Bradshaw got up and they heard the door open and saw a rectangle of outside light briefly fall and vanish. They sat and watched the movie, and after a time her head infinitesimally and slowly settled toward him until at last they touched, the weight of her hair against his shoulder, not an unpleasant burden to bear. He could smell the girlish scent she wore, clean odor, some floral cologne. When he turned to kiss her she was waiting. Her eyes were open and questioning. She did not speak.

Arm in arm they came out into the mothflecked night amidst a crowd of darting and yelling children and into a world of brightness and noise.

Bradshaw was sitting on the hood of the Chevrolet with his arms crossed waiting. He was a little drunk and he had a sullen look on his face. He looked all around him appraisingly as if he hoped someone not too big or skillful might goad him into a fight but no one paid him any mind at all.

On the way home he did not say anything at all except to refuse Sudy a trip to the Daridip. He glanced at her a time or two as if he had things on his mind but he kept them to himself. She had settled herself against Edgewater in the backseat as soon as they were outside the city limits, as if she had been awaiting darkness. Streetlights fell away. He crept a covert hand across her thigh, pressed between her legs a weight she neither spurned nor acknowledged. Her lips against his throat were wet. Bradshaw halfglanced at them. He accelerated.

There was a stockgap of old railroad rails across the road past the trainbed and he hit it at eighty, a harsh clanging of reverberations that rocked the car so that it squatted and sprang. He hit second gear and the wheels spun, night fed the road at a dizzy pace.

Her cool hand was in Edgewater's and he laid it on his penis. When he did she did not move the hand but she raised her face and looked at him. Something of calm acceptance in her look touched Edgewater in a way he did not care to analyze. In some infinitesimal way he did not like, the world was altered.

She had a reputation for being dour and practical. What she could not use she did not want. Even Harkness, not one for aesthetics himself, said of her, If she can't eat it, fuck it, or bust it up for stovewood she don't want no part of it.

She had long been parsimonious and the older she got the harder she squeezed a dollar. Dollar bills passed through her hands with painful slowness, they might have had glue on them. Bradshaw would spend them and have to wait agonized in limbo till she parceled out more. He grew tired of bills that trickled to him in twos or threes. He searched for her purse before he asked her but apparently she had anticipated him.

I need some money, Bradshaw told her.

You might get you a job, she said. They pay off ever Friday for that, I hear.

Mama, I got in applications everywhere from sawmills to garment factories. They ain't nobody hirin.

They ain't hirin drunks in poolrooms and beerjoints, that's for sure. You must be afraid to ask sober. She changed the subject. How long's that Edgewater boy goin to be in my house?

I couldn't say. I don't think for him.

Nor for yourself neither, seems to me. What do you mean bringin trash like that into your sister's house? Puttin him in her very bedroom?

What's the matter with it?

Jails and asylums and unrespectable houses is full of the evidence of what's the matter with it, she said.

I don't see it like that. Besides, you don't know what all me and him's been through. Me and him's tight. Don't you go sayin nothing to hurt his feelins neither. You do and I'm long gone from here.

You better keep a close eye on your sister, she told him. I can't be with her all the time with you haulin her all over the county.

Don't you trust her? Ain't you brought her up right? Don't she know right from wrong?

No answer. Bradshaw had on his town clothes, his hair wet and slick, a knowing look in his eyes, they wandered out to where the Chevrolet waited. Time in its flight seemed dizzying, the world with its myriad diversions spun past him. He trapped here pleading poverty.

Daddy had ten thousand dollars insurance. What happened to that?

Why Lord he never had no such a thing.

Yes he did. How do you get by then? How do you pay the house payments ever month?

Her voice stopped him. Don't cuss me. Not if you expect anything when I'm gone. I'd as soon leave it to Sudy as not.

I need some money.

She had produced as if by legerdemain a folded bill: a ten. He reached for it but she was not yet through with him.

I want you to swear on your daddy's memory to watch her around him.

I ain't no spy. She's my sister, and Billy's my friend. He saved my life.

She gave him the bill. I'll give you ten dollars a week.

Fifteen, Bradshaw said.

The old woman heard her footsteps in the hall, soft, careful, yet somehow imbued with urgency. She waited for the bathroom door to open, the click of the lightswitch, but it never came. The steps went to the door at the end of the hall. The door opened soft on soundless rungs. She has to get something out of her dresser, she told herself. She lay taut and sleepless, held her breath for as long as she could and listened for any sound, the sliding open of a drawer, the reclosing of the door, heard at last only the expulsion of her own breath, the cries of the night beyond the walls. So it's tonight then, she thought.

She made to get up but something stayed her, something perhaps subliminal, some old halflost knowledge of other times unknown and unacknowledged, some kinship with others of her sex that ran deeper than pride or anger or even blood and recognized without admitting it what had made her daughter lie sleepless till this hour of the night and then move with wraithlike stealth to the bed where Edgewater slept or waited, understood wordlessly the urgency she had already half suspected and feared and seen in her daughter's transparent face. She turned her eyes to the wall, the face old and bitter, dark and tearless and wrinkled as an apple left to rot in the sun.

What? Edgewater asked. What? He had raised up on his elbows at her touch on his shoulder, lay peering out wide-eyed at her in the darkness, still half asleep as if he did not recognize her. Her hair was unbraided, fell to her waist. Between the pale loose braidcrimped strands of it framing her face, her features were paler still, the eyes alone were direct and intense. Be quiet, she said softly, stopped his mouth with her palm. There was a faint smell of soap or perfume on her hands.

Get up, she whispered. She removed her hand, stepped back for him to arise. When he got up she looked quickly at him and then away while he pulled on his pants. She took a blanket from his bed and folded it and he followed her out the door.

That dry summer the woods were afire and the air had a taint of woodsmoke. The yard was full of moonlight. She started toward the car but he caught her hand, led her down the path to the back of the mulberry tree. Its branches shrouded the ground; there the earth sloped down an embankment and when they sat on the spread blanket the house was lost to his sight. She had her arm around him, he could feel the bulk of her body, the weight of her heavy breasts through the thin gown. Her breath was warm against his throat, a baby's breath.

I was afraid you was goin to leave, she said.

When he kissed her, her eyes closed, fluttered open to meet his own, turned away in their sockets to the dark. He pulled down the gown about her shoulders, studied the smooth cool mounded flesh with something akin to detachment so that she said, What's the matter?

How far would you have gone, he thought. What would you do if I hadn't come here, if I didn't do what I'm going to?

Nothing.

He stroked the nipple, pinched it gently between forefinger and thumb, felt the barely perceptible pressure of erectile tissue growing beneath his touch. A vague and momentary elation touched him. Here in the moonlight her white and Nordic body was a country he could explore at will. She sat half erect, pulled the gown over her head. Her body was lush and white. She opened her legs for him and when he penetrated her she made some soft sound in her throat, neither pleasure or pain, perhaps just acknowledgement. The shadow of his face threw the lower part of her face in darkness and her forehead and eyes in stark moonlit relief, an early sere leaf had caught somehow in her hair. Her eyes were wide and unobstructed and he studied them as he moved, as if there was hidden in her depths an answer to a question he had not dared ask.

She lay totally submissive while he labored above her, her legs out-flung like some beached life from the ocean depths, some grotesque beast dividing, joined only at the crotch, struggling for life in this other-worldly medium. Or yet some wanton sacrifice in a pagan rite yielding to whatever dark ritual the gods inflicted upon her.

He lay on his back, stared into the depths of her above him. He could discern the rolling shards of the treehouse, felt momentarily that the timbers might have hung poised all these years full and awaiting him, childish carpentry turned lethal by whatever fates dogged his steps, dropped soundless and ironic to impale him where he lay.

She touched his face, dropped her hand to where sweat pooled in the hollow of his throat. Next time we'll go down by the creek, she told him. Nobody'd see us on that sandbar down there. He did not reply. He arose, pulled on his trousers and walked down by the brook. He washed his face in the cold water, his hands, felt sand list past his fingers in the cool depths, his hands beneath the surface like white aquatic spiders, his reflection rippled and unrecognizable as a specter. Soundless she came up behind him naked as he arose facing the dark hill where the cemetery lay; he felt the warmth of her body lay on his back like a brand, felt her breasts pool against him, her arms encircle his chest, wisps of her sweaty hair against his neck. It was a weight not to be borne.

An unease touched him, and a need to be elsewhere as sharp as fear. An apprehension, as if he had spent money that he did not have, made some unspoken commitment he could not keep.

It was two nights later, far into the night, the girl was just a white shape standing quiet beside the bed, peering down myopically to see if he was awake. He was. He got up, picked up a quilt from the couch, led her out of the house. It was lighter outside this time. Moonlight fell flat and white, shadows ran deep and infinite. She moved to open the car, but Edgewater said no, spread the quilt where the moon threw the car's shadow black as bottomless water, drew her down to the dewy earth.

I can't do this, she said, breathing hard, the voice kept saying, I can't, even while she was. You've got me to where I don't know what I'm doin, excusing herself as she thrashed and struggled as if for breath, silvered by the moonlight. Then she lay quiet, the pale hair curled and damp at her temples, her body slick with sweat. He looked down into her face but the look was gone, would never have the exact same look again for him.

He got up, leaned against the car, his folded arms resting across its top. The metal was cool, comforting, a soothing hand. He stood so a long time, wished vaguely for a cigarette. After a while he heard her stir, come up behind him. What's the matter, she wanted to know. There was nothing wrong. Her body was a slack, definitive weight. A total dependency shifted onto him so that he felt a familiar disquiet. He was looking toward the west, and now she looked with him. Somewhere distant the woods were afire, just a line of red fire pulled tight as a burning thread, easing over the horizon, pulsating, contracting, then widening faster down the slope as if it were feeding. As if it were alive, as if it were the only thing left alive in all that dark.

Decorous and cleanshaven they left the next morning to find work, the old woman watching the car as Bradshaw backed it carefully out of the shed, touching its polished surface with apprehensive fingers, as if she regretted her offering it already, as if she dreaded seeing it roll out of her sight. The girl came up beside her, stood watching her brother with a cynic's eyes.

You drive careful, the old woman said.

Of course I will, Mama, Bradshaw said abstractedly. He was easing the clutch out a little, pushing it back in, rolling the wheels impatiently, eager to be gone. In a hurry to find work to busy idle fingers lest they fall to the devil's purpose. He turned, scanned the driveway behind him. Sudy, will you run them chickens out of the way?

You better not run over my Dominicker, the old woman said. The girl had begun throwing pebbles ineffectively at the chickens pecking in the grass. Shoo, shoo, she was saying.

Oh, hell, Bradshaw said. He popped the clutch and spun backward, began to cut the wheel toward the driveway.

And you better not be drinking that old whiskey, her voice rising to be heard over the throbbing motor, ending in a breaking shriek, her face contorted, some mad old harridan shrieking unheard imprecations on deaf ears.

Yeah, yeah, yeah, Bradshaw said, easing into second gear. The last thing Edgewater saw was the girl in white, watching them go for a moment and turning back toward the house, somehow forlorn.

Yeah, a job, Bradshaw said, fumbling out a cigarette and pushing in the cigarette lighter. Hands that neither sew nor spin are an abomination in the sight of the Lord. You write that down, Edgewater. At the switch-back he spun off the railroad in a cloud of dust toward town.

They weren't hiring at the poolroom but they tarried there anyway. Save for a lethargic barkeep talking drunkenly and ferociously to himself, they had the place to themselves. He seemed to be berating himself for some gross and ancient wrong. After a while the door opened and an old woman pushed a cripple in a wheelchair and Bradshaw and Edgewater began a listless game of eightball. The cripple wheeled his chair up to the table and fell to watching. There was a sour reek of urine and vomit about him. He had dead lank hair like dried straw that lay flat on his skull and his legs looked shrunken, as if the flesh had been incised from his bones, lost in the castoff trousers he wore. He had an enormous bowtie replevied from the garbage of one more prosperous than he, clipped to the collar of his chambray shirt.

Hey Elmer. How you makin it?

Not worth a damn, Bradshaw. Where you been?

Better places than this, Bradshaw told him, sighting along the cue. He shot the three into a side pocket. Higher times and wilder women. What's been happenin around here?

Starvation.

Bradshaw scratched in the corner, looked all about the poolroom with an air almost proprietary. Yeah, back to my old stompin ground, he said.

You ain't got nary a cigarette on you have you?

Edgewater gave him one. Elmer put it in his mouth, sat waiting patiently, as if some vague idea of courtesy forbade him asking for a light. Bradshaw held at length a match. You want to kick your ass to get your lungs pumpin?

The cripple began to laugh, strangled on smoke, a laugh that became a hacking blue cough that wracked him until the chair shook. When he finished coughing he said, Bradshaw, you ain't got fifty cents on ye have ye?

Hellfire, Elmer. I give you fifty cents just last year. What'd you do with that? He was fumbling in his pockets, separating change. Here. Don't spend it all in one place.

Elmer wheeled toward the bar.

What's the matter with him? Edgewater asked.

Bradshaw shrugged. I don't know. Some disease. Folks say he got ahold of some bad whiskey one time and that done it, but it ain't so. He just got a little worse all the time. He used to hobble around duckfooted like and then he got to where he couldn't walk at all. Folks chipped in and got him that wheelchair. Goddamn but he used to be a ballplayer. He had a fastball you could of lit a cigarette off of.

Who was that old woman?

His mama. She's just an old whore. Or was till people got to where they wouldn't buy it. She didn't used to be so ugly. He laughed to himself. Boy, she can't stand me. Me and old Arnold had her out one time and she wouldn't give me none. Old Arnold had a dick on him about like a jack and I reckon she was spoilt. It was dark and we was all drunk and I crawled on her and put it in but she throwed me right off. Why you ain't Arnold, she said. She had her glass of snuff there in the car and I took it away from her and pissed in it and she ain't had no use for me since.

Some women are just sensitive natured, I guess, Edgewater said.

I reckon so.

By the time the game was finished and another begun, Elmer was back with a bottle of beer and a benign look on his face. The door opened and a prosperous-looking man came in and ordered a beer. He carried it to the back table and selected a cue and began idly practicing bank shots. He had on a white shirt, a necktie, and a softbrimmed gray hat. His face was florid, the cheeks mauve with burst capillaries. The face somehow imbued with excess. Too much good food and too much bad whiskey. He had the look of a smalltown politician.

Hey, Big Shawn. Elmer hurriedly drained his beer. What do you know?

Very little, Big Shawn said.

You wouldn't drink a beer with me would ye?

Big Shawn glanced at his wristwatch. I might have time for one. I got to meet somebody at the courthouse here in a minute.

Elmer waited. Big Shawn went on practicing bank shots. It'd be easier if I had one too, Elmer said at last.

Oh. Well, here then. Shawn gave him a quarter, turned his bottle up to drain it, set it back on the corner of the table. You get you one. I got to get on.

Listen. You ain't got…Here he paused, gauged Shawn's prosperous appearance…two dollars, have ye? I need me some supper.

Two dollars? I just give you a dollar Wednesday. Wasn't it? What'd you do with it?

Hell, Elmer said, shrugging. Wednesday.

Another thing, Shawn said, hanging his cue back on the rack. You know that big sack of garden stuff I brought you? Clyde Webb said he seen you going across the street here at the corner and said you just throwed that sack of stuff right out in the middle of the street and kept on going.

Elmer's face was all outraged innocence. He's a goddamned liar and the truth ain't in him, Elmer said. I carried that stuff home and Mama cooked it.

Well, all I know is what I hear, Shawn said. Like there was garden stuff strowed all over the street and cars was running over tomatoes and all that other stuff.

They said. People'll tell anything. You wait'll I see that lyin' son of a bitch. I'll set him straight.

Big Shawn had racked his cue and now he paused to relight his cigar. I got to get on, he said. I'll see ye.

I sure could use two dollars, Elmer suggested.

I can't spare it this morning, Big Shawn said. He dusted his hat carefully against his trouser leg and went toward the door. When he had opened it and started onto the street Elmer's voice stayed him.

A sack of shittin' garden stuff, he said. I couldn't give nobody nothing bettern a goddamn bunch tomaters and cucumbers, I'd just keep em to myself.

Big Shawn grinned and shook his head. He went on out into the hot street.

I just hate a tightwad like that, don't you? Elmer asked.

Boogerman came down out of the woods where the hollow leveled out and into a field of cutover cane. He walked with something like stealth into the edge of the field and halted behind a hedge of sassafras and blackjack sprouts. He peered between the broad leaves of sassafras. Two men were crossing the field approaching him, striding and as yet unrecognizable forms. Past them the field curved downgrade to a deep red gully choked with brush and the worn copper of old cedars and rusting car bodies and beyond this was the tin roof of his house glowing a warm umber in the ascending sun and a shiny black car parked in his turnaround driveway.

The figures came on straggling across the field. One dark and one light with the sun in his hair. The blond almost skipping along talking and gesturing to the dark and stolid presence like a familiar. Boogerman's eyes shaded to ascertain did they wear guns or badges. He could not tell as yet. The car was strange to him. He knelt on the cool earth. The weight of the sun was on his back. Jays quarreled from the woods behind him, crows called like watchdogs as these interlopers approached.

When they were nearing the border of the field one of them began to hail him and just as he did Boogerman recognized Bradshaw. He stood up brushing dry hay from his overalls and just let them come. He wore overalls and a chambray shirt both sunfaded to the same neutral hue like something from nature layered with years of ancient stains no longer even recognizable. He had a blearyeyed whitewhiskered face and he looked like nothing so much as some badtempered badger coming out of hibernation after a long harsh winter and blinking against unaccustomed light. He had a shotgun strung on his arm and now he broke it down and pocketed the shells.

What say Bradshaw?

What was you sneaking behind them bushes for? We seen you ease out and peep all around like you'd just done something against the law.

Weda been the law weda knowed you was makin whiskey right off.
What you ort to do is just walk out whistlin, ye head throwed back like
you just made a down payment on the world.

You tell me about it, Boogerman said. I ain't been doin it but fifty
year and I still got a lot to learn.

Yeah and how much of that fifty years did you pass up at Brushy?

I ain't never done but eleven months and twenty-nine days out of
fifty years and they hid whiskey in my front yard to get me that time.
You fellers wantin a drink or just visitin?

A little of both, Bradshaw said.

Walk on down to the house and we'll find some shade somers.

They walked back across the field toward the house. When they
passed the ditch Bradshaw said, I'se in your line of work I'd find something else to do with my syrup buckets. That ditch is full of em. That's
a dead giveaway.

I'll tell you what. Why don't I just sell out to you and you can run
the business any way you want to.

There was an enormous cottonwood shading one end of the house
and beneath it a motley collection of old lawn chairs and Coke crates and
an old broken rocking chair appeared to have been salvaged from floodwaters. They sat silent beneath the tree. The house seemed to emanate
silence, it seemed to be sleeping. A cloud passed from in front of the sun
and moving light lacquered the windows, lending the weathered wood
a depth and solidity almost surreal.

Where's ye family at? Last time I'se here they's seven or eight of yins.

Gone.

Gone? Gone where?

The old man shrugged. Just gone. Here and there. Hildy, she was the
oldest and she was the first to leave. She got wildern a mink and finally
she run off with that hairlipped Ferguson boy and I ain't seen neither
one of em since. Then the rest just started goin. I had all girls, you know.
They'd get up breedin age and you ain't never seen nothing like it.

Bradshaw knew; the girls had constituted the main reason he was
here.

Seems like ever night they's cars parked in here and a bunch of
drunk carryin on. Fightin and such as that. Little by little they just got
meaner. Took to not even kickin the door to when they'd go in em to

screw. Like a bunch of dogs around a she in heat. It got to where you couldn't walk out in the bushes without walkin up on a pair of em doin it. One night I just got maddern hell and I got my gun and run the whole bunch off. I meant to just run off the boys but hell they all went.

Bradshaw's face was somewhat rueful, the look of one listening to the description of a party he was not invited to.

What about your old lady?

Hell, she went too. Even the goddamned dogs is gone. Seems like when they start leavin everybody run out on ye. Even the cats went wild and livin in the woods somers.

Boogerman himself had a feral look about him, the look of a man too much to himself. His eyes were quick and covert, they flickered about as if to see all he could at once. He seemed eager to be alone, to continue some discourse he held eternally with himself.

Ain't you hunted for em?

I didn't lose em. They left on their own hook. They can come back the same way. I don't need em nohow. He arose, mopped his throat with an old red handkerchief. Let me get you a drink, he said. I got some around here somers. He walked around the house, moved slow and slopeshouldered towards a caved outbuilding.

So much for that, Bradshaw said to Edgewater. Last time I'se out here this place was crawlin with pussy. You had to fight it off with a stick.

It give up without a fight today.

Well, hell, you heard him. They all left.

When Boogerman came back he had a pint bottle swinging along in his hand. I don't know what the world is comin to, he was saying. Young folks. I don't know where them of mine went wrong. You have a bunch of em and then one morning they just ain't there no more. He unscrewed the cap from the bottle, smelled tentatively. Here, git you a little drunk.

Bradshaw tipped the bottle back and drank. Oily bubbles rose in the whiskey like tiny glass beads. He took the bottle down and wiped his mouth and reached the bottle to Edgewater. Edgewater shook his head no. I pass, he said. He could smell the sour sickish reek of the whiskey. He took the bottle, held it to the light. He shook it, watched a miniature storm of debris whirl silent in the bottle: bits of bug, hair, tiny green beads like weedseed. An insect leg spun like some curious dissected specimen in formaldehyde. He passed the bottle back.

Old Edgewater knows Roosterfish, Bradshaw said. His voice sounded strange. He seen him up in McNairy County somewhere.

Well, I'll be damned. I figgered he was dead and buried by now. What was he doin?

Edgewater's face clouded with concern. Painting barns, the last I seen of him. We parted in a bit of a hurry.

There wasn't a trade Roosterfish couldn't handle if he tried his hand at it. He could do a little bit of everything he set his mind to. Fore he lost his arm anyway. Boogerman drank from the bottle, stared up the road to where dust rose in an approaching cloud as if in pursuit of some as yet unseen vehicle. He set the bottle out of sight behind his leg. He could do carpenter work, mason's work. Used to build as purty a fireplace as you ever seen. He built that un down the road here where old preacher Holly lives.

A flatbed truck stacked with cordwood went by in a wake of dust. The driver saluted Boogerman with a listless hand.

Roosterfish came down here to ask about Holly. To see would he pay. He'd heard he better watch him. So I just told him. He may be a preacher but he ain't nothing but a goddamned deadbeat. He owed me for a gallon of whiskey and him claim to be a preacher. He'll pay me, Roosterfish said. I'll see to that, and he went ahead agin what I told him and built it and damn if Holly didn't do just what I said. Told him he'd pay him the first. Well, the first come but the money didn't. This was in I think June. Roosterfish didn't push it. He just waited. October come and one night it was chilly enough for a fire. Holly kindled him up one and Lord if it wadn't a sight. Smoke rolled out of his house like it was afire. It was just like he'd built a fire in the middle of the front room floor there. Well sir, he's over at Roosterfish's with his hat in his hand before good dark. It won't draw, he said, somethins the matter with it. I'll fix it when you pay for it, Roosterfish told him. Next morning Holly went to the bank and borrowed the money and went straight and paid him. He laughed to himself and Roosterfish stowed his ladder in the back of the truck and went over there and climbed up on the roof and chunked a brick down the chimbly. What he'd done was set him a big piece of glass above the throat and all it took to fix it was dropping that brick.

Roosterfish is slick, Bradshaw said.

He is that, Boogerman told him.

Listen, we lookin to haul some whiskey. You still haulin down to Vera's?

Off and on I am. The business ain't what it used to be. Sugar gittin higher ever day and everybody got a car now and just as well drive up to Mt. Pleasant and buy bonded. The liquor stores is tryin to put all of us out of business. But you might take her about twenty gallon if you a mind to. I'll just pay ye to haul and she'll settle up with me for the whiskey.

Let's load her up then. We need to be rollin.

Well, I'll have to show ye where it's at. I got it hid on old man Holly down there.

When they had it loaded Boogerman seemed loathe to let them go. Youns be careful, he said. He stood by the road's dusty edge amidst the sawbriars and watched them out of sight.

Suitably employed now, whiskey loaded and rolling again, Bradshaw fell to thinking of other women they might take out that night. I done forgot about Bonnie Serber, he said at length. I got her cherry when she about thirteen and they say a woman always keeps a soft spot in her heart for her first one. Do you believe that Edgewater?

No, do you?

I don't know. Anyway we'll get some pussy. I may have been the first but I damned sure wadn't the last.

Halfway back to Ackerman's Field Bradshaw got a strange look in his eyes and suddenly became violently sick. He stopped the car and leapt out and began to vomit in the ditch. Edgewater sat and smoked and listened to a constant chorus of birds calling mockingly from the knoll of pinewoods. Bradshaw got back in weakly. He rested his head on the rim of the steering wheel a moment and then he got back out. You'll have to drive awhile, he said. I just ain't up to it.

They went on and about a mile later he was sick again and this time did not have time to get out. He fell to cursing Boogerman, maligning his whiskey.

I was trying to kill myself I'd pick a way a little less messy, Edgewater told him. They forded a shallow creek and Edgewater stopped in it and found an old rusted minnow bucket on the bank. He threw water in the floorboard until he could not smell vomit anymore. Bradshaw got out and washed his face in the creek. Mama's gonna have a shitfit about this car, he said. I don't know what I'll tell her.

Maybe the hair of the dog would help you. We could crack one of the jugs in the trunk.

Bradshaw gagged and spat into the creek and shook his head. After a while they set forth again.

He was feeling better by the time the whiskey was delivered. They bought a case of beer at Vera's and started out toward Serber Ridge. By the time the town fell away and they were in pinewoods he was driving again, had regained almost all of his volubility and he was telling Edgewater about Bonnie and her younger sister. Edgewater rode in silence and drank beer. The sun was tracking westward now, the day beginning to wane. He closed his eyes, all the country was beginning to look the same, all the faces to be interchangeable. The road curved and dipped into lowering rushes and he opened his eyes on a bridge across a narrow stream and it seemed to him it was a bridge he had raised a thousand times. The act of raising it itself foolish and devoid of purpose.

Bradshaw was not sick anymore but the whiskey seemed to have made him very drunk. His speech was slurred and his eyes were taking on a belligerent overbearing look. They ceased at a housetrailer set atop a gentle rise and Bradshaw shut off the engine and got out. He stood looking at the trailer uncertainly. I never noticed this before, he said. You wait here and I'll rouse em out.

Edgewater could see no electric wires. He wondered idly why anyone would set up such a trailer without electricity. A beast barked at them fiercely at the edge of the yard and a woman came out of the housetrailer and stood watching him through the screened-in storm door. The housetrailer was new and it looked to Edgewater to be long as a freighttrain. Behind it stood a crumbling shack forlorn and empty, given over to woods, windows stoned out, the house itself canted leeward as if it were in the act of falling with a movement so infinitesimally slow as if to be undetectable, as if time had warped and elongated: harsh times and prosperity simultaneous and profound on this same quarteracre. Hush, Bradshaw kept telling the dog. You hush your mouth. He stood leaning a little as if listing to some gentle wind. His pants were wet to his knees and his shoes were full of creek water and made squishy sounds when he walked.

Bonnie?

Bonnie ain't here. The face was closed and bitter. Who are you anyway?

Bradshaw snickered to himself. Bonnie would know, he said.

Come on, Edgewater told him.

I know she's in there, Bradshaw told the woman. There was a wooden porch or platform constructed of two-by-fours in front of the trailer and Bradshaw walked unsteadily up to it and rested his arms there. The woman stepped back into the semidarkness of the trailer and made to close the door.

I want to ask her to go to that dance at Ethridge with me.

She ain't here I done told you.

Bradshaw fell into ruminative silence. He stared away across the field to doves foraging and a fence curving away to a nothingness lost in yellow flowers. Well, is there anybody in there that wants to go to the dance at Ethridge? he finally said.

My husband'll be in in a little bit, she told him. He might want to talk to you about it. The woman closed the door and Edgewater heard the bolt slide home. He leaned out the window.

I reckon that ain't Bonnie?

Her sister-in-law or some damn thing.

You ready to go back to town? Or somewhere?

I reckon so. I hate coming this far on a dry run though.

I'd hate gettin my ass blown off by somebody I ain't even met.

All right then. I sure wanted to see Bonnie though.

They were not halfway back to the blacktop when they met a car coming flatout in the middle of the road. Edgewater took the ditch run and went steering through pokeweed and blackberry briars with Bradshaw grabbing at the air with his hands, climbing half out the window as if of a mind to jump. Stop, stop, he kept saying. It's her. They ceased crosswise in the road and Edgewater backed up to right the car. The other car had stopped as well and was slowly backing up the road toward them. There were two girls in it.

When they were parallel with them the girl shoved her sunglasses up on her forehead. She was a slim girl tanned very darkly from the sun and she had black hair that gleamed sealike and sleek, wound up smoothly at her bare shoulders. There was a vestigial and faint prettiness about her but her eyes were old and wise and Edgewater had seen eyes like them in bars and countries far removed from this backroad. Well hello, sweet thing, she said to Bradshaw.

I see you still takin your half of the road out of the middle, Bradshaw said.

I got things to do and people to meet.

Where yall been?

Over to Napier swimmin.

Why hello, Linda. You too stuckup to speak?

The other girl raised a disinterested hand. She was less pretty than the dark haired girl. She was very fair and had bleached-looking platinum hair. You got a cold beer in there?

We got one but you have to come after it. We want to see what you look like in your bathing suit.

The girl got out and came around the car unselfconsciously. She had on an orange bathing suit as brief as a heretic's prayer and as convention permitted. Her body gleamed with richly scented oil as if she were the sex object of some holy embodiment who had prepared her vessel to preserve it for other ages. She looked like trouble to Edgewater, but that was only a thought in passing. Trouble had never meant that much to him.

What say, jellybean, she said to him. Water from her wet hair beaded slickly on her smooth white stomach.

Bradshaw handed her a can of beer. Listen, he said. Me and Billy's goin over to Ethridge tonight to the dance. We lookin for a couple of volunteers. How about it?

She lowered the beer can. Edgewater could not see her face: he saw the can descend and the orange hemisphere where the car door breached her breasts and her belly and her tilted hips. There was a faint gold down on her stomach below the navel. She rested against the warm metal of the car. He could smell the warmth of her.

You'd have to talk to Bonnie about it, Linda said.

I already got a date, Linda. Sorry, Bonnie answered from the car.

Hellfire. You mean I come all the way out here from where I come to see you and you won't even break a date to go with me? Who's it with?

Chief Aday.

Aday? What you going with a burntout old cop like that for? He must be sixty year old. What's in it for you?

Twenty dollars, she told him.

Bradshaw fell momentarily silent.

I'm goin with him all the time now. He helped me get that trailer. If you was out to the place I guess you seen it.

Yeah, I seen it. Bradshaw got out and walked around to the other car to where Bonnie sat. Edgewater heard him say, Now you ain't done forgot me this quick, have you?

I ain't forgot you but I still got a date.

Between the girl's slim arm and the hourglass curve of her waist Edgewater saw Bradshaw lean down, a hand on either side of the window, bracing himself, bend to the girl's dark face as if he were whispering secret knowledge in her ear, some occult password that would grant him passage across some ephemeral border. Then he seemed to be gnawing at her neck, chewing her ear.

Quit, she said. Now quit that. I told you I can't and I can't really.

You know damn well you can if you want to.

No I can't. He'd whip me. He'd lock you up too.

Sure he would. You know he would. He'd shit and fall back in it too.

You don't know him. He's crazy about me.

Well, I am too and I want you to go with me tonight. What if I died and you didn't go with me. What if I had a car wreck and was laid out all mangled and bloody. Think how you'd feel. You'd wish then you'd of went with me.

I hate to hear a grown man cry, Bonnie said to no one.

You don't have much to say do you, jellybean? Linda asked Edgewater. Has the cat got your tongue? Edgewater was still staring at her stomach.

Sure I do, he said. What do you want to talk about?

Bradshaw had said something they had not heard. Then Bonnie said: Well that's how it is. You can root hog or die.

Hell, I ain't payin for something you laid on me for nothing time and again.

She pulled the sunglasses back down over her eyes. The last fleeting glimpse of them revealed them hard and unaffected and as removed as if she were already miles away. Yet she grinned at him, a flash of white teeth. No tickee no shirtee, she told him.

Bradshaw kicked the side of the car as hard as he could. Dust flew from the rocker panel, there was a whumphing sound and a dent appeared in the door. He grimaced for a moment, surveying onelegged, clutching his right foot.

Piss on you, Bradshaw told her. I knowed all along you was a whore. I wouldn't fuck you with a borrowed dick. God knows what I'd catch.

You just keep on. Go back to fuckin Mama Thumb and her four daughters, she told him. You always been safe enough that way. She had started the motor. Linda, get your butt in the car.

I got to go, Linda told Edgewater.

Don't rush off in the heat of the day.

She gave him a little wave with her fingers as she went around the car.

In a childhood nigh forgotten by everyone save Bradshaw, she had been his sweetheart. She was the daughter of a judge and her blood ran back to forebears who long ago came up the Natchez Trace and settled the county but somewhere along the line things went wrong; a streak of wildness going back perhaps to these very forebears, to a time when the country was vast enough and wild enough for one to do anything he felt like. Her name was Caren Ricketts and along about the seventh or eighth grade she started growing breasts and by the ninth grade nothing was the same. The breasts had risen perfectly into separate and improbable cones that the tight sweaters she affected showed to an advantage almost breathtaking. She had learned to paint her lips a glossy red and her hair was bleached to a burnished platinum. She had discovered a way of crossing the study hall that drew all eyes to her, a loose-hipped walk that disrupted whole classes and inspired masturbatory fantasies on a plague-like scale.

She had discovered older men as well. Servicemen home from Fort Campbell, sailors home from the sea. Aging alumni with nothing to do all day but shoot pool and drink splo whiskey all night and home nowhere save the memory of the hometown crowd chanting their names like a litany. Riding with these gangling long-legged heroes of near mythic proportion to the fabled places of the surrounding counties. Club Cloverdale, Elkin Springs. Dancing there to the local band, riding through the summer night to Napier Lake, Firetower Ridge. The moment of sweet surrender eternal, a loop tape she could and did play again and again.

There were things to be kept, things to be cast aside, she was a juggler high on sex and country music and white whiskey and she could not hold onto everything. One of the first things to go was Bradshaw.

Bradshaw was nothing anyway, a nobody. In fact he was worse than a nobody, on her scale he was a somebody with a minus sign, because his father was a preacher; preachers did not figure very high in her scheme of things. Once as a child she had gone with Bradshaw to church. His father was preaching at the Primitive Baptist Church and when he knelt and prayed at length nigh interminable and then arose he had left in the wake of his raving a circular area of the floor wet with spit. Caren had looked at him with a kind of detached revulsion and she told it all over school that he had spit all over everybody in the first three rows.

Bradshaw had his memories, or perhaps they had him, for they would not please him: once in the seventh grade they had been behind a chainlink fence watching the football team practice. The players were lying on their stomachs, backs arched, hands locked to their ankles, rocking back and forth. They look like they're screwing the ground, Caren had mused, and hearing her say the word had the force of a blow. Screwing. Her soft ladylike voice. The word was branded whitehot onto the smoking lobes of his brain. It was eternal. It had fueled countless secret and sweaty nighttime fantasies, it would fuel countless more. To him she was Eros personified, as if all history's musky female sex had been distilled and cast in her image.

He used to try to keep up. By the time he discovered whiskey and shantytown gangfucks and niggerized cars running on luck and stolen gas she was already out of his reach. She had eloped with a pipeliner and went to Nashville to become a country music singer. She was gone two years. Whatever craft she plied in those years no one ever saw her name on a jukebox, heard her sing on the Grand Ole Opry. When she did come back she had lost the pipeliner somewhere along the way but she did not seem to miss him; she had learned that the world is wide, pipeliners easy to come by. After a while she went to work as a waitress in first one and then another of a series of county line beerjoints and she had stories of the seamy side of show business. Nashville was her Hollywood, her Babylon.

Bradshaw would still try his luck from time to time, but he was hopelessly miscast in her mind, she refused to update the picture she had of him. He kept track of her, was subtly obsessed with her slide down the social scale. He could not rise to her level, perhaps she'd fall to his. He kept up with each abortion, each lost boyfriend. They were all points in some elaborate game he played in his head.

The last he'd heard she was married to a truck driver and he thought her lost but one Saturday night in July he walked into Goblin's Knob and there she was coming through the kitchen door with a tray of freshly washed beer mugs. Bradshaw could not believe his luck. Somewhere a god had smiled down on him. He ordered a mug of beer and drank and wiped the mustache of foam off his lips and just looked at her.

Hey, Buddy. How you been?

He strove to keep calm. The sight of her maddened him. She had set the tray down and begun to remove the mugs and stack them upside down on a towel beneath the bar. He watched the movement of her breasts as she worked. His mouth felt dry.

I been all right. Been travelin around some. What you doin back around here? I heard you was married.

Well, I may have been when you heard it. I'm not now.

What happened?

It's a long story. Ain't they all?

Damn, Caren. Me and you ort to get together.

Why?

Why...for old time's sake. We go back a long way. We could talk about the times we had.

We never had any times, she said. Her eyes dismissed him, wandered over the few drinkers at the scattered tables. Refugees from dog day heat. Her appraising eyes ceased on a rawboned man wearing a gaudy cowboy shirt. Then they turned back to Bradshaw. Old times are gone anyway, she told him. New times are all there is.

Bradshaw drank in silence for a time, watched in the wonky barglass the camaraderie about him, himself alone at its center in the mirror, no part of it.

Come on, Caren. Let's me and you step out tonight.

She smiled at him. I can't, Buddy. You know I always had bigger fish to fry.

He drained his mug and arose. You'll come around.

When hell freezes over, she said, then smiled to take the edge off it. No hard feelings.

He winked at her. We'll see, he said, and wended his way toward the door, glancing once toward the man in the cowboy shirt.

Late of an evening then you would see them begin to gather in the poolroom like an enclave of the damned, taking pause at some lost waystation of doomed souls. Seated at the bar awaiting night and whatever promises it would ultimately leave unfulfilled, they had an air of wistful patience. Surely the night held more for them than darkness. Yet there was something anticipatory about them, something lost, they were like worshipers drawn to this curious tabernacle as if it alone would shelter them from whatever apocalypse fell beyond the reach of its diastolic neon. Grim faces in some medieval mural of freaks and jesters, curious and animate statuary sought out by a collector with a bent for the grotesque.

Old men with vague war wounds and metal plates in their skulls held a drunken discourse with themselves and when their rheumy eyes did focus on the world about them it was as if they viewed it across some chasm unimaginably wide and as if it were some land they had left and could not remember the way back to, no more tangible than the plot of space and time that had been their childhood.

Old spent whores devoid of pretense and their young protégées patinaed with guile moved alike among them with a ribald and pred-atory ambiance. Edgewater could sense there was a kinship here, a curious brotherhood of the forsaken, the unwanted, the obsolete. Yet their coarse laughter that drew Edgewater near to them out of whatever darkness mocked him, was a story that he could not quite overhear, a joke that was missing the punchline, a voice, no more.

Crippled Elmer cadged beer with a sort of wistful desperation while his mother searched faces foreign enough to these shores as to be unaware or desperate enough to be unmindful of her generosity with gonorrhea spores and body lice. Her wrinkled face powdered and rouged grotesquely as if her cosmetologist was a failed undertaker so inept as to be drummed from the craft, her hair an electric orange red so absolutely divorced from anything that ever grew on a human head that it appeared something purloined in haste by mistake from the trunk of a clown. She wore brash and groundless confidence like some bright garment of youth that did not fit anymore. She forced on Edgewater a drink of Bobwhite from a halfpint she wore on a string about her neck like some gross bauble. Hauled up from whatever grubby depths of her garments and warmed to body temperature by her collapsed and withered dugs. The bottle itself lipsticked and scented alike with dimestore perfume and the acrid musk of her body; the bottle tilted to her upraised face and upon his ears like some backdrop or soundtrack to whatever drama he played out came through the graffiti-ridden walls of the men's room the click of the pool balls. The clanging of the pinball machine, the drunken voices crossing boast with complaint, farther yet and lost a wailing ambulance was shuttled down the endless walls of the night.

Bradshaw and Edgewater fell in with Arnold and he had a place that he would show them. A honkytonk where the women were easy and the whiskey cheap and the music loud. They piled into the Chevrolet and commenced a drunken wandering journey through backwoods and timbered ridges, Arnold's voice a confident buzz of promises.

I wouldn't take just anybody out here, he told them, his face sly and foxlike by the yellow dashlight. Oh, you'll like this place. Its pussy wanders in and out all night long with a glass of whiskey in its hand and all you got to do is ask. Now how does that sound to you?

Bradshaw was unconvinced. I lived here all my life and never heard of no such place. I ain't hid under a washtub all that time or my light under a bushel neither.

As if already half demented, Arnold had slipped into some occult realm of dreams and conjured up by telluric alchemy a fantasyland to his order: available pussy and whiskey without end, the law here unarmed or feeble and no questions asked, no papers to be looked at.

The foraging headlights showed them a land of blackjack and shadows and canted shanties more akin to lairs than dwellings and down winding hills through deep hollows where the faces of politicians stared blandly back from telephone poles, old churches with scripture scrawled like threats of dire intent. Coal oil lit shacks and straggling lines of blacks along the littered shoulder of the road who turned to stare them past with expressionless faces.

The hell with this, Bradshaw said. I'm going back and try to get Bonnie to go to Ethridge to the dance with me.

It ain't much further, Arnold reassured him.

Then ultimately to a clearing where there were four or five old cars ringed about a sprawling shack through whose slotted walls and boarded windows spilled out yellow light and the sounds of an unamplified gutbucket guitar and a loose and heavy shuffling of feet.

Hell, we got a dance right here, Arnold said gleefully. He had a proprietary arm about their shoulders. You boys git out and I'll show you around.

They stood uncertainly in the bare front yard. Two or three starved-looking dogs sniffed at them about their cuffs to see were they edible. While they stood as if awaiting invitation, voices arose inside, rose higher still as others joined in, female shrieks of distress. The door flew open and banged against the wall, there was a man framed briefly against the interior light. There were doorsteps there but he did not use them. He leapt out in the yard, his face terrorstricken. It was all instantaneous. His head whirled in one desperate search for cover and he ran for a scraggly stand of pines bent forward, arms flailing the night, his footfalls the only sound there was. Then the door filled again and a big black man leapt down the steps with an unbreeched shotgun in his hands, fumbling shells into it as he came, eyes white and wild and searching among the crouching shadows. He breeched up the gun.

Out my motherfuckin way, he told them.

They needed no such advice. He ran a few steps and dropped to one knee and fired one barrel into the spinney of trees. By the time the blast had died away he was again running toward the woods. Bradshaw had turned around spinning back onto the gravel road.

Arnold was apologetic. I just don't understand it, he told them. It was real quiet last time I'se out here. Bradshaw gave him a withering look of contempt and made no other reply.

It was late when they got to Ethridge and things did not go right here either. Bradshaw had grown sullen and uncommunicative. He drank steadily and watched the night slip away, replace unwanted scenery with yet more of the same. He had come to dimly suspect some vast conspiracy of his enemies. Some plot concocted by Bonnie and Chief Aday to keep him from getting bred. The dance was being held in an enormous long building that had once been a roller rink and it was surrounded by rows on rows of cars. They could hear the music long before they got in, discordant shards of guitars and fiddles, a lachrymose hillybilly voice. *I'd walk for miles, cry or smiles, for my mama and daddy*, it sang.

Bradshaw was pointing out a car to Edgewater. It was a yellow and black Mercury with enormous mudflaps and hubcaps designed to look like wire wheels. That goddamned Bobby Yates's new car, he said. Sniffin around after Sudy. I may just whip his sorry ass.

That ain't Bobby's car, Arnold said. Bobby's in Michigan or someres.

I wish you'd sort of hold it down, Edgewater told him. I'm gittin a little weary of this shit. You keep on the way you're going and you're gonna have us all in jail.

He may even have Sudy in there tonight. I've told that son of a bitch the last time I'm gonna tell him. Next time I'll show him.

Hell, Arnold said. Settle down a little. Let's go in and pick us out one. I bet there's women in there stacked three deep.

Behind the restraining arm of the bouncer couples closedanced and swayed to the music of the bands. A rotating ceiling light bathed the dancers in a dreamy and romantic glow. The bouncer shook his head. No stags allowed, he said firmly.

Bradshaw shook his head in disbelief. He gathered his faculties. I'll give you to understand I'm not no goddamned Staggs, he finally said. I'm a Bradshaw and have been all my life. I got a drivin license in my hip pocket here to prove it.

The bouncer's face was almost pitying. Edgewater was grinning, trying not to laugh. He turned and watched girls' soft faces dreaming past him on the dancefloor.

I don't care what's in your hip pocket, the bouncer told him. You don't get in here tonight unless you're a couple and at the best I don't see one. You ain't but half a one. If you want in you'll have to bring a girl like everybody else.

Bradshaw became inarticulate with rage. Edgewater and Arnold grasped his arms and pulled him bodily out the door and down the steps. He jerked free and fell upon the yellow and black Mercury and began kicking the side of it.

Fuck this shit, Edgewater said. Who needs it.

Then Bradshaw ceased and went and set down on the concrete steps.

It may be some girls'd come in by themselves, Arnold told him placatingly. We'll just ask em and take them in. Bradshaw was staring at the Mercury in deep thought.

I need me a possum, he told Arnold at last. You ain't got one on ye have ye?

A what?

Bradshaw was getting in a better mood. Ain't you never put a possum in nobody's car you didn't like? Hell, they'll shit all over it and tear up the upholstery tryin to get out and make the damnest mess you ever seen.

In a kind of detached unbelief Edgewater drove them around looking for possums out the residential area into the country on little winding backroads. Bradshaw and Arnold hunched forward peering at the roadside as the lights illuminated it. But they could not find any possums. Apparently they had all stayed home.

It beats any goddamned thing I ever seen, Bradshaw said savagely. You don't want a possum you're kneedeep in the sons of bitches and when you need one they ain't one to be found nowhere.

The only decent thing that happened to Arnold all night was that they let him out at his home. Thus he was not there when the cruiser fell in behind them. It followed them from the city limits on toward town, stalking them, somehow predatory, an insolent and arrogant beast suffused with confidence of its prey. Bradshaw's hands were rigid on the steering wheel. He sat with an uncustomary stiff erectness, eyes straight ahead, some besieged statue.

Don't look back, he cautioned Edgewater, peering into the rearview mirror. Act like you don't see em. They may not do nothing if we just ignore them.

The red lights came on even with the water tank and Bradshaw drove dumbly on. The siren came in one brief burst and he pulled over to the curb and ceased. He sat, pounding the steering wheel gently with the palms of his hands. I guess ignoring them just don't work anymore, Edgewater said.

He turned to see. The car had halted behind them and there was an officer getting out. Someone else remained in the car, a diminutive shape, perhaps a girl. Bradshaw was looking too. Hell, it's Aday. That underminin little slut put him up to it, he said. He told Edgewater to act sober.

Hell, I am sober, Edgewater said. The unperceptive world would have seen in the face at the window something fatherly, benign. A middleaged face with sagging jowls, mildly quizzical watery blue eyes, the face of the law, all of authority standing between the sleeping in their beds and such amoral miscreants as even now sat silent under his stolid stare.

Something the trouble? Edgewater asked him.

There may be, the man said agreeably. We'll see. Could I look at your license, Bradshaw? Bradshaw had it ready. Aday read it carefully, front and back, as if its manufacture was somehow foreign to him, as if its secrets eluded him. He did not hand it back. He ignored Bradshaw's reaching hand and stood holding the license.

What was you wobbling so for back there?

Wobblin? I didn't know I was.

Didn't know? You looked like you'd lost something and was drivin along lookin for it first on one side of the road and then the other.

Well, that's news to me.

In your shape that may very well be. You been drinkin, ain't ye?

No.

Then if I'se you I'd sure feel hard at whoever it was poured it all over me. You smell like a hog that fell in a malt barrel.

I might of had a beer or two.

What about you there, Silent Cal?

I'm not drinking either, Edgewater said.

We ain't done a goddamned thing.

Maybe, maybe not. But how about usin obscene language to a lady? Aday's face tightened and anger flared and died in his eyes.

I been up since six o'clock this morning, Bradshaw said. Any ladies seen since I left the house must of scaped my notice.

How about public drunkenness then and disorderly conduct? How's that suit you? How about driving while intoxicated and how about what all you got hid in this car I ain't even searched yet?

Shit, Bradshaw said.

Aday opened the door. How about you boys takin a little walk out in the street here and back. So I can sort of judge if you're in command of your faculties or not.

Edgewater walking. The girl watched, a small malign presence by the dashlight. He looked away. The dark bowl of the night was full of stars, full constellations rising far and far. The red lights from the watertank illuminated above him a smooth metallic ovoid, great arachnid legs of girders and beams descending lost in mist, some intradimensional insect descending to spirit him away to other shores. A car paused to watch him, pulled slowly around him, pale faces on their way to freedom.

Bradshaw when he walked felt called upon to execute some cocky variant on an about face and ended disoriented and uncertain of his bearing, leaning, appeared poised for flight into whatever meager cover might lie beyond the throbbing redlight. Edgewater leaned tiredly against the car, heard already the final clang of steel doors. Git on over here and get in the back, Aday said.

Aday drove Bradshaw's car and Bonnie followed in the cruiser. Bradshaw turned once to watch her. He looked back to the front, studied malevolently the cropped hair on the back of Aday's neck. You needn't be so goddamned smug, Bradshaw said. I'd a been in your shoes if I wanted to lay out twenty dollars like you did.

A man with a mouth like yours could fall down that staircase goin up to the jailhouse, Aday told him. More'n one feller got banged up pretty bad like that.

Hell, no hard feelins. A poor son of a bitch falls for a whore like that's got enough troubles without my addin to em. You just remember the sun don't shine up the same dog's ass every day.

Aday was turning into the courtyard, before them the courthouse rose up stark and forbidding, its dark bricked edifice sinister as some bastioned medieval castle.

It does when one dog's the chief of police and the other one ain't, he told Bradshaw mildly.

Reality touched Edgewater only in places of transiency, jails and bus stations, the highway. Horizons and locks and timetables spawned in him a desperation, an aching need to be gone.

Asleep in the harsh and whiskeysmelling dark, he saw his mother's face, the weight of his father's hand, dreamed old childhood words and deeds long past recall.

In a long ago December dark his grandmother died behind weathered stone walls, he could hear through the canted screen door her noisy dying, the rasp of her breathing from out the cool oily air like some malign beast panting faint and fainter from its lair. From the porch the breathing became no more than the rattle of such leaves as were left in the still and frozen trees. From out of the dark too came still and profound the soft voices of the mourners, her sons and daughters brought back by death like flung stones regathered, and in the yard winter light on freshly minted cars with northern tags, inside them a smell of newness, a smell of distances crossed, of strange and prosperous lands.

This same still and silver light on his cousin's face, so surreal and clear that he could trace with clarity the intricate veinery of her eyelid, the eye itself closed, the lash a sooty pooling shadow, her naked breasts as white and poreless as marble, as chill as December stone flowers that perhaps bloomed only on such winter nights as the scythe was abroad in the land.

Her touch as soft as any before or since, her lies as sweet: the uncle opening the door on them then, its near soundless click itself a testimonial to the quality of his work on Detroit assembly lines. Perhaps he bolted on this very door, had no foreboding that he would one night open it so that moonlight would fall oblique on his near-naked daughter as no light ought to fall as no father ought to see his daughter, standing necktied and awkward and halfapologetic before anger seized him.

Yet his father had cried. The face turned away when Edgewater mounted the steps to the Greyhound bus and to whatever lay farther beyond it and the harsh face had crumpled, eyes mirroring his own with surprise as if his face would not do his bidding, with the shock of it surprising them both. The old man never cried. Yet he turned away, there was the worn chambray of his back, across his shoulder bisecting the face of his mother which did not exist anymore in any form approaching this, existed only in such dreams when reality and fantasy swirled like ink spilled in water, clouds of ever paler black fanning outward and lost.

The window he peered through was the eye of a world that he was forsaking or that was forsaking him. Through the window of the bus, the town falling away pathetically sudden and faces burning there as if his mind had by some dark alchemy etched their likenesses eternally into the glass. Beyond these images that watched him with benign unconcern, a backdrop like juryrigged scenery of amateur devising, a threadbare tapestry of houses thinning out, woods beginning and deep hollows from whose cedared mouths a mist of time itself rose like smoke. Faster now and dusk hard on his heels and the maw of the night opening before him, a rushing collage of the mountains and the scattered yellowlit windows of the woods and the trees, the trees, the trees.

The jailer brought them plates and set them on a long benchlike table and then he fetched up from his overalls an enormous ring of keys and opened their cells. Breakfast was fried bologna and eggs. Two slices of untoasted light bread and coffee so translucent Edgewater could see the bottom of the tin cup. The eggs were fried hard, done to a rubberlike texture and their edges were burnt lace in congealing grease.

Bradshaw stuck a fork in an egg, dissecting with the tines and cutting them up. Busily shaking out salt. Just add ye tip onto the bill, he told the jailer. Me and Billy here'll settle up when we check out.

What I hear that may be some time, the jailer said. He relocked the bullpen and went out of sight and they could hear his steps on the stairs.

They were halfway through with breakfast when the girl came. She came up silent and stood leaning against the bars watching them as if what she saw did not please her greatly. Her face was calm, her gaze appraising. If you ain't a finelooking pair, Sudy said evenly.

I can explain everything, Bradshaw said. His effervescence seemed to evaporate. His eyes were slick and evasive. He chewed endlessly and swallowed and the mouthful seemed to lodge in his throat. He could not meet her gaze. He sat staring at the tin plate where his loaded but unraised fork was at rest and he waited, perhaps for her to leave, or to deliver whatever message she had brought.

Any explanation you got you can save for Mama, Sudy said. I imagine you could use the extra time to study one up anyway. You don't owe it to me, even if it was me up half the night listening to her ravin about you bloody in some ditch somewhere with that car wrapped around you.

Hell, ask Billy here what happened. He'll tell you. Goddamn miserable excuse for a law they got in this town.

She turned on Edgewater a look of exaggerated attention, as if she waited breathless for whatever such wonders he was about to reveal. Then the expression faded and there was nothing there at all, the face bland and innocent and the eyes deep and blue. It was a strange look, as if the face had no emotion of its own to reveal but awaited Edgewater like a mirror, willing to reflect whatever images he chose to cast there.

Edgewater laid his silverware down and arose and walked into his open cell, stared out the window at the roofs of buildings below him, flat tarred rectangles outlined by cinderblocks. The courtyard seemed far below, the bars too tight to squeeze through. His chin rested on his forearm. The windows faced east and he could feel the warm comfort of the sun, see it fall knifesharp through the edge of the window, see spectral motes of dust spin weightless in elliptic orbits, feel its weight on his face like the palms of a woman's hands. Unseen pigeons cooed softly, he could hear them scrambling about the roof over him, then the beat of their wings.

When do you start to work? the girl asked Bradshaw.

They not hirin right now, he told her sullenly. How'd you know where we was anyway?

Some woman call the house way in the night and when I picked up the phone she just said you was in jail. When I asked who was it she just hung up.

Now who'd pull a sorry trick like that?

I figured you'd come nearer knowin than me.

Damn meddlin busybodies. Did Mama send any bail money?

All she sent was seventy-five dollars and I had to prize it out of her hand a bill at a time.

Hell, that ought to be enough. Have you been to the judge's office? How much is my bail?

They fined you seventy-five dollars. Mama called before I come out here.

Bradshaw sat for a time in awkward silence. He glanced at Edgewater still at the window. Edgewater seemed lost in the study of whatever Saturday commerce moved below him in the streets and appeared not to have been listening.

Well, what about Billy here? Didn't she send the money to get him out too?

I told you all she sent was seventy-five dollars.

Me and him was in this together. You go tell her I said loan Billy enough to pay his fine. How much is his?

Twenty-five dollars. But she won't do it. She paused, looked obliquely at Edgewater. She said he was the one got you in here in the first place. As if you ever needed any help and I told her so.

Damn, Sudy, how come you always come down so hard on me?

She stood clasping the purse. Edgewater had turned, watched her. Their eyes met and she stood awkwardly, somehow like a little girl playing grownup, the grace of womanhood always just out of her reach. She dropped her eyes from Edgewater.

I'll see if I can get some more money, she said.

Get it where?

I'll go try to cash a check.

I always thought you had to have money in the bank to cash a check.

Just let me alone, all right. I'll be back in a little while. Just wait here.

We wasn't planning on goin anywhere, Bradshaw said sarcastically.

This time when she came the jailer was with her. He unlocked the cell and motioned them out. They followed her down the stairs, their footfalls hollow and echoing in these sepulchral halls of justice and onto the first floor. Idlers they passed glanced at them without much interest and they pushed through the heavy door and out onto the steps. Edgewater took a deep breath, already there was a smell of autumn in the air he filled his lungs with.

Bradshaw went to get the car and they waited for him at the front of the courthouse.

Where'd you get the money?

I wrote a check and signed Mama's name to it.

Why?

She pretended to misunderstand. Because she had money in the bank and I didn't. What do you think?

I'll pay you back.

Let it go. I'll just try to beat her to the mailbox when the checks come back. If I know Buddy it was all his fault anyway.

Edgewater was going through his pocket. You hadn't got such a thing as a cigarette on you have you?

She opened her purse and at last took out a half pack of Camels. I guess you can have one of these. I don't smoke. They're a keepsake. A souvenir I guess you'd say.

He took the cigarettes, tilted one from the pack, handed it back to her. She put it back in the purse. The tobacco was dry, a cylinder of tinder that flared when he lit it. The tobacco smoke tasted stale, weak. A souvenir of what? he tested.

Just a keepsake. Here comes Buddy.

Edgewater followed her to the car and got in. He pondered on what sort of memory had left only a half pack of cigarettes to keep it alive.

In spite of getting up in the mornings with the intention of going he stayed on all through the summer. He would be thinking of leaving and Bradshaw would say, How about easing over to the Knob for a brew? Or would draw him aside and say, Swalls needs a little whiskey. Let's pick him up a load in Hickman County and make a little pocket money. By this time the old woman had come to see him as the fruition of some grim curse cast upon her by her enemies, some maledictive embodiment of evil come to lead her son down the red cherted road to hell, her doling out dollar bills grudgingly and one by one, then rehiding the old purse somewhere Bradshaw would not look, wishing he was gone and afraid he would leave at the same time.

It had been a wet spring that year but when the rain ceased and the clouds dissipated it would not rain again, as if all the year's allotted water had been dispensed, the sky clear and infinitely blue. July went out hot and harsh and dry. Corn that had been green and richly promising withered and yellowed, less than waist high, forlorn and hopeless. The stalks twisted on themselves as if they would by main force wring water up from the parched earth.

Long used to the vagaries of the weather, folks were still touched by an unease, a disorientation, an aberrance in the way of the world. Leaves starved for water turned yellow prophesying an early fall. Taproots crept ever deeper, searching for the sustenance locked in the earth's keep. Vines wilted and their tendrils curled and then blackened as if frost had seared them. The earth grew harsh and then harsher. Faultlines came in it and fissured microcataclysms crept through the fields and the sun bore down a fierce and vindictive retribution. Cisterns dried up, streams fell and shrank, left fish beached goggle-eyed and gills faintly pumping to drown in fetid sloughs. Ponds dried to a slimy green scum that was a wonder to young boys, marvelous primeval life forms the sun sucked the water from so that in time it became a dry fibrous mass coating the slick clay. Then the clay dulled and dried, became an intricately faulted surreal waste as barren as anything that must shuttle through the stellar depths.

Old men would come out that year at night and stare at the sky as if some sign might flare there briefly: stood out in the hazy blue dusk while fireflies moved like spirit lights among the dark boles of trees and heat lightning flared and died, faint mocking thunder tumbling roll on roll down the well of the sky. They listened to the sounds of the night as if encoded in the cries of insects might lurk some secret knowledge of the earth's complexities, surely creatures of the night dwelt deeper in God's favor than they. Sometimes along toward dawn clouds might form and offer surcease. Then the sun would rise over the jagged trees orange and malefic and its heat would fall like a weight. What clouds had formed would dissipate into faint wisps the sun burned away and ultimately the sky would be marvelously clear, a hot mocking blue.

Old carbodies lost in the rank sweetsmelling jungle of honeysuckle and kudzu became unbearably hot to the touch, tar on the blacktops bubbled soft and viscous, became a quagmire drawing into itself the tracks of children and bottlecaps and hapless insects and whatever befell it. Heat at midday fell flat and malign and the concrete highway curbings took on a glint as if they were encrusted with jewels, a highway of diamonds.

Preachers hinted apocalypse in Sunday sermons to rows of limp parishioners among whose ranks fans fluttered listlessly as leaves in the vagaries of the wind. Saturday corner gospelmongers were more direct. Demented and hydrophobic they ranted of man's dark side. I told you and you wouldn't listen, they said with satisfaction. Maybe you'll listen now. The wrath of God had kicked aside a rotten log, bared the sun's white agony onto a motley of writhing grubs, sexton beetles scuttling for shelter. The earth wearying of its tenants, shuffling them off into the eye of the sun. Choking with vitriol these men of God looked savagely about for such souls as Saturday night might bring within the range of their voices and saw little worth sparing. Mad faces turned toward the hot sky, they demanded God smite all these whoremongers and adulterers, honkytonk brawlers, whiskey drinking fornicators. That not even the young be spared for evil already ran through them like a fault line.

It became a summer of random violence. Tales carried tense and breathless backyard to backyard with a kind of anticipation, each day new horrors.

Forsaken by sleep, Wallace Suggs lay and listened to the tin pop with heat and the slow drone of dirt daubers about the rafters and to the breathing of his wife beside him and katydids beyond the unscreened windows told him of old wrongs she'd done him, old cuckoldments, old lovers on other nights as slow and sweaty as this one: told of burnt-up corn and notes due and at length he got up naked and barefoot and took down his shotgun. He shot her while she slept and went down to the children's room and shot them as well save the oldest boy who sprang out the window. A figure mad with desperation fleeing toward the barn through latticed moonlight and gone in the haysmelling dark. Gun aloft and barefoot Suggs leapt tenderfooted over rocks and briars and killed his boy in the loft, turned the gun last on himself.

In later years they called it haunted there, shunned, plagued. Boys taking dares stoned such windows as there were and fled, and at night blue lights were said to flit about the cottonwoods and a globe of phosphorescence to rise above the graveyard. Cries of old violence crossed and commingled, rage and entreaty warred ceaselessly in the listening night.

Another: Stella Weatherspan held back the curtain and peered past the yard to where her husband Clovis worked on his truck and a deepest rage seethed within her, apocalyptic visions flared behind her limpid eyes. He had a bottle of beer aloft and eyes squinting into the sun as he drained it and set it on the angleiron rimming the truck flat. He was bare to the waist and bronzed from the sun and despite the slack gut there was a look of indolent violence about him.

The truck was jacked up and both rear wheels off and he slid under it.
I told you to bring me a beer, he called without looking toward the house.
I told you they ain't one.
Then you better shit one.
Beyond the cordwood truck sicklooking cotton drowned in Johnson grass and she had not been able to get him to so much as file a hoe, he seemed always to clutch a wrench or a beer bottle, to be always leaving for Goblin's Knob. He half raised one elbow and peered toward the house. There was a curious look on his face: not contempt or dislike

or even anger but simply a kind of dismissal, a denial of existence. An arrogance that transcended her and this cottage with its gingerbread scrollwork and the giveupon cotton. It was a look gone in a flicker but by such moments are the thought and deed welded to one.

She had already noticed the jack cocked slanting but he would ever defy fate to smite him. She was close enough to see the slick sheen of perspiration on his upper torso and the tattoo of a naked woman lost in a thicket of suncoppered hairs and he was reaching an arm toward the brake line when she took up the galvanized pipe he used for a fulcrum and warped the jack as hard as she could.

There was some insurance money; she soon discovered there was no shortage of good old boys to help her spend it. A strange new world opened itself to her. Grief stricken, folks said at first, taken to drink and to riding in topless cars and slow dancing at Goblin's Knob to honkytonk songs and to high brittle laughter devoid of humor. By the time the money was gone she was living with a gangling youth named Ray Tanner who left a cancer-ridden wife for her.

They sold the house when there was nothing left to sell and with the money embarked on a monumental binge. They closedanced at the Knob through an alcoholic haze while he mentally computed how much money must be left. Wayne Raney sang, *My hair's still curly and my eyes are still blue. Why don't you love me like you used to do?* The homilies of Hank Williams fell on deaf ears: *Take my advice, or you'll curse the day you started rollin down that lost highway.*

With the last of the money they bought an old silver housetrailer angular as a tinfoil box and set it down on rented land, a cornfield bare of tree or flower. They set it on cinderblocks and she dug up a bed at the end of it for hollyhocks. Then one day he was just gone. There were long lonesome days waiting for the mailman but there was not a letter ever.

She lived all alone then and with the years a kind of bleak austerity settled itself upon her, as she grew older she looked with disapproval upon the doings of the young. She was saved at a traveling tent revival, all her sins absolved, washed white as snow.

Swalls drew up two dripping brown bottles of beer and uncapped them. You ever see weather like this in your life? It's a hunnerd and twelve degrees out there.

They sat on the high shaded porch and drank the beer. Edgewater glanced toward the road. The blacktop was overhung with shimmering waves of heat and the fronds of sumacs hung wilted and thickly talcumed with dust.

Arnold drank from his bottle. Hell, Edgewater brung it with him from California. They have this kind of weather out there all the time.

Swalls looked at Edgewater. I hope you plan on carrying it with you when you go, he said.

They were down by the creek when she told him, hesitant to be the bearer of such ill tidings. She was reticent at first, he later wished he'd kept his peace. He wouldn't have had to ask her what the matter was. Yet she would have told him anyway, she was bound to get it said. They stood in light dappled by late summer greenery, the creek catching and refracting the sun like a stream of moving light. As she talked she spoke faster, her face lit with a bright and fragile anger.

Are you sure?

Yes.

Well, goddamn.

She fell silent, shredded dried bark in her nervous fingers, dropped it into the creek, watched it list and slide. It was a long time before she spoke. I thought you was doin somethin, she said apologetically.

I guess I was, he said. I guess I done a little more than I thought.

He was shaking his head. That's crazy, he told her.

It may be crazy but that's the way it is. What's crazy about it, anyway? It happens to people every day.

How do you know you are?

How do you think I know? The way people always find out.

You mean you've been to the doctor then.

Of course I hadn't been to a doctor. Quit makin fun of me. You're the one talkin crazy.

How late are you?

She flushed, her eyes turned away to follow a cardinal's flight, bright drop of blood in a world of green. I don't know what you're talkin about.

He had knelt in the yard, laced his arms about his knees. She remained standing before him, still, accusatory. Yet watchers from a

distance would have seen in this silent tableau something courtly, a car-
ryover from a simpler time. Knelt so in the earth perhaps pled her hand.

Come off it. When was your period supposed to start?

Around the twentieth.

Good God. You're not hardly a month late. What are you getting so
excited about? A lot of things could have caused that.

I just know the one. Her face was pale but there was a stubborn core
at her center, there was no give to her. Why do you keep saying me,
askin about me? You're in this too, you know. I thought you was doin
something.

Doing something? Doin what, for Christ's sake?

You know what I mean. Wearin them things. Somethin to stop it,
to keep it from happenin.

Edgewater was quiet. I am doing something, he thought. I am moving down the line, infinitesimally slow, you cannot detect my motion
yet. You're setting me up, he told her.

She began to cry, there was a brittle desperation about her. She was
looking at the ground before his feet, at meaningless marks he made
there with a stick. She would not meet his eyes. I knew you'd try to get
out of it, she told him.

Goddamn it. I never claimed to be a genius but at the same time I
don't have to be hit over the head with a stick. I don't have to hear bells
ring or have a light bulb appear over my head.

I guess you'll deny doin it to me all those times. Ever night nearly.
I guess you'll deny admittin you never used them things or done anything to stop it.

I guess you'll deny practically dragging me from my chaste and con-
tinent bed.

You wanted it.

Well. It doesn't matter now. None of it does. I'm just a little foggy
on just what it is you want me to do.

You ought to know without me havin to beg you. I want you to do
what a man has to. If we're going to have a baby it has to have a name.
Was everthing you told me just lies?

No, but I still don't like being played for a fool.

Why do you have to make it seem like something dirty? I oughtn't
said anything to you about it. I ought to've told Mama and Buddy and

had them do what it is you do. Let the sheriff serve you with the papers or somethin.

The hell with a bunch of papers, Edgewater said. You better be thinking this over. You better be making some other arrangements.

She was still crying. The only other arrangements I know is to kill myself, she said. Kill it or myself and I don't know how to kill it.

Edgewater was looking around with a kind of desperation. He arose and laid an arm about her shoulder, touched her cheek but she twisted away.

Sometimes I think how good it'd be just to go to sleep and not wake up, she said bitterly.

Stop talking crazy.

I swear I will. I'll kill myself and it'll be on your head. I'd rather do it as tell Mama, it'd kill her. You've got to help me, Billy.

I don't have to do anything but die.

Then what'll I tell her and Buddy? What'll I tell everbody?

Just deny everything and tell them you don't know how it could have happened.

You think you're so smart because you don't care about anything or anybody. Like that puts you above everbody else.

Well. I don't know. I'm just like everybody else, trying to get by as light as I can. It seems to me it took awhile for things to come to this; I guess it'll take longer than a few minutes to figure out what to do. Quit crying and quit thinking about it till I work out something.

It's all I can think about. It's all I've been thinking about.

We'll work something out.

That's easy for you to say. You're not real, she told him mockingly. If they was taking a census I doubt they'd even count you.

When they started to the house she hung back, there was a kind of mournful dread about her, and all the way back he was thinking: If I'd left yesterday I wouldn't know any of this, none of it would exist.

Edgewater drank a beer at the Knob, saw his reflection wrought twisted and strange by the bar glass, the past suddenly all about him as if it existed still, a strange world peopled by his past and present and future, a triple exposure crowded with magic.

It had been Jenny. She said his name and her voice trailed off, faltered, the phone fell and banged against something.

Here was a deadfall laid in time: the phone had rung in National City. Jenny was in Chula Vista and he had not let anything slow him down but by the time he got there it was too late anyway.

All the lights were on and he wandered from room to room like a harried burglar until he found her in a bathroom. All his mind would register at first was blood, an inordinate amount of blood, pooled where she lay dead on the tile floor on rags and towels and bedsheets and delicate drops of it about the floor in a widening mad pattern of desperation, a puddle of it by the phone, a spoor for the damned to interpret and follow.

She was curled on her side with a towel clutched between her legs and she had died trying to hold life in, would defy it to flow out of her, had chinked herself with cloths like rags stuffed in cracks against the winds. There was a half fifth of vodka open on the dinette table and a glass and he judged she'd gotten herself drunk before attempting, her drinking to the edge and past it. Long lonesome hours, as lonesome as it ever gets. He drank half a waterglass of the vodka and walked out into a day bright as any day ever was, a day in which the mechanisms of the world meshed just as smoothly as they had ever done, he detected no changes. One soul, one mote, spun off its orbit into the abyss, a thing of no import. He walked up the street in the hot sunshine with the vodka burning in his stomach and imbued with a mystic wonder that his feet did his bidding. He went back to his apartment because he could not think of anything else to do.

A neighbor turned in his name and the SDPD picked him up for questioning but they did not seem to have any questions he had answers for. An abortion kit, they called it. Somebody picked it up in Tijuana. It hadn't been him, he hadn't known they existed. Imagine asking for one in a, what? Drugstore? Had the baby been his? Well. It could have been. It could not have been. The things you never know about a person you think you know. She was a jigsaw puzzle he held only one piece to, did not really care to compare notes with the holders of the rest of the puzzle.

He was in Chula Vista when the private detective her father had hired found him. He had never seen a private detective and so studied this one with interest while they rode, disappointed in this laconic young man who looked more like a CPA than anything out of Chandler.

Her father was very well off. He studied Edgewater across an immense shiny escritoire. Edgewater stared at the desk. Its top was formed by blocks of different rare woods, rubbed and polished until it gleamed.

The man looked at him from a vast distance, as an entomologist might study some new but unimportant species of insect.

I just wanted to see for myself what kind of piece of trash you were, he said.

Edgewater had no words to say.

Why didn't you take precautions and why didn't you take her to an abortionist? How could this thing have happened?

I didn't know, Edgewater said, felt how inadequate that was.

Why didn't she come to me?

Edgewater shrugged, arose.

Sit your ass down.

Edgewater starting for the door, already reaching for the knob.

Was it yours?

Yes, Edgewater said, though he did not know, could not have known.

He was in Arizona before he came to himself, before he felt right. He had slept on the desert and when he came out onto 66 the sun came up. It came up all at once and in it the highway was as straight as a chalked line and gleamed as if it were made of crushed jewels. He had never seen it so before. It would take him anywhere in this round world he cared to go.

Bradshaw covered all Edgewater's haunts but he could not find him. A kind of embryonic unease lay in him, a feeling that things were not right, that the world was full of things going on that he was not privy to, things that he could immediately bring to rights did he just know why they were. A feeling that the ground he stood on was plastic, warping, that the center of things had shifted subtly from its orbit.

Where's old Edgewater? he asked Swalls.

I couldn't say, Swalls told him. I never set myself the task of keeping up with him.

Bradshaw drinking, the upraised beer bottle a receding cone of amber light he sighted along. He set the bottle back. I need to find him. That old boy get out by hisself in the world and no telling what'll happen to him 'thout somebody been around to look out for him.

Swalls shrugged. He's three times seven. I guess he can take care of hisself.

Late of an evening, out in the yard and away from the old woman, Bradshaw asked Sudy about it straight out and she just told him. I'll kill the son of a bitch, he said.

The old Chevrolet rolling again and Bradshaw halfdrunk, a sack of beer riding in the seat beside him, watching the road reel to him, a road barren of hitchhikers and of Edgewater's malign presence. In these long hours he played out what he would do. What he would say, what Edgewater would reply. Talking to himself in a kind of soliloquy of anger. He felt betrayed.

The next morning he wordlessly left home again, still alone, poor, bitter company. The highway this time, across the county line, bearing on east. Idling with grocery store loungers, shadetree mechanics, filling station attendants. Have you seen a feller looks like this? He wished for a photograph. He began to feel that Edgewater was laying low, had took to the woods one last time, traveling off the shoulder of the road to avoid the pursuit he must surely expect. Yet in a part of himself he did not even acknowledge the existence of, he was glad that he did not find him. It was far easier to try and fail, to tell Arnold, I'da killed the son of a bitch if I could of caught him.

He was going into a land of hills. Behind Edgewater there was a long sloping straight road. Ahead of him, it rose and fell, wound toward the far mountains in a series of undulations and was lost from his sight. A sere summer was going serer still, already the leaves were dying. The scent of them in the haze, a ripe bitter scent of premature autumn. All the world seemed dying, death ran through it like the veins in a leaf. The far hills were bright, they seemed to flame with reds and yellows and oranges, bright as if their coloring had been left to the hands of children. Above them the sky was a hot metallic brassy blue and the horizon seemed to waver as if it were incorporeal, as if composed of some element transigent as mist or smoke.

He turned at a distant sound and stuck out a thumb and watched coalesce out of some like matter a shape at first near liquid and wavering down the shimmering highway and then it solidified into a car as it approached, as if it had undergone some curious metamorphosis. The car hurtled past him without slowing, a brief wind soon lost, a glimpse of an old woman with harsh purple metallic hair. Some kind of small furry dog watched him disdainfully from the fleeing back windshield. A few scraps of discarded paper, dust covered, settled themselves back covertly amidst the encroaching sumac.

He went on. The world warped here, some vast declivity in its surface, himself at the epicenter. At last starting up the other side, an insect struggling on glass, he grew short of breath, paused among the roadside refuse and looked back the way he had come intently as if he expected pursuit. The road lay barren and silent. The very air seemed leaden and still. Below and to his right a vast hollow stretched and curved away. In the distance a mist rose from its depths amidst cedars blueblack and hazy. Above him buzzards or hawks wheeled. He walked on.

It was his second day and the distance he had covered meager. He had been on the road before good day and although he had been thumbing whatever had passed, once even with amused desperation a wagon, nothing had stopped. The day wore on. The sun past its zenith, began a swift recession sliding down the mauled red of the western world. The air was full of the acrid smell of dried leaves and golden with some sort of haze half translucent that rendered the sun small and distant, a distinct orb the color of blood. Clouds boiled up breathlessly then rose to obscure it. Its hot red glow lit the clouds from behind as an intricate and rococo thread of fire traced their outline against the heavens. Like minute fractures in the serene face of sky limning farther and yet more awesome fires, hunting some vaulted space where perpetual holocausts flamed behind the cool deceptive blue.

Before dusk he finally got a ride. A truck transporting something covered with ropelashed tarpaulins coasted by on a long careening downgrade, stopped with a hiss of airbrakes and waited. Edgewater ran the last few steps and got in, glancing sharply as he did at the shapes on the bed of the truck, rectangles the size and configuration of caskets stacked beneath the green tarp. Then he was in and the door slammed and the truck eased on. The door would not catch. He slammed it again.

It's broke. You got to raise the latch up here and then shut it.

The driver was small and redfaced. Tiny crisp curls covered his head, everything about him seemed red save the mottling of brown freckles and the muddy blue eyes.

Where you headed?

Up in East Tennessee but so far I ain't havin much luck.

It's gotten dangerous to stop and pick up hitchhikers. Man might end up in a ditch with his throat cut.

I guess so.

The driver was downshifting for a broken line of hills that came out of the dusk chimerical and indistinct, a dark Rorschach world they were driving off into. He had turned the lights on. Edgewater stared into the frieze of shifting images striding past the window. A house floated by swimming in blue watered ink, as if everything beyond the truckcab was immersed in deep water, had lost reality and definition, all distances seeming on some common level the same. A series of lean-tos had been added to the house, the roof line of each adhering to the original structure so that it sloped perpetually earthward. The final addition appeared to Edgewater to have been useless to anyone over three or four feet in height.

The company won't have us pick up nobody. What do you think about that?

Edgewater turned to look at him. The man was young but already his face looked frozen, cast into some permanent expression of anger. Acne spread out from his cheeks in a harsh scarlet rash. The eyes were fierce and congested, as if unable to handle the turbulence of emotions assailing them, a great snarl of them bottlenecked seething within the bony little skull. Above them his brows were arched as if the world were constantly besieging him with a series of surprises, none of them pleasant.

I think it's a hell of a note, Edgewater said. From my viewpoint anyway.

You goddamn right it is. You see what I think about their goddamn rules, don't you?

What?

You settin here ain't you?

Edgewater glanced down as if to ascertain his whereabouts.

The hell with em, the man said, an invective so bitter and all inclusive as to fall alike on all the world save himself and Edgewater.

Who do you work for?

The Iron City Casket Company over to Iron City, tightfisted bunch of son of a bitches.

So that is what you're haulin back there.

Yeah. Hell of a load ain't it?

I guess so. How many you got?

I don't know. I don't load em I just haul em.

Oh.

Not bein smart with ye or nothing, it just ain't my job to load em is what I mean. How many would you say?

It looks like thirty or forty.

I reckon so. Enough anyway for a lot of cryin widder women and grinnin undertakers ain't it?

Edgewater did not reply and the driver fell into an uneasy tense silence. He glanced occasionally at Edgewater as if awaiting further comment, as if he would draw him into whatever forge shaped his rage. They were coming into a community of some sort; faint lights flared across bare fields. They passed a church all lit and ringed with cars. Finally the driver said: You know what the markup on them mother-fuckers is?

What?

They got maybe thirty or forty dollars worth of lumber and mate-rials and then they sell the son of a bitches for three or four hundred dollars. Don't that sound to you like a good business to be in?

I guess so.

You guess so. I guess so too. All they need is a fuckin mask and a pistol. Then the undertaker puts his markup in there and gets his slice of the pie. Don't it look like some of that profit would get passed on? Don't it look like somebody as far down the ladder as me ort to get a taste of it? You know what I make a hour? When Edgewater did not reply he said, Seventy-five cents a hour, by God.

Edgewater was trying to envision a casket factory, imagining what a solemn duty this must be. Imagining an assembly line of blackclad workers of soberfaced visage armed with screwdrivers and saws through which a casketloader conveyor moved soundless and stately. It seemed a strange vocation, a craft perpetually reminded of death, steeped in it. He could not conceive this but he did not need to be reminded. A man did not need constant reassurance of his fate, did not need to have his final shelter about him as a terrapin carries its shell.

Why don't you just quit?

The driver gave Edgewater a brief sullen look, as if Edgewater had in some subtle way aligned himself against him. Times is hard, he finally said.

I got to get me a donut and somethin to eat, he said again after a while. He stopped at a store in some town so small as to be nameless and unknown to mapmakers. A community set on the rim of the hills with a grocery store and a filling station, below it lay truckers' lights like spilt jewels. Edgewater went in with him, got a drink from the red cooler by the door. He laid a nickel on the counter. The old man ensconced behind the counter nodded, took it solemnly.

The driver was waiting at the meat case. An old woman sliced off thick slices of ham and cheese onto white butcher paper, she was dealing out crackers one by one from a carton. Edgewater went out into the warm summer dusk. Dusk was deepening. It was almost full dark now. You could see night coming. Above him the sky was clear and an orange-red crescent moon hung above a line of jagged black. Stars were strewn random and happenstance above him. Here in these higher elevations he felt himself more akin to the galaxy that stretched beyond comprehension, felt an eerie timelessness, a clock not begun to measure. More remote from the earth, from its plagues and its weary duties. A denizen somehow displaced eternally halfway between, unable to belong fully to either dimension. A familiar of memories that were more than the metal he rested against, more corporeal than the bottle chilling his fingers. Conjured by faces already dead or just waiting in the wings.

Far off in the dark a line of fire crept over a ridge on the horizon, burned itself into his retinas, ebbed and quaked like lightning frozen in perpetual arc, widened then and spread, a hot acid dissipating the night. Moved down the slope as if feeding, the only thing left alive in all that dark.

He lit a cigarette. There was a loose corner of the tarpaulin and he lifted it. Beneath the canvas the surface of the casket was cool and smooth to his hand. Starlight fell on its burnished bronze luster. He touched it with his other hand, saw dimly the reflection of his fingertips appear there like a hand reaching to clasp his own, of a self already lost and mouldering, disembodied from the desolated wastes of dementia. The surface of the casket hummed beneath his fingers as if charged with some tellurian current and then it warped before his eyes and ran like melting glass, solidified to wood ancient beyond reason, moldcrept and wormscarred pine and the cold finality of the grave lay on him like a nameless and unspeakable embrace.

He turned away. He sat on the running board and drank the last of the Coke and finished smoking the cigarette. After a time he got up, set the bottle on the gas pump, and walked toward the truck. He had his hand on the door handle when he turned back the way he had come. Beyond the point where light from the store windows failed, the way lay dark and secret. The darkness writhed with shapes he could not discern. To hell with it, he said. When the driver came out wiping his mouth on his sleeve Edgewater was standing on the opposite side of the highway with an air of infinite patience.

You ready to roll?

I reckon I'll roll back this way if I can.

The driver looked at him in disbelief. Hell, you said you're goin east.

I was then.

Goddamn feller. I knowed you was just out joyriding up and down the road I'da left you where I seen you. Youda been better off.

Thanks anyhow, Edgewater told him.

The driver shook his head and got into the truck. It rolled away. Edgewater stood quite still in the pooled light and waited. Then after a time the light there clicked out and the old man and woman came out. They glanced at him and then they went on their way. He sat on the curb. It was a long time before he got a ride.

Edgewater had been gone for a week when Bradshaw came into Goblin's Knob and there he was, drinking a beer and listening to Swalls tell lies as if he had been there every day and not somewhere Bradshaw could not find him. He was not drunk, just sitting, and when Swalls moved on down the bar he offered Bradshaw no explanation, no word at all.

The jukebox was singing about honkytonks to two old men in overalls. *Honky tonkin, honey baby.*

Edgewater sat and nursed his beer while Bradshaw stood there, searching for a way to say what they both knew he had to say. For she would be showing by now and the old woman in a killing rage, the air filled with recriminations and threats.

She's my baby sister, he said at length.

I know who she is, Edgewater told him. You don't have to pimp for your own sister. Is there anything you want me to do?

He waited for Bradshaw to swing, hoping he would. You would have thought him retarded but he was not. The balls of his feet felt light and his head shiningly bright and clear as if some astringent had washed all the fog away and his left shoulder began to tingle, all the way down to his fist. There was no expression at all in the empty eyes.

But Bradshaw seemed to slacken, just shook his head from side to side.

They were married the fifteenth of September by a county judge in Ackerman's Field. The judge intoned the words in monotonous rote and Edgewater found his attention wandering to a calendar just behind the judge's left shoulder which bore smiling and benign portraits of the city police department and to the folded wad of greenbacks that seemed to warm a small rectangular patch of thigh beneath his pocket. The old woman had cosigned a note at the bank that morning. She had attended the wedding by necessity, it was she who must give Sudy away.

It had been a busy time for Edgewater; he had been moving in the world of commerce, toying with the playthings of the respectable and moneyed. Small entrepreneur borrowing money at the bank, renting a house, dickering with old man Grimes at the carlot over a beatup green Chevy Fleetline and leaving in its stead a not inconsiderable portion of the fresh green bills.

When they came out of the courthouse after the ceremony a front tire was flat. He could not believe it. He stood uncertain of how to proceed. Then he unlocked the trunk to get out the spare and the jack, knowing full well what he would find. The trunk held only two empty beercans and a bent tire spud, all furred thickly with oily dust. Wait on me, he told them as if they might drive away with a flat. I'll be back in a minute. They got into the front seat and seated themselves, the old woman poised and dignified as if in some chauffeured limousine, moving protectively at Sudy's side as if she would protect her thickening body from the snide eyes of the world.

He crossed the street diagonally to the service station and sent a mechanic to fix the tire. He bought three cans of beer and drank them seated on the commode in the tiny men's room, one after another, and stood the cans carefully in the corner.

Assessing his face in the mirror on the towel rack, he looked strained and curiously desperate, harassed. The eyes were saturnine, wolfish. Bought and paid for, they mocked him. He straightened the shoulders of Bradshaw's old white sport coat. I can handle it, he told them and went on out.

They carried the old woman home and with the backseat and trunk piled high with groceries and her castoff plunder they drove late that afternoon to Grievewood where the rented house waited. Grievewood was not a town or even a settlement and it was a community only through grace of them choosing to live there. Grievewood was just a geographical location, a name. Halfway to Goblin's Knob and then left down a winding dirt road.

Even with all their household artifacts unloaded and inside, the house still seemed somewhat vacant. It was a huge old steep-roofed farmhouse with seven rooms and what they had only made it look like some children's playhouse or a place tramps had slept then moved on: mismatched crockery with chipped edges, worn towels and quilts. A blackened coffeepot with the glass missing.

I guess we can seal off part of the rooms, Sudy said doubtfully. It'd be easier to heat anyway. When you start getting paid we can buy us some new furniture.

I guess so, Edgewater said, not as if the prospect fired him with ambition. He looked around the room. A blackened stone fireplace taking up much of one wall. An old couch and chair a previous tenant had left and that Edgewater had paid the landlord ten dollars for. The kitchen held a stove. Another room a bed. The air seemed damp and chill, it was colder inside than out.

You want me to try to build a fire? Are you cold?

A little bit. She determined to put the best face on things. It might be nice to have a fire in a fireplace, I never lived in a house that had one before. I'll make us some sandwiches or something for supper.

Edgewater walking about his grounds, surveying by dusk his new dwelling. The house was set atop a rise and the yard sloped gradually away to where a wovenwire fence bordered a creek. There was a wooden bridge on concrete pylons spanning the creek, and from this bridge the house patinaed with the opaque air of dusk became more opulent, its faded paint and dusty windows were obscured and it seemed impressive and brooding, an abode befitting some country squire of an earlier time.

Inside the squire's wife prepared his evening meal, fragrant kettles steamed and meat roasted on a spit, drops of grease flared bluely and died in umber coals. A larder of provisions to dull winter's threat. Windows chinked

to stay the wind and a cedar backlog on the fire. The squire's young wife
leaned to tend the fire, left hand to her long hair, a funnel of sparks shot
up the flue, there was a bright expanse of glimpsed thigh. Lean red hounds
ranged restlessly in the dogtrot, ice from their feet littered the oak parquetry
and would not melt. The night drew on and on.

In days gone his grandmother had owned such a house, who slept
there now? Did old gentle voices recite transgressions, whisper old secrets better untold?

Once in his youth his mother had had a thing to tell him, con-
spirator's eyes bright with portent. He had not wanted it on him. Old
weights better borne by the dead than passed to the living. I will skip
my turn, let the earth cover it forever, whatever it was, whatever it is. I
handpicked enough burdens of my own, cut away the straps but they
would not fall. Old mouths now long impacted with earth would have
drawn me into their tawdry intrigues, used me to people the broken
landscapes of their dreams. Hard now to learn that hands beyond the
grave still retain their grasp.

There was an old oneroom clapboard outbuilding with a door canted
on the remaining hinge and within an air of sheltered gloom, the earth
floor strewn with a welter of broken and abandoned tools, darkness already
crouching in the corners. Old plows and castoff wheels and geared devices
locked in rust and unidentifiable, an old sheetiron heater with the sides
devoured by longcold fires. A scrapiron monger's dream. A leaning flue
of claymortared bricks, a tiny window still intact were testament this had
once sheltered men. Through the moted glass the spare and bitter light fell
on windbrought leaves clumping among these purposeless works of men.
Summer home of copperheads and rattlers.

Leaning in the corner was an old axe near worn away with use and
grinding. Edgewater took it up, wiping away the spiderwebs. He went
out into the yard.

Above the bridge an enormous sycamore had been uprooted and
beached here by floodwaters. Worn and barkless as driftwood, old
branches gleaming white as bones in the dusk. The wood was so dead it
broke when he began to chop it.

Till after full dark fell he carried wood and aligned it on the high
porch. The sycamore he could break and from the hill above the toolshed old cedar stumps leached colorless and near weightless. The lights

were on now in the house. Once she called to him from the porch. He went in and laid a fire. He lit it and went to gather more wood. When he went back in this time the room was warm.

She had quilts spread before the fire, they lay on them. Here at the tailend of this portentous day, silence seemed to have settled on them. Her hair was undone, she'd put on a gown. He lifted it over her hips, felt the cool mound of her thickness. He lay an ear against it, perhaps he could hear what life swam in these seas. Unmarked, white pristine, virgin. As if no eyes had ever beheld her, no sun shone here, repository of ancient wisdom.

Turn the lights out.

Why?

I just don't like it with the lights on, she said.

How do you know?

I just know I wouldn't. I don't like you lookin at me.

He kissed her navel, turned his cheek then and pillowed his head against her as if listening for the roar of distant seas.

Whose is it?

What?

Whose is it?

You know it's yours.

All right. I'll take it then.

He lay with his cheek there for a long time and she lay beneath him motionless as if she were sleeping. He thought she might be crying and after a while he looked to see but she wasn't. She was just lying there with the gown tabled about her breasts, staring at the whitepainted ceiling as if she thought about nothing at all.

A new world of the senses opened up to Edgewater, a world of comforts he'd forsaken or never known. Soft flesh in the morning, compliant, scented. Her breasts above him bobbing with her motion, her face abstracted, a stranger's eyes. Somehow intent on her mark as if she had forgotten him, had never even known him. Her mouth open a little as if she could not breathe, the hair sweated at the temples, strands of it stuck to her brow. She was a face seen through the wrong end of a telescope, unseeing siltrimmed eyes staring at him from the sandy seabed, strands of seaweed twined in her fanned out yellow hair, a seasnail nestled in the hollow of her throat.

There was frost in the mornings now and a chill icy clarity to the light. Some mornings he'd build up the fire and go back to bed. When he'd go out to bring in the wood the world was all white ice, the bridge glittered. The sun above the cedared slope had moved farther away, there was a quality of remoteness to the air, to the silence. Crystals of ice glittered. There did not seem to be any world beyond the ridges that bluely bound them. The porch was icy to his bare feet. He'd crawl back in bed and she'd come awake with his shivering.

He had a job now. Every day save Thursday and Sunday he sold cars for Grimes in Ackerman's Field. The old woman had gotten him the job, hauling in some old marker for a favor her husband had done Grimes long ago. Each day at seven-thirty he was there at work in his neat clothes, prepared to discuss the merits of various automobiles with whatever customers the day brought him, take their down payments, fill out the notes Grimes used. At noon he'd eat a sandwich in the Belly Stretcher Café amidst other merchants like himself and listen to them talk of vagaries of dealing with the public. That old woman had pressed order onto his life, forced events into a routine. He'd go to work and drive home in the evenings and Sudy'd be there. Days were shorter now, the house would be already lit, a cheering homey glow set against the umbered hills and that was the way October came that year.

When he got off work he went behind the garage where he'd parked and crippled Elmer's chair was stationed beside the old green Fleetline. Elmer himself ensconced inside with the door closed and Edgewater's radio playing away. Edgewater went around the front of the car and opened the door and got in.

Edgewater had a paper bag on the seat containing a carton of cigarettes and a whole strawberry pie for Sudy. He looked into the sack. The cigarettes had been opened and there were two packs gone and there was none of the strawberry pie left at all.

I done you a big favor, Billy, Elmer said. How about givin me a ride home?

I'll take you home but I'd just as soon not want to know about the favor. He got out and folded the chair and put it in the backseat and then he got back in and started the motor. Then he looked over at Elmer.

Two fresh packs of cigarettes showed clearly through the thin material of his slacks. He had one in each front pocket. Edgewater looked up. His mouth was smeared thickly with some sort of red jellylike substance and crumbs of sticky piecrust clung in his weekold beard. His eyes were clear and innocent.

You have anything in that poke?

Cigarettes and I had my wife a pie.

You better look and see if it's all still all right. They was two niggers out here goin through ye stuff when I come up. That's what I'm doin here. I thought I'd set and watch ye car till you come.

Thanks, Edgewater said dryly.

I like to never run em off. I throwed rocks at em and cussed em but they won't hardly nobody mind a cripple.

Bradshaw was sitting on top of the world.

He had had his hair cut and a barbershop shave and he fairly shone with cleanliness. There was a closecropped expanse of naked flesh at the back of his neck where the clippers had been and you could have smelled him coming from the Bay Rum alone. He had on a white nylon seethrough shirt and black beltless slacks and a pair of Winklepicker boots he had long admired through the plateglass of Ellis Drygoods. He had money in his pocket from a check he had forged on his mother and it would not be back for at least a week. A week is seven days. Who knew where he would be in a week? Empires can topple in seven days, wars be won or lost, a civilization tilt and slide into silent seas.

He had had a halfpint of peach brandy at Big Mama's before he set out and he could tell the cards were falling right. There were times when he could do no wrong and he felt in his nerve ends that this was one such time.

On top of everything else it was Thursday and business was slow at the Knob on Thursday nights. Old men past working age who did not have to arise early on Friday mornings and whom he did not even consider competition anyway and loggers stopping by for one quick draft and a sixpack to go. He saw the evening as a chance to get reacquainted, reignite old fires. Even Swalls might not be there. Watching the highway snake away beneath him and night falling beyond the pines and with the peach brandy a warm nucleus of comfort within him he gave himself up to fantasies better left alone. One or two beers and then she'd come around the bar and pass him to the jukebox. Let him help select the songs. Bathed by the cool blue neon of the jukebox, turning, she would let her breast brush his arm. I got to be goin, he'd say. A restraining hand on his arm, the glossy scarlet mouth pouting. Why? Drink another beer or two. Old Swalls is gone and I'll set em up to you. No, I got to go. Where you goin, Buddy? You got another girl somers?

There was an iron cot in the back Swalls sometimes used and she would lead Bradshaw to it. There in the musky tousled blankets the essence of her, the core square root of her being. He would arise like a phoenix from the tangled quilts untouched by her flames and haul up his trousers, make ready to go. Her supine body trying to draw him back into the shameless sprawl of her legs. Somehow I thought it'd be better, he'd tell her, and just let the screen door fall to behind him.

When he crossed the county line and came onto the pinebordered clapboard building it was even better than he'd dared expect. Not a single vehicle sat in the parking lot. Not even Harkness, whom he had for a moment dreaded. D.L. Harkness was an unknown quantity, a man who had transcended clocks, a man above the clocking of timecards and the rising of the sun. He parked and whistling tunelessly went up the steps and inside.

He was somewhat taken aback to see Swalls behind the bar but he went up anyway and seated himself and ordered a beer. He sat without speaking to Swalls and drank his beer and stared toward the kitchen as if he could by some occult telekinesis draw her bodily through the swinging doors. He sat for the length of time it took him to drink the beer and gaze thoughtfully at the label and then as if interpreted there his next movement, he said, Where's Caren?

Swalls looked up from the newspaper he was reading and adjusted his glasses. His gaze lingered on Bradshaw's sartorial splendor and his nostrils twitched delicately at the smell of Bay Rum. Thursdays is slow, he said. I give her the night off. He went back to his newspaper.

Well shit a brick, Bradshaw said. He sat in indecision, half off his stool, as if he needed to be gone somewhere else but could not remember where. His reflection in the barglass seemed to steady him, he seemed to draw reassurance from it. Give me anothern, he said.

Swalls slid him the bottle. You tryin to get out of your class, he said.

Yeah, and I reckon you wouldn't jump it in a goddamn minute if you had the chance.

Me? I'd let her squat and piss in my face if that was her heart's desire. But I'm a man always been aware of his limitations. That ain't a bad thing to learn.

You seen Edgewater?

No. You mighty dressed up to be lookin for just Edgewater.

I reckon a man can clean up if wants to.

I guess so.

I never come here to talk about your philosophy of life, Bradshaw told him.

For lack of anything better to do he sat for a long time drinking beer and hoping someone he knew might show up. He played the jukebox and the morose homilies of country musicians soothed him, changed him in some subtle way so that his haloed reflection staring back at him seemed to go into the stature of myth, the raw material tragedy is made from. Unrequited love, she would never know the pain she caused him, the suffering he rose above.

He sat for a time alone on the porch in a canebottom chair with the beer bottle cradled in his lap, his feet propped on the porch railing, staring off across the valley where the river flowed unseen, and if he strained to hear, it seemed to him that he could discern the murmur of distant water. Across the bottom there were scattered lights, vague and undefined, coal oil yellow windows. As the night drew on they went out one by one, sleep stole hushed and ephemeral across the face of the land.

Cars went by sometime, indecipherable shouts occasionally as they passed the Knob. Dropping off the sloping curve the rattle of glasspacks, the hot throaty popping of burnt-out mufflers. Headlamps arching upward, leveling out, flaring across deep sleepy hollows, coon trails, the domain of owls and foxes. A few people stopped briefly, no one he knew or cared to know. He began to get drunk.

He was back inside when Caren and her date came in. She was laughing, untying blond scarfed hair. They seemed a little drunk. She was with the man in the cowboy shirt Bradshaw had seen before. The cowboy and Swalls went out into the pines where the whiskey was hidden and Caren went behind the counter and began to fill a carton with bottles of Coca-Cola. She looked up and smiled at Bradshaw. Hey, Buddy.

For some reason the smile enraged Bradshaw. Who is that?

What? Oh. Bobby Seiber from Beaver Dam. Why?

He looks like a goddamned queer to me. Wouldn't nobody but a shittin queer wear one of them shirts.

He used to be a Golden Glove, she told him. I'll tell him what you said and let him take you outside and show you how queer he is.

He wouldn't get no cherry.

You're drunk, Buddy. Go sleep it off.

She shrugged and started from behind the counter and Bradshaw said all in a rush: Caren why won't you go out with me?

What's in it for me?

Well hell. You go with everybody else. What's the matter with me?

There's nothing the matter with you, she told him, but I go with who I please. I give up fuckin for charity a long time ago.

She started toward the door and met Swalls and the cowboy coming back in. The cowboy had a halfpint in his hand and his face was flushed and he seemed drunker. Nothing would do him but he must dance. He put money in the jukebox and opened his arms and Caren fitted herself smoothly into them and they stood swaying, her smooth head pillowed against the tapestry of steers and lariats and wide open spaces. Her hips thrust against his pelvis, arms around his neck. Their eyes were closed.

Shit, Bradshaw said. He went out the door and unsteadily down the steps to the parking lot. He breathed deeply to steady himself. Frigid air stung his nostrils, there was an icy weight laid against his lungs. He had forgotten it was nearing winter, he did not even know where summer had gone. Yet now the winds of late November sang in the pines, many mournful voices with age-old tales of northern snows and sleet hissing soft among the branches.

He sat down dizzily and for a moment thought he might vomit. He leaned against the cowboy's car, rested his face against the cold metal of the quarter panel. Even after he began to feel better he continued to hunker in the gravel staring at the ground. After a time he began to pick up gravel stones from the parking lot and pour them from hand to hand. He could still hear the jukebox, another song began. He unscrewed the gas cap and began to drop the rocks one by one down the gas tank, listening to the sounds they made: first a hollow skittering rattle down the neck of the tank and then a faint splash when they struck the gas. He sat bemusedly dropping stones for some time.

When the couple came out Bradshaw had arisen and was leaned against the car pissing into the gastank. When he saw them he leapt back adjusting his clothing and there was a look of demented glee on his face.

Hey you son of a bitch. The cowboy began to run down the steps three at a time. Bradshaw angled for the pines at a dead run, darting between needled paths he knew from times past but deep into the pines a low strand of wire he did not foresee threw him face forward onto a litter of bottles and cans. He half arose to listen and could hear no pursuit. He held his breath. Lightheaded he heard the car start, saw lights flicker among the trees. He exhaled. Chickenshit, he snickered to himself. He took out a book of matches, struck one to examine his injuries. Black blood welled sluggishly from a V-shaped tear in his ankle.

After a few minutes he came out of the pines looking covertly all about but he did not see anyone.

She finally agreed to go to a doctor. He took off half of Monday to drive Sudy to the doctor's office, but she would not allow him to accompany her inside. He sat in the car and watched her slowly climb the steps reluctantly, an unrepentant prisoner approaching the bench. He did not see how she could function in the world so little did she speak. Still waters, how deep did they run. Surely she must need an intermediary to plead her cause. He could not imagine her talking to strangers, though he knew she must. She parceled words out as if she hated to see them go, might have better use for them later. Or perhaps it was just with him. She leant slightly to open the door, looked back at him once and then she was out of sight into the doctor's office.

He sat facing the quiet sidewalk and watching the early morning's business slowly accomplish itself. Young girls cutting school passed wreathed with bold laughter, all the world must seem a joke. They eyed him briefly as if practicing on him, just keeping a hand in, then went on. An old man came very slowly and patiently down the sidewalk supporting himself with a cane, progressing toward the steps with infinite care as if he conveyed something of marvelous fragility. What brought him here alone? Edgewater wondered. What news awaited him here? With time allotted a day at a time the news could only be in degrees of mediocre or bad, though he guessed any day was good as long as it was there at all. A young couple passed hand in hand and went up the steps. The wind brought him bright scraps of their laughter after the door closed behind them.

He waited a long time. The morning wore on and finally the day began to clear, a wornlooking sun broke through the southeast quadrant of the sky and gave forth a frail light that barely cast shadows. The wind whipped along the streets and sang Coke cups and scraps of paper along the asphalt. A world wearing itself out, unsure of renewal. He turned when the door opened again and saw her come out on the concrete porch and down the steps.

She got in and set her purse on the seat and sat waiting. He cranked the car.

What'd he say?

He said I was pregnant.

Well that's a relief. It's nice to get that straightened out. He didn't happen to mention when it would be.

She paused a moment, as if doing some mental calculation. He said it'd be sometime the last of March or early in April.

He was negotiating his way back out into the street. Have you got to go uptown to get any medicine or anything?

No. He give me some vitamins in there.

Is that all he said?

He said it looked like everything was going all right. He wondered why I didn't come before.

So do I.

He drove her back to Grievewood and went on in to work.

He sold cars for almost a month and he had some success with it. He wore slacks and a sport shirt and his hair combed neatly and he could talk with persuasion when he was called to but it was not usually necessary. James told him he was a born salesman and assured him he'd go far. As far as he went was a day in late November when Grimes sent him out to pick up a car.

Grimes sold cars to hardup people who could not buy them anywhere else and he sold old juryrigged cars held together with spit and baling wire and stopleak, dissonant gears packed with grease and sawdust. When asked how long he guaranteed his cars he used to smile a huge smile showing his gold teeth. He'd put his cigar back in his mouth and wink. Six months or till you get it off the lot, whichever comes first, he'd laugh and say. Dealing with people he dealt with he had some problems. Payments were not always met on time. Cars had to be repossessed or stolen back under cover of darkness. If he'd got a large enough down payment he could resell a car till it finally fell apart or he hit some customer prosperous enough or ignorant enough to pay for it.

When he came in that morning he handed the wrecker keys to Edgewater. You need to go over by Clifton this morning and pick up that Buick from old man Weiss. It's a long way over there so you need to get you a early start. He pulled a sheaf of folded papers out of his breast pocket. Here's the title and a copy of the note and everything you need to get it. He ain't paid a dime in over three months and I want the money, all of it, or the car. If he gives you any shit just hook on to it and drag it off.

I don't know. I thought I was selling cars, not repossessing them.

It's just something that's got to be done. It's a part of business. You better stop over there and get directions. He lives way off the road.

I don't think I'm cut out for that sort of thing.

He laid a stepfatherly hand on Edgewater's shoulder. You'll just have to make up your mind. It goes with the job.

I don't know.

He bought coffee to go at the Belly Stretcher Café and set out.

It was not cold that day but brisk and the azure sky was marvelously clear. There a look of distance to the horizon and an Indian summer haze to the air and Edgewater drove through the countryside not thinking or planning, just holding the wrecker on the road and sipping his coffee.

Past Flatwoods where the Clifton road branched off he stopped the wrecker and sat parked there for a time, as if undecided what to do and which way to proceed. The road to Clifton fell away in a series of downward curves and deep hollows and where the river lay in blue distance were houses and farms and tin roofs winking, the sun so far away they looked like mockups.

He got out and stood there leaning against the truck smoking a cigarette and just staring across the hollows as if he might be waiting for someone. Once an old car stopped and its driver wanted to know did he have trouble. Edgewater shook his head.

I guess you're equipped for it if you do, the man grinned, gesturing toward the wrecker.

Edgewater grinned too and the man drove on.

Old man Weiss had some disease that was consuming him and that Edgewater did not inquire the nature of. This false man of dried sticks and rags sat with a shawl across his lap and rocked in the wintry sun in a willow rocking chair. His face was bright with fever and his eyes gleamed with something that was not life but a mockery of it. There was a calm look about him as if he had made his peace with everything that mattered and was already a resident of some country so far and lost that Edgewater had not even heard it rumored.

Edgewater did not see anything that looked remotely like a Buick and he did not ask after one. And say you don't know anybody around here named Jackson? he said, arising from the edge of the porch.

Not no more. There was a Jackson feller used to live around here ten or fifteen year ago but Lord he's dead and gone.

Then I guess it's not him I need, Edgewater said. Thanks anyway.

You mighty welcome. Come back.

I'll see you. He picked his way through moiling hounds back to where the wrecker set idling.

What are you doing? Swalls asked him from the front porch of the Knob. Out drummin up business?

Edgewater grinned. Grimes sent me out after this son of a bitch he said was behind on the payments.

They went inside and Edgewater drank a Coke at the bar and sat drumming his fingernails.

For some reason or other you remind me of a man fresh out of a job.

I guess I just quit.

You don't look too pleased with yourself.

I don't know. I hate telling my wife about it. She's gonna have a shitfit.

Swalls had no reply. Victim of four marriages and scarred in all the ways two people can scar each other he felt no call to advise others. He knew more about almost everyone than he wanted to and he had learned that there are some things that are born faulted and the sooner done with them the better.

In midafternoon Bradshaw came in. When he saw Edgewater he retreated four or five steps and threw a hand before his face in mock horror. Don't take it, he pleaded. I'll be in the first of the month, I swear.

Fuck you, Edgewater said. Anyway I already quit.

Edgewater's brother-in-law came up and put an arm about his shoulders. I seen ye out on that carlot in ye sellin suit, he told him. You looked mighty prosperous. I thought a time or two about comin in and borrowin some money but I figured you had the bighead and wouldn't talk to me. How come ye to quit?

The notion just struck me.

I figured you'd be smoking them big long cigars and have Grimes runnin around with a grease rag in his hip pocket by now.

I reckon not.

There was a look of prosperity about Bradshaw himself. His cream-colored slacks had razorsharp creases and his oxblood loafers gleamed a rich burgundy. He smelled alike from Bay Rum and the expensive cheroot clamped in his jaw teeth. You want to make a little money?

Doing what?

Help me haul a load down below the state line.

Help you? What are you doing, pushing it in a wheelbarrow?

I just meant mainly for the company. You could help me drive some. Give you half my profit.

I don't think so. I aim to keep as low a profile as I can till I'm sure all that jailbreak mess has blown over.

Lord, Billy, we won't hear no more about that. If we'd been goin to they'd a got us when Aday locked us up.

I still don't think so. I'd have to leave Sudy by herself.

Oh come on. We'll be back by night anyway.

You'll have to follow me into town and pick me up. I've got to give Grimes his wrecker back.

Going down the steps Bradshaw paused and hoisted his trouser leg and pulled down his sock to show Edgewater his wound. Look here. Got in a fight out here the other night and I sure missed you, I looked all around but you wasn't nowhere to be found so I had to go ahead and do it my ownself.

Edgewater peering down, examining the scabbed-over cut. You mean he stabbed you in the fucking foot? He must have been a little on the short order.

He pulled his sock back up and gave Edgewater a sharp wounded glance. Hell naw. He was a big burly son of a bitch. He was a Golden Gloves. We got into it over that Caren tends bar in there.

What happened to your foot?

Hell, I was runnin him through the woods back there and run over bobwire fence. You ort to seen it. It was night and he was runnin over half-grown saplins and everthing else. Sounded like a bear lumberin around.

Edgewater parked the wrecker by the side of the garage and went into the office and handed Grimes the keys. Grimes winked at him and arose and walked over to the door and peered toward the wrecker. He frowned. Since I don't see no Buick I'm assuming you got a pocketful of money for me.

Edgewater shook his head. He was hauling out papers, the title, note. He handed them to Grimes. I quit, he said.

You what? You quit?

Yeah.

Well that's a hell of a note.

Edgewater shrugged.

What's the matter? That old man out there get to you? You getting squeamish on me?

I just quit.

You think everthing's supposed to be laid out nice and polite. Everthing run along smooth. You're full of shit, too. Life's hard. It's dog eat dog out there.

Tell me about it, Edgewater said. He was walking away.

I ain't payin you for this morning, Grimes called after him but Edgewater didn't turn.

Bradshaw was waiting for him with the motor running. Edgewater got in and slammed the door. Let's go to Alabama, he said.

We got to go pick it up where I got it hid. I ain't been haulin it no more than necessary.

They took the whiskey aboard and went out Highway 20 to 31 and through Lawrenceburg and rolled on toward the Alabama line. Through

Iron City and Edgewater saw with interest the Iron City casket works. Tightfisted sons of bitches, he said aloud.

What?

The Iron City Casket Company.

Oh. I never had no dealins with em myself.

The day drew on and they drove through slant afternoon light, the hills gave way and so onto a clay banked land of a smoother cast, the highway flattening out and running slick and chalkline straight, the earth here red as if ochred by the blood of old lost battles.

Whose whiskey is that anyway?

Bradshaw smiled, the tip of the slim cheroot cocked higher. Yellow feral eyes narrowing to conspiratorial slits. Mine, he said. I bought it from Boogerman and he give me this feller's name been buying some from him along. Feller named Skelton, down in Lawrence County. Boogerman drawed me a map and done talked to this Skelton on the phone. I got thirty gallon I give seven dollars a gallon for and I aim to sell it twelve. I might take ten.

You got it all laid out. Where'd you get so much money?

I borrowed it from Mama. Told her I was buyin half interest in a fillin station.

You beat anything I ever saw.

If I don't now I soon will. I aim to get rich in this here whiskey game. I done put me in some helper springs so she don't set down so. You notice how she sets with her ass cocked in the air?

At Wheeler Dam they came upon an enormous traffic jam and Bradshaw fell to worrying. A crane truck with a great boom atop it had tried to cross the bridge. There had not been sufficient clearance and traffic stalled behind it had boxed it in, it could go neither backwards or forwards. There was a din of honking horns and ahead of them where the bridge rose stark and skeletal revolving red lights pointed out two Alabama highway patrol cars, order moving within chaos. The state troopers were flagging traffic back, the truck negotiating laboriously backward through a volatile melee of angry travelers.

Be just our luck to get caught with all this shit.

Edgewater didn't reply. He was staring far below the embankment to where brush tended away and the lake began. The water was choppy and cold-looking, the color of slate, and a few birds wheeled above it, as if tethered by invisible wires, darted down to skim the surface, rose effortlessly on the updrafts of the wind.

You don't seem too worried.

Grimes said it was dog eat dog out here and I guess it is.

Here comes one of them now, straighten up.

Hey, tell him I'm a hitchhiker you just picked up.

But the cop had no words for them, he was busy flagging the truck back, it passed, the driver's face a pale harassed ovoid through the glass. Traffic began to creep forward.

I bet that poor dumb son of a bitch don't never get where he's goin, Bradshaw said. He ort to bought him a boat. Bradshaw was cheering up, felt that the jaws of a trap had snapped shut and narrowly missed him. He nodded gravely to the patrolmen as he passed, solid citizen, young businessman on his way home from the office. A Jaycee meeting tonight perhaps. Wife, children, dog, slippers, evening paper. He knocked ash from his cigar and accelerated. Sweet home Alabama, he said.

Towns with only names to distinguish them one from the other fell away in their wake. Town Creek, Courtland, Hillsboro, little sleepy towns with dusk falling on them all alike, they drove into a darkening cloud. At Moulton they inquired directions at a service station, pored over Boogerman's map. Edgewater turning it this way and that, undecided which way was up. It made as much sense one way as another. Its secrets securely locked.

Was he drunk when he drew this?

He was drinkin.

I see he draws a map about like he makes whiskey.

Across a sea of dead cottonstalks with sharp empty bolls like aberrant flowers. Knocking at a stoopless door at a slatwalled shack set atop crumbling cinderblock pillars. An aged black man behind peering suspiciously, receding backwards to where darkness began. I knows him but if you just wantin a drink I can fix you up.

Naw. We just need to see him.

Oh. Well. It's a mile or two back towards town then. Little brick sidin, right close to the road. Got a mailbox with a picture of a rooster painted on it.

When Bradshaw blew the horn the porch light came on and the door opened. A man came out and pulled it to behind him and came down the step. He had a flashlight in his hands. A big black dog fell in at his heels and followed a pace or two behind. The man was slight, unshaven, as surly-looking as the dog that paced him. He wore overalls and a wool hat.

Country-looking peckerhead, Bradshaw said. He got out, Edgewater following.

We got it back here in the trunk.

Let's take a look at it.

The trunk aloft. Light playing on the volatile colorless liquid in gallon jugs with fingerholds on the neck. A veritable cornucopia of visions, nightmares, delirium tremors, a drunkard's dream. A lifetime supply of hangovers.

Skelton opened a jug, smelled, shuddered. I'm glad I'm sellin instead of drinkin, he said. He shined the light toward a small gray outbuilding. I generally keep it back yonder in the crib. You can back down through the yard there, it ain't nothin in the way. I'll walk along behind and I'll shine the light for you.

The wind whipped across the flat field, sang in a loose piece of tin somewhere, a faint few drops of cold rain. Edgewater shivered, wished for a coat.

Don't they bother you keepin it so close?

Not as long as I make a little trip into town about the first of the month.

Easing backward across the yard, the light pinpointing the crib door. When the whiskey was inside and Bradshaw awaiting mention of money, the man said, I reckon Boogerman told you how I do business?

No. I reckon he figured I knowed they wadn't but one way of doin it.

I don't know about that. What I been doin is taken his whiskey on consignment.

Done what?

Keep it here and I pay him when I sell it.

The hell with that. This ain't no goddamn bread truck I'm runnin. Consignment. If that ain't the goddamn beat of anything I ever heard. You think I ain't been around?

I don't know where you been. I guess you folks may do it different up in Tennessee.

You fuckin A we do. And Tennessee's where this whiskey's headed for right now. Help me load er up, Billy.

We done made a deal.

I ort to deal you up the side of the goddamned head. Drive all the way down here with thirty gallon of whiskey and you whip this crazy shit on me. Who ever heard of consigning bootleg whiskey?

You won't never make the Tennessee line.

Bet me.

I got a brother-in-law a deputy sheriff. All it takes is one little phone call.

I don't care if you and J. Edgar Hoover go coonhuntin ever Friday night. You try to stop me from loadin my whiskey and we'll knock you on your gimlet ass. Less you got a phone right handy. I don't see no wires running out of ye pocket.

You might do that, the man said agreeably, if you was about fifty pounds heavier and twenty years meaner. And if I didn't have that dog here and somethin in my pocket a hell of a lot handier than a telephone.

Edgewater looked at the dog. It stood highshouldered and wary, its black eyes watching them, sharp little ears pricked up. It did not look like a dog at all. It looked like a weapon.

You cocksucker.

Take it or leave it. I do all my out-of-state business on consignment. They might be something wrong with that whiskey. I'll pay ye when it's gone.

Sure you will.

Or you can explain to the law what you're doing with thirty gallon of untaxed whiskey in a dry county.

What kind of dog would you say that was?

A big one, Edgewater said.

It looked like one of these here Doberman Pinchers to me.

They were nearing Moulton, a scattering of random lights. Bradshaw had fallen into a deep depression worrying about his money. Here I am broke, he said. No whiskey and no fillin station neither. I'm ashamed of myself. I never thought I'd live to see the day I'd stick two hundred and ten dollars up a wild hog's ass and holler sooie.

Coming up on the city limits he pulled off the shoulder of the road and ceased. I can't do it, he said. I'm quittin my whiskey or money one.

How do you plan to do it?

Hell, I don't know. I just aim to.

If you had the whiskey could you get rid of it anywhere else?

Hell yeah. Cates'd take half of it and Early maybe half. But I had planned to make me four or five extra dollars a gallon down here where it's scarce.

It's not scarce now.

Have you got a flashlight?

They may be one in the dash pocket.

There was but the batteries were dead. Edgewater took them out and rolled down the glass and threw them out the window. Let's go see if we can find a hardware store open.

They walked around the square in Moulton but all was shuttered and barred. All save the sidewalks rolled up and a few strolling young couples, a lit movie marquee and a tired-looking old woman in the ticket booth sat like something preserved under glass. We need a crowbar, Edgewater said. What's in the trunk?

Just a spare and a jack and like that.

Drive on out the road.

They found a little country store open outside of Moulton but they did not sell crowbars there, the merchant a little curious perhaps about what emergency this time of night necessitated a crowbar. He did have flashlight batteries and Edgewater reloaded the light. Out of sight of the store they stopped and checked the trunk.

Edgewater handed him the tire spud. Maybe that'll prise the boards loose. He was taking the bumper jack apart. He took the foot off the bottom and clicked the jack to the top and off the post. When it was all apart he was left with a length of rectangular steel almost four feet long and an inch and a half or so in diameter. He tried it for heft, then threw everything back into the trunk. Let's see if we can find anything to eat.

They ate hamburgers and French fries at a café on the Decatur highway. They had apple pie with melting cheese on top for dessert and coffee and then watched the clock's hands crawl on.

I dread that damn dog. What we ort to do is buy a can of arsenic and about a pound of hamburger and mix up a part of it. Drive by and throw it out and come back in an hour or two to see if he's got a stomachache yet.

I don't know about poisoning a man's dog. Always seemed a little sneaky and chickenshit to me.

You'll think chickenshit when he uncouples ye damn leg and runs off with it.

They were the café's last customers and the waitress began locking up. They got one more coffee to take with them and sat in the car watching the lights go out one by one. *Nick's Café, Nick's Café,* the neon blinked in cool purple urgency. It blinked off in mid blink and the white stucco café stood identityless and abandoned. The dark from somewhere inside a pale glow from a streetlight. The rawboned waitress came out with a ring of keys in her hands and locked the door.

Well, Edgewater said. Let's kill some time. This is a hell of a day. Start out repossessing cars for old man Grimes and end up repossessing whiskey for you. There's got to be a lesson in there somewhere.

They parked a hundred yards or so below the house in a curve where the road widened. Raise the hood up, Bradshaw said. If the law comes by they'll just think somebody had car trouble and went on.

Well, you better take the keys.

They started across the field fording a mist of vapors that seemed to be rolling out of the earth through stubble of cutover cane stalks and here and there rearing politely shocks of bundled cane like phantoms or an audience of mutes. Edgewater looked up once and the sky was clearing, a high swift press of vaporous clouds caught in some wind that bore them transparent across the face of the stars: the clouds seemed still and behind the firmament in motion a rush of stars streaking toward the edge of the universe, a vast armada of warships with running lights gleaming through the fog pressing swiftly on to the void at the world's boundary.

They paused before they got in hearing of the house. What'll we do if it starts barkin? Bradshaw whispered.

Get behind some of these cane stalks and try to wait it out. He won't think too much of it. A bootlegger's used to getting woke up in the middle of the night.

The dog did not bark at all when it came. They were easing up behind the crib, keeping it between them and the house. It came loping and near soundless around the corner of the corncrib, lethal, ears laid back and muzzle aloft. Lord a mercy, Bradshaw said to himself. Black dog of folklore and legend, warning of death, Satan's fires, hellhounds on their trail.

Edgewater shifted his weight, imagined that he was Babe Ruth, having pointed out the right field bleachers and thus committed. When the dog leapt he imagined it a hard fast one across the center of the plate and he swung the steel jackpost with all his might. He put his entire body into it. The weight of the dog bore him off balance and backward and to the wet earth but he scrambled up still holding his weapon. He had caught the dog alongside the head or shoulders and it lay inert, its feet moving a little as if it dreamed pursuit. He could not tell whether it was dead or unconscious and he did not look to see. Bradshaw was already prying at the slats with his tire spud. The boards were old and rolled off like jagged teeth at the bottom and came free with ease. He tore three of them loose and pulled away from the wall and crawled through them and disappeared. Edgewater could barely see the light, a mere ghost of light. He could hear a soft cautious bumping inside and almost immediately Bradshaw began to set out whiskey and align it beneath his makeshift door.

Edgewater began to carry the jugs across the canefield four at a time, bent like a broken field runner. After the whiskey was all out Bradshaw set through the aperture three half gallon cans of peaches and crawled out carrying an old Malacca walking cane he'd found inside and he was wearing an ancient black derby with cobwebs depending from it.

You can have ye pick, Billy.

Goddamn it. Let's get back to the car before we argue over the spoils. I don't see why you all the time have to pull this crazy old shit.

Hell Billy, you logged the day out. You pick.

Oh, all right. I guess I'll take a can of the peaches. This other stuff seems slanted toward a more esoteric taste than mine.

Suits the shit out of me. I wouldn't take a purty penny for this mahogany cane.

Tripping across the field, Bradshaw was so lifted by getting the whiskey back his feet barely touched the ground, a mad pantomime clown with hat cocked and cane atwirl, fleet and soundless.

———

After Edgewater quit he hung around the house and there were days when they stayed abed almost all the day, times that he would remember as idyllic in light of what came. She swore undying love to him and she'd come to him with a kind of frantic desperation, a longing that would not be satiated, a wound that would not heal.

There were other days when the hours went by in silence and they moved so slow you could almost see their passage. The day might pass without her talking and her eyes looked far away and self-absorbed as if she'd gone somewhere he couldn't follow. There was a serene and complacent look about her as if she'd been visited with some duty to perform or some task to execute that rendered her unmindful of the minutiae of life. She could shut him out without a word. If she noticed his touch at all she'd just move the hand away in annoyance, turn away, but the eyes would not change at all. There were worlds in them no one went but herself.

These days he might sit for a time on the stoop in the cold wind and translucent winter light. The wind was in the brittle leaves, it told him old tales of winter snows long melted and cold's privation and a need for security seized him. He felt in a sort of limbo, he dawdled while the fates decided his case.

He borrowed Swalls's bucksaw and with it and the axe began to lay in winter's wood. There was an umbered slope behind the house and he'd cut trees there, saw cuts off and roll them down the hill through the gray sedge and watch them mound up against the crib wall. He sat and smoked and rested between cuts in a detached kind of contentment, aware simultaneously of the cold and of her below him moving about the kitchen and the pot of coffee warming on the stove and the blue smoke rising from the brick flue.

He chopped dead pines and cut them to kindling length with the bucksaw and stacked them chesthigh on the porch. He split the cuts of red oak with the axe and stacked wood until the porch was ringed with it, like castellated battlements he'd peer across toward an enemy held at bay.

You must expect another ice age, she said, but he had no time to answer. That morning there'd been a frozen glaze along the borders of the window, a thin white skim, candied sugar scrollwork so fragile it broke beneath his fingers. The last of the geese went south in a shifting V and he read something akin to desperation in their cries.

Long after he had more than enough wood and on days when she'd no need for him, he'd sit on the crest of the hill as if he were waiting for something and watch what of the world he could see. The hill was high and steep and from its summit he could see far in the distance through the winterbared trees, the highway, broken lines of it between the hills.

Commodities were given out on the third of the month. This was always a windfall for crippled Elmer. He had traded a five-pound box of cheese for eight bottles of Red Top ale and he drank them all alone down by the tie yard. He drank them slowly, rationing them out to himself, his wheelchair parked in the narrow alcove between two stacks of crossties. Uptown someone might see him and ask for one of the ales. It was easier to avoid than to refuse, for he had only rice left to trade and rice was a slow mover. He could not have given it away. The alcohol gave him a sort of convivial desire for companionship, but not enough to make him give up the beer. He drank the ale and with only what thoughts he had he watched the slow drift of fall constellations above the rim of the ties and listened to the pitch of voices he knew ease to him from the boxed walls and pasteboard windows of shanties across the tracks.

He had nowhere to be, no one awaited him, so he sat still in the balmy night, talking to himself, occasionally laughing softly as if at some old joke. All the beer gone, he sat cradling the last empty bottle and listening to the diminishment of sounds, the town going to sleep about him.

When all was still, he wheeled himself out and looked covertly around him and when he was satisfied he went up the incline to the blacktop and past the streetlight through fogging bugs to the corner and left there. Skirting the square he went down past the shoefactory unmindful of signal lights, for the streets were empty now. The way was declivitous here and the wheelchair picked up speed, dizzily he could feel a breeze drying the sweat on his face lifting the strands of lank hair, hear the near silent hum of the tires. With a kind of careless drunken skill he negotiated a curve onto Pine Street, drew from the ratty folds of the shawl covering his withered legs a length of wood worn slick with friction and sweat and applied pressure to the tire spokes, slowing himself with a mental admonishment about speedcops lying in wait and the knowledge that a cornfield lay near here.

It was not a proper cornfield but a dozen or so canted stalks planted at the end of the garden but it would serve his purpose. So unproductive as to preclude harvest, the stalks still held the half-formed nubbins, hardened now in withered shucks. It still had not rained and the earth in the garden was as hard as the street so he had no trepidation about easing the wheelchair off the blacktop, wheeling himself with some effort through dry weeds and across the rockhard clods and fossil-like marks of the plowshare. He could not raise himself to the ears of corn but grasped the stalk and bent it to him and broke the ears free. He looked at them disgustedly. Were he a farmer he would not even allow to mature sick puny specimens as these. He would long ago have chopped them down with a hoe before someone saw them. He put the corn on his lap beneath the shawl and backed himself out through the brittle stalks that broke beneath his wheels and back across the sidewalk to the street. There was a smell of the sere cornstalks, of the earth.

A city policeman pulled him over on Vine. He had been wheeling down the middle of the street, imagining himself a truck driver, and had not even heard the car, steered abruptly for the curb when the lights hit him. The cop stopped and looked him over. A not unfriendly face, a face of gentle admonishment, but implacable, the voice a kind of benign malice.

What have I told you about driving that thing in the middle of the street? You gonna kill yourself or cause somebody to wreck and maybe kill them.

Elmer didn't reply. On his face was a look of spurious respect that would not have deceived a child. Under the shawl his hand clutched the ears of corn, began to rub them together and shell kernels from one hand to the other.

Where you goin anyway?

Just ridin around.

You goin a roundabout way to be headin home, that's for sure. You know what time it is?

I ain't got no train to catch. What's it to you anyway?

The cop got out and stood by the back door.

Come on and I'll run you out to Sycamore Center. We'll just fold your chair up and put it in the back here. Save you a mile or two.

I'll go home when I want to and when I do I'll go under my own steam. Ain't you got no bankrobbers to catch? Ain't you got nothin to do but worry cripples?

You up to somethin, ain't you?

Hell no.

Then why won't you let me take you home?

I can't go home for a while. Mama's got a customer out there.

The cop sighed and pushed the car door to and got back in. You just see you stay out of trouble, he said.

Elmer was quick to sense appeasement. You got a cigarette? he asked.

The cop started the car. I don't smoke, he said. The cruiser began to roll.

You got ary chew of tobacco? Elmer called after it.

The chicken house he sought was set in the backyard of a white frame house off Vine and Mill streets and repeated nocturnal visits and knowledge of its inhabitants had rendered him bold enough to wheel past dark sleeping windows and to pause only a moment to listen. All he heard was the quiet hum of a refrigerator compressor. A watchdog came around the corner of the house and stood stifflegged watching him but he and Elmer were old friends and at length the dog came and laid his head in Elmer's lap to be petted. Elmer stroked his ears for a moment and then shoved him away, mind on bigger game. He wheeled toward the doorless chicken house, his anticipatory face not unlike the face of other more able predators, sharp, foxlike, cunning little ferret eyes.

When at length he backed out through the dark aperture he was swearing softly and wiping chickenshit off the wheels onto the shawl. The inert bodies of three pullets mounded the shawl over his lap. Where the feeling began above his pelvis he could feel the heat of them, their hot blood still yet somehow vibratory with the shock of life so suddenly gone.

Wheeling about to turn his eyes suddenly widened with momentary fear and he was face to face with a man in the yard across. There was a scraggy thigh-high hedge that separated the two yards and across it a man stood watching him, a look of mild amusement on his face. The man had on an old suitcoat too small for him and one sleeve of it dangled empty and there was about him as well something secretive, something that allied them as cohorts in some conspiracy. The figure nodded formally as if he had met some acquaintance in the street and turned and walked across the yard without looking back. He glided into place next to the adjoining house, peered through a bedroom window.

Elmer was back on the street with his chickens when it occurred to him to wonder why Roosterfish was skulking about his own backyard like a burglar, staring through his own windows like some perverse windowpeeper of the night.

The old house was cold and drafty when the weather began to turn chill. Edgewater looked about it to see what could be done. In a bedroom piled high with broken furniture and boxes of junk he found a stack of window panes and part of a can of glazing. He got a case knife and pried open the can. It was still pliable enough to work with. He took out all the broken panes and replaced them, used the knife to putty the panes in the sashes. He built a fire and climbed up in the attic to see was the flue sound, sniffing for smoke, watching for light through the old brick, found a can of tar and patched a leak he had found in the roof.

He had planned to seal off some of the bedrooms so that the house would be easier to heat. Prowling through the junk stored in old pasteboard boxes he fell to reading old newspapers, magazines, clippings saved about folks long dead. Keepsakes and souvenirs put away and forgotten, memorabilia of other years. In a boxed envelope: a collection of old-fashioned valentines, old-fashioned sentiments, childish scrawls in faded pencil. Old memories he took to himself like debris out of his own past.

An old album yielded up portraits of folks, unknown to him, men stiffly posed, standing perversely among plowshares and squinting into the sun in Sunday best. Little girls self-conscious in lace and crinoline, flowered hair, eyes a little frightened, the eye of the camera fixed with a wary and distrustful stare. A world of pictures, old faded images from out of time lost and unmounted by those who mourned themselves as well. A graveyard cleaning. Women in long dresses looking up from rakes or hoes, a hand raised to hair lifted by winds that blew out of spring long shuttled down endless and irrevocable corridors of time. A banquet table from a length of woven wire stretched between two trees. A backdrop of graves, always the graves, the living attendant and respectful to the dead, guilt at still being among the living, a throwback to old cultures long layered under the sand. Others, a young girl and boy, hands clasped, faces bright. Tomorrow a promise and not a threat. Children playing by the selfsame creek that fronted his house, perhaps this same couple's children in later years, kneedeep in water, mouths open, he could very nearly hear their shouts of laughter. Others more somber still. A heavyset woman lay serene on her deathbed, eyes closed, brow unruffled, hands clasped, unreal, a swollen mockup left by tricksters in her stead. A preponderance of dead babies in funeral wraps in diminutive caskets, banks of carnations. Here one saved, pressed. It powdered under his delicate touch, gave forth a musty smell of ancient doom. Death must have dogged their tracks, camped at night somewhere in the bottomland, must have worked this place on the shores. An age of morbidity without apology.

Other souvenirs kept from happier times, no less poignant. A young man in uniform and tam, brown belt, cropped hair, a brave smile. Affixed to the bottom of the picture was a stick of spearmint gum, hard and odorless, someone had written on it: JIM. Whatever happened to you, Jim? We all remember old Jim, he went to the wars. Where did you go, Jim? What did you see? What befell you? Did the French girls smile sweetly with their eyes or did you get blown apart in Belleau Woods? Did the birds pick bloody scraps of you from the shattered trees and did you die a hero's death across waters or did you die in debt and consumptive on a hardscrabble Horn? Did they close you into an insane asylum where strangers grudgingly saw to your wants or did you die rich and fawned over, was your will contested? She saved your gum, Jim. She must have liked you. Did you ever get any of that?

He heard her call him, looked up and out the sun-lacquered window. More accustomed to this fragile sepia world of silent people than to these bright colors and harsh sounds, dim through the faded curtains, through a lace scrollwork of shadows. He folded the album and laid it back in the pasteboard box and went out.

He took stock of what money he had accumulated and he decided to lay in winter stores. He bought a barrel of flour and a stand of lard. He bought sugar and coffee and dried beans and tobacco. Candy and a case of peaches canned in heavy syrup and he bought everything he thought they might need to see them through till spring. The grocer had to send it out on a truck. Edgewater catalogued his provender with satisfaction and stored it away in cabinets. He had visions of sitting with his feet on the hearth while the snow flew.

Just what are you doing, Billy? she wanted to know. She was looking at all this largess with amazement, as if Edgewater had gone into the grocery business. Why did you buy so much? Are you not goin back to work?

He had not thought about it. Why? he asked.

It took her a moment to frame an answer. Because everybody works, she said. That's what people do. They get a job and they work at it and they make a livin.

We'll get by.

I don't want to get by. You're not supposed to just get by. We've got a baby on the way. And anybody can get by. I want nice things, pretty clothes, things other people have. Don't you care what people think?

Edgewater was silent, but he realized that he did not. He had come to think of survival as an end in itself, not something to be taken for granted. Anything beyond that was just frosting on the cake.

I'll see what I can find, he told her.

Some days she would go visit the old woman and when she did or on days when she was in a bitter mood he would put on his coat and prowl the woods. The timberland went he knew not how many miles before there were other houses. Some days he was in them all the daylight hours and past nightfall but he was never lost. There was a calm silence to the woods, and acceptance. They had nothing to prove to him and they did not ask anything. When the woods swallowed him time lost all meaning, it was the same here as it had always been, perhaps it would always be. Daylong he'd walk through this silence till it permeated him, seemed to soak into his very clothes. When he was back he'd have nothing to say to her, no defenses to offer, as if little by little he was taking on the qualities of the country he moved through.

Following a rutted road grown thick with blackberry briars and cut by gulleys deeper than his height, he came upon old signs of civilization. He passed graves rounded with cairns of stones and an abandoned church or schoolhouse with its roof half caved and windows sashless and dark. He peered in. It was a church, here were the pews and the pulpit, old hymnals swollen and hard from rain. A scholarly and pious gloom. Sanctuary now for a congregation of predators and night prowlers.

Further there were mineral springs and the ruins of a veritable community. A post office. What seemed to have been a grocery store. Then down where mineral springs boiled out of limestone rock near a derelict hotel in opulent ruin. The hotel had been built on both sides of the stream and spanning the creek was what appeared to have been a dance floor, half stripped of its oaken flooring by vandals or inclement weathers and when he crossed the timbers it swayed and creaked eerily in the wind, old cables protesting his unaccustomed weight. The railing had been stripped away by wind and lay with broken windows among flower bushes grown mutant and strange.

He walked amidst all this ruined splendor and something unnamable touched him. The wind stirred velvet drapes long rotted to mildewed shards as colorless as funeral silks and to this music he envisioned dancers swaying lantern lit and graceful. Easy laughter floated over the waters and he heard voices in slow and refined cadences, eternally carefree, locked or frozen in time. Down a curving staircase of ruined oak came ladies of quality on the arms of men of means. Long gowns swept the parquetry floors and diamond earrings winked in the light of revolving chandeliers. Old doomed watering hole of the rich. Its benefits proved false. Its waters had not saved them. These dancers were long dead, their bones no more than the gnawed bones of rabbits predators left like an offering on the marble foyer, their voices just the winter wind singing through their skulls.

The past stirred all about him like something he had awakened from sleep. Old meaningless intrigues were played out here, the smiles and flirtations on those long-gone summer nights. Cuckoldments and betrayal perpetrated here with grace and style. Dalliance among the rich had come to no more than among the poor in the long run. And this was the long run: velvet wallpaper brought from foreign shores that lay in watermarked and rotted sheaves for rats to nest in.

The sun tracked on and the air grew thick and oppressive as amber and he went down the stairway on the other side of the creek and back out into the world.

He'd taken to staying gone as if he kept more curious work hours. He would come in at four or five after being gone all day, in the woods or perhaps at the Knob listening to Swalls and Bradshaw swap lies. She never asked him where he had been. He came in one evening and she had been crying. She was sitting in the rocking chair he had bought her to ease the pain in her back. He put his arm around her and she did not pull away. He could feel her shoulder trembling through the cloth of her blouse.

I want to move, she told him. We have to find another house.

Move? Why? What's the matter with this place?

I'm scared here, she told him. This place is haunted.

Oh for God's sake.

I heard a baby cryin in that shutoff bedroom, she told him. This evening. It kept cryin and cryin. I unboarded the door and went in and it quit. It was just old boxes of stuff in there, clothes and things. There wasn't a baby in there.

Of course to hell there wasn't a baby in there. Didn't you watch me board it up when it started turning cold? Didn't we look in all those old boxes?

I don't care. I know what I heard and I heard a baby cryin in there. And that's not all.

Oh good God.

I seen a warnin, she told him.

A warning of what?

I don't know. I seen like a shadow on the ground. I went out and got a stick of wood and started back in the house and this shadow, like a great big bird, come over and just swooped down and flew along the ground. Not a bird, just the shadow of one. I looked up and there wasn't anything there and looked back and it was still there.

Well.

Laugh if you want to.

I'm not laughing, Sudy. I don't think it's funny that you're scared. But I think it's just your nerves. I don't think there's crying babies and big black birds around here.

Somethin's goin to happen.

He sat before her, laid a hand on her knee. Of course something's going to happen. Something's always going to happen. Thousands of things, an infinite number of things. Some good, some bad, to us, and to everyone else. And they're locked in, set, they'll happen whether babies cry or birds fly or whatever.

Somethin bad.

Well.

You don't believe me.

I believe you're scared and worried. That's all I'm concerned about.

Are you concerned enough to move?

All right, Sudy, I'll look around for a place.

You won't do it.

He asked around town for an empty apartment the next day and when he came in Harkness's truck was parked on the bridge. Harkness himself leaned against the truck drinking a beer and listening to the baying of distant dogs. He turned and threw his empty can into the bed of the truck and raised a hand to acknowledge Edgewater's existence. He did not speak. Edgewater sat for a moment and waited for Harkness to move the pickup but he made no move to do so. Edgewater got out.

I live over there, he said. I need to get across the bridge.

Harkness nodded and got in the truck and pulled across the bridge. This time he did not get out but cut the switch and opened another beer and sat watching Edgewater get out of the car. Runnin my deer dogs a little, he said by way of explanation.

Edgewater didn't reply. He went up the steps and into the house. Sudy was reading by the waning light of the western window and she didn't look up. Edgewater turned the light on and picked the coffee pot up from the stove. It was empty. He filled it with water and put it on to boil.

What's he doing out there?

I don't know. He said he wanted to run his deer dogs.

Did you tell him that he could?

Well, I didn't tell him he couldn't, I didn't see any harm in it. Do you?

Of all the land in the world I don't see why he has to run his deer dogs in my front yard.

He's known Mama and Daddy of years, Buddy. All of us.

Not quite all of us, Edgewater said.

He went into their room to change clothes. When he couldn't find any clean socks he pulled open one of Sudy's drawers, pawing through stockings and brassieres and panties. Out of a tilted box of Kotex slid a half pack of Camels. He hadn't known she still had it, or why. What moved her to it in such a fashion. He put his shoes back on sockless and went out.

He made coffee and carried it to the window. It was near sunset, light the color of blood mottled the windshield of Harkness's trunk and burnished the bullhorns mounted on the hood. Harkness was out now and leaning against the tailgate with an air of patience and staring toward the hollow where the dogs ran. There was about him a comfortable attitude that suggested that he was making himself at home and that he might be there for some time.

Fuck this, Edgewater said. He set his coffee cup down hard on the windowsill and arose. She was watching.

What's the matter.

Nothing.

He went out and down the steps and when he came into the yard Harkness looked up.

I don't want you hunting here.

Do what?

I don't want you running dogs or parked here or drinking beer here, I want you gone.

I reckon you own this land here, then.

I don't own it but I've got a rent receipt in my pocket.

Let me tell you something, good buddy. I've lived all my life in this county. I know ever soul in it and most of the cats and dogs. No man ever denied me permission to run dogs on his land or cross his fences.

I wouldn't know about any of that. All I know is I pay the rent and I want you off it.

Harkness's face was heavy and florid, the sun lacquered it as well, bathed him in rich deep colors, purples and reds, out of a more resplendent time. One eye was somehow a little higher than the other and it lent to his face a mismatched look, as if it had been cleft and imperfectly joined.

You're just a goddamned troublemaker, ain't you? And don't think I ain't got your number. Why I've knowed that little girl longern you have. I reckon you ain't lived around here long enough to learn me. I'm the bullgoose in this poultry yard, Harkness said. I'm the steed in this barn lot. You understand me?

You may well be, Edgewater said. You're certainly handy enough with the bullshit.

Don't fuck with me young feller, I've got nothing against you but don't fuck with me.

Harkness got in and cranked the truck. Edgewater started back toward the porch. He turned when he heard the truck shut off. I guess you got the goddamned road rented from the county, too, hadn't ye? Harkness asked. He cranked the truck and spun it backward, pulled across the bridge. Edgewater climbed the porch steps and went in. He came back out momentarily with his coffee. Harkness had stopped the truck fifty or so feet down the road. The door was open and yellow light spilled onto the gravel. Edgewater could hear the radio, then the baying of Harkness's dogs. He went back in.

The pain in her back and side worsened sometime before dawn and it did not cease all day. This day seemed endless, it wore on and on. He stayed inside with her all day, kept urging her to let him drive her to the doctor. It'll get better after a while, she'd say. I might as well get used to it. In midafternoon it grew more severe still and he went to the store at the junction for aspirin. She took some and after a while he asked her, Is it any better?

I believe it is getting some easier.

He asked her again later and she said the same thing but he knew she was lying.

At suppertime he heated canned soup and they sat at the table but she hardly touched it.

Do you want to go to your mother's? Or me go call her to come over here?

Why? I don't see what good it would do.

Well.

Dusk fell and then dark. He listened to the radio awhile and read and watched her where she rocked and he'd see little glimmers of pain flicker across her face. He threw the book aside but did not rise. She sat watching the fire, crocheting some small garment. When it was time they went to bed. Then he got back up. He found the flashlight and with it he went out naked and cranked the car to see would it start. He checked the tires and the water and the oil. It was clear and very cold and there was not a breath of wind. Off in the dark he could hear the creek running. He exhaled and his breath plumed palely. He inhaled and the air was sharp and icy. Starlight gleamed reassuringly on the old car.

He went back in and lay down beside her. The lights were out and all he could see were the luminous hands of the clock. He lay beside her still and quiet and after a long while he would begin to think she had gotten easy and fallen asleep. He half dozed: then he would hear her breathe in a sharp intake of air like a gasp and he would come wide awake again, senses all alert, intent, staring into the blackness.

He dozed. Billy? He came awake again and she had a hand on his shoulder, fear in her voice. Billy?

He leapt out of bed and turned on the light. He was hauling on his trousers, getting sockless into his shoes, struggling with his shirt.

Damn it you're going if I have to drag you.

She was huddled under the sheets watching him. Her eyes were wide. I think I'm havin it, she said.

You can't be.

I think I am.

He helped her into her gown, wrapped a blanket about her against the cold, and carried her outside, holding her onearmed while he wrestled with the door, at last kicking it wide, lowering her onto the seat gently. So fragile a burden, already faulted.

Just hurry, Billy.

Across the bridge and so into the night. The speedometer didn't work but he kept it floorboarded, seldom braking, feeling the Fleetline drift beneath him on the graveled curves, her frightened eyes, the ragged elongated tapestry of trees at night. Slowing going into the curves, speeding up coming out, the headlights burning away the night.

There was a long hall gleaming with floorwax and set in a room or alcove at its center a square nurse's station. A bank of telephones. Busy women in starched white imbued with purpose. A grayhaired woman listened to his tale with no anxiety, calm, she'd heard it all before. It's nothing to get excited about, she told him. Perhaps a little secret, amused at the prospective father, sockless and beltless and shirt wrong side out, dressed on the run.

He had to count money into a waiting palm before attendants spurred by some imperceptible signal that he'd paid hastened past him with a wheelchair and out to where she waited in the car. He'd been across this country and now back again but he was naïve in the ways of the world.

Fetched up against the wall to let them pass, he watched them speed silently by with her and down to the end of the hall, her face turning toward him as they went by, pale, a frightened face uncertain of where she was being taken. He started that way as well but the sliding door closed after the wheelchair went through and he stood uncertainly in the hall.

The doctor's on his way, the nurse at the station told him when asked. The nurses are back there prepping her for delivery. Everything's being done, you can relax now. She's in capable hands.

He sat in the waiting room and looked at a magazine. He had half finished an article on bass fishing before it came to him that he was not remotely interested in bass fishing and did not even know what he was doing with it. He smoked a cigarette and drank a cup of cardboard flavored coffee poured down from a machine and sat and watched the night's emergencies come and go.

For a fugitive of order he had come to a strange pass. A world of cohesion here, of symmetry as if all the world's order had been distilled and ended up here. Nurses and doctors came and went, faces calm, here no one exploded with anger, everything was contained well under control. In capable hands, she'd said. If there was a place in all the universe where mishaps were brought to rights, then surely it would be here. Even the voices grow calm within the walls here, steady weights are lifted, has the money not already been paid.

Here in this glow of cold white fluorescence even time was held in abeyance. The sun neither rose nor set. The lights never went out, so day never ended, nothing marked time's wheeling save the changing of shifts, the hours of births and deaths, hello and goodbye. The changing faces of the nurses.

A wail of ambulances made him restive and he walked the halls of this resort for the maimed or dying. Standing near the emergency room doors he saw them suddenly explode inward, simultaneously with this moved aside for two attendants running down the hall. Two uniformed city cops held the doors wide and the attendants fled into the night where an ambulance set with rear doors already sprung wide and reappeared almost instantly bearing between them a stretcher where lay an enormous and bloody black man. Seemingly beheaded he lay in a great welter of blood with his eyes open and alive. He was turned on his side with the slashed side of his throat upward and agape and faintly pumping like the gills of a fish. As they fled past Edgewater he could smell the coppery odor of blood and see in the man's hip pocket a smashed bottle and a spreading stain of whiskey and blood. They were gone down the hall to another door that opened and closed behind them.

Is it all right if I make a local call?

Go right ahead.

He took up the phone and then realized he did not even know the number, had to search it out in the directory. It seemed strange seeing the name in print: Emma Bradshaw. It rang and rang and still she slept on. At last it ceased and he heard her voice, querulous and apprehensive, tinged with dread. The phone that rings deep in the night.

He told her what she had to know and hung up. Bradshaw was gone as he was wont to be when the bells of need tolled so Edgewater called the cabstand and had a taxi dispatched.

I need to find out something.

Well. The doctor's here now, and he's with her in the delivery room. There've been some complications but everything's being done that should be.

What sort of complications?

She's just having a difficult delivery.

Well. Thanks.

Back in the waiting room there was a boy who was like a caricature of a prospective father. Edgewater watched him and seemed to grow calmer himself. The boy smoked and chewed his nails and behaved precisely as if he were some actor awaiting imminent fatherhood in a film.

Sometime in the hours of early morning he slept and awoke to find the old woman watching him with bleak eyes. There was a bad taste in his mouth and his eyes hurt and sleeping in the chair had given him a dull ache at the base of the skull. He rubbed his eyes. Asleep he'd forgotten where he was. He picked a cigarette out of the pack and lit it.

Have you seen her?

They let me go in a minute but they've got her all doped up. The baby didn't make it. They wanted me to tell you. They said to let her rest.

They fell silent, wary of each other. Curious that it should have come to this. Old enemies honoring an armed truce perhaps. Gamblers just waiting for the next card to fall. Edgewater stretched his feet out, tried and failed to get comfortable. After a while the door opened on its near soundless hinges and a nurse beckoned to the boy awaiting news of his wife. You've got a little girl, she told him. He arose to follow her and her eyes glanced once at Edgewater and met his momentarily then sidled away.

Edgewater sat for a time in the Fleetline and watched the night wear its weary way out but it was too cold to stay outside for long and the heater did not work. He stayed long enough to wake himself thoroughly for in the morning hours before dawn the cold grew bitter and then he went back inside. Nothing seemed to have changed, he felt he'd been there forever. A familiar of the waxed halls, the closed doors, the soft hushed comings and goings. The constant hum of unseen machinery, a distasteful smell he could not identify.

He went back to the waiting room and stood staring out through his own dark still reflection to the neat rows of box elders and beyond, the asphalt slick and wetlooking under the lights, and past this further the streetlights running along the highway with their quaking coronas of nearblue light and the infrequent passage of cars, headlights flaring soundless and ghostly though the thick glass. A backdrop of sleeping houses, an occasional window lit, sickness or trouble in their night as well. The focus of his gaze shifted and this vision faded and beyond his reflection was a waiting room with its rows of empty chairs and the old woman with lowered head, hand to her brow, asleep or praying. Weary Madonna. That it should come to this. Mother and daughter linked by a circle of pain.

Near daylight he drove downtown and circled the block until he found a café open. Entered and sat among early morning deer hunters, a few drunks out all night and afraid to go home or perhaps they had none. He ordered coffee and a grilled cheese sandwich, sat half entranced waiting at the counter, staring unseeing at tiers of sectioned pies under plate glass, cardboard mockups of sandwiches and carbonated drinks.

He ate the sandwich without really tasting it and when it came sipped the hot coffee, absentmindedly wiped his buttery fingers on a paper napkin. He paid and went out. On the street he paused for a time and then he went back in and ordered a bacon and egg sandwich for the old woman. He paid for that and a container of coffee and went out again.

The town still slept. He sat in the car amidst a calm silence and watched. The sun was just rising over shantytown, the railroad tracks gleamed as if they had been polished in the night. He closed his eyes and felt the spare warmth of the sun through the glass and began to hear far off as yet the approach of the train. The sun crept on. It crept across the jungle of kudzu until the tie yard commenced itself out of light colors appearing. You could watch them come, the trees rising up burdened and grotesquely disfigured by the weight of vines, the sun's slow slant sweep across it and past and across the tarpaper roofs and cindercolored walls of shacks and yawning porches with swings dependent from lengths of chain and bare earth chickenscratched, with trees from whose branches hung lank and motionless swings fashioned from automobile tires. On trucks with splayed tires and stone-shattered glass and wrecksprung doors and from thence onto moted glass in curtainless windows onto the sleeping faces of drunk and whore and child alike, night's dreams were ending, sweet day had broken.

Mr. Edgewater?

Yes.

Dr. Klein would like to see you. I believe he's across the hall in the emergency room. He would have seen you in his office but things have been pretty hectic around here this morning.

All right.

He walked on down and across the hall to where the emergency room was marked by a row of lights about its door and a metal placard. He pushed the knobless door and it opened on freeswinging hinges, he went on in. He felt enormously hollow inside, empty, cold winds sang there like winds singing off stone.

A man in white standing by a table while a nurse was applying a compress of gauze to the arm of an old man sitting up on a metal stool. There were drops of blood on his pants and on his shoes. The doctor turned when the door opened, a wry little man with thinning hair.

Mr. Edgewater?

Yes.

I'm Dr. Klein, your wife's physician. I wanted to talk to you in my office but I guess you'd gone to eat breakfast? Your wife is rising now. We've moved her to 11-B and of course you can see her, but she's heavily sedated. She won't be coherent. She's had a very difficult time. He was snipping the gauze, tucking it under, a neat workmanship job, taking up a roll of adhesive tape.

I know.

An extremely difficult time. She seems to have a kidney infection.

What about the baby?

There was a pause, indicative, if the conversation had ceased here Edgewater would still have known. It was a stillbirth, Mr. Edgewater. I'm sorry. The baby was already dead. That was one reason things were so complicated.

I see.

I'm sorry. It goes without saying that we did everything we could.

Of course. You said she was in 11-B?

11-B, yes.

Sudy was sleeping. The old woman was sitting in a chair by her. It was a small room with two beds, two sinks and two chairs, a green curtain on a rod suspended from the ceiling separating the room so he couldn't see who was on the other side. He glanced at Sudy and then approached the old woman and proffered the paper bag and she stretched out something more claw than hand and slapped it from him. It hit the floor at his feet, he could see the dark brown spread of coffee staining the bag. He picked it up. There was a wastepaper basket with a black plastic liner in front of the radiator and he threw the bag into it.

The girl was white, she lay pillowed on her blond hair, the hair was damp at the temples, darker there, ash tendrils against her cheek. She stirred momentarily in sleep or whatever drugged state she inhabited. She looked helpless, vulnerable.

Sudy? He leaned above the haggard face.

Her eyes fluttered and she said something. He leant to hear but he did not understand it: one word, it had sounded like a name, but if it was, it was not his own.

————

Late in the afternoon, weary and desolate, he drove back to Grievewood, a place so aptly named. The house cold and dark, shadows gathered within and it seemed some old house abandoned long ago to nightprowlers and the elements, no one living here at all. The front door stood ajar still, the fire in the fireplace dead and burnt to a powdery white ash the wind through the front door lifted and stirred like flakes of dry snow. There was a steeped-in smell of old smoke.

He put on a pot of water to boil for coffee and when it was hot he heated water in a pan for shaving and sat at the kitchen table drinking the bitter coffee and waiting for the water to heat. He peered through the kitchen window to the old garden spot thick with spears of brittle weeds, beyond it the bleak gentle roll of winter hills. The house seemed cavernous, emptiness multiplied by itself, old voices called down the sleep starved corridors of his brain and he thought he heard her voice, her laughter. His own voice saying things he wished he'd said but hadn't.

When the water was hot he carried the watermarked mirror he'd found and his soap and razor out to the dogtrot where better light fell through the screened entrance. He lathered his face and shaved, the soap drying quickly in the windy hall. He went back in and washed himself and put on clean clothing in the room with its still-tousled bedclothes, her shoes at the foot of the bed, the aspirin on the seat of a kitchen chair by his side. A halfglass of water. Here time seemed not to have progressed at all. Even the alarm clock had stopped, though not to mark her hour of travail: it had trundled on a few more hours before ceasing. He viewed the room as a stranger might, already felt a bitter remove from it, as if the pleasures and the ultimate disquiet of this bed had befallen someone else.

He gathered together a few things he thought she might want or need, a clean gown and underwear, her hairbrush, toothpaste and a toothbrush. He worked hurriedly, like a thief expecting interruption. When he had all the things in a paper bag he went on out to the car. During the day clouds had moved smoothly in from the west and the sky was a dull gray. A band of lighter gray lay on the horizon and he thought later it might snow.

He pushed open the door to 11-B and saw not Sudy but an elderly woman appended with wires or tubing in her wrist and nose, an old shocked-looking woman with wild tufts of irongray hair and frightened eyes. For a moment he thought Sudy had died and then he backed out and made inquiries at the nurses' station.

Mrs. Bradshaw had her moved into a private room. She's in 16-B, down and across the hall.

He went down the hall with the brown paper bag. She was alone and she was sleeping when he went in. In this room there was a view of the outside, he sat in a folding chair by the window and stared across the gray winter world. A few cold-looking birds foraged the grass near the building's edge, rose fluttering to the bare branches of a mimosa tree, sat disconsolate and uncertain as if they wished they'd followed their brothers south. True to his premonition a few flakes of snow fell, tilted in the wind and listed soundlessly against the glass. A cold wind tilted the branches of the tree and the birds rose out of his sight. He sat for a long time while the light waned and the day drew on.

Billy?

He turned. She was just lying there watching him. He arose and carried the paper bag over to the side of the bed. There was a metal nightstand there with a shelf in the bottom and he set the bag there.

It died, didn't it?

Yes.

It was a little boy.

Well, it couldn't be helped, Sudy. Are you feeling all right?

I just feel real weak and everything.

When you get tired tell me and I'll go or just sit and let you sleep.

I slept all day.

He sat awkwardly beside the bed and he seemed unable to think of anything else to say. He turned toward the window to see was it still snowing but he couldn't tell, dusk was deepening and the world closing in.

I'm not going back down there, Billy. I'm going home.

You won't have to go back. I'll find a furnished place here in town and rent it. I guess that place wasn't too good an idea to start with.

No. That's not what I meant. I mean I'm going back home. I'll stay there awhile and then I'm going to get a job. There are things I want, things I need you don't even know what are. Things we'd never have.

You won't work. You quit a perfectly good job over something that had to be done and money don't mean a thing in this round world to you.

When you've got it you throw it away and when you don't that's all right too. You're just as happy. I can't live like that, Billy.

He sat listening to all this with no trace of surprise, with a kind of tired inevitability, a vague ache of emptiness.

You never wanted to marry me anyway, Billy. You had your own reasons for what you done, you always do.

And all you wanted was a name for the baby.

She was crying a little. The little thing don't need it now, she said. I wanted to be respectable.

Respectable? he asked in disbelief.

See? You don't even know, or care. You don't care about anything. You're…just all to yourself, there's not enough to go around. You don't need anybody else. It's like you're not even there.

There were things he could have said but he did not say them. He sat silent as if under some edict or judgment, as if he awaited some invisible presence to arise and speak in his behalf, the natural order of cause and effect itself to plead his case. Or awareness that things once set in motion must one day cease.

Edgewater crossed a trestle spanning an overpass and from this height he could see the city. He sat for a while dangling his feet in empty space and peering out across the tops of a vacant lot given over to a spreading hedge of mimosa, bare of leaves and in the cold clear air their delicate branches looked bonelike and fragile. Past their tops and farther there were two boxcars tilted on their sides and being swallowed by hedges like some old undiscovered train wreck of long ago and he thought for a fey moment he might kick among the bones of the victims for their coins and jewelry. Beyond the boxcars a thin and near translucent border of willows and past that as if it were some ambiguous border marking the beginning of civilization a few scattered houses and the tarred and graveled roof of the Cozy Court Motel with the sparse scattering of cars and the café sat cattycorner by the highway to the right and taller than buildings of the town he could see the courthouse set on its rows of hedges and symmetrical square of asphalt and he sat for a moment trying to pick out the barred windows he had stared out from that day. If time were eternal and looped there might come an instant that time veered and stopped into a momentary synchronicity and he thought for a moment he might see his face at the bars or his face there might see him here on the trestle in the wind but he doubted one face would recognize the other silhouetted dimensionless and profound against the bluegray sky. He got up and walked the rest of the way across the trestle down a ramp of riprap and slag and cut past the tilted boxcars with their air of old doom and toward the scattered houses and ultimately the Southside Café.

He went down a dry gully half filled with old car parts and tires made outsized and grotesque by its embroidery of vines as if the hedges were in the act of devouring them, drawing nourishment from them. He crossed a field of cheap wine bottles and beer bottles and cans and up a steep bank he stopped in someone's backyard. There was a boy of four or five there playing on his knees in the dirt and pushing along a hoescraped road some small vehicle rusted and dented as if it were the survivor of countless miniature highway catastrophes. The boy looked up at Edgewater with no surprise or anything at all on his face and Edgewater nodded at him solemnly and walked on past the house.

From within the house noises flared in threatened violence and he abruptly veered away from the brickhedged wall and quickened his pace as if whatever violence this house possessed might be contagious. Something glass broke against a wall and fell and a woman said, Here go ahead and drank it up goddamn you. Schoolclothes money and all. A deeper voice replied something unintelligible to Edgewater or perhaps just incoherent. The female voice gained volume and stridency almost a wail of despair. If I don't get away from here I'll lose my fuckin mind, she said.

Edgewater set out toward another house where wetwash hung frozen on a wireline but a door banged behind him and as he turned a young man naked to the waist and barefoot threw a pan of water onto the grass. For an instant the water was opaque and silver and a mist of steam rose off the ground.

Hey you.

Edgewater didn't stop.

What the hell you doin sneakin around my yard?

Just passing through, Edgewater said without slowing.

I wonder if a load of birdshot in the ass might hurry you along?

Fuck you.

Why goddamn you. The voice was enraged as if he had focused on all the grudges he bore against all the world. Edgewater ducked under the clothesline where a shirt rose all in a frozen sheet like some surreal door and he could hear the man running across the yard. Edgewater stepped behind the corner of a shed where stood a motley of tools should he need them. He waited for a time until he heard the door close and he went on.

At the Southside Café he ordered a cup of coffee from the redhaired waitress and sat idly reading the menu.

Sugar? she asked.

You might just stick your finger in it.

She winked at him. I'll do better than that, she said. She set the coffee somewhere out of sight beneath the level of the bar and he heard a lid unscrewing and a soft liquid sound of pouring and then she set it atop the formica with a flourish.

There you go. Should put lead in your pencil on a day like this.

He didn't care for the taste but he drank anyway. The first sip seemed almost all whiskey. He picked up a copy of the thin county paper and carried it to an empty booth near the window and sat facing the outside and unfolded the paper to see what news the world held for him. It seemed scant. The first page was taken up with notices of birth and obituaries as if all that transpired in between these two absolutes was ambiguous and of little moment. The society pages then perhaps. He was idly reading the advertisements when she approached and laid face down an oblong cut from a newspaper. The back held the picture of part of the frontend of a car and the word Plym. He turned it over and the heading read: RITES HELD FOR EDGEWATER INFANT. He read the short notice but it was dates and names and it told him nothing he did not already know and perhaps far less. He folded it carefully and slipped it into his shirt pocket.

Thanks.

I just thought you might want it.

Well, thanks again.

You want some more coffee?

If there's any of that same pot left.

If there ain't we'll brew up another one, she said. She gave him a slow wink with a gray eye and walked back to the counter letting him watch the backswing shift of her hips and his eyes could trace abstractly the elastic of her underwear. When she brought the coffee she sat across from him and sipped her Coke and they sat quietly looking out at the day waning where it lay behind her like a backdrop or projected image, she like some drunken instructor or interpreter who might make it coherent to him. As they sat a few cars went by with their lights on and after a time she arose and turned off the neon sign and came back.

He offered to pay her for the coffee when he got up but she waved his hand away. Forget it, she said. You want the bottle? she asked in a lower tone.

I guess not. See you later.

She followed him to the door like some host loathe to be left alone. When you gonna walk me home, Billy? Sure is dark and scary when I get off at midnight.

One of these nights.

You still livin up there over the poolroom?

Yeah. He stood half in and half out the door, dividing the warmth from the cold like the old witch in a childhood weatherhouse boding ill seasons.

Bet it's nice and quiet up there. When you gonna let me find out what sort of place you got?

His reflection in the glass door was superimposed over the darkening outside world like some brooding ascetic, the lines of his lorn face horribly delineated, he appeared some old monk or hermit, possessed by some esoteric belief not adhered to in all this world. Any time, he said and stepped into the cold.

Tonight? she asked but the pneumatic door closer cut it short and he pretended he hadn't heard. He turned and raised one hand and saw her own raise doubtfully beyond the steamed up window and he struck out across the yard toward the highway.

He was tempted but he knew all things have their price and he just did not have the coin of the realm. Talk, pretense, excuses. He did not feel like saying that he did not think she was cheap and that he knew she was not that kind of girl.

It was just one of those crazy things. Just one of a thousand nights of those crazy mixed up things. He was dry, talked out, empty. Inside he felt dark and shrouded and bitter and overdrawn at whatever arcane bank account had kept him solvent these long years.

———

Coming down past the hotel Edgewater saw with some interest that traffic was snarled under the redlight. Approaching he came upon corridors blocked up, some sort of disturbance in the street, horns blowing and he could hear angry shouts and curses. A policeman pulled up to the curb and got out and strode purposefully to the intersection.

Crippled Elmer was abysmally drunk and he was directing traffic. His wheelchair was in the middle of the street and he wheeled himself madly first one way and then the other, waving his arms meaninglessly in the air. Somewhere he had come upon a whistle and he blew it shrilly. His head lolled drunkenly on his shoulders, he stopped blowing the whistle and gave unintelligible directions to the line of factory workers backed up by the traffic.

The policeman grabbed the wheelchair by the handles and whirled it around with no trace of ceremony and wheeled it angrily to the curb where his car sat. Onehanded he threw open the door and spun the chair around facing it and laid hands on Elmer's shoulders.

Where you takin him?

Hell, I'm takin him to jail. Where'd you think I'se takin him? He's so drunk he don't know he's in the goddamned world.

Elmer's eyes stared unfocused between Edgewater and the cop while his fate was debated. He began to sing tunelessly some old song. He had vomited on himself.

I'll take him home if you won't lock him up. If he gets home he's too drunk to get back up here and cause trouble.

Who are you, his guardian angel?

I just hate seein him locked up. He can't pay any fine to get out.

I know it. But what the hell can I do? I can't let him run that thing wild. He's gonna kill somebody.

I promise you I'll get him home.

When Edgewater came pushing the wheelchair up to the porch the old woman with matted hair and snuffjuice around her mouth came out and stood watching him try to hoist the wheelchair up the steep steps. He couldn't make it. Elmer's sodden and boneless weight shifted like water and he was about to spill out of the chair. Edgewater was holding his breath because of the smell and his face grew red. He lowered the chair back to the earth and backed up a step or two and stood breathing deeply.

How about giving me a hand?

Just leave him there. He sleeps in it.

It may rain.

He could use it, she said. If you get him up here he'll just roll off the porch and hurt hisself.

He'd freeze to death tonight. Edgewater turned the chair and backed it to the edge. He got up on the porch and lifted Elmer with a hand under each armpit. He drug him across the back of the chair and his feet fell lifeless and askew on the rough boards of the porch. Myriad small shoplifted articles fell from his pockets in a curious rain. Quit goddamn it, Elmer said. The old woman sniggered as if he had done something of infinite cleverness.

The room was unlit and fetid. Heavily curtained windows stayed even the light from the sun. When his eyes adjusted to the dimness he could see that the room was furnished only with crates and boxes and old mismatched chairs with burst upholstery and gangrenous padding.

He hoisted Elmer into an old armchair and looked about for something to cover him with, at length he laid a throw rug across his lap. One bleary eye opened and closed like a lens taking Edgewater's picture.

The old woman had followed them in. Her eyes were bright and fey on alcohol and pills.

Keep him here. If he gets back uptown they'll lock him up.

She was doing something to her hair. A look almost coy on her wrinkled Kewpie face. How about me and you havin us a good time?

Edgewater doubted she had a good time left much less one to share but he did not say so. He didn't say anything at all. He went out into the grown up yard.

He was almost back to the crossroads when he heard someone hail him. He looked back. Elmer had drug himself onto the porch, was struggling to reseat himself in the chair. When he was in he started across the yard. He grew tangled in the weeds. Edgewater could see his hands spinning the wheels, he could hear him swearing. He was free, coming on toward the road. Hey, Billy. Wait up.

To hell with it, Edgewater said. He went on.

He walked down to the blacktop and crossed it and took a shortcut along the railroad track, walking the ties with a wind at his back that seemed to hurry him along. As he walked he kicked a can along the rails, the world here seemed lost and forsaken, there was only the sound of the wind whipping and the hollow rattle of the can skittering when he kicked it. The eerie silence of these old rails with weeds long grown up through them. As if they were some ancient and inexplicable anomaly of nature instead of the works of man. Perhaps in times past hobos had run along here pacing the train, swung themselves up by the catwalk and flattened in out of the wind, but a man would grow old here waiting for a freight to come highballing out of the night.

Dreams of why troubled him less and less these days but he dreamed he woke far in the night and the room was full of light and sound. *Red light backed the room with a strobic intensity and washed even the tangled bedclothes where he dreamed. He sat washed scarlet and all the world was a circular wall, a world of sound, sitting so amazed and rapt his mind began automatically to sort and identify them, prowl cars, ambulances, perhaps a fire engine, as if all the earth's emergency vehicles had been summoned to preside at his demise.*

He dreamed he arose and dressed to go into the world to see what was all this commotion. He stood by the window hauling up and belting his trousers. He saw speed below his window, low and squat, an ambulance with siren, an undulating wail and lights bathing the white façade of houses and porches, a rich velvet claret in a measured start and cease as if geared in some manner to his heartbeat.

Down the street and through the alley and the cause of all this disorder seemed to be near the railroad tracks. All manner of official cars and trucks were there and the train stood black and long and halted with only a measured hiss of escaping steam to mark its presence and a vast crowd of folk rubbing the sleep from their eyes and staring toward some mishap ahead of the engine. Far up the track the headlight gleamed like a searchlight searing the night out of the way and here he came upon the remnants of a wheelchair, wasting warped and shredded chromium and the mangled scraps of a man scattered among the ties like scraps some feeding beast had dropped and he fell to his knees in the gravel.

With the curious illogic as dreams sequence and implement themselves, he had a flashlight and he unpocketed it but a man in white laid on his arm a restraining hand. Don't shine that light, he said. Have a little respect. Far up the track Edgewater could see an old railroader in a striped cap walking toward him with a lantern swinging along in his hand from side to side hypnotically, but though he watched for some time and though he could see the railroader's legs scissoring through the misty night, he did not seem to get nearer and the bill of his cap kept his face in shadow.

That's Crippled Elmer, he dreamed he said.

It's Elmer, the man agreed. But he ain't crippled. He's a baseball player. He's got a fastball you could light a cigarette off of.

What was he doing in a wheelchair then?

He just had it tricked up where it would ride on them tracks and he got his schedules crossed. A laugh came out of darkness, for this man's face was in shadow as well and something dread lay cold on Edgewater and it came to him that this was some tableau arranged for his benefit by all these faceless men and the dream was so stark and vivid and moved on so many levels of reality he grew afraid. A caution seized him; he felt he must think this out carefully. He felt he had to see a face, any face, something familiar out of all this dark. Then as if reading his thoughts the man released his arm and Edgewater sat holding the light and knew he was afraid to illuminate the disembodied head lying between the ties. The man beside him chuckled a little to himself in some secret amusement and looked toward the heavens and, as if his glance engendered it, a skiff of clouds rolled from across the face of the moon and a steely pale light began to inch across what of the world he could see. He turned to peer up the gleaming track where the old signalman still walked like something mechanical fixed in position and back to where light crept up the ties and he could trace the splits and grain of the ties with his fingers and see tiny starshaped spatters of blood and the cold light on the rails and even as he sat waiting for the light to reveal the face he dreamed he awoke.

But he did not awake. He was walking up a road out of his childhood and he felt he had been away for a time but he did not know where or for how long. It was summertime and he was barefoot and the road lay thickly accumulated with fine dust that felt soft as velvet and this dust powdered the fronds of sumac depending into the road from the wall of encroaching greenery; all the sounds of summer fell on his ears as clear and tranquil as they ever had in life.

The road ahead curved, lost to his sight as it always had and he knew all he had to do to get home was walk around the curve and climb the rising bank up stone steps laid into the loam but when he progressed around the bend he stood halt and wonderstruck by what he saw. There was nothing, no mailbox and no steps and no house atop the bank, only the smooth rolling verdant countryside with no houses anywhere in sight and just a limitless expanse of incremental shadings of green all the way to where it grew misty with distance and met the deep blue of the sky. All the country he looked on was sown with some sort of wheat or wild grain that looked thigh high to him and a wind blew a little out of the south and ripples ran on infinitely across the field like a wave on water. He went a little away into the grain and then stopped undecided and he turned to the four points of the compass and even the way he had come had closed behind him, gone elastic and shimmering. As he watched, the image solidified like rippled water clearing the grain field as well and he felt he was seeing the world as it was before civilization had a mark upon it or else untold millennia after civilization had perished.

Uncertain where he was or what to do, he climbed the bank where he had been to the top and peered all about and then sat to rest awhile and think about things. He lit a cigarette and sat smoking and pondering his fate and after a time he looked up and he could see in the distance a man wending his way through the grain and by the time Edgewater had finished the cigarette and carefully blackened out the butt in the damp earth the man had neared him and climbed the bank and squatted by Edgewater. He had a grainhook or scythe with a crooked handle and two wooden handholds on it and he unshouldered it and laid it carefully beside him.

I don't guess it'd hurt to breathe a minute, the man said agreeably.

Edgewater peered at him closely. The man seemed to be about forty, a tanned, healthy country-looking face. Anglo-Saxon, one of Agee's famous men perhaps. High cheekbones, thin blade of nose, a day's growth of stubble. The eyes were squint from the sun but the irises were a deep guileless blue and the face looked all in all like someone who might give him directions. As he made ready to speak, the man withdrew a sack of Country Gentleman from the pocket of his chambray shirt and sitting on his heels began to build himself a cigarette.

You live around here?

The man shrugged, licked the cigarette paper and made fast the paper with his index fingers and brought out a kitchen match.

Here and everywhere else, he said.

I used to live right here.

The nut brown skin around the eyes crinkled with amusement.

I guess you don't no more?

I guess not, Edgewater mused. What happened to all this? The house and the family that lived here?

I tend all this now, the man said. He blew out pale smoke. I got all this land. You must be talking about another time.

Well, yeah. It was another time.

He waved an expansive hand. I tend all this now.

It seems like an awful lot for one man to do.

The man laughed dryly.

I always been adequate to the task. I get a little help from time to time, people working on shares, so to speak.

I'm lookin around for work. Maybe I could get a week with you? This looks like a world of grain to take care of.

You doin all right where you are, the man told him. Maybe in time. All in good time.

I wish I could have found who I was looking for. I had something to tell him.

You can tell me, the man said.

He leaned forward and spat onto the earth and laid his cigarette stub in the spittle and watched the slow crawl of moisture up the paper. Satisfied he pushed it from him.

The world is full of fools lookin for places ain't there no more. He arose and took up the grain hook. I'll see ye, he said.

Take it easy.

The man climbed down the bank and started off into the sea of grain leaving behind a diminishing trail that smoothed itself out like a wake a man might leave swimming and after a time he was only a dark moving dot in all this green.

Edgewater awoke and lay bathed in sweat for a moment before he arose and washed his face in the bathroom. He came back out and sat in the chair by the window wishing for daylight but this night seemed timeless. In these clockless hours before day he knew he'd overstayed his welcome but he didn't know what to do about it. He knew he was leaving but there did not seem to be anywhere he wanted to go or any face left in all the world he cared to look on.

———

Edgewater's room above the pool hall was across from the doctor's office. He had but one furnished room in the attic where the walls sloped like a truncated V inverted but there was an enormous window facing south and there was a radiator painted with aluminum paint that complemented the décor of the room and sometimes even put out heat. When it did not Edgewater shivered under his blankets and swore at it and sometimes rapped it with a piece of wood a former tenant had left and had perhaps used for this selfsame purpose. There was as well a little stove with kerosene burners and early on these winter mornings he made coffee and had his first cup by the big window in the sun and watched the day's crop of sick folk wash up below him.

On these cold near-zero mornings cars would park before the brick two-story building and set with motors idling, white puffs of exhaust rising and dissipating. The healthy would sometimes get out and assist the old or infirm up the steps and then return to the warmth of their cars, sit and smoke with a kind of bemused country patience until the old man or woman at length hobbled back down with their ration of pills or tonic, stood alongside the car fumbling with the door. Their clean faded overalls, their town bonnets and dresses. Something in their faces that touched him, a look of acceptance, of calm resignation. Whatever illnesses and complaints not registered here he figured not worth mentioning. On these bitter mornings when everything seemed bleak and austere to him, it seemed that all the world's old and resigned and doomed must eventually come to his front door. In these early long dreary hours of December he fell to searching faces for folk he knew, saw none familiar.

Save one morning near the end of the month when he saw approaching a figure he recognized, a onearmed man walking springily along the sidewalk and halting and peering up toward Edgewater's window with a shaded hand. The window had sidepanels that cranked outward and Edgewater opened one of them and stuck his head out into the cold.

Hey. Around at the side.

Roosterfish waved his hand in acknowledgement and passed from Edgewater's view of the black shingled roof and he heard the door open, after a time measured footfalls on the stairs. He unchained the latch and opened the door onto the cold and drafty landing. Roosterfish's head and shoulders appeared above the railing.

Come on up.

When they were inside Roosterfish shook hands with him solemnly, pumping his hand up and down as he'd seen old folks do. Roosterfish stood peering all about the room, eyes soaking up all these uptown wonders. Even a picture on the wall. Aswim in gaudy greens and reds Longfellow's village smithy raised a sledge beneath the chestnut tree. A mighty man was he.

Get you a seat. You want some coffee?

Roosterfish selected a chair, aligned it near the hissing radiator. I could use some. I don't believe I've ever seen it so by God cold. I come as nigh freezing to death last night as I ever want to.

Edgewater poured steaming coffee into a cracked porcelain cup. Remnant of other days. He passed it to Roosterfish. Where are you staying?

I got a room in that goddamn roachtrap they call a hotel but I'm plannin on leavin. I spent most of last night with my mattress wrapped around me and the rest of it beatin on the goddamn walls for heat. Tonight I plan on takin my blanket down by the tie yard where it's warmer.

Bunk in here if you want to.

I don't want to put ye out. I just kindly wanted to see ye. We split under unusual circumstances.

Yes we did. What did they do to you? Whatever happened about all that?

Not much. There was a plague of fire hit McNairy County there for a while. Barns went up in the night. Squally times. I spent many a night laid in the brush while the law kicked through ashes huntin for clues.

I guess by you being here they never found any.

Oh, they knowed who it was all right. They had enough people tellin. And I expect maybe they's a warrant or two layin around somers. But knowin and hangin don't necessarily sleep together. All that old shit ain't nothin new to me.

Edgewater was looking him up and down; Roosterfish looked much as he remembered him, except that he was thinner, the bones in his face more pronounced, the eyes perhaps more deepset. Roosterfish had always put a neat and clean appearance, and even now he was freshly shaven, his cheeks slick and gleaming. Clean clothes, hair neatly trimmed. A smell of talcum, Bay Rum.

I would of come looked you up sooner but I didn't want to bother ye. First they told me you was livin way out in the tules somers and all married and settled down. Then I heard about ye bad luck and I didn't figure you much wanted to see nobody.

Well. I guess it happened more to other people than it did to me. I'm still alive anyway. Elmer said he saw you way back in the fall.

Yeah. Him and an armful of stolen chickens. Ah, I just passed through that night. Runnin me a little reconnaissance, like the army does. My main interest here was the cockfights, and they don't have em that time of year, so I had to wait for cold weather. Is they any of that coffee left?

Edgewater refilled his cup. What did you find at home?

What I expected. Her gone. The house all tore up and everthing worth anything stole. Winders busted and a dead cat on the kitchen table.

Edgewater seated himself on the windowsill, a weight of cold glass lay on his back. And you never heard where she went?

Oh yes. I heard several places she went. I even checked a few of em out. Each one of em just a little shadier and a little further down the line than the last one.

You never found her.

I quit wantin to.

Well. Anyway I'm glad to see you.

We had a few times, didn't we?

Yeah we did.

I had some after you left, too. Got kind of squirrelly there after they killed my rooster. They purely kicked the hell out of me, too. That old pistol hadn't of blowed up I believe they'da killed me. They wanted you as bad or worse than they did me. They hated your ass, son. They could understand me; they couldn't figure you out for shit.

I yelled at you before I jumped. There wasn't time to do a whole lot of planning.

Oh, I know, I know. I was a little addled or somethin. I just couldn't believe they was a son of a bitch alive mean enough to kick my rooster in the river.

Roosterfish fell silent, seemed not to want to dwell on the details of the past. He laid an arm across the surface of the warm radiator. It sure is tricked out nice here. Beats the hell out of sleepin under a bluff. Lord, I bet it's cold on that old river this morning.

Like I said, bring your blankets and stuff around and bunk here. You can have the bed or the floor either.

They might throw ye out.

Edgewater shrugged. I need to be gone anyway. Seems like I can't get started. That might be just the thing to get me down the line.

I was aimin to ask you about that. What are your plans?

I don't have any plans.

You not still goin on east?

I just don't have any plans.

I reckon you could do worse than settle here. You reckon your old lady'll come back?

No, Edgewater said. I just guess her life was sad. I never knew what to do to keep it from being sad.

It ain't none of my business, I'se just askin.

Who told you all this? I didn't think there was five people here knew my name.

I'se talkin to Buddy Bradshaw.

Edgewater smiled. Yeah, that figures. No, I don't think she'll be back. I doubt I'd be here if she did. Are you going back on the road? he asked.

No. I'm through with the road. I don't look back, when a thing's settled it's over and done with. I done it a long time and I ain't got regret one, even the whitecaps, but I'm through with it.

What about Harkness? Do you not call that looking back?

No. I don't. That ain't back, it's here. It ain't settled yet, how could it go anywhere?

In the afternoon they walked down the street and through an alley and cut across a backyard to the hotel and picked up Roosterfish's things. Roosterfish burdened with his bedclothes, coming up the sidewalk with a great bundle of clothes and blankets athwart his thin shoulders, like a derelict or evictee or survivor escaping with all the effects he could salvage from fire or flood.

He made himself a pallet on the floor near the radiator and late in the afternoon they went down to the Snowwhite Café for supper. After they ate they walked in the poolroom, stood a moment in indecision before the door. You want a beer? Roosterfish asked.

It doesn't matter. I guess I could drink one.

Tell ye what. I got a couple pints of Gypsy Rose in my stuff. How's that sound?

Like old times, Edgewater said.

I got somethin to tell ye I ain't told nobody else.

Waning light of late afternoon frangible on the wall. Roosterfish already wrapped in a blanket, shoulders against the wall, his bottle of wine a deep opaque purple. He had a tale he must tell.

I seen the damnest thing down there one night I ever seen. I was laid out in the woods in front of Tyler's house kinda keepin an eye on things and tryin to decide what I was goin to do to him. I'd done set fire to his car but hell that didn't tip the scale. I was laid out late one Saturday night waitin for him to come in from wherever he was and his old lady was home, you member that young gal over at Simmons's looked like she was half crazy? She come out a time or two and looked up and down the road and then she'd go back in. Wadn't a sign of a light on nowhere and I got to kindly wonderin what she's doin in there in the dark. Time drug by. I had me a bottle of wine and I was stretched out there waitin and takin me a little nip now and then. I figured he'd done me a pretty bad wrong and I'se makin my plans. I had my gun. After I got beat nearly to death like I done I'se about half crazy. I could of burnt him in his sleep and never turned a hair. There wadn't nothin left of me but meanness.

Anyway, after a while he come. Somebody pulled up and let him out. Bunch of men and women too, a whole damn carful. Drunk, sounded like. I just laid there watchin. He got out staggerin and sniggerin to hisself and wanderin around the yard. Seemed like he couldn't find the porch. Directly he got up the steps and kindly squared his shoulders and prissed on in. You member how he walked.

Roosterfish took out his pipe and clasped it between his knees, packed the bowl with roughcut tobacco. He took it up and popped a kitchen match on his thumbnail and lit the pipe and sat with eyes unfocused, staring at nothing.

He stepped in that door and all hell broke loose. It was the god-damndest thing I ever seen or heard tell of. It looked like all the winders just lit up at once and somethin went like dinnymite goin off. It went *whoom. Whoom.* The goddamned doors blowed open and here come

Tyler sailin backwards through em and lit plumb out in the front yard. It got quietern hell. Just that dark house and the doors gaped open and her probably settin there with a scattergun in her lap.

Jesus H. Christ. What'd you do?

I can tell you more what I didn't do. I didn't hang around for the inquest. I didn't step down the road and call the law. You talkin about a man clockin the miles, I clocked em. I figured they might be some way they could work it around where I done it and I felt a dire need to be elsewhere.

He blew out smoke, smoothed his thin bird's wing of gray hair. I can't tell you how it made me feel seein it. I can't describe it. There I was layin in that brush hatin him and she just cut him in two with a shotgun. I felt like God Almighty. It was scary.

They came down the slope onto the highway, detoured through the yard of the concrete plant, gray concrete trucks set in rows like some arcane beasts at pasture. A dozer with its tracks frozen deep in the whorled and icy earth. Above them the great mixer still and silent as if it were some monolith abandoned by a prior race unable to survive in so winterlocked a world as this one. A great frozen mire of sand and gravel and loaders parked with buckets dropped, old piles of wornout or obsolete machinery Edgewater had no inkling the purpose of. Through a hedge of fragile weeds that broke with their passage and up the bank of a ditch toward the Southside Café past the county garage where gravel trucks idled white smoke and men stood with hands over a fire in a fifty-gallon drum as if they were charged with its protection.

Roosterfish had a plan. A plan of stark simplicity yet it was a day or two in coming. Hints must be dropped, reactions gauged. Walking down South Elm past the water tank he looked all around to see were there spies about and decided to reveal it all to Edgewater. All there was were the bleak empty streets of December, a vacant lot with the restless stirring of wintersered weeds.

I wouldn't give a chance like this to just anybody. It's big money. But I kindly took a likin to ye and I know for a fact you ain't loose at the mouth. I figured you ort to have a shot at it.

Roosterfish.

What?

I don't want a shot at it.

Why hellfire. You don't even know what it is.

And don't want to.

Why shitfire, Billy.

And you ought to be forgetting it right now.

You don't even know what I plan to do.

You're going to tell me, whether I want to know or not, I expect.

I owe it to ye, son. He looked carefully about again. I'm goin out there and clean out Harkness and that bunch at the cockfight. If I can't do it one way I'll do it another.

Good God. I knew it.

Sure you did, Billy. That's why I want you in on it. You're smart.

I'm damn sure smart enough not to get mixed up in some halfbaked scheme like this.

Hell, it can't fail. Just give me the benefit of the doubt, Billy, have I ever steered you wrong? Now listen. Robbin a cockfight, whoever heard of a thing like that around here? That'd be the last thing they'd expect. And cockfightin's against the law. What're they gonna do, run to the sheriff?

I can tell you what they're going to do. They'll blow your foolish ass away, Roosterfish. You better think this over.

I been thinkin it over. I got it all planned.

I don't want to hear it.

Roosterfish took a drink of wine, wiped his mouth with the back of his hand. I got me a gun, he said after a time. I'm just goin in to watch the fights, see? Just like anybody else. When everbody's inside watchin the fight you're out there stealin all the rotor buttons out of their distributors.

The which? Edgewater asked in disbelief.

Stealin the rotor buttons. That way they ain't goin nowhere. We'll have money and be haulin ass for warmer climates. I can't stand this goddamn cold weather. My blood's getting thin or somethin. This wind's cutting through me this year like a knife. I'm getting me some money and headin someplace got some sun about it.

Edgewater seemed in deep study. What I could do is jack up their cars and trucks and take all the wheels off them, he said at length. Roll them off in some holler somewhere. That way they'd still be stuck even if they found where we hid the rotor buttons.

Son, I don't believe you understand the magnitude of the money we're talkin about here. I told you they was some highrollers shows up at them cockfights. We could wind up with eight or ten thousand easy; that's Mexico, son, or Arizona. Layin in the sun and some gal smearin ye right good with tannin oil.

What we'd wind up with is the graveyard or the penitentiary one. Now I'm going to say this just one time as clearly as I can. I want no part of it. I've spent all the time I plan to in jailhouses. And if you've got any sense at all you'll give this up and never let it cross your mind again.

You might be right.

You know damn well I'm right.

I ortn't tried to bring you into this. It's between me and Harkness. No hard feelins. I guess I ortn't even mention this neither, but I will. I been keepin my ear pretty close to the ground where Harkness is concerned and I hear he's been campin on ye old lady's doorstep. Did I tell ye he was a lowlife son of a bitch, or did I?

You told me.

Billy, don't it make you mad?

I don't know. I guess not.

Why?

Why should it? You look at things and you don't see just one thing, you see a…a progression of things. One of them leading to the next. The inevitability of things.

You may see that, what you said. All I see is a lowlife son of a bitch and a way to take him down a notch or two.

Edgewater did not reply immediately. In the darkness he could hear the soft, almost furtive sound of Roosterfish drinking, the cap being screwed on.

How do you drink that treacly shit? Edgewater asked. You could pour it on pancakes.

It grows on ye. Are you tellin me if you had a chance to even up with Harkness you wouldn't take it?

I guess I am.

How come?

I just told you. The inevitability of things. There are things that are going to happen, things already set in motion. They'll happen no matter what I do. And to do what you're talking about, you have to care about some particular thing a hell of a lot. You have to be obsessed. I guess I'm not. Look at it this way. If somebody else had took your old lady you wouldn't even be thinking about Harkness.

Roosterfish took a slow drink, thinking. No. It has to be Harkness.

All right. The way you told it he never held a gun on her, never kidnapped or raped her. Why aren't you hunting her? She's the one that said all that love, honor, and obey stuff, not Harkness.

No. You've got it all balled up. It's between me and Harkness. It's just somethin you don't do, and he done it. I don't care if it was in her all the time, ticking like a time bomb. Harkness set it off.

You may be right, Roosterfish. It's none of my business. No hard feelings. I just thought I'd tell you my position.

Well. It don't sound like you've got one. But you won't be sayin nothin about what I told you?

Hell no. But I still wish you'd forget it.

A voice he'd come to think of as mad or near mad bespeaking him out of darkness from the pallet where he'd thought Roosterfish slept. A wineblurred reenactment of old wrongs and injustices he'd thought he was done with. A new note creeping slyly in tonight.

You ever get any off that old woman? Roosterfish's voice from the floor, from the dark by the radiator. He'd been silent so long Edgewater had thought him asleep.

What old woman?

Mrs. Bradshaw. Ye mama in law.

God no. Why would you say anything like that?

She used to cut a pretty wide swath in her younger days. I guess she's changed some now though. It's been near eighteen year since I had anything to do with her.

Edgewater had arisen on his bed but he could not see Roosterfish. He leaned back on his elbows. Dim light from the streetlamps fell on the north wall but black shadows from the windowsill bisected it and Roosterfish's voice came out of the darkness.

I don't believe any of that bullshit, Edgewater said. That old woman's washed in the blood.

You ever see anybody washed cleaner than the ones needed it the most? They ain't nobody harder on whiskey than a reformed drunk.

That woman used to really like it. But she was a Jesus shouter even back then at the same time. Used to nearly drive her crazy, she couldn't decide whether she was saved for the streets of gold or doomed to the fire pits. Lord, them was some times. Used to be them traveling tent revivals come through and they'd hold em out in the woods wherever some farmer'd give em leave to camp. Brush arbors. That preacher'd get wound tightern a mainspring about ten o'clock hollerin and speakin in tongues and all you'd have to do is just take her arm and kindly guide her to the bushes but she was of two minds about it. She'd act like she didn't want it. Screw ye and grit her teeth all at the same time. Her folks plumb give up on her. Time she married Bradshaw both them kids was a walkin. Little woods colts.

Roosterfish?

Yeah?

Roosterfish, I don't need a history lesson. All that stuff is dead and gone to me.

Well. That may be. I'se more thinkin aloud than talkin. But it's somethin to me. You told me you saw the inevitability of things but I doubt you do. It's all preordained to you. I doubt you see how a man'll set his path to deliberately ruin another man. Take coverin up the trail a man left through sand. Kick through all the tracks and rake sand in em and scatter a few leaves around over em, it's just like nobody walked through there at all. Ever place a man's been or everything he touched stomped down like he never was.

Roosterfish, Edgewater said after a time. Is there not any way I can make you forget all this crazy old shit?

A man's accountable, Roosterfish said, and then he was silent. After a while Edgewater thought him asleep but then he heard the unscrewing of the cap from the wine bottle, the soft sound of drinking. The cap going back on.

That winter Bradshaw was much on the road, the old Chevrolet a familiar sight at Goblin's Knob, Sycamore Center, Crying Woman Hollow. All the habitats of bootleggers and whores and gamblers, those who followed these crafts for a profession and those trying to lose their amateur standing. Anyone who would indulge him, include him, not make him the fool when like accrued to like. Was one fool more or less than the other?

Sudy was back home and the old woman accepted her return with a grim silence, a silence that Bradshaw felt he could not endure. The house seemed to turn hateful, cursed with a stillness that seemed to impart old regrets and dissatisfactions and forlornly keep them eternally fresh, surreal emotions that transcended human tenacity, would leave the very atmosphere charged and telluric long after they were gone. Silence was the mortar the brick was laid with, silence chinked the cracks to thwart the winter wind.

His face in a watermarked mirror, cutting the part in his hair keen as a knife edge with his comb. A smell of aftershave, faint effluvia of beer. The door filled, blocked the light. Even to his eyes a harridan draped in black, already tendrils crept from the grave to ensnare and draw her down.

Where you goin?

I got a date, he said.

Where at?

The part suited him. He turned his head slightly, the light fell in a soft sheen across the Brilliantined waves on his head. Where the lights is bright and the music is loud, he told her. He was looking for passage out and she was standing in the door.

When you comin in? What time'll you be back?

When you see me comin. He stepped past her and she turned in silence to watch him go. The door to Sudy's bedroom was closed.

Palpable reprieve when he stepped onto the porch and pulled the door to behind him. He was in another world, a world with sharper colors, brighter sounds. Beyond the door silence whispered to silence, a relieved conspiracy of ennui and atrophy said, At last, he's gone, he's gone. The house seemed to settle itself, to sigh.

And gone.

Gone in a brief burst of smoking rubber to McAnally's, drinking halfwarm homebrew and listening to old men's tales of winters past. The creak of chairs the soft slap of wellworn cards. McAnally's sloe-eyed daughter standing hipslung in the door framed by a coal oil lamp and eyeing him with a kind of tremulous arrogance, the planes and angles of her face all light and shadow from the lamp. Her eyes alone clearly visible, dark holes drawing off all the light. Hungry, wise. Her legs and hips outlined through the thin cotton shift, black like some pornographic negative held to the light. The bitter hot taste of the homebrew going down. The road again, the sound of slewing gravel, the weight of a thigh against his, a breast beneath his hand. What was real and what was fantasy that winter swirled and ran like watered ink. He adapted for himself a kind of homemade reality.

A girl from Beaver Dam so utterly unwashed that he could not believe it. No stickler for hygiene, even Bradshaw must have the windows down. The wind off ice, a rattling of frozen trees.

What's the matter? You raised in a barn?

The strong odor of fish, raw, tainted. I just need me a little fresh air.

Apparently she could not smell it or perhaps she enjoyed it. You freezin me to death.

Looking down past her mounded breasts and belly, the kinked pubic hair, he watched his penis disappearing into her, imagined it set upon and devoured by vast hordes of microscopic piranha that swam in the seas of her body. When he was finished he got out of the car surreptitiously and washed himself off with whiskey, the pain a kind of catharsis. He felt himself cauterized, did a little soundless dance, limp penis shrinking and strumming in the December wind.

In a burst of entrepreneurism he saw himself rising Horatio Algerishly in the world of bootlegging. Finding Boogerman drunk and sleeping it off, he stole twelve gallon jugs of whiskey from him and sold them to Cates Burcham. Under cover of darkness he stole them back from Cates and sold them to Big Mama. He figured all he needed to become a millionaire was perpetual night and several hundred more bootleggers, an infinite number.

You would see him on the streetcorners, a White Owl Tiparillo firmly clamped in his lean jaw, yellow feral eyes, slits that narrowed to appraise the eternally passing possibilities. Holding forth in the poolroom, younger boys drawn to him by his stories of things he had not done in places he had never been, improbable women who had said to him unlikely things. He with his tales like some old lecher with suspect candy.

Yet driving through winter dusks it came to him that some great exodus was leaving the land, he drove past old deserted houses with blind windows and canted hardware, robbed doors and past untended fields grown with dog fennel and beggarlice and scrub brush. The world was in suspension, gone south for the winter. With winter, malaise lay on him like a stone. He longed for warmer climes, better times. Even the weather seemed to conspire against him. The sky was slate gray. It began to rain a steady ceaseless drizzle and the temperature fell, beaded drops of water hung hesitant on winter trees and froze on looping telephone wires, there was a cold in him whiskey would not warm, no fire would dissipate.

He went to look up Edgewater. He climbed the stairs and knocked at the door. Hey, Billy, he called, but there was only silence. No light beneath the door. Perhaps Edgewater had already gone. He tried the knob but the door was locked.

Back outside he drove aimlessly through near empty streets. In the rain garish plastic Christmas candles and roped tinsel looped pole to pole looked tawdry, sodden, the wind funneled scraps of paper up the alleys like dirty snow. Spurious Santas from shop windows brought back knifelike and bitter the snows of his childhood.

Arnold was at the Southside Café drinking coffee when Bradshaw found him. He wore an enormous greatcoat that near swallowed him and whatever myriad moths it housed. He looked peaked and depressed, wizened and morose victim of whatever plague had befallen Bradshaw.

I been ridin around this son of a bitch, Bradshaw said. All it needs is somebody to kick the dirt in. If there's a sign of life around here I missed it. He fumbled a nickel from his pocket. Gimme a coffee, Sue. Arnold, you seen Billy?

Not in several days. I seen him with Roosterfish. They looked like they was cookin somethin up. Then last Wednesday I went up there to see did he want to go drink a beer but he didn't. He was readin a book.

What?

I ast him did he want to go drink a beer and he said naw. He was eating chocolate candy out of a box and he was reading some big old thick book.

I'll be damned.

He's a funny feller.

Yeah he is. He's all right though.

You not still mad about Sudy?

I can't live nobody's life but mine.

He cupped the coffee mug in his palms, felt the rising steam warm on his face. He looked about him, saw nothing that promised to relieve the boredom the night threatened.

Let's ride around awhile. He arose, left the coffee unfinished.

All right. Arnold drained his cup.

Keep it between the ditches, Sue said.

Live hard, die young, and leave a beautiful memory, Bradshaw said.

Who for? she wanted to know.

They circled the Daridip. It was deserted save a forlorn waitress who watched them without interest through waterbeaded glass.

Ride out to Cates's and get a halfpint.

I'll pay if you'll go in and get it. I'll go on down the road and let you out and you go in like you've come on foot.

Why?

He's pissed at me, Bradshaw said.

How come?

I don't know. He just don't like me.

They say somebody stole a bunch of whiskey off of him.

I wouldn't doubt it. People ain't got no morals anymore, Bradshaw said. He pulled out into the street, turned at the corner. He started to accelerate, then he slowed and pulled to the side of the road. Florida, by God, he said.

What's the matter? Arnold asked.

Let's go to Florida.

What?

Hell yes. I've got the money to get us there. They's work down there. Hell, we'll lay up and take the sun and anytime we get hungry we'll just reach up and pick an orange.

Goddamn. You reckon we could sure enough?

You fuckin A we can go.

What'd we do in a big place like that?

Hell, give a pair of highrollers like us a week and we'll own the place.

I'd sure like to go. Damn, just head out.

Bradshaw released the clutch, pulled back out onto the pavement. We're as good as gone. I'll run you by your place and you put your shit in a pasteboard box and get ready. I got to see somebody a minute.

Don't change your mind. How long's it take to get to Florida?

I don't know. But we'll find out. I'll pick you up in a little while.

———

He fortified himself with a pint of peach brandy at Big Mama's and was underway again. With the decision to leave, a heady euphoria had lifted his depression. He did not even mind the rain he drove through. He felt that all that was wrong or complicated or too much trouble to worry about was being lifted from him, placed on more responsible shoulders than his own. He was being given another chance, the slate was being wiped clean, he could begin somewhere anew. Who knew what Florida held for one as ambitious as himself.

A vague and foetal plan had crept into his mind, formed itself without his conscious effort, as if it were some misbegotten and deformed offering of his subconscious. He slowed, stopped where a farm road turned off the blacktop where charred cinderblocks and rusted shapeless metal marked an old houseplace, parked under bare branches of an ancient shade tree.

The rain was soft on the rooftop, mesmeric. He drank from the brandy, fancied he felt the progress of its slow warmth through miles of veins, capillaries, until it seeped through his entire body. He could feel a warm and comfortable layer of it beneath his skin. He thought of walking into the Knob, not as some experience he dreaded but a curious kind of anticipation, and he forced himself to sit for some time, drawing out the implications, its possibilities. When at length he had finished the brandy he got out and threw away the bottle. There was an old ungathered cornfield he knew about below the house site near shapeless in the dark and there, like some supermarket shopper gauging size and quality, he moved from stalk to stalk feeling among the ears of corn that had survived foraging crows and tenant farmers with tow sacks.

He was searching for just one particular ear that he felt he would recognize when he found it. He searched almost the entire field before he pulled one and raised it, judged its size against the pale and dripping heavens. It looked to be sixteen or so inches long and as thick around as his forearm. It suited him. He walked back to the car swinging it along in his hand and with the light of his cigarette lighter began to fumble through the contents of the glove compartment until he came upon a half roll of black electrician's tape.

Trousers pooled about his ankles he stood taping the ear of corn to his upper thigh, spindly legs glowing ghostly in the murky dark. A spectacle worth comment should the headlights of a passing car seek him out where he stood like some erotic revenant engaged in a tableau of the obscure and sadistic. Already tight, the trousers barely fit when he pulled them up and adjusted them to his satisfaction. He stood unsteady for a moment feeling with his hands this addition to his wardrobe. He wished for a mirror. At last he walked stifflegged to the car and got in.

What few drinkers were out this rainy night gave Bradshaw scant attention when he seated himself at a corner table and awaited service. He lit a cigar, appraised the room with his reptilian eyes, catching her eye and nodding when she raised a mug.

She set the beer down and scooped up his change and turned to leave but he would not have it so. Tonight there was something subtly different about him. An air of confidence tonight, the easy calm assurance of a man who has dwelt on the riddles of the cosmos and found them not so insoluble. I'm leavin for Florida tonight, he told her, leaning back a little in the chair. I just thought I'd drop by and say goodbye.

Goodbye, she said, but she did not move. She waited to see if there was more.

There was. I just wanted to see you again, he told her. I may not be in this place again and I just wanted to see your face, to kind of place it in my mind like a picture.

She did not reply. He waited for a moment as if to give her opportunity for speech and when she did not take it he said, You got a date tonight?

I don't know yet. I got to get back to the bar.

She was barely back behind it when Bradshaw drained off the beer and began making urgent beckoning signals at her. She did not turn toward him for some time. When she finally did he raised the empty mug aloft and made beckoning gestures with it.

When she brought the fresh mug he had his chair cocked against the wall and his coat off and draped across his lap and he was inclined toward further conversation. Sit down awhile, he told her.

I can't sit down. I got to tend bar. Swalls don't pay me for shootin the breeze with the customers.

I never seen nobody like you, he said as if he had not heard her. I can just look at you and it just runs all over me. I just wish you'd look at the way you got me tore up. He moved the coat, drew her eyes with his hand to his crotch.

Her eyes widened, a face with a stunned look of incredulity, near slack with surprise and disbelief. Then she looked quickly away, turned on her heel and went back to the bar. Perhaps he'd misjudged her, he thought. Perhaps he'd offended some delicate propriety not heretofore in evidence. But in a minute or two he looked up and she was watching him across the room with a curious calculating look on her face, as if she were mentally reevaluating him. He ignored her and sipped his beer, studied the patterns of his socks, stared through the hazy smoke at the other drinkers.

On her rounds about the room she would glance at him covertly and he began to make gestures at her. He would pull at his trousers, try to draw slack between the tight material and his great pinchbeck erection. Scoot around the chair in some grotesquely exaggerated vain search for comfort. She'd look away. People began to glance curiously at Bradshaw. After a time she brought a fresh mug over, although he had not called for it, and when she set it down she just stood there. After a moment he looked at her and suddenly he felt he was seeing her for the first time since they had been in the seventh grade: he was aware of changes he had not noticed, the face of a budding girl vanished and here were minute crowsfeet at the corners of her eyes, a sooty telltale dark at the roots of her platinum hair. But her body was still ripe and her breasts still thrust against the cloth of her blouse.

What time you getting off?

Eleven o'clock. I reckon you can take me home if you still want to.

He took her not home but down the intricate scenery of dogwoods on Firetower Ridge, as if he were unused to the comforts of home and bed and unable to function save in some extension so symbolic of the highway.

Halfdemented he was tearing at her clothes. An act perpetuated so endlessly in myth that it took on texture of the surreal. Each moment seemed frozen in icy clarity. A breast sprang free, his fingers were hooked in the elastic of her drawers. Surely pubic hair such as this must have been spun in the night by Rumpelstiltskin. Some curious aberrance of time. Here were a lifetime of memories being accumulated helter skelter in the space of moments.

Slow down buddy, she said. We got all night. A hand on his spurious cock, apparently detecting there nothing to deter her. Her breath
hot in his ear. He banged his head on the door, paid it no mind. He was
trying to haul down her panties, she lifted her hips to aid him, he felt
her hands at his zipper.

Her tongue tasted of ambrosia, he knew with a detached and rueful
sadness that this was a feeling that would never come again.

Onehanded he was trying to force his trousers down over his hips.
There was a slack acquiescence to her legs. What light there was fell
across her face and illuminated it twisted as if in pain, the eyes vacant
as holes charred and hungry. When the trousers were in her face, down
his fingers worked briskly at the windings of tape.

She was keening some high note through her nose, a mindless siren
song of want and she grabbed his hand and shoved it between her legs.
Her hips were lurching, her crotch wet and slippery. He had two fingers
inside her, three. She writhed under him, pulling him blindly toward
her, her lips were sucking at his neck.

You want it? he asked her.

Yes, she whispered, yes.

You sure you ready for all of it?

Give it to me.

He thrust himself into her, came almost as soon as he did, a series of
spasms rocked him, he felt caught in some vast tide that hit him wave
on wave and beached him. When he was through he lay drained atop
her while she pitched and bucked and clawed at him. Slowly he stopped
spinning, the world righted, clicked into focus. He noticed with annoyance her nails were hurting him. Finally motions began to slow as if she
were winding down, some great erotic doll with a mainspring broken
and then she was still save for an occasional spasmodic jerk of her hips,
as if they moved through no bidding of hers. Her face twisted away
from him. Did you come? he asked her solicitously.

No.

Funny, I thought you did.

You lyin son of a bitch, she said.

I fucked you.

Not by a damn sight you didn't, she said. She was rising, trying to
see him in the dark.

Is something wrong? he asked her. He picked up the ear of corn from the floorboard and laid it across her breasts. She looked as it dumbly. You through with it, he told her. You can keep it for a souvenir and use it any time you want to.

She was beating at his face with the ear of corn, half crying. You dirty bastard. You're crazy or something. He grabbed her hand, shook the corn free. Get off me and let me up.

Bradshaw raised himself off her and hauled up his pants. He still had on his boots. She was cursing him steadily, slipping her panties on. He watching with something akin to regret, the flash of pubic hair abruptly gone. She was buttoning her blouse.

Get out of the goddamned way and let me out.

Suit yourself. He opened the door, kicked it wide, it rocked on its hinges. A cold breath of the night came in, scent of rain and wind and of trees. She got out while Bradshaw was fumbling around for the ear of corn. Here, he said, tossing it to the ground beside her feet. Absentmindedly she stooped and picked it up, as if in a daze. Frozen by the domelight, she looked momentarily uncertain about the wisdom of getting out in the rain so far from home. Miles of dark yawned like an engulfing chasm. But she didn't speak.

I got oranges to pick, Bradshaw said. He slammed the door and cranked up and spun backward and the last time he saw her she was standing in the diminishing glare of lights, one writhing shadow among many, just watching him go and with the ear of corn dangling from her hand like some impotent and forgotten weapon.

There were few evenings now that the pickup was not parked in the Bradshaw yard, long about dusk you'd see him slam its door and saunter toward the house, cap in hand. The old woman said, Here he comes.

At first when he came it was ostensibly to talk to the old woman. Reminisces of times past. To see did they need anything, now that there was no man in the house. He would sit and smoke his pipe in the old armchair by the window, eyes half closed, and watch the girl. He was an impression of stolidity, who could believe those tales they whispered? Solid. Substantial, a man of means and a not inconsiderable amount of power, an employer of men, renter of houses, a grocery store in Flatwoods.

After a visit or two he made no secret of his purpose. Then the old woman would retire and leave them like some courting couple to their own devices. Harkness plied her with gifts, with attention, with all the wiles the years had sharpened, lacking looks or charm or even common decency, he fell back on other methods. There were few nights when she did not find him awaiting her when the Dewdrop closed and she stepped into the chilly night. She was ashamed he came, that people thought she would leave with him. There he was waiting again, wiping a clean space on the steamed up window, peering with speculation at her, at the absurd horns on the pickup truck, while he knew the only thing waiting for him was the cold rented room where the silence vibrated so that you strained for voice you could not quite hear.

You need to get out more, he'd tell her. See what the world's like. Perhaps at night she lay awake and thought. She, who had so few of the world's frivolities, could see from where she lay in bed the box of candy shaped like a heart, bottles of cheap scent a whore would have thought tacky. But no one had ever given her even so tawdry presents as these, her riches doubled effortlessly by the dresser mirror behind them. Knew them not as simply ends in themselves but harbingers of others, more opulent, wonders springing from an inexhaustible source. And most of all she felt the deadly weight of silence, the nearness of the two graves the past year had brought.

She would walk back toward town and he would follow along behind, cruising at four or five miles an hour past the sleeping houses and locked and nighted businesses without trying to get her to talk, just watching her as if he would shield her from whatever might befall her, some grotesque guardian angel in a tricked-up pickup truck.

Perhaps in some way he could not articulate, he saw her as his lost young girl, dreamed of her slavishly with soft flesh after years of women with sagging breasts and bellies, thighs that the flesh listed on like water, felt in her a rekindling of youthful fires, alloy he could heat and shape to his choosing.

Then one night he waited for the traffic light to change and she walked on a few steps and then ceased. There were promises of money to be considered, of soft gowns and see-through underwear and warmth on winter nights. Even now it would be too warm in his truck, yet here on the sidewalk the wind whistled hollowly off the asphalt, sang eerily in the highwires looped above her. When he reached across to open the door on the passenger side there was nothing at all on his face.

Harkness owned some land in a part of the county named Sandy Hook and he bought a secondhand housetrailer and set it up there for her. Sandy Hook had once been part of the vast holdings of a phosphate concern, empty soils gleamed coldly where trains used to run laboring through the desolated countryside. The land here looked as if some ancient cataclysm had befallen it, its moors and rocky barrens absolutely lifeless, even the trees singed and dead, standing branchless and black, as if they had been scorched. Old brick furnaces and half fallen walls winding nowhere rememberable lost to kudzu and ivy channeled the hollows, remnants of artifacts of some old ceremonial magic. You would drive for miles and you would not see a house, a hunter, a fence.

It was country that befitted him very well. Here he was answerable to no one, any trespassers were answerable to him. Perhaps he felt she would be safe here, safe from the younger men he knew must someday come along, for the ways of the world were his as well. An enforced solitude like a parody of fairytale fortresses, a fairhaired princess amidst her radio and truestory magazines awaiting him. Glad to see even so remotely human a face as his, to hear any human voices.

Roosterfish was driving an old titleless Hudson about the color of dried blood and it wore tags borrowed from a Hardin County junkyard. But if he was a fugitive he did not act like it. He came and went as he pleased in Edgewater's room, as if he had some appointed rounds to keep. He'd drive the Hudson around town and if he met the law he would just nod at them and keep on going. He seemed to have crossed over into some land of unconcern. Edgewater decided he must be mad.

Everyone knew Roosterfish. He'd hold court in the poolroom, a great favorite with the daytime idler. His illgotten gains flowed from him in a seemingly endless supply, buying beer for the crowd, maybe drinking one himself and telling his tales and listening to theirs. These old men and young with nothing to do but sit about the pool hall resting from no exertion in particular and possessed of little past and no future and endless talking, settling among themselves the vagaries of human nature.

Ofttimes the talk would turn to D.L. Harkness, all the old myths and new ones more recent than his memory: him and Clyde Warren was down at McKnight's one time drinkin and they got to arguing about this old dog Early had. Just a stray cur somebody dropped on Early and stayed cause he fed it. Bout eat up with the mange. Anyway, they got to arguing about that dog. Whether if you skint a dog it would die or whether it would live. They kept on an on and getting louder all the time and directly Harkness bet him twenty dollars. He's mad. He got out his knife and helt that dog and skint it. And it alive. They said it was so sickenin Warren got to tryin to renege and Harkness wouldn't let him. Well sir, he completely skint that pore old dog and it died like Warren said it would. Harkness just wiped his knife on his britches and pulled out his pocketbook and paid off. People's to blame for it. People's just let him get away with all such as that till he don't even pay no mind to it anymore. They've let it get to where he thinks whatever he does is right.

They shot pool but Edgewater soon gave up trying to beat him. Roosterfish walked the balls with a graceful careless ease, breaking the rack and running them in rotation, breaking again.

You ever do that for a living?

Not in a good long while. I learnt there ain't no man good enough but what he don't come up agin one better. Best pool shot I ever seen come in this very poolroom one time wearin raveled out overalls and brogans you could nearly smell the pigshit on and he had this round, innocent face like he hadn't been off the farm but about fifteen minutes. I shot a pretty fair stick back then but I wasn't as good as I thought I was. Anyhow, he stood around watchin me with his eyes bout like goose eggs and he kept tryin to get me to play him. I ain't got time to play ye, I'd tell him. He kept on. Finally I give him a good lookin over and I'se drinkin a little so I told him I'd play him one game for fifty dollars. I fig-ured he'd took off a load of hogs or somethin and his money was burnin a hole in his pocket. Well sir, he went back out to his old rattletrap car and brung in a custombuilt cue stick I bet cost three hundred dollars. Come in a plush-lined case look like a snake casket. When I seen it I felt like somethin kicked me in the ass right hard and I never got a shot. He just blowed me away. Turns out he was going all through the South takin on all these fellers that thought they was hot like I did.

———

On Sunday morning, when Edgewater awoke, Roosterfish had rolled his blankets and gone. As if he were some hard traveler with vast distances to cover and who must be on the road before good light. The only sign he had been there at all was an empty Gypsy Rose bottle tilted against the wall. Edgewater went with his morning coffee to the window and peered across the street for the old Hudson but it was gone too.

The last time Roosterfish'd been here, there had been only a stomped circle of earth with the brush bush hogged off, but now there was a square windowless building framed up of unplaned yellow poplar set in a glade where the stumps of the trees it was built from still gleamed white and truncate and the tops and brush were in piles yet unburned. The building had a concrete floor and a new tin roof glittering in the winter sun. A bluelooking stovepipe pierced its roof and thick smoke rose and dissipated before the stiff wind and above the pipe hovered a transparent flux of quaking hot gasses.

By ten o'clock a motley of trucks and cars and even a wagon or two littered the newground, like some congregation of worshippers gathering for arcane service. The glen rang with the crowing of cocks. They seemed to be everywhere, strawlined coops in the backs of pickup trucks, the trunks of cars, overalled men moved to and fro under the shadeless trees with cages under their arms. Here and there buying and selling and swapping, but the main business was inside where the cocks were. Here and there a halfpint glittered in the sun.

Slouched against the south wall of the shed for what fugitive warmth there was, Roosterfish looked them over. A crop of hardankles for sure. Some pretty roughlooking good old boys here today. He kept looking for Harkness. He could feel the weight of the handgun in his jumper pocket but he did not figure to need it. He had his unbreeched shotgun slung casually across his arm and no one had even paid it any mind. He had parked the car and simply walked up as if he had been doing a little rabbit hunting. He idly scanned the gunracks in the windows of pickup trucks. A deer gun or two he might have to do something about a little later.

In this fragile light there was about the fighting cocks a sinister beauty. Something ancient and unchanged, predatory qualities held over from more primitive times. Their bottleglass eyes cold and remote and at an absolute remove from fear. Calm, certain. A worn sun from the winter solstice laying across their feathers a sheen of iridescence, brilliant fiery orange, scarlet, sleek bluegreen. Long tailfeathers rippling with the wind. The purest glossy jetblack, cool creamy yellow about the breast, as if they had been shuttled through a color spectrum swirled and molten. He watched them with a long practiced eye, felt some old kinship stir within him. A similarity of qualities here perhaps. The old traits of arrogance and independence, obsolete save in these cocks bred solely for the purpose of maintaining these very bloodlines.

Inside the building there was a hot fire in the heater and he stood warming his backside and idly watching the progression of fights in the cock pits at the other end of the room. There were three pits. A fight would commence in the first one, move to the second when both combatants were so weary or near death as to cast the outcome of the fight into question, then a match with other owners and fresh opponents would commence in the first. A flurry of betting, side betting. Fifty dollars here, a hundred there. He watched with no great interest. He figured it mattered little who won or lost, in the end the money would reside within his own coat pocket.

A boy of fifteen or sixteen with a near dead rooster on his hands. The boy was loathe to admit defeat, a dispute was rising. He kept urging it back to the fight, but it no longer suspected where the fight was, its eyes were pecked out, it seemed preoccupied with some more important war being waged inside its brain: some miniature power failure there, cataclysm on a minuscule scale, whole sections going into blackness, an icy wind down empty corridors. Its head lolled loosely on its neck. The boy pried its beak open, forced breath into its lungs, he squeezed water from a rag onto its head.

The pitman was a short stocky man with gartered sleeves and a hand-rolled cigarette appendant to his bottom lip. That rooster's dead, son, he said.

The boy knelt with the rooster and began removing the cockheels from its legs. Die, goddamn you, he told it. He arose with it and carried the cock out the door to where rose a mound of dead or dying cocks. He pitched it outside.

The fights went on, the roosters weighed atop delicate scales and so matched accordingly. Money endlessly changed hands, Roosterfish watching with his acerbic jaundiced eye. The day drew on, bottles were tipped back. He waited impatiently for Harkness. There was a harsh burning in his stomach, his throat felt tight. He wanted it over. The pile of dead roosters grew higher. A fight erupted near the cock pits and boiled by him with meaty sound of flesh falling on flesh and a cane-bottom chair splintering and flattening beneath their thudding feet. The air seemed to fill with flying chickens and feathers, the disquieted cock's quarreling. Watch the goddamned heater, the pitman yelled. First man turns it over answers to me. Roosterfish flattened himself against the wall while the pitman took up an axe handle and brandished it threateningly, the fight progressed across the floor and the wall of men that contained it flowed through the wide door and out into the yard.

Roosterfish stayed by the stove, hand above it, palm lowered over the rising heat. The pitman winked at him. Outside he could hear the cursing, the grunts of blows dealt and received. The pitman at last shrugged and went out with his axehandle and Roosterfish could hear him berating the men in the yard. After a time a truck coughed and started and then another and the pitman came back in, heading a straggling crowd, and the fights commenced again.

A man he vaguely knew but whose name he could not remember offered him a drink. He accepted the bottle, shivered involuntarily and handed the bottle back. Where's old D.L.?

The man laughed. D.L.'s pussywhipped, he told him. He drank from the bottle, a spiderweb of spittle he wiped away with his jumpersleeve. He's found him some young stuff I guess got him purty well housebroke for a while. Got it set up in that trailer he's got by Buttermilk Ridge and I spect he's sleepin in today.

By one o'clock he had decided Harkness was not coming and was forced to reform his plans. He went outside again and sat in the car and ate a lunch of sliced cheese and crackers he'd brought wrapped in waxed paper. He washed it down with wine from a bottle he brought out from beneath the seat and slid into his jumper pocket. Twin paper-crimped cylinders of double-ought buckshot were fed into the open chambers of the shotgun. Their brass primers staring back at him like two expectant eyes. He got out, made ready his plan, checked to see was anything blocking him in. There was not.

There was a blue GMC truck with a racked deer gun near the woods and upon ascertaining no one was looking he crept inside. He had the door open and he had cocked the barrel under his stump methodically levering out the shells. Dry little metallic clicks.

He was making plans about Arizona. He was thinking about the white orb of the sun, the way the sand glittered, the way a shimmering haze of heat hung over the lights. He was thinking about sitting by a motel pool with a moneybelt comfortably buckled around his middle and a tall glass of something varicolored and potent in his hand and a lissome girl by his side in a lawn chair and anticipatory to his every need.

Hey. What the goddamn hell you doin?

He turned with heat in throat and eyes wild toward a young man who had been urinating against the side of the shed.

Zip up ye britches and let's go around front a minute. He raised his shotgun.

What the hell's goin on here?

I'm robbin this son of a bitch, Roosterfish said easily. Suddenly he wasn't afraid anymore. Walk ahead of me a step or two and go in and let these other fellers in on it.

He had the stock of the shotgun cocked easily back under his arm when he threw down on them. The pitman turned from the scales with a rooster in his hands and just stood holding it for a moment, then set it gently down. He was eyeing his axe handle.

Roosterfish figured it was a good a time as any. He maneuvered behind the pitman, lifted the shotgun and fired a blast through the ceiling. The only sound after that was the soft wisk of movement from a couple of roosters in one of the rings.

All right boys if any of ye want to get out of here alive better do what I tell ye. He handed a brown paper bag to the redhaired boy next to him.

I am kindly in a hurry and I ain't sayin this but one time. I want all of ye to get ye pocketbooks and take the bills out. I want that redheaded boy there passin in front of yins with that poke there and sack it up. I don't want drivin licenses nor huntin licenses or pictures of ye old lady. All I want is the money.

The boy picked up the paper bag. He stood holding it and staring at it as if he expected to find there a set of directions advising him how to proceed.

Go ahead, son, Roosterfish said. They ain't nothin to it. You've picked cotton, ain't ye? Just like that. Pullin it off the stalks and putting it in the sack. Two or three of the men had already unpocketed their wallets. The rest stood staring at him stolidly.

I'll tell you another thing. I got my back against the wall. I'm between a rock and a hard place and I don't give a damn which way things work out. So if you got a notion about callin my bluff, you just save it. Cause I ain't bluffin. He moved with his back against the wall until he came to the door.

The boy was sacking up money, thin sheaves of precious green grudgingly given up and only then to the sweet persuasion of Roosterfish's doublebore shotgun. Tithe up, boys, he said easily. I don't want no IOUs nor holdouts. I got a long way to go.

Outside he heard the throb of a car engine, the bump of wheels taking the dropoff from the main road: the motor ceased, he heard the cries of people and of roosters. Gimme that poke, son.

The boy handed it to him. His face was very white and his freckles stood out like spatters of thick brown paint. Don't come out of here till you hear me leave. And the first car on my ass gets its windshield blowed out. On the driver's side. Roosterfish started easing toward his Hudson.

He eased backwards out through the lot rapidly stuffing the money into his shirt as he skirted the shed and came to his car and thence upon a nightmare scene not conceived by or allowed for in any variation of his plans: an ancient Chevy stakebed truck with bundled cornstalks for homemade siderails set blocking his way out. Both doors were flung wide and three crates of chickens had spilled onto the roadbed and broken and the pinewoods seemed to be full of escaping chickens, crowing, cackling, fluttering, unable to get aloft with their cropped wings. An enormous woman done up in black muslin and two or three gangling boys were trying to catch them. She whirled an angry face upon Roosterfish.

Hey. Help me get my roosters caught.

Goddamn a bunch of roosters, he said. He looked wildly about him, peering back as if expecting around the corner of the shed the cautious arrival of faces more brave or foolhardy than the rest. Lady you better get that rollin scrapiron out of my way.

You'll just have to go around, mister. My chickens is all got aloose.

They ain't no around. The goddamned fence runs right up to ye truck there. Now how about backin up and lettin me out?

She gave him a fierce preoccupied look. You can just wait.

He waved the shotgun. Lady, I just robbed the goddamned outfit and I ain't got time for smalltalk. Now will you get that thing out of my way before I blow it out?

They Lord God, she said. She threw her arms heavenward in an attitude of mute supplication toward some higher power and her eyes grew round and huge. They rolled back and closed and she seemed to melt, the very earth to absorb her, she slid black and enormous and slack to the frozen roadbed.

He looked halfdemented, he couldn't think, a panic seized him. He leapt into the woman's truck and began grinding the motor, patting the accelerator, peering wildly toward the shed where he detected a lurking movement of overalled men into the yard. A pair of level blue eyes met his across the truck door. A thatch of straw-colored hair.

Hit won't start. Hit's hot, hit's got a bad coil wire.

Goddamn it to hell. Roosterfish leapt out and kicked the door too hard and started to run and spun back the way he'd been and steadied the gun across the cab and paused and aimed low. He fired one barrel and sent toward the contingent of fading men a veritable wall of earth and shredded leaves and sticks. He whirled and ran. She was arising from the earth, turned upon him eyes wide and horrible as he leapt past her. He was going at dead run. He ran into the pinewoods at an angle bisecting the corner and he came out in a cornfield where the going was smoother and he leveled out, breathing deeply and listening to the slap of the handgun and the increasing frequency of warping cornsticks breaking and what of the sky he could see tilted and bobbed crazily as if the horizon was in turmoil.

He fetched up short breathing raggedly at the field's edge and looking back through the field to the woods where a dark stain of cypress bled into the pine. He saw them running along the roadbed. He heard a distant shout and a man separated himself from the throng of men and brought a rifle to his shoulder. There was a puff of blue smoke and almost immediately the chunk of a bullet going to earth and then the flat slap of the report the wind rolled to him. He steadied the gun against the tree and fired low again and saw the air fill with shredded cornstalks skitting away and above the twin barrels, the men fading back into the cover of the pines.

He felt better in the woods. He followed an old log road back through country he'd squirrel hunted as a boy and the lay of the land came back to him, it was unchanged. He figured they'd follow the road. He slid down an embankment to where the country flattened itself out then fell away in a hollow. He did not slow up. He pushed himself, wanted as much distance as possible between himself and the cockfighters.

It was the second day before he came upon even so much as a trail or road, any sign at all that others had preceded him in these deep woods. The first day he walked steadily, angling what he judged to be southeast. He paused to rest, his back against the bole of a tree, the shotgun cradled across his knees. He stopped only long enough to catch his breath and then he was off again, up a slope so steep he must progress from ledge to ledge from the trunk of one sapling to the next. The leaves were wet and slick and as the day wore on they began to freeze, creaking dryly, accompanied him under his feet as he climbed.

He topped out at last on the crest of the hill and stood trying to get some idea of where he was. He knew vaguely the way he had come but he was unsure of how far and even of which county he was in. All below him were misted hollows and umbered hills going blue and distant, dusk rendering the air smoky and opaque. He breathed deeply, the cold hurt his lungs. Even as he stood it grew colder. He turned the four points of the compass. Bound by a gunmetal sky, he was in a bleak and austere winterscape, an incomplete world, the only life not yet colored, unpigmented save for delicate brushstrokes, shades of black and muted grays. He stood listening, though for what he was unsure: bloodhounds, shots, the distant shouts of the cockfighters. He expected to hear nothing at all, and all was silent save the gentle rattle of sleet in the leaves above him. He shouldered the gun and went on.

Full dark fell on him caught up in a hollow's undergrowth. Tired of climbing, he had tried to follow it to its mouth, found himself chest deep in a thick growth of brambles, honeysuckle that choked his movement. He held the gun aloft and trudged on like a man fording deep water. When at length the bracken showed no sign of diminishing he angled again up the slope until he could see the sky. Beyond the inkblack pattern of trees the sky had lightened as though some obscure light flared beyond it and it had begun to snow. He could feel the flakes sitting almost weightlessly on his upraised face, beginning to melt in his growth of beard.

The wind was worse on top of the ridge. It was out of the north and stiff, and caught in a brief whirlwind of snow he stood disoriented, uncertain as to which way to go. He could find no break in the timber, no sign of a road or a light or a house. Nothing of shelter in all this dark. Only a series of inky horizons falling away from this lofty height that were only shapes, no more than accumulations of night.

Sometime in the blackness he came upon an old stone wall winding its way along the backbone of the ridge. It was chest high and a foot or so thick, chunks in places fallen away from the effects of time and weather. He climbed it awkwardly, leaned the gun against the stone and slid down into a deep winddrift of leaves.

He was weary, his legs ached from walking. Hunger gnawed at him but he paid it no mind. The wind was not bad here. He burrowed into the deep leaves, half sat with the stone wall behind his shoulders. He sat with the gun clasped in his hands and thought about nothing at all. After a while his eyes closed and he went to sleep to the sound of the wind whipping the snow off the coping of the stone wall.

Perhaps at one time the wall had formed some sort of boundary, the domain of a landed gentleman from a wealthier time. Day showed him a skiff of snow on the ground, other signs of human habitation. He tarried idly, exploring. There were great stone chimneys high rising against the gray of the heavens but they framed a house that was not there anymore. Perhaps a fire so long ago that even the blackened earth had been leached clean by the seasons. Poking about he found shards of blue broken glass and a few old label-less bottles with rings of rust about their necks where lids had been. They might be money buried here, he told himself. He looked, slipping about but there was no one to see, listened but there was no sound save the wind sighing in the pines.

Stepping through an old hedge he fetched up short and swore. He flailed at the air, caught himself in the tangled hedge. Below him the earth fell away in a well eight feet or so in diameter, its round walls smoothly bricked and sloping away to where water gathered at the bottom black as ink. Old cautionary timbers laid across it and weathered stumps lay about the opening. Goddamn, he said. Who knew what bones slept dreamlessly here. He retrieved the gun from the tangled hedge and retreated. Blowing across the well the wind moaned hollowly, played on the harp of the earth, an eerie wailing that followed him down the skeleton of a road and faded finally out when timber thickened and hills came between them.

By near noon he was following a cherted road that did not seem to go anywhere. It was just a road. It wound around curves but when he negotiated them there was only more of the same, red clay banks rising into scrub pine and blackjack. But later he began to hear the sounds of labor, hammering, the whine of a chainsaw. At last he came upon a crew of men by and by rebuilding a bridge. Five or six of them who ceased working their labor to stare at his approach. There was a flatbed truck with a canvas doghouse on the back parked on the shoulder of the road and he saw then lunch boxes aligned alongside the water cooler. The men nodded to him but did not speak. Hidy, he said. He passed them, down the embankment and through the shallow creek. He could feel their eyes on his back. After a time he could hear the hammering commence again.

A quarter mile or so from the bridge he came upon an old gray farmhouse. Curtains at the windows. Gourds strung on seagrass twine from the porch joists that the wind keened through. Woodsmoke hovering above the ground, sharp and nostalgic in the damp air. A bugeyed Bichon Frise came down a cobbled walk and barked at him fiercely.

Roosterfish looked about him. Across the road a branch wound and the ground sloped away and he stooped and laid the gun out of sight on a ledge in the flintrock. He crossed into the yard, ceased when the dog snapped at his trousercuffs. Git, he told it. It barked ferociously. Hush goddamn you. I'll cut your thoat with a pocketknife. He kicked at it ineffectually. Or maybe eat you, he added.

The front door opened and an old woman came out drying her hands on her apron. Hush, she screamed at the Frise. The dog lay on its belly and with its tongue lolling, watched Roosterfish, malevolent with its black protuberant eyes. Roosterfish stepped around it and went on up the walk. How do, ma'am, he said. He already had his hat off.

How do, she said. She was a tiny little woman with bright berry eyes, short frizzed gray hair. She adjusted wirerim glasses and waited for him to speak.

Ma'am, is that your dog there?

Yes sir it is. It didn't bite ye did it?

Oh no. I hate to even bother you with it. Roosterfish was humble, polite, you might say courtly.

Well, what'd it been into?

My crew's fixin that bridge up the road and it eat my dinner. I had my lunch in a poke there on the bank and it got into it and eat it ever bite.

They Lord. Why didn't you take a switch to it?

It had done eat it.

Well. I don't know what you had but maybe I can scrape you up somethin fit for ye dinner. You want to warm a minute while I look in the kitchen.

Just anything atoll, Roosterfish said, crossing the sill. He stood reading homilies from the wall, reproachful. He warmed his hand at the potbellied stove, leaned over as if he could absorb heat and store it against cold to come. He looked about the room. The floor was littered with wood shavings, mounds of white long curls of ash or hickory and aligned against the walls were leaned axehandles in varying stages of completion and the worn velvet of a draw knife. On the mantle of a boarded up fireplace was a box of kitchen matches and he pocketed a handful.

She came through the kitchen door carrying a brown paper bag and handed it to him. Its weight was comforting. When I seen you I thought maybe you come to buy an axehandle, she said as if she lived in dread of some shortage of axehandles.

No ma'am. You make all them axehandles?

Me and my husband used to make em but he died.

Oh, you sell many of em?

Not anymore. I guess I make em mostly out of habit. It makes the time go by.

Roosterfish had the bag under his arm. I reckon I better get back to work. That bunch don't do nothin less somebody's watching em.

And say you don't want to buy no handle?

I reckon not.

He was already on the porch when she followed him out with an axehandle in her hands. Here. I won't charge ye for it. If you ever see anybody needs one tell em Bessie Littleton's got em.

He did not tell her he owned no axe. I thank ye, he said.

He went down the walk with the bag under his arm and the handle clasped in his hand. The bag felt warm against his ribs. He could smell fried ham, spicy smell of sausage, apple pie. When he heard the door close he leaned down the embankment and laid the axehandle atop the gun and picked them both up. He went on down the road. He looked back once and saw the curtains fall against the window and he wondered what she thought when he did not go back up the road. His arm tightened on the bag. After a few minutes the road curved and the house was as lost to his sight as if it had never been.

Two or three miles from Harkness's trailer there was a steep hill and cutback, so steep a vehicle must stop to make the curve, take low gear to begin the long climb up the rutted and rainwashed road. Off the left side of the road was a descending thicket of halfgrown cedars lost in vine-encrusted hazelnut bushes and then a dropoff of eight or nine feet to a narrow and longfallow field. This was where Roosterfish took up his vigil.

Roosterfish had become as desolate as the country he moved through, a haint. He suspected madness at his heels but had neither the strength nor desire to flee it. He let it engulf him, warm muddy water lapping about his thighs. At night strange noises whispered in his ears, the memories of old unforgotten wrongs crawled like succubi into his blanket wherever he made his bitter lonely bed. Sinister thoughts wormed into his half asleep mind like serpents, took on the configuration of animals unknown to him.

By day he watched hawks wheel against the mute and limitless heaven. At night owls and doves called to him half asleep in brushpiles and the hollows of uprooted trees. Nearly two weeks later Aday and his deputies tromped through the undergrowth, found where he had lain long hours in wait for Harkness. There was evidence here, though unneeded, of the hours stacked one on the other like tottering blocks, pitifully insignificant when weighed against what came after. A crumpled cigarette pack, an empty Gypsy Rose wine bottle, gnawed bones of rabbits or chickens, hollowed out places or worse where he must have slept his troubled sleep, tromped out places in the willows where he had squatted and shat. Who knew what thoughts dwelt in his mind, what games filled the hours through which he waited as if some power higher than he had charged him with a watch he must keep.

He waited almost a week for Harkness. On the sixth night while he hunkered watching, lights appeared on a distant curve and swept the tree branches like the tangible and immediate result of some prayer; the truck came on until he could hear it, Harkness rawhiding it as usual, impatient, slurring in the gravel, heading not as he thought for the life waiting in her bed but for its nether pole that Roosterfish took up when first he heard the truck.

At the moment the truck slowed almost to a standstill to negotiate the curve, Roosterfish arose like a grim and harried necromancer from the brush and raised the gun aloft and in almost the same motion fired both barrels into the windshield. The moment the glass blew out he was instantly assailed by a wall of sound, the explosion of the gun and glass splintering and rushing inward engulfing Harkness's ruined face like some perverse and twisted warping window peered through to find Harkness blind and already dead and still clutching the wheel, the sharp cacophony of country music rushing over him like remnants of a world he had abandoned, the sawing fiddles and twanging guitars and maudlin gospel songs from the truck's radio as if he fired not on Harkness but into some complete hillbilly band that supplanting Harkness bore the truck on toward where he still peered down the shotgun.

Perhaps he thought Harkness had already cut the wheels for the curve, perhaps he did not think at all, acted through instinct and nerve and memory of his deed committed countless times in fantasy, calloused by the endless commission of it in his thoughts. He stared unbelieving as the truck leapt the shoulder of the road and bore on toward him through brush that slapped against the rockerpanels and over headhigh saplings warping under the bumper and headlights. He cursed and threw the gun from him and leapt aside into the darkness just as the fender caught him knocking him off balance as if the headlights froze him where he stood. He pushed vainly at the slick metal with an arm he did not have, gibbered mindless at the night as the bullhorns hooked his coat, as if some beast of myth as remembrance already doomed had constrained to take him with it, impaled him, dragging him into its mad descent. He spun off balance, the very earth he stood on tilted, ran like liquid beneath his feet.

Some nights Edgewater would climb the stairs to the apartment over the poolroom and stand outside the door and sit for a minute on the top step and wait. The stairwell was ancient concrete, a green lichen grew there, faintly phosphorescent. It might have been carved from some underground stone, a passageway cut by troglodytes in some subterranean world. The stairway was concrete as well, blackened by generations of feet, carpeted by a film of ground-in grime and debris and cigarettes and the accumulated filth of years.

He would sit on the top step, patient, as if he waited for a homecoming, and stare down to where the lichened steps descended to streetlevel and to the sidewalk beyond where cool neon fell perpendicular to the darkframed oblong of light the opened door made. Wind blew a scrap of newspaper, old news of separation and reconciliation, hands-on violence. There would sometimes be the sound of sirens as the police ministered among the restless, telltale fragments of disquiet like faulted splotches of the night: siren wailing, an ambulance unmindful of redlights came past the Snowwhite Café and he could hear the rattle and slap when it hit the railroad tracks and saw in his mind it rock back on its shocks and spring flatout into the long sloping curve past the tie yard, drawn by violence, like a moth to flame, unifying folks' troubles, a carwreck, a shooting or cutting in Sycamore Center.

He woke to an unaccustomed silence. He'd fallen asleep to the muffled jukebox lamentations about the wild side of life from the jukejoint below and the disembodied voices coming through the ceiling and floor that were full of imprecation, rebuke or entreaty that had never separated themselves into words. His eyes moved in their sockets. It was dark in the room and for a time he couldn't remember where he was or how he'd come to be here, but sometime in the night he realized that he had loved not her but the child and past that maybe not even the child itself but the idea of it.

Then the pale ceiling materialized out of the void and the blind eye of the ceiling light bulb formed itself as if the room needed his perception of it in order to take its place in the scheme of things. Then in the silence he became aware of a soft whispering, slurred words beyond all deciphering. Sleet at the windows sang harsh on the glass front of the poolroom. It was a bitter wind along curfew emptied streets.

He got up. It had turned very cold in the night and he swore when his bare feet touched the linoleum, immediately feeling around for his socks and shoes. With the blanket hooded about him he crossed to the windows. He pressed his face against the cold glass. He could see the back streets, the car lot down the way, no soul about. He could hear the wind whipping hollow up the alley. In the white photoelectric glare of the streetlamps nothing moved save the wind-driven sleet scouring against the windowpanes. Then a garbage can lid turned soundlessly into the street like some strange wheel come unmoored and spun away like a tossed coin.

He crossed the room and flipped the lightswitch but the light just flared once like a flashbulb and died and he dressed hurriedly in the darkness and with a cigarette lighter held aloft plugged in the hotplate. He held outstretched palms over the burner until it glowed red and turned and filled the coffee pot from the sink and set it atop the coil. Shit it's cold, he said. On his knees then, waiting for the water to warm, he looked like some penitent object before an electric god. Praying for heat, for the mercury to climb.

Edgewater seemed outside himself, absorbed into some Ur world. With his head cowled still and his innocent luminous eyes he looked an acolyte to some obscure and aberrant offshoot of Buddhism.

There was no clock and no way to know what time it was. As if it mattered. He thought, This moment is all there is. What I have in this moment, like the very moment itself, is all there is. There was nothing before this, and nothing after. I am hemmed in and trapped by this moment, by now. Where was I before, where will I be again? Even as I saw now it is gone, but where? How can I hold it to me, how can I delay it? But it is too late. Late is late and it's late. Inside his mind time grew soft and elastic and stretched a shifting skein of thread that bound the clock hands and would not break. He stuck a finger into the coffee water but it seemed not to have warmed at all. Fuck, he said. He unplugged the hotplate, rose and found his coat and folded the blanket nearly military style in the darkness and tucked it under an arm. What now?

The possibilities swam in the wavering yellow glare of the lighter. What to take, what to hurl overboard to lessen the weight. There seemed nothing to take he could not do without, nothing that would diminish his holdings for being left. He crossed to the door and opened it and slipped onto the landing. He closed the door behind him for the last time. Some switch had clicked in the night, in the moment before his eyes came open, some circuit breaker had blown, time to roll, time to move down the line to where the water tastes like cherry wine.

Edgewater stumbled down the stairs and into the windy night with misbuttoned shirt and untied shoes. He stooped and tied his laces and fumbled out a cigarette and lit it and leaning against the wall stood smoking. At length he entered again into the cold night, shoulders hunched. He crossed the empty parking lot and there was no sound save the hollow scrape of the wind turning a paper cup against the frozen asphalt, a scuttling keening like a ship's hull scraping ice. The sky was an inverted bowl of dark above where the streetlights tended away and the lights in the residential streets burned blue, cold and soulless, illumination without comfort or warmth, a cool otherworldly glow.

High looping winter winds sang lonesome through the telephone wires and moaned as if dialed there, filled with disembodied voices of despair, the wires were hurrying along their way. He looked like a man waiting on an overdue bus. Even as he watched in the cones of yellow light from the streetlamps, the sleet began to change into snow, huge feathery flakes that rode the updrafts of wind and bellowed in the alley-way's windy mouth and settled in the frozen streets and rose again and accumulated in shapeshifting windrows.

He crossed the street and struck out south with the wind at his back. Past jewelry stores and five-and-dime variety stores with Christmas cheer under plateglass like red and green tinseled memories out of the lost country of his childhood. No cars passed. The traffic lights shifted, directing ghosts of traffic to their phantom destinations. Ackerman's Field looked like some town under curfew, some plague beset place abandoned, the last one out forgot to turn out the lights.

Past the parking lot and the alley black with shadow the tie yard loomed, its stacked ties all chinked with sleet and the railroad tracks curved shining and ran on and on infinite as a promise, an invitation to be taken up at will. Tarpaper shacks where the disenfranchised of both colors lay dreaming, rocking in the lee of more gentle shores. The nights would not replace what the day had taken away. The nights were never long enough.

High and dolorous, a dog howled from behind the darkened shacks and was taken up howl on howl by whatever strays have accrued themselves to the human flotsam lodged here, little more than strays themselves. A cry passed on and shuttled down in staggered relays like news of some dread import, sinister discarnate shapes or voices not designed for human ears. Far out past shantytown an awakened cock cried a false dawn and at the deserted Mobil station a stopped clock proclaimed it twenty past seven forever. Time blank and meaningless here. All there is now is night.

Merchants' windows brightly lit and piled with wares waiting like baited deadfall traps to snare the day's customers. Celluloidish jewelry for ladies of taste, men of means wink coldly from its backdrop. His own image shrouded in this crushed velour, eyes black and shadowed, recessed, the eyeholes of a skull, an ancient pharaoh's skull among faded and tattered funeral silks. Behind his reflected right shoulder a cruising prowl car almost ceased, crept interminably along in the street, a featureless reflected face studying him from beneath the blue cap. A beefy sinister face with no expression, save that of threat, as if he would lift this provender through shards of glass. As if they had anything he wanted. He half turned without looking at the police car, continued a few steps on. A restaurant. Rows of tables stacked with chairs. The sleet had turned to snow. It was snowing hard and swirling in the streetlights. There were thin wisps of it in the street, drifting in the bitter wind. The cruiser had stopped and sat idling, blue puffs of exhaust dissipated in the snow, the face still watching, a window rolling down.

Hey.

Edgewater stopped and turned.

You got a home you better be headin that way.

He walked toward the corner, turned by the First National Bank. He passed on by the florist's with its wreath of tacky piety and past the dentist's office with windows filled with carded arrowheads like some arsenal of weaponry for whatever ancient warriors were still extant and drumming. Into the alley with the wind at his heels, hurrying him along: slapping some loose shutter or boarding at the back door of these merchants' warrens and a displaced garbage can lid clanged harsh and hollow and atonal on concrete and then no other sounds save these.

Lights wheeled on at the alley's nether mouth and came on slow and implacable and stately. Illuminating garbage cans slowly being covered, wearing thin cowls of snow and a fluted glimpse of a black cat and Edgewater trudging hands in pocket and head lowered into the snow. He glanced up and through the glass it was the same cop's face, the same calm look of suspicious insolence. Vague recriminations for crimes dreamed or imagined. A look such as would deny even the existence of innocence. The brake lights came on briefly surrounding him in a bright red haze of drifting snow and he looked at his feet, at the crisp fresh tracks the cruiser had made. He watched. Then it went on.

Out of the alley onto South Maple and the wind was at his face now and it was snowing harder. He looked once passing a streetlight and the snow looked infinite, a soft feathery hush sifting endlessly down from a void that went on forever. Some phenomena that had survived time, was as old as earth. There were no lights he could see anywhere save the streetlights and he stood halted a moment listening, as if he were being inundated in silence and trapped in some snowfall paperweight perpetually tilted.

He went on. Past picket fences white in the streetlight and shuttered windows glowing from the soft inner nightlights. He felt already gone, outward bound. A hunger for a world where he could make some connection struck him. The world you see in four-color advertisements in the *Saturday Evening Post,* father and mother and two freshfaced children admiring the new Buick, the new Frigidaire, basking in the warmth of the new Amana forced air furnace. Later they'll tuck the children in their beds. Where visions of sugarplums dance. Reckon what you have to do to get the *Good Housekeeping* Seal of Approval. A world only told about, only rumors reach the hinterlands there.

He went on, past the schoolyard and the converted funeral home where the souls of the numberless dead drifted aimless or spoke and whispered without purpose into the ear of the living.

He came out on the highway and then he could see the neon from the Cozy Court Motel. No one about, things slow tonight in the motel trade. His feet felt frozen, he hoped she had the heat on, he'd lost the feeling in his toes.

The restaurant at the motel, cheery light burning in the night, stayed open all night and he crossed the red and green yuletide neon and ordered a cup of coffee. There was no one there save the waitress and she looked as if she had been or was asleep or wanted to be. She set his coffee down and wiped with dull persistence some nonexistent stain with the damp cloth she was holding.

What's the matter, Billy? The big boys take your coat away from you?

He was spooning sugar into the steaming coffee. Three spoonfuls, four. Not eating right, needing energy. Pouring cream up to the lip of the cup. It wasn't this cold when I came out. I wasn't expecting it to snow like this either.

It said on the radio it's already four inches on the ground in Memphis. Is it sticking here yet?

Beginning to.

They looked out the windows but they were steamed up and there seemed no world at all beyond the harsh yuletide neon.

You want a little drink?

I don't reckon tonight.

Do you mind if I have one? Will you not say nothin to nobody?

It's nothin to me.

That cheap sonofabitch comes in here prowlin and sniffin around tryin to smell it on me. I have to hide it a different place ever night.

She was kneeling behind the counter with rounded knees bared and reaching into a cabinet and she had her mouth open to say something when the door opened and she leapt up, a hand smoothing at her red hair, a dark roan bristle at her armpit.

But it was not the manager. A thin youth in a too small suitcoat stood rubbing his hands together briskly and blinking, his eyes toadlike at this unexpected light. Snow crowned his lank strawcolored hair, began to melt there.

He looked all about the diner inconspicuously. A curious sullen face, sharp and narrow as an arcbit turned sideways. Eyes scanning the flyspecked list of sandwiches. Hamburger, cheeseburger, BLT. Apparently no favorites there. Gimme two coffees to go, he said, holding up two fingers as if she suffered some hearing impediment, or he some speech defect. He turned to the jukebox, stood hipslung reading the song titles, his lips moving as he read. As if he studied the list for some obscure purpose, as if great and transcendent knowledge were inscribed there.

He crossed to the counter when she set the coffee down and he laid a dime on the counter with a soft and final clink. The coffee came in brown paper cups with twin flaps appended on them to hold them by. He had his fingers through the slots and both coffees aloft and stood studying Edgewater as a tailor might use his eyes to measure a man for a suit of clothes. The eyes were more yellow than any other color.

Good buddy, lemme talk to you a minute out in the yard.

Edgewater turned to see but there was no one there save himself. What about?

I just need to ask ye somethin.

Outside the wind had died and the world was going white and soft, a blurry fairyland beneath the glare of light. He began to wonder idly how he was going to get home, if he was.

What is it?

Buddy, what about some pussy?

What?

He said it again.

Edgewater stood studying this diminutive lecher. This curious apprentice pimp. Perhaps taking some esoteric test in a college for pimps, being graded at a distance by some professor of this craft. Some strange whore in mismatched drag. He felt displaced.

Where is it at?

Right over there. The pimp was pointing. The motel was a long barracks-like building divided into units and there were two or three cars parked facing it. It was toward these cars that he vaguely gestured.

How much?

Five dollars.

There was an old claycolored Ford. The door opened onto it. The backseat was piled up with a jumble of suitcases and clothes and blankets and there was a girl curled sleeping in the front seat. She was very pretty.

Here. He handed her a cup of coffee when she opened her eyes and she sat holding it numbly for a moment and looking dazed as if she did not quite know where she was or as if in waking her he had drawn her back from some more pleasant land. She had been resting her cheek on her hand as she slept and the prints of her fingers showed white on her face. She had brown curly hair and looked about fifteen. She was wrapped in an old army blanket.

When did it get so cold?

It's been turnin cold all night. It's snowin too.

They Lord. We won't never get home. Did you find any gas?

I don't know. Not yet.

You don't know?

Not yet.

Edgewater was shivering in the cold. In the warmth inside the motel he could hear a compressor or thermostat kick on and a heater start and he thought of the summer air blowing through the rooms where implement salesmen and more experienced whores than this one lay dreaming. Dreamed satiated and ginsoaked and limbs interlocking in tousled blankets. Did they dream of lost times that would not come again? Of chances lost, roads not taken?

Come around here a minute, Edgewater said. I want to talk to you.

The boy closed the door and opened it back when she said something.

What?

I said could I play the radio?

You know I said it'd run the battery down.

You won't let me do nothin.

He closed the door hard and a small avalanche of snow fell from the window trim. He brushed it from his hand and they walked around to the back of the Ford. A prowl car passed with its tires hissing in the snow and dipped off the hill and out of sight in a white slipstream of exhaust.

What is it?

What kind of deal is this? Edgewater asked.

No kind of a deal to it. I ask you if you wanted some pussy and told you how much it was. Do you not think it's worth five dollars?

That's no whore in there.

You damn right it's not. That's the freshman queen of Lawrence County, Alabama.

I take it's also your wife.

We're on our honeymoon. We been to Nashville and we had nothin but hard luck. To top things off, the car tore up and it took all our money to fix the shittin thing and then nothin wouldn't do her but she had to see the Grand Ole Opry. That's a hard town. We're flat broke now and the car's out of gas. They throwed us out of the motel at eleven o'clock this morning when our time was up.

Couldn't you wire home for money?

Our folks washed their hands of us when we got married. Strangers as well and I know strange. I've ask for help and all I've got is hard looks and kiss my ass. Fuck it. Do you want it or not?

Edgewater took a five-dollar bill out of his pocket and handed it to the boy, who glanced at the denomination and shoved it deep into his pocket. There was a yellow gas can in the car, he took it and turned without speaking to Edgewater. He opened the door on the driver's side. You do like I said, he told her. He turned without closing the door and Edgewater watched his thin and angry figure retreating under the streetlamp, the sound of the gas can bumping his leg rhythmic with his walking. Carrying his gasoline like some amateur arsonist trudging on toward the kindling point of the world, distanced from the throes and turmoil of life as if long blackballed, like some soul doomed from its membership not to inhabit the world, only to bear witness to.

She sat beside him without moving, stoically staring out the windshield at the mounding snow and beyond that, further to the stucco wall of the motel, as if it were something they were speeding toward. He put an arm about her shoulder and gently drew her nearer. She came grudgingly but without protest, a leaden weight stiff against him. He could smell the warmth of her, curiously intertwined, a little girl smell of spearmint and a woman's perfume and lipstick and he thought he could divine through the bone structure of her face the way she had looked as a child. Her profile was clean and bright as the profile on a newly struck coin and she was very pretty. There was an ache in him, a regret for all the coinclean profiles, all the slender grace, all the lost homecoming queens of youth. Snowflakes fell on the windshield and lay without melting and formed patterns of wondrous intricacy. She was crying, still without moving. Tears moved down her smooth cheeks, he stopped one with his fingers and they came faster.

Stop crying.

I can't.

Say you're from Alabama?

Yeah. Lawrence County. You ever been there?

Yeah. Town Creek.

We were supposed to go down to Mobile and see the ocean but I'll never see it tagging along with him. Have you ever been to Mobile?

He had, yet there was no one person or deed to recall it to him but a series of separate pictures like snapshots from a summer vacation, holographs of marvelous clarity, a montage of shifting images: *a ravaged land of limestone and red clay bleeding through like old blood, honeysuckle pinewoods dark and still and moribund days in the sweet hot sun and naked breasts he could trace the blueveined heartbeat in.*

A mosaic of desperation. He remembered backwaters of the Tennessee River, brackish and tepid. A motorboat knifing the water and a waterskier bent and briefly airborne spanning the wake with careless grace. A girl with a vacuous face looking stricken in the sun, in a yellow bathing suit and later when he removed the halter of it the breasts were shockingly white; soft against her, tan and even as he watched the nipples pucker and draw taut, as if some chill wind blew across her supine body, as if she drew from his touch some occult cold that started there and fanned outward and would ul-timately destroy her, a slow arterial movement of dark heart's blood slushed with ice, slow and slower and cease.

A bootlegger. A black bootlegger with an enviable Sunday afternoon business, an unbelievable string of cars going around his house like some great dislocated traffic jam and coming out the other side. Going in he had met a car of the Alabama State Police. A casual wave of the hand, he'd waved back. Two enormous back porch coolers set filled with nothing but tallboy Bud at fifty cents a bottle. It was told he had a halfwhite daughter in a New England finishing school and it was told the fix was in so high and wide that the Budweiser truck dropped below the Tennessee line into the land of prohibition to make his deliveries.

He tasted her stiff lips, a musky taste there of sleep. Her eyes were open, a welled black enormity fringed with dark lashes that would draw him under.

Quit foolin around. Just do it if you're going to.

Do you want me to or not?

I just want it over with. I want to go home.

He released her and lit a cigarette and smoked in a thoughtful silence but she did not move away. She seemed drained of all volition, a weight to be guided and controlled.

You want to go in that café and get something to eat?

He oughtn't to have made me.

No. But he just told you to. He's not making you.

He'll beat me if I don't.

Then tell him you did. Tell him I couldn't get a hard on, tell him whatever he wants to hear. Or just tell him to go to hell.

He opened the door. It was not much colder outside than in. As he got out she took his arm and moved to forestall him. Don't go. Go on and do it. He'll whip me if you don't.

He wanted done with her as well.

He got out anyway and returned to the café. He foresaw other stops for her before she was in Alabama.

His coffee was cold. He drank it anyway, a bitterness tempered with sweetness.

What'd he want? the waitress asked.

He's down on his luck, Edgewater said. He had something to try to sell me.

You buy it?

I couldn't afford it, he told her.

He went back out and wanted to be moving slowly homeward through the night. It was surely near day but no sign of it or any indication anywhere that the snow would cease or even slacken. It was already halfway to his knees and from beneath the domelit water tank a dog came out and stood bellydeep and perplexed. Her face was in his mind, her clean sweet youth like the shards of a dream or a taste in his mouth. She might have been his last young one ever. The last one with a gossamer shred of innocence still restraining her. Dweller of some halfway house between. He wondered idly why he had simply given the boy the five dollars but he did not know why he had not used her anyway. A seed of doubt had been sown. He would never believe her and the seed might grow and drop the fruits of it. A chill wind blew up from the west, lay on his back like a weight. He was chilled to the bone, felt half frozen. The wind drifted the dry snow, swirled it about him like a blizzard. He felt a chill beyond the capability of weathers, beyond the ice the December night lay on him. The world is indeed wide, surely highways led to Lawrence County, Alabama.

He climbed back in the car, leaned and kissed her lips, her eyes open, fringed with thick lashes. Her lips clasped together, prim, she twisted her face away from him.

He'll be back in a little bit. Do it if you're going to.

Do you want me to?

I just want to be anywhere but here. I want to go home. You heard him say for me to, you gave him money.

He got out again and walked slowly across the parking lot, hesitating at the door of the café, looked back at the girl in the car and opened the café door.

Harold hasn't got a gas can back in there has he?

I can look. Why? the waitress asked.

I just need one a minute. They're out of gas.

She disappeared through the door and after a moment returned with a yellow can. You better bring this back, Billy. He'll have my ass if it gets gone.

Outside he carried the can back to where the car sat and stood peering speculatively at the other cars. He looked about. Last summer's watering hose tending down from a spigot and with his pocketknife he cut a length from it. While he beat it against the sidewalk dislodging from it lozenge-shaped pellets of ice she got out and watched with interest. The car across was a new Cadillac and apparently full of gas for he refilled the can four times, each time setting it in the snow and siphoning the gas into the tank. When he was through he turned without speaking to her and carried the can back inside and when he returned she was still outside shivering and watching it snow as if it was some wonder she was unused to.

Get in. We'll see if it'll start and get the heater going.

She got in beside him and the car cranked on the first try. While it warmed up he got out and scraped the ice off the windshield and when he got back behind the wheel he seemed heightened in some way, a curious euphoria had seized him. For no reason at all he thought of Bradshaw. Sweet home Alabama, he said.

Reckon what time it is? What could he be doing?

It must be near daylight. I guess he's waiting for a gas station to open.

You mean there's not one?

I doubt it.

You knew that all the time. She shifted her weight in the seat, slid a little nearer, just a suggestion of weight against his shoulder. How many cans of gas would you need between here and Town Creek? he wondered aloud, but she did not reply. He was lost in study of her mintclean profile against the beleaguered glass and perhaps he saw more than was visible. She was time and generations of forebears moving halfperceived through the warped glass of the past and in the planes and angles of her face he read their tale, their travails and ultimate indomitability. For this, at once cause and result, there was about her and about the past she lead like some dread familiar an air of blooded dissolution of sweet gentle ruin.

She turned and watched him as a bird might return the unblinking glass stare of a serpent at the moment when the identities of victim and predator shift and merge, become one duality of violence.

How many times would you have had to stop between here and Decatur? he asked her.

She halfsmiled. I dare you, she said.

He released the clutch and the car spun backward through the snow. In this instant he saw in his mind's eye a snapshot, the old image of himself merging with the image of himself now, a black and white Polaroid of a young man standing before the edge of a wood. And even as he watched and attempted to hold the image steady in his mind the edges blurred, it microscopically shifted, began its escape: a furtive order sliding from the scenery that has locked it toward the white and pristine void at the picture's edge.

Afterword

Finding *The Lost Country*

by J.M. White

In the last few years of his life, William Gay would read from a forthcoming book he called *The Lost Country*. He had signed a contract and had a deadline of February 2012 to turn in the manuscript. The publisher announced that it was forthcoming; it was listed on Amazon. William would talk about the main characters, named Edgewater, Bradshaw, and Roosterfish. He liked to remark that Edgewater was the most autobiographical character in all his books. As February approached, I asked him how the book was going and he said he had written it but now he couldn't find it.

Within a week of telling me this, William was dead. In the last year of his life, he had been having seizures and then a heart attack, which he survived only as a result of some good paramedics who jump-started his heart in the ambulance on the way to the hospital. After that, he had a pacemaker, but within a year he was gone.

The day after he died, the publisher for *The Lost Country* called to ask me to go to Hohenwald and see if I could retrieve the manuscript. I tried calling William's kids, but no one was answering. A few days later, the phone rang. It was William Junior, who said he had a tub full of notebooks and wanted me to help go through it. I went to Hohenwald at the earliest opportunity, where Junior showed me William's ashes in a cardboard box on the mantel. Then he brought out a plastic tub full of William's handwritten notebooks. He and his brother Chris had gone into William's bedroom and found the notebooks piled on the floor of his closet. They put them in three plastic tubs; William took one and Chris kept the other two.

I started looking through the tub, and almost immediately I spotted Edgewater and Roosterfish in some of the notebooks. Junior gave me the tub to take home, and I stayed up most of the night sorting the notebooks into piles based on the characters that appeared in them. William's writing was not easy to decipher. The notebooks were filled front to back with tightly written script; notes were written on the sides of many pages and across the top margins. He didn't cross his t's or dot his i's, so many of the words were difficult to make out—the letters t, i, a, and e were nearly identical.

The next day, I got some expandable folders and organized the notebooks. There were *The Lost Country* notebooks, notebooks of published short stories, music writing, and notebooks from *Provinces of Night*. I made an archival list describing each notebook and labeling it. I took the tub back to Hohenwald and picked up Junior and we drove over to meet Chris. Once there, Chris brought out the two other tubs. I offered to do the same sorting process with these, and he sent them home with me.

I could tell there was a significant amount of unpublished material, including twelve notebooks from *The Lost Country*. In one of the notebooks, I found a synopsis in a letter to an agent. Once I had everything archived, I carried all the papers back to Hohenwald. All together, Junior and Chris had fifty-eight handwritten notebooks. I called the publisher. He was excited to hear about the notebooks and asked me to get a copy to him. Within a week of sending copies of *The Lost Country* notebooks, the publisher called saying they were rejecting the manuscript. I was disappointed but was totally undaunted. I knew that until we had all the material typed, we just didn't know how much was there. The synopsis laid out the plotline, so I had something to follow. A small group of William's friends started typing *The Lost Country* notebooks and passing the material back and forth. We all agreed it was as great as anything he had written. I began laying out the typed sections based on the synopsis.

Each time I visited Hohenwald, different family members urged me to go visit the house that William had built in 1978, where he and his wife Diane raised the kids. Finally one day I drove out and found the house. It is built like a log cabin, using four-by-four beams stacked like Lincoln logs. William's daughter Laura had been living there with her husband and their four kids, but she passed away from cancer a month after William died. I pulled up in the yard and Kory, Laura's husband, assured me that it was all right to go up into the attic. Dallas, one of the older kids, went with me. The opening to the attic was covered with loose boards. Dallas pushed the boards aside and we climbed into the low attic.

I have never seen so many spider webs, they were hanging from the rafters like Spanish moss, the air was thick with them like gossamer curtains suspended from the beams. There were magazines strewn all over the floor three and four layers thick. There were cardboard boxes filled with *Rolling Stone* and *Playboy*, along with more literary stuff like *Harper's* and *Atlantic*. Dallas was pushing around through the magazines and came up with an old spiral-bound notebook.

One wall was lined with bookcases that ran the length of the room, stuffed full of thousands of books. I knocked down the spider webs and looked at all William's old books. At one end of the shelves I found a cardboard box with the lids folded shut. When I looked inside, it was filled with typewritten sheets of paper—hundreds of pages of old cheap typing paper in various stages of decay and yellowing, lots of them bent and crumbled. I looked through the pages and saw the names of the characters from *The Lost Country*. It was a total mess; some of the pages had numbers on the bottom, but most didn't, and the pages didn't seem to be in order. I closed the box and sat it by the steps. It was getting dark in the attic. Dallas had come up with a couple more notebooks, so we piled everything together and headed down.

Kory agreed for me to take all the materials home and figure out what they were. I couldn't believe my luck. I had found a typed copy of *The Lost Country* and a bunch of handwritten notebooks. The box smelled like stale cigarette smoke mixed with mouse dung and it was covered with a deep layer of grime. When I carried it into my office and sat it on the floor, my cat circled it, sniffing it and looking it over very intently. I opened the box and laid the papers out on the floor. It was a jumble, a hodgepodge, the pages totally out of order.

I brought in a box of plastic sleeves and put all the pages in plastic protectors. I started sorting the pages on the floor. Each time I found a character name, I put that page in a pile. It took me a couple of days to make it through the box. When I came to the end, I had four stacks, a couple of them quite substantial. I had three for each of the main characters and then one large stack for all the pages without names.

I found one page that had "The End" written in pencil at the bottom. Some of the pages had handwritten page numbers in the bottom right-hand corner, and the page that said "The End" was 231. I put the pages that had numbers in order and read through them and then read the unnumbered pages and started fitting them in. Only about half of the pages were numbered, but it wasn't too difficult once the storyline became apparent.

The team of Susan McDonald, Shelia Kennedy, and I started comparing the material from the notebooks with the pages from the attic. Shelia entered all the pages from the attic into a computer file. Then we were able to take material from the notebooks and compare them to the typescript. It was plain to see that the notebooks were the source of the typescript, since it followed the notebooks word for word. Then we were able to fill in any missing pages of the typescript with the material from the notebooks. After a few weeks of sorting and arranging, we had all the material integrated. We had the entire manuscript, except for a few pages leading up to "The End."

I printed a copy and headed back to Hohenwald and showed it to the family. I wanted to get back in the attic and see if I could find more material. William's ex-wife Diane and all the kids reviewed the draft we had done. Diane said William did his greatest writing during the seventies, and she thought these pages were from that time. She thought Laura had typed those pages, although his oldest daughter Lee also helped from time to time. When I mentioned the names Edgewater and Roosterfish, Diane immediately knew the people the characters were based on. She went on at some length about Roosterfish and how he was based on two different people, both now dead, who were the most reprehensible people in Lewis County.

Diane's trailer sat beside the house William had built, and she was living there helping Kory with Laura's four kids. I walked next door and showed Kory the draft, and he was very pleased to see that I had found something useful. He got a flashlight and we went up the narrow steps, pushed aside the boards, and there I was again with all those books and magazines. I started digging through the boxes. The first one was full of old *Ramparts* and some *Esquire*. Kory's flashlight was getting weaker by the moment. I picked one last box, and bingo, there was a sheet of crinkled typewriter paper sticking out between some magazines. I dug deeper. There was a pile of typescripts near the bottom. I showed them to Kory; it was nearly dark and he was ready to get out.

Then I noticed a few pieces of sheetrock leaning again the end wall. I peered behind them and saw a plastic tub sitting there, wedged against the wall. Kory held the sheetrock while I pried it out. It was filled to the top with old notebooks.

I had gotten to know William's brother Cody who lived nearby, so I dropped by his place to show him the manuscript of *The Lost Country* and these latest finds. When he looked at the pages, Cody remembered that he had read them when William originally wrote them. He confirmed what Diane said about when the manuscript was written. When he saw the name Roosterfish, he asked if I knew what it meant. I said I had never heard it, and he said it was a term they used when they were kids—common slang in Lewis County in the fifties for cocksucker.

Now I knew that William had started writing *The Lost Country* nearly thirty years before. I remembered him telling me that he couldn't find the manuscript, that he had looked through his papers and he didn't know what had happened to it. Here it was, in a box in the attic, yellowing with age. Finally it had surfaced, too late for him to have any personal benefit from it, but not too late for his readers, who had been anticipating the title for years. I found notebooks with material from *The Lost Country* in this newest tub as well. To our surprise, the ending to *The Lost Country* was in one of the notebooks that had been hidden behind the sheetrock. We celebrated. I assembled the entire novel into a first draft and then called a couple more friends, Lamont Ingalls in Florida and Paul Nitsche in Wisconsin, who were great admirers of William. Lamont, a native Tennessean, has been working as an editor and reviewer since Wild Dog Press published William's collection, *Time Done Been Won't Be No More*, in 2010. Since then he has been involved with recovering and publishing all of William's works. Paul Nitsche has also worked tirelessly, reading the manuscript repeatedly, editing, proofing, and helping in all aspects of preparing *The Lost Country*, and all of William's posthumous works, for publication.

I contacted the publisher, who was thrilled to hear the news. But they no sooner got a copy of the manuscript than the publisher died of a heart attack. Suddenly we were entangled in a huge mess. The publisher left his business in total disarray, owing all his authors, including William, huge sums of money, and the company had nothing but unpaid debts. Some of the staff tried to salvage the operation, but it was hopeless. It took over two years to work through the legal morass and get the rights to the book back. Finally the rights reverted to William's family, who were anxious to get it into print. But it wasn't a simple matter to place it with another publisher. After many months and what seemed like endless delays, we placed the manuscript with Dzanc and now, more than six years since his death, William's greatest work is seeing the light of day.

There aren't many stories about great books that show up after the author has died. *A Confederacy of Dunces* by John Kennedy Toole springs to mind. Typically, posthumous works are a bit piecemeal and have an unfinished feel to them. However, William is a special case. He completed his first novel at age twenty-five and continued writing nonstop, though he didn't get published until he was fifty-nine years old. He honed his skills over all those years so that, while he revised slightly in his handwritten notebooks, once they were typed he did few if any revisions. It wasn't until I had access to his entire archive that I realized the extent of his unpublished writings, which included four unpublished novels and a collection of unpublished short stories.

William's writing was the driving force of his life. He cared about little else. He was a free spirit and lived like a true artist in a self-ruling world. To many people, he seemed aloof and detached. He lived a hardscrabble earthly life, rugged and simple. It really didn't matter to him where he was, he lived in a writer's trance. He served his art and let his art serve him. He was creating something original, something brand new, high energy, cut to the bone, coming out of the darkness with an element of danger, exploding onto the page. He was a gentle person but in his books life is cheap. Sitting up writing in the still of the night, he wrote prose that is heartfelt and melancholy. In a world that didn't seem to care, he was an earth angel singing from some imaginary corner of the universe, which he imbued with beauty and concern for all life.

J.M. White